P9-CLU-628

THE SISTER-IN-LAW

ALSO BY PAMELA CRANE

Little Deadly Secrets

THE
SISTER-
IN-LAW

A NOVEL

PAMELA CRANE

WILLIAM MORROW
An Imprint of HarperCollins*Publishers*

This is a work of fiction. Names, characters, places, and incidents are products of the author's imagination or are used fictitiously and are not to be construed as real. Any resemblance to actual events, locales, organizations, or persons, living or dead, is entirely coincidental.

THE SISTER-IN-LAW. Copyright © 2021 by Pamela Crane. All rights reserved. Printed in the United States of America. No part of this book may be used or reproduced in any manner whatsoever without written permission except in the case of brief quotations embodied in critical articles and reviews. For information, address HarperCollins Publishers, 195 Broadway, New York, NY 10007.

HarperCollins books may be purchased for educational, business, or sales promotional use. For information, please email the Special Markets Department at SPsales@harpercollins.com.

Originally published as *The Sister-in-Law* in Great Britain in 2021 by HarperCollins Publishers.

FIRST U.S. EDITION

Library of Congress Cataloging-in-Publication Data has been applied for.

ISBN 978-0-06-298493-7

21 22 23 24 25   BRR   10 9 8 7 6 5 4 3 2 1

To Angie, the inspiration behind the story. Thank you for making your brother single for me, you evil genius.

To Missy, the inspiration behind the characters. Not because you're crazy, but because you're crazy awesome.

To Jamie, the inspiration behind the family bond. You set the bar high for all sisters-in-law to follow.

To every sister-in-law out there, this book is dedicated to you. May family drama never drive you to murder.

No matter what you've done, I've done worse. I've been a thief, a liar, a killer. But I'm also a wife, a mother, a sister. They see me, but don't really see me. Not the real me, the darkness under my skin. And I'll do anything to ensure they never find out.

Chapter 1

Harper Paris

I didn't believe in therapy, but I believed what my court-mandated therapist once told me: *You are what you leave behind.* According to this logic, we were a composition of our choices. You leave trash? You're trash. You create beauty? You're beautiful. As I ran from the living room, I left behind a blood-bath, but I wasn't sure what that made me as I sobbed at the sight of crimson residue staining my hands.

The sight of my husband of twelve years sprawled out on the sofa, a knife jutting from his chest cavity, palms loosely circling the hilt—that was the reason I screamed. It was a howl that shattered my voice, the wail flowing up from my chest and out into the empty air. When the last bits of my cry wafted away, I pressed frantic fingers against his neck, his wrist, finding him deathly cold. Then I ran. And kept running until I found myself on the front porch, the scent of metallic blood singeing my nostrils and the taste of bile burning my throat.

Don't ask me why I ran to the porch. Not the bathroom, not the kitchen sink—both more reasonable places to purge my stomach—but outside, where a floral scent lingered with my vomit. One never knows how you'll react in any given situation until you're in the midst of it. I was in the midst of my husband's gruesome death, and all I could do was scream and cry and run out my front door into the night, apparently.

I needed to go back inside, but I was terrified. Terrified that it was real.

"God help me," I whispered, drawing in a shaky breath. My voice was drowned out by the cacophony of crickets.

By now I was certain I was having a heart attack, as the panic thrummed against my chest. Every beat physically hurt. The fresh air, soaked in lavender and honeysuckle, helped a little, but not much. Feeling faint and feverish, I raised my hand to my forehead, damp with sweat that drizzled down my temples. My body pulsed, hot and cold all at once. Delirium started to set in.

My temples drummed with a terror of something unnamed and unknown. I didn't know what to do. There was no way Ben could still be alive. I had checked, several times, pressed my fingers to his neck searching for a pulse. Ran my hands along his wrists, his face, begging for him to come back to me. It was the call of regret for a mistake I couldn't take back. And now he was dead, because of me.

The only man I had ever truly loved was nothing but cool skin against my warm touch. I'd realized he'd been long dead when his stiff arm fell against my leg, causing me to yelp. Mere hours ago I had relished the feel of his flesh; now it scared me to touch it.

It. My husband was no longer *him* but *it.* Dead, rotting flesh.

I relived it again and again, that first moment when I arrived home. The living room was black, under night's spell. *He fell asleep on the couch again,* I had grumbled to myself when I vaguely saw Ben's form cocooned under the blanket I had custom made with a family photo woven into it. While I tidied the coffee table of an empty potato chips bag and a half-drunk bottle of vodka, his arm had fallen off the slippery leather cushion, thumping against my thigh. I jumped back at the rigidity of his limb, then gasped at the sight of the knife in his chest, and that's when I noticed what the shadows had hidden: he looked gray.

Gray like death.

I cupped his unshaved cheek, only to find it cold. The husband I had snuggled up against in bed to keep me warm, the father whose arms wrapped effortlessly around our children, now rigid. That's when the wave hit me—this was real. I screamed. I searched for life. Ben was dead.

Holding myself upright against the porch railing where honeysuckle vines wrung around the posts like leafy fingers, I used the breathing technique my therapist had left me with. Smell a flower—in. Blow out a candle—out. In, out. In, out. Eventually, a calm mellowed the panic after about forty in-outs, forty flowers and candles. My fingers brushed against the Christmas lights we had never taken down. A classy white LED string that took Ben four hours to individually wrap around the railings and up the Corinthian pillars. Removing them would have been an all-day project, which Ben had never made time for. And never again would.

My stare settled on the lit window across the street and two doors down, half hidden by an azalea bush in full bloom. A sweet but sad elderly woman lived there, the neighborhood night watch. Miss Michelle, I called her, because I could never remember her last name, even though I knew it was something simple with an *H*. Hall? Hill? I didn't remember much these days, as each one blended into the next in a hurried blur. Miss Michelle had often kept late hours since her husband passed from cancer. *I can't sleep with the emptiness next to me,* she once told me.

Would I ever sleep again?

A breeze ruffled my hair, sticking curly tendrils to my lips. After wiping the bile from the corners of my mouth, I returned inside, petrified to look at him. Tears mixed with mascara stung my eyes. I pressed my palms against my face to stop them falling, but it only made it worse as yesterday's makeup scraped against my eyeball.

I needed to call someone. But where was my phone? In the kitchen? I couldn't remember.

I headed into the kitchen, fumbling in the dark for the light switch as my fingers, wet with blood, slipped across the wall. When I finally turned on the light, the room glowed eerily. The mahogany cabinets soaked up most of the brightness. My obsessive-compulsive brain gave me two orders: wash the blood off my hands, then make the call. I turned on the faucet and watched the pink swirl of blood circle the drain while I scrubbed the smear of guilt from my hands.

My palms were clean but my shirt—and my soul along with it—were not. I wanted to change clothes, but I knew better.

No wife reeling from the unexpected death of her husband should have time for a wardrobe change. I searched for my purse, where my phone was tucked inside. As I passed through the kitchen, clinging to the mottled granite counter to hold me upright, a flutter of paper crinkled under my hand, then tumbled over the edge of the countertop. A single, yellow, lined page floated down to the polished oak floor, the kind of paper Ben used for scribbling notes during investor meetings and money management seminars. It had been ripped from his legal pad. I picked it up, immediately noticing the salutation: *My darling Harper.*

A letter. Of course Ben would leave a letter. Anything to heap the guilt on me as his corpse decayed on our Ethan Allen sofa. It was his final hurrah. Ben always got the last word, and up until this moment I never minded. It's what made our marriage work—I was always right, but he always got the final say. We'd often laugh about that.

My fingers trembled as I squinted away the sooty tears and read through the haze:

My darling Harper,

You saw this coming, didn't you? You knew one day you'd walk into our home and find me like this, taken by my own hand. You had to, after all the suffering. All the secrets. All the pain.

You can't blame me for this. You put me here, after all. It was only a matter of time before I escaped the pain of this world, because it was all that was left to do. I couldn't carry on anymore . . . not after what happened. What you did. What I could never forgive. I tried. I really did. But in the end, trying isn't enough. It's not enough to erase the past. It's not enough to blur the memories.

You've spent the last year hating me, and I've spent the last year missing you. We're not who we used to be, and I realize now we'll never find ourselves again. When you lose too much of yourself, there's no way to rebuild. Moving on without you wasn't an option, but this was.

I loved you, Harper, but love isn't enough to vanquish the cruelty of life. Death is, though.

Your ghost for eternity,

Ben

My lips mouthed those final words—*your ghost for eternity*—but no sound came out. Our love couldn't *vanquish the cruelty of life*? Waxing poetic wasn't Ben's style; football was. Golf was. Beer brats on the grill was. These words didn't sound like the man I knew. But it could only be him, because only Ben knew all of our secrets . . . well, all but one. The biggest one. The one I'll take to my own grave.

The scrawl seemed to match the handwriting I'd seen on hundreds of permission slips and to-do lists and meeting notes. A businessman's neat print, the letters capitalized. It had to be Ben, but a version of Ben I'd never glimpsed until now. I actually liked this broody, raw, profound edition of my husband I had never met, because it was better than the lying, cheating one I had spent the last year living with. I hated how I had always loved him, no matter how deep he cut me. Love was the ultimate dichotomy—it tore the heart apart. I'd take the pain of heartbreak over no pain at all.

I felt his haunting words, and I wondered what his last

moments were like as he wrote them. I guess when a guy like Ben ponders death, something else takes over. Something deeper and darker, something that uses words like *vanquish* and *cruelty of life.*

What you did. His message flooded me with guilt and regret. The blame was clearly on me. I did this to him. I nudged him to the edge, then shoved him off it. If only he had known the truth . . . but would that have changed anything? Or would knowing only have pushed his goodbye sooner? It was a question I'd never know the answer to. A question I could never ask him.

The letter slipped from my hand to the granite as I swiped away a trickle of snot. I felt myself slipping. I needed help. Should I still call 911? What then, after the police showed up? What if they asked questions?

Where were you when he died? What were you doing when he died? What does this letter mean? What secrets is Ben referring to here?

No, the risk was too great. My brain was too cloudy to make a thoughtful decision. I was drowning in deep water. There was only one person I trusted in chaos like this, one person who could help me. The same person who helped me the last time I faced Death.

Lane Flynn. My brother, my best friend, my savior. That's what a brother was for—to help his sister when she locked herself out of her car, or forgot to pick up the kids from school, or when her husband turned up dead. Lane would know what to do.

I couldn't find my purse on the counter where I usually dropped it—along with a stack of mail or my grocery haul—

when I got home from running errands or shopping. Where had I left it? For the life of me I couldn't remember. I could only vaguely remember anything prior to this moment. All I remembered was cleaning up, being hit by that awful stench of death, then seeing Ben properly. I must have dropped my purse then.

I didn't want to venture back in there, near the body that had once been my husband, the kids' father, now a skin-wrapped shell housing flesh and bones. I didn't want to relive the reality that he was gone—the kids' hero, our financial security, the handyman who kept our home running smoothly. Who would fix the leaky sink in our master bathroom? Who would remember to change the oil in my car? Who would replace the lightbulbs in that ridiculous light fixture hovering twenty feet high in the entryway? God knew how much I hated heights. Ben knew too.

Selfish bastard. Taking away the one thing I depended on—*him*.

I rounded the corner into the living room, bracing myself for the sight and smell and aura of decay. Sure enough, I found my purse—and a tipped vodka bottle—at the foot of the sofa, right below where Ben's head hung crookedly off the cushion. Anger rumbled from an unknown place deep within me, and I picked up the bottle by the neck and threw it at the wall. It smashed into a ring of liquid that dribbled to the floor, joining the shards of glass.

How dare he do this to me! How dare he do this to our kids! How dare he make me a widow! How dare he, how dare he, how dare he! Hot, furious tears rolled down my cheeks, the tears of a scorned woman. Ben had rejected me, had rejected our life together.

Through the sobs I grabbed my purse strap and rooted

through tampons and a wallet and lipstick until my fingers felt the slickness of my phone. I pulled it out and ran to the bathroom, hovering by the toilet in case I threw up again. I dialed, praying through one ring, two rings, three rings, that Lane would pick up. On the fourth ring, he answered.

"Hey, Harp. What's up?" Husky with sleep, Lane spoke so casually I almost forgot I wasn't calling about dinner plans, but about my husband's suicide.

"It's Ben." Thick and unsteady, I didn't recognize my own voice.

"Hold on." The line crackled as Lane shifted the phone. "What time is it?"

"I don't know. Listen to me, Lane. Ben's dead!" They were the only words I could push out before I slipped into a blubbering stream of sobs.

"Slow down, Harp. I can't understand you. What's wrong?" Lane spoke coolly, evenly, his calmness tempering my frantic nerves, but only momentarily.

"He's gone, Lane." I didn't believe it as I said it. It couldn't be real. And yet the reality of it was painted on my shirt in blood.

"Who's gone? Harp, what happened?"

"Ben." The tears flowed freely, but I found a sliver of my voice, just enough to say everything I needed to say. "On the couch . . . he killed himself."

Lane stopped me with the urgency of his tone. "Oh my God. Ben's dead?"

"I don't know what to do. How am I going to tell the kids?"

"Where are Elise and Jackson, Harp?" Lane intercepted. "You can't let them see that."

"They're at Mom's for the night. What do I even say to them? They'll never understand. And Jackson . . . this will destroy him, Lane. How will I pay the bills? I don't have a job, and Ben's life insurance won't pay out for suicide. We depended on him for everything, and he took it all away! How could he do this to his family?" One after another, the worries scrambled to get out of my mouth.

"Harper, listen to me carefully." Lane broke through my hysteria. "Do not call 911. The police cannot know about this. And don't touch anything. I'll be right over. Stay there—I'm on my way."

As the line went dead, I knew what would happen next. Knew what Lane would tell me to do. And I'd do it all, down to every last detail. That was when I realized what all of this made me. The pain and suffering I had left in my wake was enough to make my husband kill himself.

I was a monster.

Chapter 2

Lane Flynn

"It's going to be okay," I told Harper.

It was anything but okay.

It was worse than I imagined, seeing my brother-in-law like that, stiff and ashen and tinted with blood. The knife sticking out of Ben's chest looked more like a prop, and the scene was comparable to any number of zombie shows I'd binge-watched, his face waxy and fake. But the smell . . . there was nothing fake about the stench of an hours-dead corpse.

I knew the smell because I experienced it almost daily at the hospital where I worked. Most people were terrified of the dead, but gore and blood and death were my everyday life. I just never expected it to be my brother-in-law. And not like this.

I stood over the body formerly known as Ben Paris, trans-

11

fixed by the awful display while Harper broke down in my arms, her sorrow soaking into my shirtsleeve. I doubted she could survive a second round of pain so soon. It wasn't fair how life discriminated against her. Kissing her head and rubbing circles on her back, I tried to comfort her.

"It's going to be okay." I had recited this same line a year ago, not knowing if it was true. It felt like just as much of a lie today.

"We'll get through this together." It was the best I could offer and—this time—the truth.

"Lane, can't you do something for him?" she asked.

"Harp, I'm a nurse, not Jesus. I can't bring him back from the dead. I wish I could, but I can't."

She pulled away and looked up at me, cool air rushing into the gap of space between us. Her watery eyes searched mine. It was familiar territory to me, the pleading eyes of those left behind seeking answers about their departed loved ones. *Did he die peacefully? Was there anything else you could have done for her? Why, why, why?* As a nurse, I watched countless sick people arrive on their feet but depart on gurneys. Questions always followed. Answers rarely offered solace. For my sister, I had only one answer. One she would hate, but one she would accept, because Harper accepted everything I fed her.

"What I can do is try to protect your family," I said.

"How, Lane? He's gone. The kids have no father. I don't work. I would be lucky to find a minimum wage job. Without the life insurance money we'll lose everything. I don't . . . I don't know what to do."

I placed my hands on her shoulders, forcing her to see me, hear me. "You're strong, Harp. You'll get through this. I know this is horribly difficult, especially so soon after . . ." I didn't finish my thought, because she already knew. She didn't need the reminder. "But I promise to take care of you. I have a plan, okay?"

She nodded wordlessly.

"First of all, get rid of that suicide letter. That can never be spoken of again. Understand?"

Another nod.

"I'm going to stage the house to make it look like it was a robbery. It's very important that you tell the police you came home to this and have no idea what happened. Ben never killed himself, got it? He was murdered during the robbery."

She covered her mouth as a gasp slipped out. She was un-raveling, and I could barely keep my own emotions spooled right now.

"Please listen, Harp. I need to know you understand me."

"Why murdered? Isn't suicide better?"

Murder, suicide, both ugly words. There was no easy out, and Harper needed to accept that if she was going to get through this without losing everything . . . or facing jail time.

"Not if you want to get your life insurance payout. They don't pay out on suicides, Harp, which means you'll lose everything, just like you said. Considering what you've been through in the past year, I don't think you'd be able to handle that big of an adjustment right now."

Her gaze drifted as she considered my words. "What if the police think I killed him?"

"You didn't kill him, so there won't be anything that points to you, right?"

She glanced at the floorboards, her eyes shifty. Stepping out of my grasp, she ambled across the room and sunk into Ben's lambskin armchair, the one she had bought him for their fifth anniversary and made me pick up and deliver as a surprise. Everything in this room screamed *Ben,* from the oversized leather sofa with gaudy nailhead accents to the hideous abstract artwork on the walls.

Folding her legs up, she cried into her knees. She was beaten, crumbling apart. I could always tell when she was defeated, but this was something else altogether.

"*Right,* Harper? Nothing should tie you to this. You weren't home . . . were you? You have an alibi." This was my sister. It had to be true. But then again . . . I knew what she had done a year ago.

"Yes, Lane, it's just . . . what if something goes wrong? They always suspect the spouse, don't they? Maybe it'd be better to hide his body or something. No body, no crime."

I laughed mirthlessly. "This isn't *CSI.* We can't just hide a body. A missing husband will look more like you did it than anything else. Just follow my directions, okay? A break-in is your best bet. This house is a realistic target for a thief wanting a big payday."

"How are you going to fake that? The cops will find out, Lane."

"Not if we do it properly. It's the only option. You came in the front door, first noticed the broken window in the dining room as you walked by, then ran into the living room looking for Ben. That's when you saw him lying on the sofa—already dead."

Her eyes narrowed curiously. "What broken window?"

Grabbing a hand towel from a kitchen drawer, I wrapped

up my fist and went outside, with Harper on my heels. Years of *Matlock* and *Psych* reruns had taught me everything I needed to know to execute this with a semblance of believability. Break the glass inward for authenticity, then reenact the crime to ensure it all fit in place. It was still dark enough outside to cover us in shadow. I glanced up and down Hendricks Way, the quiet rows of sleepy homes . . . except for one glowing window across the street and a couple doors down. The neighborhood busybody. I doubted the old hen could see us from there through the darkness.

Along the wraparound porch were two windows that faced the side yard. I paused at one of them, raising my arm to determine the easiest place to break the glass.

"Whoa, are you serious?" Harper jumped between me and the window. "These are the original walk-through Italianate windows! They cost a fortune to replace. You're not going to break one, are you?"

"Harper, a thief isn't going to care about your fancy windows. If you want to sell this story, it's got to look real." I nudged her aside and aimed for the lower part of the glass, near my knee.

Thank God for single-glaze glass, which made it easy to break through, first with my hand, then kicking an opening large enough for a man to walk through. I stepped into the opening that led to the dining room as Harper winced at the crunch of glass beneath my boots.

"My floors . . . ," she whimpered. "Ben and I spent an entire summer refinishing these floors. Now you've scratched them all up."

I shook my head at her, incredulous that she was worried

about some wooden planks at a time like this. "It needs to be believable, Harp. You can replace the glass and fix the floors with your three-million-dollar life insurance payout."

The dining room was across the house from the living room, far enough away that if Ben had the television on and blaring, as he usually did, there was a good chance he wouldn't have heard the glass breaking. Plus, the windows were easily accessible from the porch and hidden behind dense shrubs—a perfect entry point for your everyday thief in the night. It seemed believable enough to me. I hoped it was enough for the police.

Harper followed me through the opening, her footsteps light as she stepped around the splintered carnage. A robbery needed to have things robbed, so I searched the first floor for anything of value—an antique mantel clock, several expensive vases, a painting from someone famous whose name I couldn't, and didn't care to, remember. I pulled the painting off the wall.

"Hey, put that back!" Harper demanded, seizing the framed art from me. "That's a Jackson Pollock I got at auction. Ben practically had a fistfight with the other bidder to get me this. I can't replace that."

I should have remembered Jackson Pollock, considering it was the artist Ben and Harper had named their son after. I grabbed it back.

"Which is exactly why the thief stole it. We need to hurry. The more time we waste, the more you risk. Go upstairs and grab your expensive jewelry and any valuables that you can easily carry."

"What are you going to do with my stuff?" Harper whimpered when she returned, carrying a plastic bag of jewelry.

"I'll drop the small stuff off at Goodwill and hide the painting in my attic until things blow over."

"But these are family heirlooms!"

"Jewelry is useless if you're in jail or living on the streets, Harp!" How was this so hard for her to understand?

Ten minutes later the "stolen goods' were tossed in the trunk of my car, which I had pulled into the garage to avoid any neighborly observations, and everything looked the way I expected a break-in should look. There was always the chance I had missed something, but as I re-created the events step by step, I thought—and hoped—it was convincing enough.

The last—and hardest—part was the body. The knife sat rigid in Ben's chest, a pool of blood around the wound and a drizzle of it snaking to the floor. One hand still clung to the hilt; the other had flopped over the edge of the sofa.

I didn't want to risk messing with the body more than Harper had already done, so I decided to let it be. It seemed plausible Ben was sleeping when his attacker snuck in and stabbed him. Perhaps Ben had reached for the knife to try to pull it out . . . but was too weak with impending death to succeed. Then it was lights out, and here we were. Anything was possible . . . I hoped.

"Here's what's going to happen. You're going to call 911 now. Then you're going to call me, so that there's a call record of you phoning me after them. It's important they think they were the first immediate call made after you found Ben dead."

"Uh-huh." Harper's voice trembled, her gaze was unfocused and wild. She was barely hanging on to my instructions. The concern about the windows and floors, how she'd clung to the painting . . . it was how she compartmentalized. I had seen her get hung up on silly details the last time this happened. It was her coping method during extreme duress, focusing on anything but the real problem at hand.

"Hey, sis, I got you. You'll get through this." I hugged her, absorbing the shudder from each breath.

"Thank you, Lane . . . for always saving me."

"I'm your brother. It's what brothers do. I'm going to slip out the back, so give me a five-minute head start before you call the cops. Don't call my phone for another five minutes or so. I don't want them tracing the call to a nearby cell tower, in case they're able to do that. I need to be home for the call. Got it?"

A mute nod from Harper, then I was off.

I had no idea how call tracing actually worked or if the extent of my efforts would prove relevant, but I figured better safe than in prison.

"I'm heading out now," I called over my shoulder as I left.

On my way out the back door, I noticed the small rectangular window right below my eyeline. It wasn't so much the unique midcentury design of colored, patterned glass that caught my eye, but the lack of it. A hole had been punched through, and from it the glass splintered in every direction. A heap of rainbow shards had scattered beneath the door, a toy truck among the glass.

"What the hell?" I muttered. How had we missed this? "Harp, get over here."

I felt her walk up behind me. "Yeah?"

"What happened here?" I pointed to the window.

She shrugged. "I don't know. I hadn't seen that until now. It might have happened when Jackson and Elise were playing outside. You know how destructive Jackson can be."

I knelt down, examining the details. The truck sat on top of the glass—not beneath it—as if someone had placed it there after breaking in. This wasn't good. How would the cops explain two break-in points? It was downright suspicious. Or maybe... maybe it only validated our work. Was it true after all? Was Ben Paris murdered? If that was the case . . . who did it? And why? Because a robbery gone wrong sure as hell wasn't it. Nothing was missing, and Ben didn't look like he even had a chance to fight back. Unless Ben forgot his key, broke in, randomly placed the truck there, then killed himself?

It sounded ridiculous even in my head, but I couldn't worry about it now. What's done was done.

"Did you notice if anything was missing, Harp?" I asked. If someone had broken in, they were looking for something specific. Had they found it? I suspected not, because if there was one thing I knew about my sister and her now dead husband, they knew how to lock up their secrets tight.

"No, everything was in its usual place when I got home."

Maybe the broken window was nothing. Maybe it was something. I didn't have time to dissect all the possible scenarios.

"Um, let me think." I headed into the kitchen, opening and shutting a few drawers. With duct tape in hand, I ripped a piece of plastic wrap the size of the window and sealed it shut with the tape. "Here's what happened if the cops ask. The kids were outside playing and threw the truck in through the window. You haven't had a chance to fix it. Got it?"

I carefully swept up the glass shards and moved the truck.

"What if the cops ask the kids to corroborate that? They'll say it's not true—even if they did do it. Why can't we just say it was broken when I arrived . . . which is true?"

"Because it doesn't make sense that there were two break-in points, Harp. The fewer the questions, the better."

"No kidding," Harper grumbled under her breath. "You should have listened to me before breaking my window."

"Hey, I never claimed to be a crime-scene cover-up expert. I'm working on the fly here." I handed Harper her cell phone, then cupped her hand. "Give me a few minutes, then call 911. Sound frantic. Sound scared. Make it believable."

"That won't be difficult, Lane. I *am* frantic. And scared. My husband killed himself and I have no idea why."

"No, your husband was murdered. Remember? That is your truth now."

I didn't tell her my suspicions that Ben might *have*, in fact, been murdered. I'd been tempted to do it myself after what he'd done. But I didn't need to heap more on her than she already carried. I had a feeling the truth would spill out soon enough. I just had to hope my sister survived the whiplash.

Chapter 3

Candace Moriarty-Flynn

To my beautiful Candace, whose name means "clarity."
You've given my life clarity and purpose: to bring you joy.

Six weeks later . . .

There are two kinds of women in the world: those who buy throw pillows, and those who don't. You know the ones who do. Uppity housewives who wear Ann Taylor. Etsy-loving homemakers. Prudish moms who suck in bed but bake like a fiend.

Not me. I hung out on the other end of the spectrum. Chaotic. Go-with-the-flow. Free-thinking. Fun. My ex called me a "trailer park hippie," as if that were an insult. Give me all the bohemian vibes, thank you very much. I didn't make my bed each morning, let alone worry about decorating it with overpriced, uncomfortable pillows that I would just toss on a floor that I never swept clean. Who cared about a little dust when there were more fulfilling things to do with your time?

So when the doorbell rang, forcing me awake from my afternoon nap, I opened the door and instantly knew I was looking at a throw pillow kind of woman. Her three-quarter-sleeved blouse was buttoned way too high, and her form-fitting khaki capris did nothing to compliment her flat ass. One look at her told me all I needed to know. There was a void inside of her that she covered up in boring, beige, brand name pride. She offered a polite but empty smile.

"Can I help you?" I asked, expecting her to be a Jehovah's Witness or some other religious groupie offering spiritual wares that I didn't want or need.

Her face, caked with foundation, drooped with a frown as she spoke warily. "I'm looking for Lane. Is he home?"

"Who's asking?" I felt like I should recognize her, but I couldn't quite place where I knew her from.

She extended her hand across the threshold, but I ignored it. "I'm Harper—Lane's sister."

So *this* was Harper. My new sister-in-law. "Oh, hi. I thought you looked familiar."

Her hand dropped to her side. "Yeah, we've met before. Over dinner. It's Candace, right?"

Oh yes, the awkward interrogation dinner of a million and one questions, all aimed at me. "Wow, that's quite a memory you have."

Her gaze felt intrusive. "Yep, I don't forget things easily."

Harper had an unmemorable face to match her unmemorable personality. Now *she* was the kind who made her bed every morning—sometimes even before coffee. Her red hair brushed against her chin. I hadn't remembered her being a ginger.

"You look different from when I last saw you."

Her hand flew up to her hair, touching it self-consciously. "New haircut. I needed a change, you know? It was either this or a pixie cut."

"A pixie cut is great if you want one day of feeling cute and three months of regret as you grow it out."

Her smile flicked on, then off, and her judgment traveled up and down my body. "You're quite tall, aren't you? I didn't remember you being so tall . . . and thin."

I was well aware of my five-foot-eleven height. "I suppose."

"Lane never dated anyone so . . . modelesque before. I mean that as a compliment. You're quite stunning. And young. A little young for Lane, though, don't you think?"

"Age is just a number, as they say."

Her lips rose in a grin that didn't look natural. "As long as you're happy together, that's all that matters, which I'm sure you are."

Clearly Harper liked flattery, but she doled it out futilely. It was all so unsettling, her obsessing over my looks and age. I muttered a questioning "Would you like to come in?" for lack of anything more interesting to say.

"I was wondering when you'd offer," Harper said for appearance's sake, as she was already inching her way through the door.

"Sorry. How rude of me." How rude of *her* to show up unannounced. I stepped aside, only now seeing the two tiny creatures that had been hiding behind her hips, all elbows and knees.

The little boy encompassed every creepy child in every horror movie ever made—oily black hair and pale skin. I wondered if when he smiled he'd reveal a mouth full of fangs . . . though he didn't appear to be the smiling type. A grin would probably crack his face.

"I'm not sure if you remember Elise and Jackson. Guys, come in and introduce yourselves. This is Uncle Lane's girl-friend, Miss Candace."

The three shuffled into the narrow foyer, the kids still cling-ing to their mother like I was about to eat them.

"Hi," Elise whispered. She flashed a meek smile, avoiding eye contact. Definitely shy and annoyingly timid. I wanted to yell at her to speak up, but instead I grinned back at her. Based on the snug, sparkly *Purrfect in every way* kitten T-shirt she wore, I guessed her to be about seven. A platinum blond, her hair looked borrowed from a Barbie doll, with knots all through it, as though her mother never brushed it.

I pegged Harper with my gaze. "Wife."

"Excuse me?" Her face wrinkled in confusion.

"I'm Lane's wife, not his girlfriend."

Her mouth dropped, and pink splotches rose up her neck. Aw, I had embarrassed the poor thing.

"What? You're kidding, right?"

Lifting my hand, I flashed her my ring finger, adorned with a platinum band. "It's true!"

"You were b-barely d-dating . . . ," she stuttered. "When did—"

"How old are you, Ellie?" I asked, cutting Harper off before she tossed out another question. His family was his territory to handle, not mine.

"It's *Elise*," Harper corrected.

"I'm eleven, ma'am." Elise's voice was as tiny as she was.

"Holy shit, no way! I guessed seven, based on that shirt."

Harper cast me a glare. "Language, please."

I rolled my eyes and mumbled a "sorry" that I didn't mean. The kids had to grow up sometime. I would have bet my last dollar that Harper was a helicopter parent, always hovering. She probably still dressed Ellie—I mean *Elise*—and cut her hot dogs into minuscule pieces.

"I'm small for my age." Elise's lips puckered in a pout. She tugged out her shirt, examining it upside-down. "What's wrong with my shirt?"

"It's just a bit . . . babyish, don't you think? A kitten . . . *really*? Maybe one of these days I can take you shopping for a girls' day out and update your wardrobe. Would you like that?" That earned another scowl from the sister-in-law.

"I don't think so," Harper cut in.

I turned to the creepy kid. "And you're Jack?"

"Jackson," Harper corrected again, then knelt down at his eye level. "Sweetie, say hi."

Raising his gaze from the floor, he looked at me with inky eyes that bolstered my suspicions. Two abysmal black pools rung with bluish half-moons that even a cool cucumber and the world's best eye cream couldn't fix. His face hung like a white curtain, weary and sad. I saw distance in his eyes, like he was detached from this world. I definitely didn't want to be alone in a house at night with this kid.

"Sorry, he's shy," Harper explained, resting her hand on his head.

So *that's* what mothers called their weirdo kids—*shy*.

He looked like a child who appreciated horror stories. Hell, he could star in one. Maybe we could connect in that way, one thriller lover to another. It gave me an idea.

"Do you believe in ghosts?" I asked him. I wondered if he knew some personally.

He shrugged. "I guess."

"Did you know that an old lady died in this house? It took three days before a neighbor found her body after the mail started piling up. Sometimes you can hear her pacing the upstairs, haunting the rooms." It was mostly true—except for the haunting part. I wasn't totally fond of the idea of an elderly corpse rotting away in my spare bedroom, but as long as I didn't wake up to see her skeletal specter hovering over my bed, I could deal with it.

The boy seemed vaguely interested as his mouth opened, a row of baby teeth peeking through. The girl looked up at her mother with what appeared to be a cry for help.

"What was that about?" Harper's voice lowered to a stern warning. "Don't scare them like that or else they'll never fall asleep tonight! Do you not have any common sense when it comes to kids?"

"Apparently I don't. Sorry." I turned to the boy, winked, and mouthed, "It's true."

I was done entertaining, so I glanced back at the belly of the house.

"Laaaaane!" I called. The forced chitchat was simply exhausting. "Your sister's here!" Then I turned back to Harper, eager to escape. "I'll go see where he is."

I didn't get more than two steps before it registered what Harper had said: *They'll never fall asleep tonight.* Surely she wasn't bringing her family to stay in my home without asking first? Even if she did ask, the answer would be a resounding "hell no." I was still on my honeymoon with my husband, and a house full of extended family was the last thing we needed. I had planned a month of romance for us, thanks to the tips I found in a *Honeymoon Romance* book I bought. Candlelit dinners, nighttime skinny-dipping, wine under the moonlight, lunch picnics in the yard, *christening* every room in the house with our love . . . No way was I letting his sister and her kids barge in on that.

Lane appeared around the corner, sweeping past me as he pulled Harper into an eager hug. "It's been too long, Harp."

She grabbed the knob of black hair pulled back at the nape of his neck. "Clearly. You've grown a man-bun since I last saw you!"

"Shut up. You're so genderist. It's not a man-bun, it's a regular bun."

Harper raised a skeptical eyebrow, then folded the collar of his shirt down. "If you grow one of those nasty frizzled beards, I'm hosting an intervention. Did Candace inspire this little . . . hipster makeover?"

"No. I'm just trying a new look." Lane flipped his collar back up and simpered.

"Ugh. Try another one, please. Midlife crisis much?" She tugged the edge of his beanie down over his eyes and laughed. "And by the way, what's up with the hat? It's swimming weather, not snowing weather. And you're *indoors*. What's next—sunglasses at night?"

Lane pushed the beanie back up on his forehead. "Okay, you made your point. Moving on, I've got so much to tell you. I've missed you!"

Missed her? It had only been a month since the memorial service for Harper's husband. How needy were these two? It was shortly after that when Lane introduced me to Harper over dinner at a mediocre prime rib restaurant, and I was pretty sure they'd had another dinner since then.

"And Elise and Jackson—you've both grown like weeds since I last saw you." Lane crouched down and scooped them into his arms as Elise giggled and Jackson's face shifted just enough to look like he might grin . . . but thankfully he didn't.

"Guess what?" Lane said, his voice high with boyish excitement. "I just got this cool drone. Wanna try it? It's on the back porch."

Elise screeched a "Me first!" before darting toward the back door with Jackson sluggishly following behind.

When I turned back to Harper, I saw three suitcases being lugged across the entryway, their wheels leaving long scrapes across my hardwood floor.

"What's this, Harp?" Lane asked.

So he didn't know either. He was lucky that he was being blindsided along with me. Otherwise . . . I didn't need to finish the threat.

"I need to ask you for a favor." Harper paused, glanced at me, then drew toward her brother. "Since Ben died things have been . . . rough, to say the least. The insurance money hasn't come in yet while the investigation's still open, and I can't afford the mortgage until I get my payout. I wanted to rent the house out in the meantime to cover the costs . . . and I was hoping to stay with you in the interim."

"Of course," Lane said without a beat, taking the suitcase handles from her. "We'd be happy to have you for as long as you want. That's what family is for, right, Candace?" He tossed a wishful look at me that gave me no choice but to agree. But I couldn't—wouldn't—oblige them. No, I had spent my last relationship being a doormat. I'd evolved since then.

"Aren't you rich? I thought your husband was a financial investor or something." Certainly someone who could afford fancy ugly slacks and a mini-mansion where all the Durham, North Carolina, *richers* lived could afford a hotel room.

Harper's lips straightened. "Not that it's any of your business, but because of the nature of Ben's death, they've frozen all my assets and I can't access our money. So right now I am officially broke."

"What about your mother?" I offered. "Can't you stay with her?"

"Honey . . . ," Lane interjected.

"I thought of that, but with the kids? They'd drive her nuts. Plus she's in a two-bedroom rental. We need more space, a yard . . . and it'd only be temporary, I promise." But Harper's assurance meant nothing to me. I knew from experience that broke houseguests became permanent leeches.

I wanted to strangle that diamond-adorned neck of hers.

"Look," I stated, as kindly authoritative as possible, "Lane and I are still on our honeymoon. We need privacy, alone time together—"

"Honeymoon? You were serious about being married?" Harper shot a scowl at Lane. "You got married and didn't tell me? And to a woman you barely know."

Now my claws were out. "Excuse me, but I'm standing right here!"

I would have said a lot more but a loud *thump* coming from

the kitchen interrupted me. "Did you hear that?" Lane and Harper followed me toward a row of windows, where a circle of fractures splintered out in all directions from a cleft in the middle of a pane. "What happened?" I yelled at no one and everyone.

Beneath the window, outside in the grass, lay the destroyed drone. Across the yard Elise held the controller with a horrified look on her face. Turning on Lane, I gestured to the cracked window.

"Do you see why I don't want them staying here, Lane? They've been here for less than ten minutes and are already breaking things!"

Harper advanced on me. "Don't speak about my children that way. It was an accident."

"And I'm guessing you don't have the money to fix it?"

Lane stretched his arms out between us, as if holding us back. But I didn't need fingernails to cut her when I had sharp words instead. "Harper, you may not approve of your brother's choice in wife, but this is our life. And this is our home. You're a grown woman. You should be able to take care of your children. That is your job as their mother."

While my next words were for Lane, my eyes remained fixed on Harper. "And Lane, I'm your wife. And if you have any respect for our vows, you'll realize it's not good for our marriage to have your sister living with us."

Lane rested one hand on each of our shoulders. "Harp, Candace, I love you both. Yes, things between Candace and I happened pretty quickly, but our love is intense." Lane sidled up to me, wrapping his arm around my shoulders—right where it should be. "We both instantly knew we were meant for each other. I wanted to tell you in person, but things have been chaotic. I'm sorry I didn't have you there to witness it."

"To witness your stupidity?" Harper shook her head at my husband like he was a child. "Lane, you of all people should know how manipulative women are. You lived with me and Mom your whole life. What you did was irresponsible, but what's done is done. I just wish you would have talked to me first."

I had to speak up. "Don't talk down to him. He's an adult who can make decisions for himself." I could feel the fight inside me forming.

"You know how they describe love at first sight?" Lane said. "Well, now I understand what it feels like."

Harper sighed heavily and rolled her eyes. "Yes, beautiful women have that effect on men. Look, I want to be happy for you, but I don't understand why you'd exclude me. I thought we were close, after all we've been through together."

"Hey, we are close. I'm sorry I didn't consider your feelings." Lane's voice dropped with apology. I hated that Harper was making Lane feel guilty about the best day of our lives.

"When did it happen?" she asked.

"A week and a half ago. I know it's a bit of a whirlwind, but we love each other and want to be together. There was no reason not to."

"And you couldn't invite me to be there for it? It hurts, Lane." Harper touched her palm to her heart. A tear slid down her cheek, and I wondered if it was as fake as her press-on eyelashes.

"Sis"—Lane released me and comforted Harper—"I was afraid you'd try to talk me out of it. It was with a justice of

31

the peace, nothing fancy. And Candace and I decided together that we only wanted it to be us."

"We've been through everything together and you didn't invite me to your wedding. I don't know what to say. Congratulations, I guess."

"Please don't be angry, Harp. I love this woman"—he glanced over at me and smiled—"and I've never been happier."

Harper hugged Lane, casting a dirty look at me over his shoulder.

Bitch.

"Well, if you're happy, that's all I could ask for my brother. So I guess me staying here is off the table, huh?"

I watched the battle wage inside Lane's head. Wife or sister. Who would win? If only I would have known the battle was just getting started. When Lane turned to me, I already knew his answer.

"Candace, we will have forever to be together, but right now my grieving sister needs us. Please try to understand."

Sister, one. Wife, zero. So that's how it was going to be.

I would give him a free pass. But there would be no next time. If I stood a chance at winning against his sister, the best thing I could do was keep Lane happy. "Okay, I'll get the spare bedrooms ready for you. I hope you like decorative pillows!"

Harper clapped her hands together, the tear gone as quickly as it came. "Thank you. And yes, I love pretty pillows!"

Of course she did. Which meant I was exactly right about what kind of woman Harper Paris was. And so I knew exactly how to drive her away.

Chapter 4

Lane

If this living arrangement didn't kill me, my wife would. We were barely two hours into Harper's move into the house proper and already my wife and sister were at each other's throats.

Your sister has too much stuff, Candace complained in one ear. *Your wife is a slob,* Harper accused in the other. *Cut your hair to an appropriate length for a grown man,* Harper criticized. *Your sister's just jealous because you're cool and she's an old hag,* Candace retorted. Back and forth, the hostility waged with me stuck in the middle between the woman I loved and the sister I needed.

"There's more," Harper yelled down to me as she headed up the steps carrying two stacked boxes. That was in addition to the four other trips I had already made, lugging suitcases and bags brimming with clothes and toys and *stuff*. Why did women need so much crap? "Check the trunk of the car. And don't crush the hyacinth on your way down the walkway! I saw you trampled one already."

The front door was propped open, giving entry to a perfect spring breeze, and the scent of hyacinth—or was it hibiscus?—rode the wind in, filling the house. Through mounds of fresh mulch, green spikes poked their way up through the earth. Daffodils or tulips, I could never tell which until their blooms crested, and even then I often got them confused, no matter how often Harp drilled me with details. That was the breadth of my flower knowledge, and I only knew those names from last fall, when Harper dropped a couple dozen bulbs on my lawn and insisted we spruce up my garden. By *we*, she meant her, but I was happy to give her something to do. Anything to take her mind off the demons chasing her.

Making one more trip down and back up the gray flagstone walkway, I stepped over the neighbors' cat, Puddin'. Apparently, he preferred my expensive sod grass over his litter box.

"Did you pack the whole house?" I joked to Harper, dropping a heavy box, filled with what felt like hardcover books, at the foot of the stairs with a *thump*. "What the heck is in here?"

"Only the necessities," Harper called over her shoulder from the second-story landing. "I promise you'll hardly know we're here," she hollered as she rounded the corner, out of sight, toward her bedroom. A loud thud shook the ceiling, and a moment later Harper reappeared at the top of the stairs empty-handed.

"You don't mind if I clean out these two extra bedrooms, do you? They're a complete mess. Honestly, Lane, how do you live like this? It's like a teenager lives here." Harper gestured toward the kids' bedroom behind her, then trotted down the stairs.

Candace looked up from the television show she wasn't watching, her blue eyes icy. "I use those rooms to store what I can't fit in my closet, Harper. Please don't touch my stuff." It was a demand, not a request.

"I kind of have to move it if I'm going to be staying here, Candace. Clothes and shoes and junk scattered everywhere. At least let me fold and organize it for you. You might never want me to leave, you know. It'll be like having a live-in maid and cook!"

Harper flashed a wide, toothy Anne Hathaway smile. But Candace's scowl from the living room sofa said it all. She knew this wouldn't be a short-term stay. And it wasn't a welcome stay either.

I had to admit, I didn't hate the idea of Harper living with us. Not that I didn't want alone time with my new wife, but it would be nice to have someone cleaning the house, making home-cooked dinners, doing laundry. Those weren't things Candace did, and mothering came naturally to Harper. She'd had years of practice after our father died—when I was eleven and Harper was ten—and our mother was working two jobs, most of the time leaving us to fend for ourselves. Even though Harper was a year younger than me, she had always taken care of me like a smaller, more available version of Mom. It wasn't that Mom wanted to heap all that responsibility on us; she had no choice. She was a widow with two kids. What options did she have?

I remember one summer when Mom had hired an after-school babysitter, a neighborhood girl whose family had hit hard times, but the girl had set our stove on fire making mac 'n' cheese and that ended that. Since that summer Harper had stepped in to fill in the gaps, a girl born with a broom in one hand and a spatula in the other.

I didn't need Candace to be like Harper. Candace offered so much more than a clean house. She offered me a love that colored in my gray heart, then made me want to tear it out just to prevent her from breaking it. Our fights nearly killed me, but Candace was worth it.

Candace made me wax poetic when I didn't even know I had poetry in me.

In an ideal world, my sister would teach my wife her favorite recipes or cleaning tips and they'd laugh over tea and scones together. But that was the same make-believe land where other fantasies lived, like half-naked college-girl car washes and sexy pillow-fight sleepovers. I knew better than to hope my sister and wife would ever get along.

I turned toward the front door to grab what I hoped was the last of Harper's belongings as Candace aimed a hushed "Lane" at me.

"What's up, babe?" Already I was preparing to defuse the bomb I anticipated exploding at any moment.

She muted the television and sat upright. "This has got to stop—now. There is no reason she needs this much crap for a couple weeks. You know she's moving in for good, don't you?"

I leaned down to kiss Candace's reddening cheek, but she backed out of reach. I hadn't seen this possessive, earnest side of her before, but it was kind of cute.

"I promise it won't be long. If she starts to get too settled, I'll deal with it. But for now let's not make a problem where there isn't one. Please, honey?"

"Don't *honey* me. You put your sister before your wife. Not cool, Lane. I'm trying to handle this the best I can, but we're only a couple weeks into our marriage and we already have live-in guests. We need time *together*. Alone. To connect. If you can't give me that, then clearly we made a mistake getting married." She was quickly spiraling into uncute.

It almost sounded like she was threatening to leave me over this.

"You want me to kick my own sister and her kids out on the street? When her husband just recently died?"

Candace laughed with an unfamiliar coldness. I almost didn't recognize her anymore. Where was my fluid, anything goes, live-in-the-moment wife?

"The street? C'mon, Lane, she owns a house." She rose from the sofa and blustered into the kitchen as I followed her. "A huge house, by the way. And she has a mother with a spare bedroom. She's got other options. You're just too much of a doormat to stand up to her—to stand up *for me*. For *us*."

I sighed. "Tell me what you want me to do and I'll do it."

"I tried that, and you did what you wanted anyway." She picked up a ceramic plate, angrily slapping slices of cheese and crackers on it. "I asked you to say no but you didn't. Now she's already friggin' moved her stuff in and my stuff out. I'm going to have to move my winter clothes into the attic. That dank, musty air is going to ruin the fabric, Lane! And there might be mice up there, ready to chew holes in everything."

I tried to take her seriously, but it was impossible when she was complaining like a raging teen.

"You're more concerned about your clothes than your family?"

"Not my family. Yours."

"My family is part of the package, Candace. And what you're asking of me is pretty selfish."

"Selfish? Because I want alone time with my new husband? Because I want my own space in my own house?" She continued slicing cheese in a trembling rage.

"Yes. Putting your needs above the needs of others is the very definition of selfish."

With a rush of motion, she whipped the plate across the room, sending a spray of broken ceramic and crackers along the floor. I jumped with shock . . . and fear.

"I'm just going to warn you, Lane. You made a mistake. A big one. Maybe the biggest one of your life, because this might cost you everything. You know what I'm talking about."

I *did* know, and it was a horrible threat. One I would never forgive her for if she followed through with it. As a man, I knew better than to fight back; growing up with a sister and mother taught me that much about women. I'd do what I always did: Bend. Cave. Plead. Make everything better . . . somehow.

Only, I wasn't sure if this was fixable, because it was the worst kind of ultimatum. The kind that would cost me something important no matter what. Harper or Candace, my blood or my heart. I couldn't live without either.

"I'll figure out a way to get Harper to leave," I vowed, grabbing her hand and kissing her fingertips. "Give me two weeks, that's all I need. I'll find her an affordable place and get her set up. Okay?"

"Fine." It clearly wasn't fine. "You can have it your way." But it wasn't my way. "Two weeks, Lane. That's it. Or else I'm gone."

Candace brushed past me in a huff, storming through the

kitchen doorway between two small eavesdroppers I hadn't noticed until now. Elise and Jackson looked up at me, Jackson's eyes vacant, Elise's filling with tears. The kids had heard everything.

"You don't care about us!" Elise sobbed, then ran past me and out the back door.

Jackson simply stood watching, then slowly turned and slipped upstairs.

"Elise, come back!" I called after her.

I'd never felt like such an ass before. My wife had a temper, my sister was helpless, and my niece and nephew felt unwanted. Five people, each at their wits' end, forced to share four walls— how much worse could it possibly get? And this was only the beginning . . .

Chapter 5

Harper

One month ago today I buried my soul under the weeping willow Ben and I had planted together in the backyard, and I had been digging at the patch of dirt ever since. Technically, Ben wasn't buried where I had rested a stone plaque honoring him, because the police hadn't released his body to me yet. *A couple more weeks,* they kept telling me the autopsy would take. By the time they finished, I wondered if there would be anything left of him to bury.

We had called it a *memorial service,* but I didn't want to remember. I wanted to forget. Forget that he was dead. Forget the lies, the cheating, the hollow left inside of me that led him to kill himself. If only the past year had never happened, I wouldn't be standing in the bedroom that we had shared, packing up our things for storage, wishing I could erase Ben's death from my mind and replace it with our happy life *before*.

I was exhausted from missing Ben. It felt as if I had set down my heart and forgotten where I left it.

I stood beneath the only picture that remained on our Hendricks Way bedroom wall, the one taken at our wedding. Both of us were barefoot, walking hand in hand down Sunset Beach, my white dress flowing behind me as it caught on the salty breeze, Ben's hair ruffled into curls. A perfect day. The absolute best day.

I lifted the frame off the hook and stared into the past. How could he strip me of all the good memories by leaving me with only the bad ones? All the hungry kisses, gone. The passionate nights as we explored each other's bodies, gone. The weekend getaways and night swimming and reveling at each child's birth, gone, gone, gone. Holding the frame above my head, I threw it across the room, watching with a morbid satisfaction as the glass shattered and wood splintered.

"Mom, what was that?" Elise's voice echoed from down the hallway.

"I, uh, I just accidentally dropped something, sweetie," I called back, stuffing the tremor in my voice down.

The person I was *before* was different from who I became *after*. That's what grief does, steals every ounce of joy and exchanges it for sorrow. It robbed me of my future and turned me hateful. I couldn't even tell you what I was angry at. Myself? My kids? The mailman who accidentally switched my mail with the neighbor's? The waitress who mixed up my dinner order?

I yearned for my old life—the one where I didn't grieve or lose my husband to another woman. But reality has a way of eroding such hopes. This vacant bedroom was the daily reminder that I was a widow too young, with no one to share my friends' secrets with, or to make fun of television shows with, or to tease me about the gray hairs I fruitlessly dyed.

Damn, I missed Ben. Wanting to wade in the grief, yet resisting the wallow, *that* was the irony of death. I wanted the pain, and yet I hated the pain. It had only been days and I already missed my house. The Colonial floor-to-ceiling windows. Lustrous, original oak floors. Large wraparound porch. Four-poster bed with a down pillowtop. Custom-made kitchen island. I appreciated my brother opening up his home to us, but Hendricks Way had been my home for so long that it was imprinted on me, the creaks of the floorboards a part of my lifeblood.

I pressed my hand to the window overlooking the backyard. I was disgusted by the neglected state of my garden, but I simply couldn't push myself to deal with it. Weeds crowded the black-eyed Susans, overshadowing their yellow petals that contrasted against their black centers. My poor hollyhocks had been a showstopper with their apricot and purple blooms, but now they wept of thirst with their heads bowed and leaves brown. I couldn't bear to watch my passion flowers struggle for life, their bright purple tendrils a distant memory. Behind my fence the gentrified urban neighborhood sprawled out as far as I could see, homes hidden beneath ancient oak trees, connected by winding footpaths where privileged children rode bikes and moms kept up at a fast jog behind them.

Young and ambitious, Ben and I had picked this neighborhood and this house together. I had dabbled in architecture in college and instantly fell in love when I saw this run-down neoclassical Greek Revival style with a touch of Italianate—an architect's dream. It had been built in the 1860s by an eccentric North Carolinian family of means with a knack for innovation. In a time when the concept of air-conditioning wasn't even a twinkle in inventor Willis Carrier's eye, the home's designer used nature's solution. Floor-to-ceiling walk-through windows offered a consistent coastal breeze to maintain a comfortable room temperature. And for those brutal summer days, hot air would naturally rise up the grand staircase—up, up, up to the belvedere—where it exited through a row of small, open windows near the eaves. Louver vents offered an escape for the southern heat, along with vents in each of the bedrooms. This avant-garde ventilation system was pure genius, if you ask me, though Ben still preferred the convenience of modern AC.

By the time Ben and I found the house for sale—and on foreclosure!—much of the wood had rotted from the Carolinian humidity or been neglected to the point of disrepair. But that didn't deter us or our dreams. With more than five thousand square feet to renovate, it had been quite a restoration project. It took a grueling two years of backbreaking work, but in the end we had rediscovered its beauty and made it our own.

Four open boxes sat on the window seat, all of them full, all of them holding decades' worth of memories. Next to the last box was a turquoise-and-gold urn caked in dust, a portable monument to the darkness inside me. I wondered when I'd be adding Ben's urn to my collection.

I'd almost cleaned out the entire master bedroom, minus Ben's bedside table. I opened the top drawer and grabbed its meager remnants. A handful of handmade Father's Day cards from the kids. Gaudy red leather handcuffs he had bought that we hadn't even used once, the key to which was probably lost. A Stephen King book with a bookmark halfway through, which Ben would never finish. His work cell phone. And an envelope.

A bulge crinkled from the bottom of the fold, so I opened it and peeked inside. A torn corner of paper with a street address, *3 Summer Ln,* scribbled across it. A hardware store shopping list and rough sketch of the kids' playset he had started building. And a jewelry store receipt. My nervous fingers dropped the paper and it fluttered across the dusty floor, like it was trying to scurry away. I picked it up and unfolded it, mumbling the description out loud:

> *18-karat gold charm bracelet*
> *Engraved with: True love waits*

Waits for what? Was this an anniversary gift Ben had planned to give me? And where was the bracelet? Though the message was cryptic, it fit *us.* Ben and I spent a lifetime waiting. Waiting to get married until after he graduated with his master's degree. Waiting to buy the right house until after we saved up. Waiting for Ben's investment career to take off. Waiting to have a second child after years of fertility struggles. We knew all about waiting; it had been a part of our relationship since the very beginning, when I'd told him I couldn't be his girlfriend, and if he cared enough he'd wait until I was ready. It took me almost three years to be ready, but Ben had waited. Maybe this bracelet was a tribute to that—to all the waiting. To all we had endured to be together.

The stillness of the house haunted me, the silence cut by the drip of the master bathroom faucet. Ben had been meaning to fix that for months, but he simply never made the time. And then time ran out. I turned over the envelope and grabbed a pen sitting on Ben's bedside table. It wasn't Ben's anymore, because Ben wasn't here. I jotted down a to-do list, starting with fixing the faucet. Then I tossed the pen and envelope in my purse, grabbed a box, and left the mausoleum of memories.

On my way down the stairs I saw the silhouette of a person standing at the front door. The frosted glass masked all features except for the dark attire of the visitor. Then there was a knock, the sound reverberating against the vast emptiness. And another knock before I reached the door.

"Mooom! Someone's at the door!" Elise yelled from the bowels of the house.

"I've got it. Stay upstairs and keep packing."

Although the solid oak door was wide enough to easily fit two grown men in the doorway, it swung open effortlessly. The detective who had been assigned Ben's case stood on the front porch. By now I was used to his check-ins.

"Good morning, Detective Meltzer. Come in." I stepped aside for him, a man who almost fit the girth of the doorway all on his own.

Detective Levi Meltzer had missed his calling as a wrestler. At easily six foot two, this was the kind of guy you wanted on the streets fighting crime, because I was pretty sure his muscles were bulletproof. The man looked impenetrable. I imagined his ring name being *Macho Mustache,* or as Lane called him, *Pornstache,* a tribute to his *Orange Is the New Black* obsession. Lane had often quoted television shows as if he'd come up with the witticisms himself. And I always laughed as if I'd never heard them before.

"How are you today, Harper?"

Although I still called him *Detective* out of respect, for me he was on a first-name basis. *That* was how often I saw him. Right after Ben's death it had been daily, sometimes multiple times a day, that he'd drop by or ask me to come down to the station for questioning. But now, being weeks into the investigation, his visits were becoming less frequent. Which was probably a good thing. Because that meant I was becoming less and less of a suspect.

"I'm hanging in there," I replied.

"I couldn't help but notice the moving truck. You going somewhere?" He cocked an eyebrow.

So he was following me, watching me. Perhaps I wasn't as out of the hot seat as I thought.

"I'm moving in with my brother for the time being. I've decided to rent this place out until the investigation is closed. I don't have a job, and I can't afford to keep paying the mortgage on this place in the meantime."

"I see. You know not to leave town until we find Ben's killer, right?"

Of course I knew. I had only been reminded by Detective Meltzer and my attorney a dozen times. "Yes, sir. I'm just moving across town. Not even ten minutes away. I'll jot down the address for you so you know where to find me."

"That'd be great, thanks. Here you go."

He pulled out a pen and pad from his pocket and handed them to me.

I scribbled a circle, but the ink had gone dry. "I'm sure I

have a spare in my kitchen." I headed into the kitchen to find a pen, and Detective Meltzer followed me. "I haven't heard from you in a while. Have they finished the autopsy yet?"

"No, ma'am. We're understaffed, and the coroner is backed up for weeks so, unfortunately, I can't tell you how much longer until we have the autopsy results. It can take up to twelve weeks, in some cases."

"So you're no closer to finding out who did this to my husband." I added a touch of annoyance to make it clear I was frustrated. The frustration was genuine—I needed the autopsy results to determine cause of death, and I needed cause of death to get my insurance payout. Who wouldn't be frustrated by this lengthy process with closure out of reach?

Detective Meltzer shook his head. "I'm afraid we found no DNA at the scene, have no witnesses, nothing to point us to the killer. I wish I had better news for you, Harper, especially given the unique nature of the crime." He paused, and I caught him watching me root through the junk drawer looking for a pen. When I found one, I wrote down Lane's address and handed him his notepad back.

"What do you mean by 'unique nature of the crime'?"

"Your broken back window was taped shut with only cellophane and right next to the door, which would have been an easy access point for the thief to break in. And yet the thief instead chose to break through a dining room window. It makes you wonder: What type of thief would choose a loud, conspicuous option over a quiet, easy in-and-out?"

A surge of panic swelled up my chest, suffocating me. *I was caught.* "Maybe he didn't see the broken window," I said, wondering if my practiced breaths were giving me away.

"You don't do a job like this without first casing the home, Harper. So it implies one of two things. Either you have an oblivious thief with an unusual thirst to kill, or the whole thing was staged. Considering you have an alibi, and we have no primary suspects with a motive to kill your husband, it leaves us with a lot more questions than answers. However, we have found a new angle."

"What kind of new angle?" *Dear God, let it not point to me or the suicide.*

"We've gotten access to Ben's work files on his personal computer, and we found some interesting . . . numbers in his accounting. I'm not at liberty to tell you all the details, but it looks like Ben might have been investing clients' money in a promissory note scam. If he lost a client a lot of money, well, that could make someone angry enough to want him dead."

The detective may as well have been speaking Chinese. "Promissory note scam? What's that?"

"Ben's company was in some financial trouble, so the employees were asking friends and family to buy their debt. It's called affinity fraud, in which an investor exploits people who trust him. In exchange, each lender was promised a high interest rate yield on their loan. But it turns out all the money lent by these investors disappeared . . . along with Ben's CEO, Randolph Whitman." Detective Meltzer sighed. "Some of these people lost their life savings."

"Randy is gone?" I had wondered why he hadn't attended Ben's memorial, but it never occurred to me that he'd taken off. I had assumed it was too hard for him to face. The two had been close friends since college and trusted each other with their lives, enough so that they went into business together. We had celebrated holidays and birthdays with Randy. How could he have dragged Ben into something scandalous? "I can't believe that Ben would have scammed people." I shook my head vehemently. "He was an honest businessman, Detective, and very generous with anyone who asked. Certainly not a thief."

I knew my husband. He was honest to a fault. One time he had ordered a camera, the cheapest one that the company offered, and when it arrived in the mail, Ben instantly knew he had gotten the wrong model. It was way nicer than the one he had paid for. Without hesitating, he called the company and offered to return it in exchange for the lesser camera. So Ben sent it back and waited. And waited some more. In the end, we got billed for two cameras but ended up with none when they claimed they had already sent the correct camera.

No good deed goes unpunished, I'd told Ben that day.

And no bad deed goes unseen, he'd replied. That experience taught me something important about Ben's character—that he valued integrity over everything. My husband was not a scam artist. Detective Meltzer had it all wrong.

"No one ever does imagine horrible things about someone they love, Harper. It's how people like that get away with it. The mirage of good hides the face of evil. I see it all the time."

For real villains, sure. Serial killers, yeah. The Ted Bundys and Charles Mansons who no one expected were psychopaths. But not a husband who stopped at the grocery store to pick up flowers, or a father who carried his kids on his shoulders. Ben was good at heart. "You don't know Ben like I do. That's not who he was."

"Did you know he held a private bank account under another name?"

I couldn't have heard him correctly.

"I'm sorry, what?"

"We think your husband was hiding money in other accounts."

I shook my head, sending the words loose in my brain. Hiding money? Other accounts? Did he mean the trust funds for the kids?

"We set up accounts for the kids when they were born. That must be what you found."

"No, Harper. This isn't the kids' accounts."

I felt my heart seize a little. Who would he have possibly been sending money to? Maybe I didn't know Ben at all. My shock must have given me away.

"I can see that's news to you. I think you need to reconsider what kind of man your husband really was."

"What name was the other account under?" It had to be the home-wrecking whore. I knew she existed. I'd seen her. That was the only possible explanation: he was funding her lifestyle while banging her.

"Does the name Medea Kent mean anything to you?"

Medea? What kind of name was that? "No, that doesn't sound familiar." From my purse the envelope with my to-do list poked out of the top. I pulled it out, had Detective Meltzer spell her crazy-ass name, and made a mental note to look her up later. "How much money is in this secret account?"

"I can't divulge the specifics yet, since it's still under investigation. There's a lot we still have to look into. Once we have a full list of people he stole from, we'll compile a list of suspects and keep you informed. Until then, just sit tight." He rapped his knuckles on the butcher block. "We still have a lot of unanswered questions at this point, but we'll get answers, I promise you."

It was the resounding theme of this investigation—unanswered questions. Including the question of what Ben had hidden from me and why. We were never desperate for money, so why would he feel the need to steal from innocent clients? What had he gotten himself involved in? Who was this Medea person? And did it have anything to do with why he took his own life?

I shoved the one question I truly wanted answered down my throat until it stuck there. It would only paint me in a terrible light. If the investigation didn't close, would I ever see a dime of the life insurance money? Would access to my bank accounts ever be restored? But the bigger concern was what would happen when they found out what I had done, because I could feel the past clawing its way to the surface. With this investigation getting more complicated—more *unique,* as Detective Meltzer put it—and drawing more focus on our family's skeletons, it was only a matter of time before my own secret slipped out and the truth caught up with me.

Ben's voice beyond the grave slipped into my brain, quoting his favorite movie of all time. *You can't handle the truth!* Maybe Jack Nicholson in *A Few Good Men* was right. I couldn't handle the truth. It wouldn't set me free. It would put me behind bars.

Chapter 6

Harper

Detective Meltzer was not yoked to sentimentality. His heart simply beat while mine thrummed with complex feelings. I understood the difference now. For him, death was a mystery to solve, not an experience to suffer through. After the detective left, confirming that he'd find me at Lane's with any new developments, I felt that raw ache of loneliness all over again, standing at the kitchen sink, listening to the shuffle of my children's feet above me.

Like teeth gnawing on my soul, I had lost parts of me piece by piece. At first, it was the joy in small things, like my first cup of coffee each morning. Then it grew into the big things, like not caring when Elise earned straight A's, or when shy little Jackson made a friend at school. Before I knew it, I had stopped doing more than just existing, every memory and emotion leading back to a time I couldn't reach. Back when my life was whole.

"Moooom!" I was convinced Elise's voice could travel light-years. With her penchant for drama and unnaturally strong vocal cords, she was destined for the theater. "Mom, Jackson's just sitting there and won't help!"

"But I'm tired!" Jackson whined.

"Can we be done already?" Elise again.

I had lost count of her complaints. She didn't want to move to a new house. She didn't want to pack. She didn't like Candace—and refused to call her *Aunt* Candace. I couldn't blame her. I'd dragged them out of the only home they knew, told them to pack up their lives and given them no choice in the matter. After six hours of being in our Hendricks Way house, with memories encroaching on us in every room, even I was ready to leave.

Only two boxes to go and the kitchen would be done. The counter was littered with the contents of the junk drawer, along with silverware and dishes that I needed to find another box for. How had we accumulated so much crap? Upstairs, I heard the bang of toys hitting the floor as the kids—as far as I knew—organized their possessions into three piles: Keep, Throw Away, and Not Sure. I was pretty sure Elise only had one pile: Keep. The girl had inherited Ben's mom's hoarding tendencies, God rest her soul.

"Why are you so weird?" Elise screamed at Jackson from the second-story landing, then plodded down the stairs. "Mom, make Jackson answer me!"

It was time to intervene. "Elise, don't talk to your brother that way. His quiet is just grief. Be a little kinder to him." I had lost my cool two hours ago when they were fighting about a stupid toy, the details of which I had drowned out with silent tears as I sealed all our family pictures in boxes.

"But, Mom, he drew all over my Barbie's face in permanent marker. I can't wipe it off."

"You don't even play with Barbies anymore, Lise," Jackson said, pleading his case from halfway up the staircase.

"That doesn't mean I want them ruined."

I couldn't take it anymore. Constant bickering, endless whining. "I'll get you a new Barbie. Just please, no more fighting."

"He keeps destroying my stuff, then saying he didn't do it. What am I supposed to do?"

Turning to yell up the stairs at my son, I found him at my hip and startled back a step. "Hey, buddy, you scared me. You've got to stop doing that—sneaking up on people."

"I'm not sneaking. You just don't see me. No one does."

Oh boy. I couldn't add therapy to today's to-do list. I leaned down, nose to nose. "Jackson, sweetie, I am trying my best. We've all been through a lot, though. How about you go outside and play." Then I pointed to Elise. "You, keep packing up your room. If you can behave for one more hour I'll take you both out for ice cream after this."

"But ice cream makes me sick," Jackson whined as Elise stormed up the stairs.

"It doesn't make you sick," I growled. It was always something with him. Ice cream made him sick. Pizza made him sick. Food that most kids loved made Jackson sick. And anything he simply didn't want to eat made him sick. I'd lost count of how many times I had watched him force himself to throw up from something that made him sick one day, but he was fine eating another day. My mother said it was probably to get attention, but it was irritating navigating his food maze of eats and won't eats when I had more pressing matters to deal with, like how we were going to pay our mortgage.

"It does so make me sick."

"Then what would you rather have?" I huffed.

"A soft pretzel. With cinnamon."

"A soft pretzel. For real, Jackson? They don't sell those except for at the mall. Please don't ask me to take you to the mall after this. I just want to grab something quick on the road and go home."

"But we *are* home."

Oh, my sweet boy. If only he understood that Daddy was never coming back to us, that we were never coming back to this house . . . When I looked at their sweet faces, it brought back memories of little arms wrapped around my neck, kissing boo-boos away, nightly giggles during tickle-fights. I wanted to capture the past in a snow globe and live in that moment forever.

Wasn't I changing diapers just yesterday? Or laughing at their gummy smiles as I dangled a toy above them? Now I was taking them to therapists and bribing them with ice cream to leave their home. Part of me wanted them to need me forever, but my hugs and kisses no longer solved their problems. Their problems were just too big. They would never love me in the all-consuming way they did when they were small children. But the scarier truth was that I wasn't sure I could ever love them the way I used to either—with every breath, every heartbeat, a bigness vaster than space. Life had stolen that part of me, the heart of me, when it sent death after me.

"Jackson, we can't stay here anymore. Mommy needs a fresh start. We all do. So for a little while we're going to stay with Uncle Lane and rent this house out to a family who needs it."

"No one needs it more than us." Jackson had inherited his father's persistence. "And I don't want to live at Uncle Lane's. I don't like his girlfriend."

"Wife, honey," I corrected. "And I don't like her either, but sometimes we have to put up with people we don't like."

"But I don't want to sleep in bed with Lise," he whined. "She steals all the covers and kicks me all night."

"I do not," Elise grumbled as she descended the stairs and jabbed him with her elbow in passing.

"Ouch!" Jackson yelped. "Lise hit me!"

"It was an accident."

"No, it wasn't."

"Guys, knock it off!" I screamed, nearly cracking my voice. I couldn't take another minute of the fighting, the whining, the snide comments, the demands . . . I was trying to pack all my memories and dreams after losing my husband and I just needed quiet. One friggin' moment of quiet. Was that too much to ask?

"Outside, both of you! *Now!*"

They both jumped in shock or fear . . . or a little of both. Apparently they knew I meant business, as they darted out the back door without another word. I returned to the kitchen to finish cramming whatever I could in the only box I could find.

The creak of a gate drew my gaze upward to the window facing the in-ground pool. The wrought-iron fence that surrounded it was overtaken by wisteria where crispy vines clung to it in dead patches. Once upon a time it had been tenderly maintained with gorgeous landscaping and trellises of Knock Out roses and fuchsia mandevilla. Now, weeds jutted up between fissures in the concrete around the algae-infested pool that resembled a wild habitat. Vacant and neglected, much like my soul.

A movement caught the corner of my eye. Jackson wandered the perimeter of the pool patio, then paused at the deep end, staring at something in the water below. I imagined all the frogs gliding through the murky water. Jackson had always held a fondness for creepy crawlers . . . until recently, when he simply stopped caring. I understood this but, because I was a mother, I didn't have that same liberty to simply give up. They say kids bounce back, that they're resilient. Maybe for Elise that was the case, but they'd never met Jackson. No one could anticipate the toll of death on him, how it left him hollow.

I envied my son for that freedom to empty himself. Though what darkness it would eventually fill him up with instead, I didn't know. I was too lost in my own grief to pull him out of his.

I watched as Jackson opened his arms wide, as if catching the breeze and sun that both cooled and warmed the spring air. Maybe some of his childhood innocence had been salvaged after all.

Glancing down at the sink, my gaze was transfixed at the way the chrome sparkled beneath tiny water droplets clinging to the metal. I felt myself slipping, my sight glazing, my senses numbing, my brain shutting off, Elise's chatter from the porch slurring into garbled nonsense. I missed Ben. I missed our old life. I couldn't do it anymore—the single mom thing, figuring it out all on my own. How to pay bills. How to keep moving forward. How to fix Jackson. How to push through my depression. How to float upward instead of sinking under. For a long moment I hung between reality and mental space, until something dragged me out.

Screaming.

My name.

"Mom!" Elise shrieked, her voice distant.

Blinking away the tears I felt coming, I scanned for her out the window, not seeing her bright pink shirt on the porch. My eyes darted, searching the backyard. I was used to hearing my name called for the slightest offense. Elise calling me to tell me Jackson was staring at her, as if I controlled the boy's eyeballs. Or Jackson yelling about Elise calling him names, as if I could duct-tape her mouth shut. My name got more traction than a Hollywood scandal.

"Mom!"

Splashing.

Then the word that always got my immediate attention: "Help!"

Elise's voice was shrill and panicked, and I followed it toward the edge of the pool where she crouched down on her knees, arms outstretched. Through the floating debris I saw arms flailing at the water's edge, then sinking into the green waves. A ripple along the surface, a few bubbles, then . . . nothing. It took only a second . . . a second too long.

Jackson.

My mind sprung to life, urging me to run, to save my son. But my feet . . . my legs . . . they wouldn't move, as if they had been tiled to the floor. My breath caught as a dread surged through me, but my body wouldn't cooperate. I stood there, my mouth mute and my legs crippled.

Another splash, this one bigger, as Elise dove into the water headfirst. I watched it all unfold in my frozen state, a deer in headlights, my fight-or-flight instincts on pause. Adrenaline must have snapped me out of it because suddenly I ran, throwing open the back door, catapulting off the porch and through the gate. By now, Elise held Jackson up against the pool's edge, pushing him up onto the patio. I grabbed his arms, hauled him up, then pulled Elise up after him. Jackson coughed up water, sucking in breaths as I leaned him forward and patted his back.

Elise, sobbing on all fours next to me, wiped water off her face.

"Mom, where were you?"

Where was I indeed? Why didn't I react?

"I'm so sorry, honey." I wrapped my free arm around her, holding a child in each, as if I could keep us together and safe with these arms. If only I was stronger. "I didn't hear you. I'm so so sorry, sweetie."

Her tears dripped from her chin, melting into the pool water puddling at her knees.

"He fell on purpose, Mom. Tell her, Jackson." Elise's voice held an edge of anger.

Jackson fixed his eyes on the concrete.

"Is it true, Jackson? Did you fall on purpose?"

He ignored me, so I placed my finger under his chin and lifted his face to mine. He looked up at me sadly.

"Tell me the truth."

"I don't know," he answered. It was his answer for a lot of the strange things he had been doing lately.

"Did you mean to fall into the pool?" I needed to know.

"Yes," he whispered.

"Why?"

He didn't answer at first. Just stared at me with blank, lifeless eyes. "Because I wanted to know what it felt like to drown."

That one sentence brought a torrent of emotion. Did Jackson want to die too? Kissing his mop of black hair again and again, I pressed his head to my chest and wept. Elise wept. But Jackson . . . nothing. "Jackson, don't ever do that again. Promise me you'll never hurt yourself. You could have died . . . and Mommy can't take another death. Please, Jackson."

I begged, I pleaded, I needed his word . . .

"I promise."

. . . and he gave it to me.

"Mommy loves you too much to lose you. It would break me forever."

"I know," he said.

We sat for a long moment, three soaked bodies sprawled on the concrete among the weeds, while the breeze licked our skin dry. My body felt weak from the post-adrenaline rush. I needed a moment alone. "Elise, take your brother inside, and both of you put on some fresh clothes before we head back over to Uncle Lane's."

As we all rose to our feet, Jackson sidled ahead into the house while I fumbled with the gate lock, securing it while Elise hung back at my side.

"Mommy?" Her voice was tiny, exhausted. Only moments before she had transformed into a lifesaving hero. Now she was back to my little eleven-year-old girl.

"Yes?"

She didn't speak at first, a tell that something serious was on her mind.

"What is it, honey? You can tell me."

When I looked down at her, her eyes were glassy, wet.

"Part of me wishes I would have let him drown."

As her words fell between us, I saw my reflection in her eyes. And I wondered if part of me wished that too.

Chapter 7

Candace

I wake up to exist for you. I open my eyes to see you.
I breathe to inhale you. You are my reason for each
moment.

The scent of rain tangled with my organic patchouli essential oil pillow spray, nudging me toward consciousness. Somehow my body knew a moment before my alarm when the day was supposed to begin. I sat up at the sound of "Easy Street' by Collapsable Hearts Club playing on my cell phone. A touch of irony because life was anything but easy, and it sure didn't feel neat, but the song featured in *The Walking Dead* was the perfect get-up-and-go I needed this dreary morning.

I snoozed the music before it woke up Lane (he was lucky he slept so soundly, something I hadn't experienced in weeks), then flung off the covers, the chill of the floors seeping into the soles of my tattooed feet. The tattoos had hurt like a mother when the needle stabbed the bony tops of my feet, but the images represented empowerment . . . so I'd be damned if I didn't power through the pain as the artist stamped my skin. Thai characters spelled "live this life" on one foot, and a lotus flower adorned the other—a symbol of purity, strength, and grace. I needed hefty doses of all of the above in order to carry out my plan.

Although I didn't drink coffee, I always set the coffeemaker the night before so that I could bring Lane his first cup of the morning. Little details like that mattered, they meant something. I might be a terrible cook and a disastrous house-keeper, but I always took care of my man where it mattered: delivering his morning cup with a kiss, and satisfaction in the bedroom.

This morning it took extra self-will to give a crap about Lane's needs. The guilt trips over the past few days regarding Harper's stay had been long and exhausting. Lane had made it abundantly clear that I was being selfish by wanting him all to myself. Harper wasn't just *family*, but his sister—his *only* sister—and he would open up his home for anyone in my family too. That was exactly the problem, though, that Lane would open his home and his heart to everyone and anyone, when those things should have been devoted first to *me*. To *us*. By Lane's logic, *us* could include the homeless guy who stood at the corner of the freeway underpass begging for change.

Houseguests were like fish—they were only good for about three days. We were now officially past the expiration date.

"The right thing to do is to give to those in need," Lane

kept reiterating. Except that Harper needed nothing but to crash into our lives with her noisy daughter, her creepy son, and her persistent nagging.

I never dusted enough. When I cooked, the meals were overprocessed. The dirty laundry was piled too high. No matter what I did—or didn't—do, I couldn't do right by that woman, and according to her, I wasn't good enough for her brother. She hated our unconventional relationship, the fact Lane and I shared the homemaking responsibilities. It made sense for us—he was a better cook and I had never really learned how to make anything other than prepackaged meals. So sue me for not having parents who taught me basic homemaking skills.

When it came to laundry, I didn't keep up with it daily. Not even weekly. Lane had plenty of scrubs to get through the week without me running the washing machine ragged with constant loads. And who swept the floors daily? It wasn't like we had a pack of dogs running around and shedding everywhere. So this morning, as my alarm went off at six o'clock, the sun still sleeping and the coffee brewing, I decided to show Harper just how homemakery I could be.

I was doing my best for Lane, hiding my demons. It wasn't until I pulled free from my past that I had finally been able to name those demons: Fear. Anxiety. Worry. Paranoia. The past had shaped me, made me stronger, so that I could appreciate what I had now even more. No one knew just how dark my life before Lane had actually been, not even Lane. I was entitled to a few character flaws because of it, one of which was being extra possessive of Lane. If you lost every good thing you ever touched, wouldn't you hold a little tighter too?

What Harper didn't understand was that I wasn't a chameleon like her. I didn't bend and fold into suburban bondage like she did, allowing mom groups and book clubs and the PTA to squeeze the identity out of me. I was happy living in my own shadow, not theirs.

I shivered in my drapey Cyndi Lauper T-shirt and hiphugger panties, closing the window beside my bed where last night's rain had left dewy droplets along the windowsill. After slipping on a plush robe and slippers, I piled my hair into a topknot, then headed downstairs, greeted by . . . nothing.

No scent of coffee brewing.

No gurgling of hot water pouring over coffee beans.

Someone had unplugged the coffeemaker and instead plugged in a cell phone. Harper's cell phone.

Ripping her cord from the outlet, I jammed the coffeemaker plug in and pressed the brew button, cursing her under my breath. Last night's dinner dishes were already cleaned and put away—thank-Harper-very-much—but the drying rack was full of clean pots and pans. If she'd carelessly unplug my coffeemaker, then I'd carelessly put the pots and pans away. After clattering them loudly into the cupboards and slamming the cabinet doors shut, the house returned to deathly silence.

It hadn't worked.

So I headed for the closet and lugged the vacuum out. It didn't matter that the floors were mostly hardwood and a mop would work better; vacuuming would be so much more fun. I plugged it in and with the click of a button it roared to life. Zooming around the first floor, I made sure to bump into tables and floorboards, scraping chairs across the floor as I moved furniture around. It only took a couple minutes of this before Harper tiptoed down the stairs, waving her hands at me to stop.

I turned off the vacuum and smiled. "Good morning!" I doused my tone with plenty of morning chipper. "Just getting a head start on the cleaning."

"At six in the morning?" She cocked an eyebrow at me.

How *dare* she cock an eyebrow at me in my own home!

"I figured I was already up, so why not get started on the chores? The early bird gets the worm and all that." A saying I never agreed with. Birds found worms at all hours of the day; why did only the early risers get the credit?

"The rest of us are trying to sleep, Candace. Can't you wait until after the kids are up? They need their sleep."

"First you criticize me for *not* playing house, and now you criticize for doing it? What the hell do you want from me, Harper?"

She exhaled, in either irritation or retreat. "I just want you to show some consideration. We're trying to sleep and you're purposely making a bunch of noise."

Apparently Harper's voice carried louder than the vacuum, because Elise's whining traveled through the closed door, landing on my ears. "Mommyyyyyyy, you woke Jackson up!"

"Sorry, sweetie," Harper called back to her. "Try to go back to sleep."

"I caaaaaan't," Elise answered with the same annoying pitch. "Jackson's hitting himself again!"

"Thanks a lot. Now the kids are up, and Jackson will be such a *treat*, thanks to your sleep deprivation," Harper mumbled as she stormed up the stairs. "I hope you like loud cartoons."

By the time Harper reached the top landing, both kids were

crying and screaming at each other . . . and having a wrestling match, I wagered, from the thumping sound of something—or someone—hitting the floor.

Mission accomplished.

Half an hour later, Lane rolled out of bed—had I mentioned he was a deep sleeper?—as I placed a skillet of scrambled eggs beside a plate of buttered toast and crispy bacon on the kitchen table, just how Lane liked it. I preferred my bacon a little chewy and made of pig, not turkey, but this was all about Lane, not me.

"Wakey, wakey, eggs and bakey! Breakfast time," I sing-songed over the migraine-inducing *SpongeBob SquarePants* theme song. Of course Harper had picked the loudest show she could find to entertain the kids.

It was *on,* bitch.

The kettle whistled as the kids sat around the kitchen table spooning eggs onto their plates. I picked out a mint chocolate oolong tea—my current favorite—and set it to steep. Beside me, Harper poured a cup of coffee into an oversized mug, no cream, no sugar. It figured that Harper liked her coffee bitter, just like her personality.

When the scent of mint reached my nostrils, I knew my tea was ready. I added a dash of cream, two spoonfuls of sugar, and sipped it. Perfection.

"No coffee this morning?" Harper asked me, lifting her mug.

"I prefer tea. I've just never taken to coffee. It stains the teeth."

She scrunched her upturned nose. "That's what whitening toothpaste is for. And who *doesn't* like coffee? That's just wrong."

I could have retorted with everything *wrong* with her, like how her voice scratched my eardrums, or how her caked-on foundation wasn't doing her fine lines any favors or fooling anyone. Or that god-awful hairstyle that looked like a monkey with scissors cut it. But no, I kept my mouth in check. Not for her, but for Lane.

When I escaped to the breakfast nook, I picked the chair farthest from the children and their bickering over who had more bacon. The table followed a long window that overlooked the backyard. I usually enjoyed the daily visits from the hummingbirds that hovered by the feeder I'd hung from the back porch. But not even their cute squeaks or vibrating wings could cheer me up today.

Harper followed me, sitting catty-corner to my chair. I had no desire to make idle chitchat with a woman who couldn't care less about respecting me in my own home, so I returned to sipping my tea and nibbling my eggs while Harper scrolled through her phone. The cursed thing was like an extra appendage, always at her fingertips.

At last her eyes broke contact with her device and she glanced up. "I searched for you on Facebook but I couldn't find you. What name are you under?"

Searching for what, exactly? I wanted to ask but didn't. Because I knew she didn't want to be Facebook buddies. "I don't have Facebook."

Her mouth dropped open. "Are you serious? Only sociopaths don't have Facebook."

"Judge me all you want, Harper, but social media has proven to be addictive. And it's a time suck. You're not even aware of how rude it is to have your face in your phone instead of actively conversing with the people you're around."

Harper lifted her brows and glared at me. "Is that a dig?"

"Only if you're too involved with your fake news to make eye contact with the person you're sitting next to. In fact, I think people who *are* on Facebook are sociopaths. You can be offensive, but not held accountable. The things people post on there with no consequences for their words is the problem with today's society. A person's likability is based on how many *likes* a post gets. It's fake life. Detachment from real emotions or connections—that pretty much sums up social media."

Harper rolled her eyes at me, then slammed her phone on the table—facedown, as if that made any difference—with an exaggerated smirk.

"My phone's down and my eyes are on you. Better?"

I turned to her, propping my chin on my knuckles. "What is your problem with me? I let you into my home and you treat me like garbage. I don't appreciate it, Harper, and I don't *have* to let you stay. I only agreed to it for Lane, because he cares about you. But me? I couldn't care less if you were homeless. In fact, maybe you'd grow some character if you suffered a bit." I tossed my fork down, my appetite gone along with my patience.

"You want to know my problem with you?" She jutted her finger at my face, inching toward my nose. "You and Lane have known each other for, like, a minute, and are suddenly married. Why? This isn't the 1800s—no one does that without an agenda. What exactly do you want from my brother?"

I swatted her pointer away. "Isn't it possible that I fell in love with him quickly because he's a great guy, we're not getting any younger, and there's no reason for us not to get married? We both wanted to start a life together; it wasn't just me. So you can put the accusatory tone away, because I'm not going to run off with Lane's retirement fund, or whatever it is you think I want from him."

"Whatever. People don't just have whirlwind marriages unless it's to hide something."

"Well, Lane and I have nothing to hide, especially our love for each other."

Harper made a gagging sound that made me want to gag her for real. "You're too naive to understand this yet, but you can't just walk into a marriage and live happily ever after."

"Oh really? Enlighten me then." I couldn't wait to hear her explanation.

Her eyes shifted to the window with a distant gaze, like she was watching an old memory replay against the sky. "Real love smothers you and burns you. It takes everything from you and gives back very little. It changes who you are." Then she returned her focus on me. "Are you sure you're ready for that? To give up everything for my brother?"

"I already have, haven't I? I've given up my home. I've given up my voice. Because God forbid I say no and turn you and your spoiled kids away. So don't preach to me about marital sacrifice. What I want to know is why you're *really* here. Because you have a huge house with your name on the deed. You're perfectly capable of getting a job. There's no reason for you to be here, and we both know it."

"Why is it such a big deal that I'm here? I'm grieving, Candace. I don't want to be in the same house where my husband just died. Show a little empathy."

I admit, empathy didn't come easy to me. It was hard to practice something so foreign to me. I was trained in ruthless survival growing up. My father's favorite life lesson was: *show no mercy.* I was taught to eat or be eaten. My boo-boos weren't kissed better; instead dear old Dad told me to *toughen up* or *rub some dirt on it.* When you're at the hands of a violent father and a helpless mother, you learn quickly that the weak don't survive.

Empathy was for the weak because compassion required trust, and trust got you killed. Ask my mother, God rest her soul, exactly where sympathy got her. It got her dead. As my father would say, if you wanted sympathy, look in the dictionary between *shit* and *syphilis.*

"Your husband died over a month ago, Harper. I'm not saying grief is a quick process, but why do you need to dig your claws into Lane in order to work through it? Go to a therapist. Join a support group. Talk to your friends. Lane isn't your crutch anymore, so lose the obsession with him."

Harper jumped up from her seat, slamming her palms on the table. The silverware clattered and the kids scrambled out of the room. "I'm not obsessed with my brother! He happens to be my best friend, and right now the only friend I have. Maybe if you actually had a heart you'd see that and want to reach out to me. Clearly you've never lost someone you loved or you might be more understanding."

Now I felt a little bad. Because I had lost someone, a someone I had tried to replace over and over again but never could.

When you love someone, a piece of your heart takes their shape. When they're gone, so goes that piece of your heart. And nothing, no one, can ever fill it quite right. I knew exactly how she felt.

"I'm sorry. I didn't mean to be callous about your loss."

"Have you?" Harper looked at me intensely, and I suddenly felt uneasy.

"Have I what?"

"Ever lost someone you loved?"

I didn't want to answer her. It was none of her business. But as much as I disliked her, we weren't so different. We both knew love, and we both suffered heartbreak. Maybe my walls could use a little chipping away. Who knew what I'd find on the other side. Maybe a friend, not a foe.

"Yes, in fact I have. So I do understand you. But you can't let it swallow you, Harper. I learned that the hard way—you have to be stronger than death. If not for you, then for your kids."

She stood for a long, quiet moment, staring out the window. "If only it were that easy."

Her sadness touched me in a way that I could feel. Was this what empathy felt like? Harper didn't quite seem like the enemy anymore. She was far too broken, like me, to be the bad guy. With a light caress of my hand against hers, we connected.

"I don't really know much about what happened to your husband other than what Lane told me—that he died unexpectedly. Please . . ." I patted the chair, hoping she would sit back down so we could talk, so we could forgive. If we were destined to be sisters, I could at least try to get along. "Do you want to talk about him—your husband?"

She accepted my peace offering and sat stiffly in the chair, her hand under her chin. "What can I say about Ben? He kept me on my toes until the very end."

I didn't know what Harper meant by that, but I'd nudge until I found out. Maybe it was the clue to why she was the way she was. Controlling. Rigid. Anxious. Maybe it was the answer to how to fix everything between us.

"How did he die?" I asked.

The whisper in my ear and the breath on my neck crawled up my spine and jolted me out of my seat: "Daddy was murdered."

I spun around to find Jackson at my shoulder, expressionless but observant. I recently noticed that about him: he avoided contact but was always watching with those shiny black beads.

"Murdered?"

I didn't mean for it to come out so loudly, so harshly, so insensitively. But everyone knew that when a spouse turned up dead . . . well, the living one was usually the one who had done it. Harper even looked like the textbook murderess, with the downward slash of her mouth, the stiffness of her jaw. Spotless on the outside, filthy on the inside. I imagined Harper more worried about the bloodstains on her floor than the bloodstains on her hands. Yes, Harper was a picture-perfect killer.

"Yes, I'm working with the police to figure out who killed my husband."

That's the moment I realized just how urgently I needed to get Harper and her crazy family out of my house. Because killers shouldn't live in homes; they should live in jail cells.

Chapter 8

Harper

If you've never woken up from a dead sleep to the sound of a house full of smoke alarms blaring, I don't recommend it. Especially if you have a heart condition. Or anxiety. Or young kids. And if you don't already have a heart condition or anxiety, you might find yourself suddenly acquiring one or the other after such a wake-up call.

My digital clock radio—which Lane teased was old-fashioned and had gone the way of the rotary telephone—blinked 4:43 in the morning. The bedroom was pitch-black, the only light being a sliver of moonbeam white slipping through the gap where the blinds didn't quite meet the window frame. In this otherworldly gray was where the screaming started. First the piercing siren call of the smoke alarm, followed by the screeches of frightened children. I threw off the covers and ran to the kids' room to find Elise sitting up in bed, hair in a knotted mess and eyes wild and wide. Jackson's side of the bed was empty.

"Where's your brother?" I screamed over the noise, my gaze racing around the room.

"I don't know! I just woke up. Is there a fire?"

"I'm not sure. Help me find your brother!"

Dragging Elise into the hall, I checked the bathroom for Jackson. Empty. Where the heck was he? Gripping Elise's hand like her life depended on it, I rushed carefully down the steps toward the front door as Lane darted out of his bedroom in a confused bustle.

"What's going on?" Lane yelled over the alarm as he followed me downstairs.

"Do you see smoke anywhere?" I called behind me.

"No. I'll check the rest of the house."

"I can't find Jackson."

"Don't worry, I'll find him."

Lane took off toward the kitchen while I ushered Elise to the front door, where I found Jackson standing by the coat closet, thank God.

"Where were you, buddy?" I asked as I pushed the kids outside to wait on the porch while Lane sorted everything out.

"I was in the downstairs bathroom. Then the alarm went off."

How odd, when the closest bathroom was only a few feet from his bedroom door.

"Why didn't you use the upstairs bathroom?"

He covered his mouth secretively, and his voice lowered into a whisper. "Because the ghost lady looks at me in the mirror when I'm going potty." He said it so convincingly I almost believed him.

"What do you mean, honey? What ghost lady?"

"The lady who died in the house." His gaze darted around, as if the ghost could be eavesdropping on us. "I see her in the mirror."

I felt a *Sixth Sense* vibe coming from Jackson. I wondered if perhaps he had seen the movie and his imagination was playing tricks on him. Though if Ben had let our six-year-old son watch that, I would have killed him . . . if he weren't already dead, that is. "You've seen a dead woman in the mirror?"

"Well, she writes things on the glass. Tells me she's watching me."

Was Jackson seeing things again? We had been through this once before—*the hauntings,* the child psychiatrist had called it. Jackson had made such strides since then . . . until Ben's death happened.

"Remember what the doctor told you, that it's something you create in your head? Like an imaginary friend. I promise you, sweetie, there is no ghost lady here."

"I can prove it," he insisted.

Worry buzzed in my head like a housefly. It might be time for mother-son therapy again. Self-destruction was our family religion, and we worshipped at its feet.

By this point the smoke detectors had drawn the attention of the next-door neighbors and the family across the street, who stood in their yard wearing thick robes and confused looks. I shivered in my tank top and shorts, having forgotten to grab a robe on my way out. While the spring days were hot here in the South, the nights still held a chill.

The alarms continued to blare as a crowd of those within hearing distance collected on the sidewalk. I had yet to see

Candace since all this began. Her early-morning vacuuming came to mind. Was this another one of her schemes to annoy us out of the house?

I peered into the window. Nothing appeared fire-worthy. No smoke. No flames. Just the alarm . . . and then sudden silence.

"Stay here, guys. I'll be right back," I told the kids.

I slipped through the front door, running the perimeter of the first floor. Living room, empty. Dining room, empty. Kitchen, clear. I found Lane on a stepstool in his office, ripping the smoke detector off the ceiling.

"What happened?" I asked.

Lane examined the plastic casing, then popped it open. "I don't know. I'll replace the batteries; if they're low that could have set it off. They design these new smoke detectors to all be interconnected, so if one goes off, they all do. Stupidest design ever. I don't see any smoke, though."

He tossed the culprit on his desk, and I headed back to the entryway to retrieve the kids, nearly bumping into Candace on my way out.

"Where were you?" I stopped her with my question.

"Uh"—she looked confused—"upstairs, trying to figure out which alarm was triggering the others."

I shrugged her off, too tired to deal with it, and headed outside to shuffle the kids back to bed and the neighbors back to their homes.

"False alarm!" I yelled to the onlookers, embarrassed and angsty. There was no way I'd fall asleep again with all the adrenaline that soaked my veins.

Lane and Candace were already halfway up the staircase, heading back to bed, when I shut the door behind me.

"Try to go back to sleep, okay?" I kissed Elise and Jackson on their heads, then walked them upstairs.

"Don't you want to see my proof about the ghost lady?" Jackson asked when we reached the top landing.

I exhaled my combined agitation and exhaustion. If anything, humoring him could help put this matter to rest, proving just how silly it all was. "Sure, show me."

He led me to the bathroom, then pulled himself up on the sink, his tiny legs dangling below. With a big breath, he exhaled a fine mist onto the mirror, and letters appeared. When he finished, he hopped down and pointed to the words outlined in his moist breath:

I'm watching you

A chill tickled the hairs on my arms. Okay, so clearly someone was messing with him. There was no ghost lady, but there was Elise . . . and I wouldn't put it past Lane to pull a good-natured prank on his nephew.

"Oh, sweetie, you know someone is playing tricks on you, right?"

"Yeah, the ghost lady. I know it's her."

There was no point arguing with him about it now. I'd have to find out who was doing this and make them confess to Jackson. As the words disappeared back into the glass, I grabbed his hand and led him to bed, then tucked him in for what was left of the night. "Back to bed. I don't need you guys getting sick from lack of sleep."

It was inevitable, the sickness. One single night of sleep deficiency always ended first in Jackson getting sick, then Elise, then Ben. And since I took care of everyone else—disinfecting their germy bedding, wiping their running noses, feeding them soup and grilled cheese sandwiches, and losing sleep while tending to their constant needs—I was always the last to get the worst of it. Of course, while I was battling it head-on, the others still needed Mommy to disinfect, wipe noses, and spoon-feed them. It was a cycle I dreaded, so the kids' sleep was high on my priority list. I just hoped and prayed the germs would spare us this time. I could only imagine how pissed Candace would be if my children infected her too.

With the kids groggily returned to their bed, I decided I might as well put on a pot of coffee and earn my keep. I could clean the entire house and tackle the growing pile of dirty laundry by late morning. There were at least six loads' worth dumped on the floor of the laundry room. I'd need to remember to pick up some laundry baskets so that I could separate the whites from the colors. How did Candace not know such simple rules of housekeeping?

After resetting the coffeepot to brew three hours earlier than usual—I had to give Candace props for at least setting it every night—I tossed in a load of laundry to wash while I figured out where to start deep-cleaning first.

Lane's office. It was more cluttered than the discount toy bin at the thrift store. He had mentioned a couple times offhandedly how he couldn't find anything in there; it would be a nice surprise for him to wake up to a clean, organized office. Grabbing a duster and some extra folders I had brought from home, I was armed and ready.

It was worse than I thought. The windowsill was littered with dead flies, and my fingertip cut a trail through a blanket of dust on his desk. What kind of wife didn't dust? A neglectful one. Maybe Candace best learned by example.

I grabbed a pile of bills, invoices, and receipts strewn across the desk and tapped the edges to straighten them out. Setting them aside, an envelope on top caught my eye. The return address peeking out from the tiny plastic window in the corner belonged to a birthing center. Glancing at the open doorway to find myself predictably alone, I closed the door. I debated whether to open the envelope or not, but it only took a moment before I slipped the contents out and unfolded the paper.

A bill. For an ultrasound and fetal test. This couldn't be right. Candace couldn't possibly be pregnant so quickly . . . could she? Unless she had conceived right before they got married . . . which would account for the shotgun wedding.

So she had trapped my brother with a baby. Lane wasn't the type of guy to impregnate a girl then ghost her. No, he would do the *right* thing and make an honest woman of her. Except that Candace was anything but an honest woman. Every step toward friendship we had made vanished. Fool me once, shame on you. But I wouldn't let this lying, scheming snake in the grass fool me twice. And I sure as heck wouldn't let her fool my naive brother.

Thump. Then another soft *thump* approaching.

The creak of the floorboards sent my fingers to work hastily shoving the bill back in the envelope. After tucking it into the pile, I pretended to be dusting when the office door swung open. I glanced up and exhaled relief. Thank God it was Lane. It was too early for an encounter with Candace.

"Why are you still awake?" he asked, rubbing his eyes.

"I couldn't fall back asleep." I lifted the duster. "Figured I'd get some cleaning done. What's your excuse?"

He shrugged. "I'm too wired after the whole alarm debacle."

"Want some coffee?" I offered.

"You know I never say no to coffee."

I followed him to the kitchen, finding the sink I had spent an hour last night emptying and cleaning had been refilled with a mug ringed with tea, an empty water glass, a cereal bowl with flakes crusted along the rim, and a plate with melted cheese and salsa stuck to it. Candace and her midnight snacks. I was instantly filled with irritation. Lane grabbed two mugs—mine in a shape of an owl, his the shape of a panda—and poured us each a cup.

"What's up with the kiddy mugs?" I asked as I rinsed the dishes and loaded the dishwasher—again.

"Candace thought they were cute. What, you don't agree?"

I never used to worry about how I worded things with my brother. But when it came to his wife, I was forced to tiptoe around each syllable, lest it get back to her and I ignite her wrath. Right now, however, I was too tired to curb my words.

"Sometimes she just seems more like a child than an adult. I mean, look at the state of your home. She's an utter slob, Lane, while you're a neat freak. And her clothes! Her boobs are hanging out of every top, which I don't exactly want Jackson exposed to, and she's always running around in a bikini. It's not even summer yet. Who does that in front of children? Elise is so impressionable, and seeing the slut-wear that Candace struts around in . . . I'm afraid Elise is going to think it's acceptable to look like that. She should wear age-appropriate clothing, Lane."

"Whoa, girl. Slow down." Lane held up a hand to stop me.

Maybe I had gotten a teensy bit overdramatic. "Sorry, but I don't know . . . I just don't see what you see in her."

Of course I saw what any hot-blooded male saw in Candace. Youth. Carefree. Slutty. The strappy tank tops—always worn braless—and the tiny shorts that showed her ass cheeks. Skimpy maxi dresses that revealed more skin than they hid. Prancing around in nothing but a bathing suit and silk kimono, her breasts hard and fake, just like her. And that hair, an oil-spill down her back. The blue highlights just screamed for attention, as if her breasts weren't getting enough already. Candace was what happened to little girls who wear makeup and don't have a curfew.

Did she even own any proper foot attire or just flip-flops? And the tasteless jewelry, all bangles and dangles and charms and feathers. If Candace was indeed to become a mother, she needed to start dressing like one. A proper one.

Lane rested his hand on my shoulder. "I know you don't understand it, but everything you don't understand is exactly what I love about her. She's so beautifully different from everyone else. She is fluid and restless and passionate and adventurous. She's unconventional, sure, but that's what drew me to her. I wish you'd give her a chance."

"I'm trying."

Okay, maybe I wasn't trying hard enough. The problem was that I understood how girls like Candace worked the world, bringing it to their feet. They knew how to make men smile, but they also knew how to make men weep.

By this point, sunrise was approaching. I stood at the bay window, watching the sun poke its fingers through the trees. After adding peppermint creamer to Lane's coffee and daring a splash in my own, I picked up both our mugs and joined Lane at the kitchen table, wondering if I should say something about my morning discovery. This was Lane, the brother I told everything to. Well, *almost* everything.

"Did you know Candace is pregnant?" I blurted out.

His startled expression was a mixture of shock and curiosity. I couldn't read him. Was that a yes or a no?

After a breath, he nodded. "Of course I know we're expecting."

I had assumed as much. "Do you know if it's yours?"

He glared at me as if it was a crazy question, but it was no more crazy than his whirlwind wife having a honeymoon pregnancy. "Yes, it's mine."

"Is that why you married her—because of the baby?"

"No," he scoffed. "We love each other, Harp. I'm thrilled about the baby. So what if it was unplanned? It's part me, part her, and wholly perfect. I'm happy and in love and I've always wanted a family . . . even if it came a little unexpectedly."

How blissfully, ignorantly romantic.

"Are you sure she loves you back? I'm not trying to downplay your relationship, Lane, but women do that—trick men into marrying them by purposely getting pregnant. And you've got quite a nest egg saved up that could be pretty enticing to a young, single, jobless woman."

Lane had always been a saver, ever since watching our father leave our mother penniless and broke. With a pretty good salary from working his way up at the hospital, not only did

Lane earn a good income, but he loved to spoil others. Never himself, though.

In a way, his trusting nature was endearing. But it also made him blind to the manipulation that women were capable of. Hadn't our mother's own well-practiced manipulation tactics taught him to know better? I couldn't help but feel the need to protect my brother, because he simply wouldn't protect himself.

"Why are you trying to stir things up?" He shook his head with a disappointed droop. "Yes, Candace loves me. And she got pregnant after we both professed our love to each other and were already talking about marriage and children. Candace and I both wanted this, together, so please stop with the assumptions."

"I just think she's using you. She's a bad choice, Lane."

Lane pushed up from his chair. "Just because Ben hurt you doesn't mean Candace will hurt me."

I felt the jab of his words hit my heart. He saw it etched on my face, because he immediately reached for me. I pulled back, out of reach, expanding the distance between us. I couldn't handle his consolation, not after that dig.

"Are you trying to compare Candace to Ben? How dare you! We spent a lifetime together. And we loved each other. And yes, Ben hurt me, but he also loved me despite what I did. I couldn't forgive myself, and yet Ben did. *That*, Lane, is love." I didn't know if I was trying to convince my brother or myself.

"I'm sorry. I didn't mean to say that. I know how much he loved you. That was wrong of me. I'm just being defensive because I want the same benefit of the doubt." He sat and reached out again, and this time I let him rest his hand on mine. "Forgive me for being an idiot brother?"

I shrugged. "Don't I always?"

Of course I forgave his idiocy. I always did and I always would. Even when things got dark. Even when the sins were too numerous to count. We always forgave and always protected each other. He collected the needy, love-hungry people who fed on him, then discarded him when they had their fill. I had always been there to pick up the pieces, just like he did for me. But with Lane slipping out of my grasp and into Candace's, I could no longer protect him from himself.

Candace would never take care of him like I did, and as I felt myself getting pushed away, inch by foot by yard, I wanted to hold on tighter. Lane was all I had left. He needed me, just as I needed him. Candace would one day destroy him, and he might never bounce back. He hadn't been hardened by love like I had; I didn't know if he could survive the blow.

He smiled at me, the boyish lopsided grin that threw me back to when I was six years old and he was seven. Trevor Gist had pushed me to the ground for the second time that week, skinning my knees and elbows on the broken concrete of the playground. Lane watched it happen from a distance, then turned red with the injustice pumping through him, like a soldier at war. Running toward the other boy, he cried out as he slammed into Trevor's back and tackled him to the ground, then beat the crap out of my bully. After, as Lane lent me his hand to help lift me up from the patch of gravel, he grinned and said, "I'll take down any bully who touches you."

That day Lane found his battle cry. Today, I found mine.

I'll take down any woman who hurts you. Even if that woman was my sister-in-law.

Chapter 9

Harper

Ben would forever be in my heart and in my thoughts. But he wasn't much use to me there. Daily I was losing pieces of myself while juggling everything alone. And daily I was failing at life. I hadn't been able to find a job yet, not that I had spent much time looking. The past few days since moving in had been a flurry of chaos. My days were filled with cleaning the Hendricks Way house for rental, my evenings were spent helping the kids with homework and preparing dinner, and my nights were dedicated to handling Jackson's night terrors, which were growing in regularity.

The terrors had started again two nights after we had moved in, his screams echoing down the hallway, frightening the entire house awake. Crying until his voice went raw, Jackson was inconsolable, stuck between wakefulness and sleep in a terrified limbo. I would never forget the very first time it happened, almost a year ago now. Panic had surged through me when I heard a loud bang followed by wailing. My initial thought was that he had fallen out of bed, but when I found him thrashing on the floor and couldn't calm the crying, unable to shake him out of sleep, I realized it was something else. Our pediatrician explained the phenomenon and told us encouragingly that the terrors would stop on their own. Sure enough, one day they had suddenly ended, as though he were cured. I had never been so grateful for a full night's sleep. At last, peace descended on our home—no more frantic wakings, no more panicked nighttime cries.

Until now.

For months I had dreaded the possibility of ever reliving those awful nights, and yet here I was. Stuck in my own personal hell. And Candace wasn't making it any more tolerable.

I felt myself nodding off from my mere three hours of sleep the night before when Candace's voice suddenly jarred me awake.

"How about a toast?" Candace raised her water glass from her place beside Lane at the dining room table. A large, three-wick candle burned as a centerpiece, while a platter of hacked-up chicken filled one end of the table and two bowls of side dishes filled the other.

"To my beautiful wife," Lane adulated, clinking his wineglass against hers. "And this wonderful meal she cooked."

I lifted my glass in a half-hearted salute. How do you applaud a child's effort when she comes home with a big, fat F on her test? *Good job! Well done on that lovely failing grade!* Because that was exactly what Lane expected me to do with Candace over tonight's family dinner. I simply couldn't praise mediocrity. It wasn't in my nature.

Holding up their milks, the kids exchanged a confused look. They knew the meal was terrible too.

"Do we get wine?" Elise asked.

"Are you of legal age yet?" my mother, sitting at the end of the table, said with a flash of bleach-white teeth. She looked overdressed for this meal in her purple pantsuit over a gray silk blouse. But that was Mom:; always proper, always put together.

"I dunno, Grandma, am I?"

"If your mom's okay with it, one sip each."

I nodded permission for my mother to offer Jackson first, then Elise, a sip. They winced and coughed with disgust. If anything, the dry merlot would deter them from ever wanting to drink alcohol again.

"To Candy," my mother added with a flourish, her glass raised, "and this wonderful family meal."

I nearly choked on the bite I had been chewing for the last five minutes. The roasted chicken was bland, dry, and overcooked, but I swallowed it anyway with a grim smile. I aim to please. Across from me, Elise's chicken remained untouched along with her burned broccoli—how does one even *burn* steamed broccoli?—but her instant mashed potatoes were about halfway eaten. On my left, Jackson's food was stirred together in a mushed medley without a single bite taken. I couldn't blame him.

"Why aren't your kids eating?" Candace directed the question at me.

I pointed my fork at the kids. "Ask them. They can speak for themselves."

I hadn't intended such kick to my reply, but my irritation was oozing out. I knew all about women like Candace. Trap a good man with a pregnancy. Then use guilt and empty promises to force marriage on him. Top it off with a hefty dose of make-believe. Play house. Lure him into compliance with insincere efforts of date nights and adventurous sex so that you could later use it against him. This was the foreplay before ripping his heart apart when you announced you're leaving him . . . and taking half of everything with you.

I knew her game well. I had come close to leaving Ben once, but I didn't follow through. I was more concerned about losing him than I was about losing my dignity. Dignity wouldn't pay for my huge house, or keep our family together, or give me freedom to run the PTA. I liked my house, my intact family, and my status, so I turned my head the other way when Ben began drifting.

Candace, on the other hand, I could see taking everything and running. Just as I could see her faking her way through this silly family meal. *We have a big announcement to make,* I had overheard Candace telling my mother on the phone earlier today. *And I'd like to share the news with you over a home-cooked dinner tonight.* I wondered just how much Mom knew about the whole charade.

At the head of the dining room table sat Lane, at the other end, Mom. Or as Candace called her, Monica. Mom had always insisted that Ben call her "Mom," but had never corrected Candace after that first "Monica" came out as my mother swept in through the front door, unloading goodie bags into the arms of each of the kids. I wondered if it bothered Lane that Candace would never fit into our family.

Elise sat at the corner closest to Grandma, chatting about her bestie at school, her favorite class, the boy she had a crush on, Nathan, God help me. Grandparenthood fit my mother like her tailored suits. After missing out on so much of my and Lane's childhoods, owing to the stressors of single parenting and working, she certainly made up for it with Elise and Jackson.

Children gravitated toward Mom. And she gravitated toward them. Maybe it was the relatable way she knelt down, always face-to-face as she asked questions she knew they'd have answers to. *What's your favorite animal, sweetie? Do you like candy, honey?* Every child was a sweetie or honey or sugar or pumpkin. I had told her she never should have set the precedent of always showing up with gifts when she saw the kids, but their happy squeals of "Grandma!" every time she popped over muted anything I said.

"Grandparents are supposed to spoil their grandkids," she always insisted. And spoil them she did. But one look at those smiles—and knowing how sugar and toys helped bury the unjust pain they had already suffered in their young lives—and I let them have it. Kids deserved a win every once in a while, even if it gave them a sugar buzz right before bed.

"Elise, Jackson." Candace threw her words between Elise and Grandma's conversation about how all boys are trouble, especially Nathan. "Don't you like the food I worked hard to prepare?" Candace shifted up straight as she said it, as if being an inch taller than she already was would demand their respect and obedience.

As if it were that easy. If that worked, I wouldn't still be five foot two.

Jackson shook his head. "It tastes yucky."

"You haven't even tried a bite. Here, I'll help you." Candace leaned across the table, stabbing a piece of his chicken with her fork and raising it to his mouth. He grimaced and backed away from her hovering hand.

I slapped her fork down. "Do *not* force-feed my kids, Candace. If you want to do that to your own children, go for it. But you're not their mother."

Candace's face contorted into blotchy pink shock as she rested the fork on her plate and dropped her arm stiffly to her side.

"What's this about *your own kids,* Candy? Are you two planning to start trying?" Mom asked, rising from her seat.

"It's Candace, not Candy." This was only the fifth time Candace had corrected my mother about her name. Mom wasn't *that* forgetful, but she could be *that* spiteful.

"I apologize. I keep forgetting." As Mom collected her plate, I exhaled relief that dinner was done. "I'll take the plates of those who are finished."

Instantly Jackson and Elise shoved their plates across the table. "I'm done, Grandma!" they chimed.

"Actually, that's why we're hosting this dinner, Mom." It was the first time Lane had spoken since his impromptu toast. "Would you like to tell them, honey?" Lane turned to Candace, who cupped his hand and rested their suctioned palms on the table. I wanted to scoff at the blunt show of affection.

Mom froze. Lane smiled. I rolled my eyes. The kids looked at me with a plea for permission to leave. I nodded in the direction of the stairs, and the stampede was off.

"We're expecting!" Candace's excited words were met with stunned silence.

It was too long before Mom replied.

"You're . . . pregnant already?" Mom sounded as shocked as I had been.

"Yes, and we're thrilled that it happened quickly, since we're eager to start a family. So you'll be a grandmother!"

Mom dropped into her chair. "Well, I'm already a grandmother, dear." I recognized the stiff smile the moment it spread across her lips: disapproval. A firm dash with the slightest lift at the ends. "But that's wonderful news. I'm just . . . a little surprised. You've barely known each other a month and a half . . . and now you're already married and pregnant. It's a lot going on pretty quickly. How do you feel, Lane?"

Lane kissed Candace's palm and beamed. "I'm thrilled, Mom. Really. I've always wanted to be a father, and now it's happening. Life doesn't slow down, and now it's my turn to jump on and ride it."

He looked genuinely happy. In fact, he'd never looked this happy in his life. It was like he sunbathed in Candace's pregnancy glow, and for a moment I wondered if maybe I was wrong about her. Maybe she was good for him after all.

"Having children isn't a rodeo, Lane. It's hard work and sacrifice."

"I know, Mom. But I have a good job, a nice home . . . and now I'm ready to fill it with a family."

Mom gestured to Candace. "What about your parents, *Candy*? I'm sure they're excited by the news."

Candace—not Candy—rolled her eyes at Lane, who begged her for silence with a shake of his head. I forced back a chuckle.

"I don't have any family." Candace replied so matter-of-factly that it bordered on cold.

"Oh, honey, I'm sorry to hear that." Mom paused, waiting for an explanation or some kind of elaboration. Instead Candace looked down at her plate and scraped the last bite of chicken coated with instant potatoes into her mouth.

"Did something happen to them?" Mom pressed in her tactful yet dogged style.

Candace swallowed, then looked Mom square in the eyes. "I'd prefer not to talk about it."

"Do you have any other family back—where did you say you're from, dear?" Mom knew just how to pick at a scab to make it bleed. Those long, crooked fingers with knobby knuckles full of arthritis still knew how to poke. And right now they fiddled with my great-grandma's emerald necklace, a nervous habit. So, Mom was nervous; how unlike her.

"She's from Ohio, Mom. Please stop interrogating my wife," Lane interjected with a stilted chuckle.

Mom's mouth parted in offense. "I'm just trying to get to know my new daughter-in-law."

Candace rested her hand on Lane's arm. "It's okay, honey. I don't mind. That's a lovely necklace, Monica."

Mom glanced down at her chest, as if she didn't know she was wearing the same necklace she always did.

"Thank you, dear. The darn clasp is broken, so I'm always worried it'll fall off. I'd hate to lose it; it's an heirloom. My grandmother's first husband bought it for her for their wedding anniversary. He was murdered shortly after. Strange how a curse like that can travel down the family line." She glanced at me, then Lane, as if he was next.

"Wow, that's quite a family history." Candace chuckled, but I heard the fear in her voice.

"What brought you all the way from Ohio to North Carolina? That's quite a climate adjustment, I'm sure."

"I guess you could say I needed a change. And that's what I found." She gazed lovingly at Lane, a movie-star gaze you'd see in a 1950s flick. "We met at a karaoke bar where he wooed me with song. Two chocolate martinis later, I was hooked!"

"Finding love at a bar, now that's pretty unique." My mother, so tactfully insulting.

"I can't take all the credit," Lane said. "The Gin Blossoms did the work for me. All I had to do was sing 'Til I Hear It from You' and that seemed to do the trick."

"It'll be a delightful story to tell your child one day, how a song and alcohol were the recipe for your happily ever after." Mom always dared to say what no one else would.

"Does anyone want dessert?" The tension spurred Lane out of his seat. "Candace made cheesecake—your favorite, Mom." Lane busied his hands collecting the stack of plates.

Candace stood, hovering at Lane's side.

"Dessert would be lovely." But I could tell Mom was put off. Her chin jutted out in that passive-aggressive way it always did when she was not-so-secretly upset.

Lane scooped up the silverware, making his way around the table while Candace shadowed him.

"Let me clean up and serve the dessert while you rest, dear." Mom waved Candace back to her seat. "The cook doesn't clean where I come from. Especially a pregnant one."

I helped Mom finish clearing the table, carrying the cups to the kitchen sink.

"Do you know anything about her family?" Mom whispered to me as she dumped a handful of dishes into the soapy water.

"No, she's been so secretive about everything. Is it me, or does all of this seem kind of . . . *off* to you? Like she's hiding something?"

Mom glanced behind us, her forehead wrinkled all the way up to the inch of graying roots leading into fading fake blond. I'd never seen her roots so unattended. "That girl has more secrets than the CIA. I thought it awful unusual that she has no family to speak of . . . won't even explain what happened. That kind of aloofness is not normal for kids your age, is it?"

By *kids my age* Mom was referring to grown adults encroaching on forty. But I guess your kids will always be your kids, no matter how old they were.

"No, Mom, it's not normal to hide major details from family. Maybe it's something embarrassing." I pointed to Mom's roots. "Speaking of embarrassing, I distinctly remember you saying a lady never goes out in public with her roots showing. Is there something I need to know?"

She waved off the joke with a laugh. "Oh no, I just haven't had the time to make it to the salon. I'll probably schedule an appointment next week. But I can't shake the feeling that Candace is covering up something big. Something Lane doesn't even know about."

"And you can't trust a person who hides things." My mother had often said these same words to me—first about my father, later about Ben.

"So true, dear. So true."

If only Mom knew what her own daughter was hiding. But this wasn't about me and my demons. This was about the woman who had wormed her way into our family. The woman who was dismantling Lane's life.

I couldn't prove it, but my intuition was rarely wrong. Candace's past had holes filled with secrets. And we would uncover them one by one and burn her lies down to ashes. I was the match and Mom was the gasoline.

"You know how protective I can be over you and Lane," Mom murmured beneath the splash of the water. "And the good Lord has my back on this. Look at where Ben ended up." She clucked; water sloshed. "I'd hate the same thing to happen to *Candy*."

And just like that, I had no idea what my mother was capable of.

Chapter 10

Harper

Gray days reminded me of Ben, the rain dousing me in loneliness and the clouds trapping my cries. It poured the day I met him. And it poured the day I fake buried him at his memorial service. It was as if the rain mocked me.

Droplets rolled down the kitchen window in tiny streams. The *thunkthunkthunk* of the knife hitting the cutting board was the only sound in the house, aside from the pattering of rainfall on the roof and windows. I chopped the head off the last carrot, then sliced it into long, thin strips. The kids called them carrot fries, and it was the only way they'd eat them. I collected the handful of carrot sticks—I mean *fries*—and dropped them into a bowl. I didn't quite feel like inviting the kids down for their snack yet. I appreciated quiet, calm moments like this . . . maybe a little too much lately. All I wanted was to be alone. And yet the loneliness was torture. That couldn't be healthy.

Being alone took me back to life before Ben.

Before I met him, my life was darkness. I had almost given up on love when Benjamin Paris trekked into my store with his muddy boots and grass-stained jeans. Naive me, a part-time employee at a plant nursery, fell for enigmatic him, a master's-bound college kid working for a landscaping business that summer. It was crush at first lopsided grin. Beneath the caked-on dirt, days-old scruff, and sunburn lines on his neck, he had a magnetism that drew me instantly. Maybe it was my hormones blaring, *You haven't had a boyfriend in years, so take what you can get!* or maybe it was the sizzling connection we had, but I knew within five minutes of talking to him as I rang him up that he was The One.

Ben asked me out across the cashier counter while a down-pour tapped the metal roof like restless fingers. Afraid of being used by this man who was out of my league, I told him we could only be friends, but I agreed to dinner. That same night, we ran across the parking lot toward Piedmont Res-taurant, covering our heads with our jackets while droplets pelted us. We drank too much wine and ate seared tuna and shared rich chocolate mousse and kissed across the table for the very first time. So much for *just friends.* I still vividly remembered the bittersweet taste of dark cocoa on his tongue, and it was the first of many more tastes we'd share. I pushed him away after that kiss, and I offered him a deal. He'd need to work for my heart before I was willing to hand it over. The silly boy agreed, unaware that he would woo me for three years before I finally said yes. The whole time I knew what I was doing, and I was doing it well. I was securing my spot in his heart.

"You were worth the wait," he had told me. And I believed him back then. I wasn't so sure I believed that anymore. Lately I felt worth nothing.

The moment Ben lit his flame for me, he became my light. I basked in that light until he died, snuffing it out, and only gloom remained. That's where I lived now. Utter gloom. Lane told me to reach out to my friends. What friends? I hadn't heard from any of them since the memorial over a month ago. Death tended to scare people off, lest a genuine connection brush up against them and infect them with, God forbid, *emotions*. No one wanted to hold a grown woman while she cried. I was the plague everyone ran from.

Perhaps I was a little too picky. *Classist,* as Lane once put it. I made friends only with those in my income bracket, because I'd done the whole needy friend thing and ended up scammed out of hundreds of dollars before *poof!* they disappeared when the freebies stopped coming. And my ideal friend needed to also be afflicted with kids, because only another mother could tolerate the whines and irritations that came with them. But I didn't want a friend who had kids involved in a myriad of sports. I refused to spend endless hours at baseball games or on the sidelines of basketball courts or soccer fields, my tender skin frying in the sun. I had yet to find this perfect specimen of friend, and thus I remained alone.

Maybe it was better this way for someone as untrusting as I was.

Grief was the only emotion I trusted now. Grief easily drowned out fickle joy. A bite of sweet happiness couldn't compete with the vinegar aftertaste of sorrow. There was something eloquent about sorrow, how it slowly pulled you under without you ever realizing you were sinking.

And yet I was so tired of sorrow. It had been my natural state for so long that the tears had dried up. So I picked it up, shook it hard, and watched it turn into anger. Thank you, Candace, for helping me get there.

Every day I hated her a little more. She was manipulative and lazy, the worst kind of woman. She was the type of woman who lured men in with her beauty, then trapped them into a life of servitude. Once she got bored with the adoration, she would crush Lane under her hippie gladiator sandals and walk away, her maxi dress flapping in the wind and bangle bracelets jangling.

Trusting men like my brother were the easiest targets. Always eager to please, surprising her with flowers, takeout, rose-petal trails to a candlelit bedroom. What happened when she was no longer surprised? I knew the answer to that. Poor Lane didn't.

Over the past few days I'd watched as Lane waited on Candace hand and foot—God forbid the baby inside her be jostled about if she dared sit up—and when he was at work I was expected to do the same. Pregnant or not, I wasn't her slave and I had no problem telling her as such.

The kids were upstairs doing homework, which meant they were more likely playing video games on their tablets, and I had just finished tidying up the kitchen after Candace's late-afternoon quesadilla lunch. I could always tell when, and what, she cooked because she left evidence of it everywhere. The sour cream and cheese were left on the island, and the dirty pan sat on the stove. How hard was it to put the ingredients back in the fridge? It was like taking care of a toddler!

Leaning against the doorjamb, I scrolled through rental applicants on my phone while snacking on carrots dipped in hummus. I was searching for the perfect tenant, which my real estate expert mother would say didn't exist. Candace, as usual, was laid up on the sofa watching television. I looked forward to the day when her perfect, lithe body outgrew her size 0 skinny jeans and never returned. Sitting around all the time would only help escalate that end.

"Would you mind making me a cup of tea?" Candace called from the living room. "Mint oolong, with sugar and cream, please."

I could see only half of her from where I stood, the lower half that was leaving a butt indent in the couch with all the sitting.

No, no, no! Get your own damn tea! Can't you see I'm busy?

Of course I couldn't scream what I was thinking. I was too proper for that. Women who wore Estée Lauder makeup and shopped at Pottery Barn didn't *retort*. We *replied*.

"I'd be happy to," I said instead. I couldn't refuse the princess her afternoon tea. I closed my eyes, cursing her under my breath. "But just so you know, even though you're pregnant, you should still do things for yourself. It's healthy for the baby if you keep moving."

I forced a grin and hoped the hint was clear enough.

"I swim my daily laps, but the doctor told me to take it easy other than that, Harper. That's all I'm trying to do."

I hated the way she said my name, *Harper*, the *P* harsh and the *r* over-pronounced. Like *Harp-errr*. "I understand, but I've been pregnant too, *Candace,* and taking it easy doesn't mean doing nothing. You could still work until the baby arrives. Contribute to the income, or at least to the housework."

By now, I'd been living here a week, and I knew this argument would go in circles until I caved, so I grabbed the kettle and filled it up with water. I made a show of opening and closing the cabinets loudly as I grabbed a mug and tea packet. When the tea water whistled a couple minutes later, I poured her a mugful and brought the steeping tea out on a tray, along with a bronze creamer and sugar bowl set that had been my grandmother's. A single Knock Out rose from the garden climbed the wall of a tubular vase I added at the last minute.

Any other guest would have marveled at the display. Not Candace, who instead mocked it.

"A little formal, don't you think?"

"I appreciate decorum. What's wrong with that?" Without etiquette, we might as well toss out our forks and knives and use our fingers instead!

"Nothing."

But I heard something else behind the word.

"No, please tell me what's so bad about being proper?"

"It's great if you want to come across as uppity and snobbish. Is that how you want to be viewed?"

"It's better than being seen as lazy and useless."

Oops. I hadn't meant for that to slip out. Or maybe I had. Sometimes the brain-mouth connection backfired and I said things I didn't mean . . . or did mean but shouldn't say. This was one of those times, particularly because I was at her mercy, living under her roof. Correction: Lane's roof.

"Are you calling me lazy and useless?"

I didn't answer. I now knew better than to speak. That seemed to make her even angrier.

"I'm creating life right now—your brother's baby! The wiggling arms and legs, that's me. The racing heartbeat, me again. The tiny nose and sleepy eyes, all me. It's exhausting donating all of my energy and nutrients to the baby, and I deserve a little credit for what my body is going through."

"I'm well aware," I said. "But through all of my pregnancies, I still cooked and cleaned and did my part."

"Maybe you wouldn't have lost a child if you cared more about your baby's life than your homemaking."

I stiffened, uncertain of what I had just heard. Then her accusation caught up to me. How did she even know about the baby I had lost? The silence was thick with her shame. Even Candace knew she had gone too far. Swiping my hand under the tray, I lifted it off the coffee table and flung it to the floor, spilling tea, cream, sugar, and ceramic splinters across the wood. Candace jumped up from the sofa, arms outstretched as if to hug me, but too afraid to come near me.

Stay away, Candace, lest I strike that fake remorse from your face.

"I'm so sorry! I don't know why I said that. Lane told me that in confidence and I never should have said anything. That was wrong of me on so many levels—"

I raised my palm, stopping her with a curt "Enough! You know nothing about me. Get your own tea."

Tears I didn't want her to see collected in the corners of my eyes. I refused to be her target practice. As I stormed out of the room, Elise chased Jackson past me, screaming something about her diary. My brain buzzed too loudly to hear her accusations as she tugged on my arm, forcing my attention on her, while Jackson hid behind my legs.

"Mommy, help!" Jackson screeched.

"Give it back!" Elise shouted, reaching for him around my human shield.

"What's the problem now?" I yelled over them. "You were both supposed to be doing homework, not screwing around." Not that the kids ever listened to me. My voice was my only tool, and it had grown dull.

"I *was* doing homework," Elise whined, "until Jackson took my diary. Tell him to give it back."

I glared at Jackson. "Is this true?"

"She's writing terrible things. Things about Daddy. Things we're not supposed to talk about." The way Jackson said it, his tone an ethereal bass, worried me. What had she written? What had Jackson read? How much did they know?

There was an unspoken trust between parent and child when it came to a diary. A parent simply didn't look. Period. No matter how sneaky, or dark, or secretive your child was behaving, the diary was off-limits. A breach of this simple rule created a chasm that you could never cross. But if crossing that line saved your child in the end, did the ends justify the means? Could trust ever be restored?

"Hand over the diary." I held out my open palm, and Jackson dropped the book into my grasp.

The edges of the pages were crinkled and well worn, filled with all the thoughts and crushes and disappointments and secrets that passed through my daughter's mind, then out through her pen.

"Mom, you can't read that! It's personal," Elise whimpered.

"I'm not going to read it." I wasn't sure about that yet. Screw trust when my child's life was at stake. "I just want you two to stop fighting for five minutes. Is that too much to ask?"

Handing the carrots to Elise, I pointed them to the breakfast nook, telling them to sit while I sliced an apple and spooned peanut butter into a dish.

"Here, have a snack to tide you over until dinner." I set the plate between them.

The shift in the air behind me caused me to look up and find Candace tiptoeing toward the garbage can carrying the broken remains of her cracked mug. She paused and looked at me, as if holding back words that were insisting on pushing through her lips. If she was trying to avoid another fight, she was doing a crappy job of it.

"What?" I spat. "If you've got something to say, just say it."

"You'll get angry," she said.

"That's never stopped you from speaking your mind before."

"I just . . . you want the kids not to fight, but then here we are constantly bickering. It doesn't set a good example for them."

"How enlightened of you to notice."

"I think we'll all be a lot happier if you and I learn how to get along and respect each other. Don't you agree?"

I didn't owe her respect, or an explanation of my parenting methods, but that urge to defend myself continued to surface. "You think we can just all play nice and suddenly everyone's happy? I lost my husband and am living with my brother and a sister-in-law who hates me. There is no such thing as happiness when you're going through what I'm going through."

Add the guilt of what I had done to the list of miseries, and

I would never truly be happy again, and I think Ben knew that. My misery was strong enough to kill him. If life had taught me anything over the past year, it was that happiness was fleeting. Momentary. Sadness held on much longer. Happiness was the calm amid the storm. It broke through the clouds on overcast days, but it was never enough to sunbathe in.

"First of all, I don't hate you." I could detect sincerity in her voice. "And while I don't know what it's like to carry that much grief, you have to think about how it affects your kids. They're always fighting, always complaining. Don't you see what you're doing to them?"

What *I'm* doing to them?

"I appreciate your concern, but you'll see when you have your own kids that parenting is not always black and white. We don't always do the right thing or know the right answer. Sometimes we have to parent in the gray."

While my words remained calm, my thoughts grew turbulent. She was essentially blaming me for screwing up my kids. She probably blamed me for Ben's death, and for losing the baby. Hadn't I blamed myself enough already? I couldn't continue to be nice anymore. Images of hurting Candace flashed through my mind like tiny lightning bolts zapping my brain. Thoughts of poisoning her to spare her unborn baby the misery of having her for a mother . . .

I shook the awful, terrifying thought away as I fingered the pile of apple seeds collecting on the counter. One hundred and forty apple seeds would provide enough cyanide to kill a woman of Candace's size. I had looked it up; I didn't know why.

I scooped the seeds into a bowl, grabbed Elise's diary, and headed upstairs.

Chapter 11

Candace

You once told me that you felt broken beyond repair.
Let me mend you. Let me make you whole again.

I was a mirror that had been dropped one too many times. Life didn't shatter me, but it left a splinter so big that it made me feel worthless. A cracked mirror is just broken glass. Sharp to the touch, and it'll make you bleed. And when you looked at me, all you would see was an ugly, distorted reflection of yourself.

That was who I was. All the worst parts of every woman: needy, jealous, insecure. I was either too much or never enough. And then I met Lane, and suddenly the worst parts fell off of me. Maybe they didn't so much as fall off as become invisible, because Lane didn't seem to see them. Sometimes I still saw them, though.

As I stepped out of the shower, I swiped across the foggy bathroom mirror and hated the woman who looked back at me with arctic-blue eyes that had witnessed too much darkness. Wrapping a towel around my chest and tucking the corner in to hold it up, I ran a comb through my hair, the black even blacker and the blue highlights barely noticeable. Some days I didn't even recognize myself, and those were the days I was happiest.

Today I was that dropped mirror again, and I despised myself because others despised me first.

My parents were the first to drop me. *Crack!* The day they died left a fracture I would never recover from. The worst part was that I had survived, forced to live with the memory. My mother cowering over me in the corner of our trailer, begging for my life. She didn't care what happened to her, as long as her baby girl got the future she never had. It didn't matter that I didn't have a future if she wasn't in it.

I felt it before I heard it, the shift of weight as her body relaxed on top of mine, smothering me, then a sticky wetness drip-drip-dripping onto my only good pair of jeans. Justice brand, all the rage. Mom had been so excited when she found them at Goodwill with the tags still on! Only after I felt her deadweight did I hear the crack of the gun.

The memory didn't end there. That would have been too kind. After I screamed and in a panic pushed my mother's lifeless body off me, I looked up at my father's face—bloated and sweaty and red with fury, veins blue and pulsing with cocaine—as he turned the gun on himself. Opened his thick

jaw. Aimed the barrel between tobacco-stained teeth. Then . . .
crack! Both parents gone, life as I knew it skewed beyond
recognition. Just. Like. That.

Boyfriends who stole my innocence continued to break me.
Crack! Friends who used me then abandoned me splintered
me further. *Crack!* Then, one day, I found an adhesive: love.
It glued all my pieces back together into something whole.
Someone new, with purpose. Love could do that, you know.
It recycled the heart.

A knock on the bathroom door pulled me back into the
present. Then another soft knock. The knock of a child's
knuckles.

"Yes?" I said to the door.

Again: *knock . . . knock.* Slowly, intentionally.

I swung open the door, but the hallway was empty.

"What the hell?" I spoke into the dead air.

I glanced up and down the hallway—nothing. Maybe the
kids were playing a prank. Or maybe I was just hearing things.
It wouldn't have been the first time. When I closed the door
and returned to the sink, the mirror dripped with condensation
like it was crying. Most days I felt like crying too.

I rooted through my makeup bag for my essentials. A dash
of bronzer, a swipe of mascara, Burt's Bees shimmer lip gloss.
Less is more when you have the taut skin of a woman in her
twenties. A couple days ago, when passing Harper's room, I
caught her mid–makeup routine. There couldn't have been
fewer than fifteen products on her face. The sight made me
dread my thirties.

Heading to my bedroom closet, I still hadn't decided what
to wear yet. Outfit number one was a surefire way to piss

Harper off—a bralette showing underneath a strappy floral maxi dress—but we were supposed to be working on our friendship today. So I picked the more conservative outfit number two and hoped it would appease her bland sense of style.

The sacrifices one makes for family.

By the time I made it downstairs, dressed, game face on, and purse in hand, Harper was waiting by the door.

"You finally ready?" she asked.

The woman was perpetually in a rush. I was perpetually not. Already we were clashing.

The eerie knock on the bathroom door still echoed in my mind. "Yeah. Um, did you knock on the bathroom door while I was in there?"

"No, why?"

Strange. "Are the kids around?"

"No . . . I think they're outside with Aubrey, the babysitter. Lane's heading to work shortly." Her voice lifted with concern. "Why do you ask?"

I shook away the strange thoughts floating around in my head. "It's nothing."

I wondered if Jackson was rubbing off on me.

"You look nice." Harper grinned with approval at my conservative jeggings and retro Fleetwood Mac T-shirt. Her gaze caught for a moment on the holes in the knees and the frayed hems, but at least she wasn't commenting about my cleavage under her breath. Wearing an adequate bra in public seemed to have scored me an even higher approval rating.

"Thanks. You do too."

And she did look nice . . . for a sixty-year-old lady, not a late thirties woman. I checked my hobo bag. Lip gloss, wallet, cell phone, all-natural mood stabilizer. Everything I would need to endure a day with *sis*!

A week ago, I would have never agreed to a *Sisters' Day Out!* as Lane called it. He had been begging me to make some "girl time" with my new sister—*in-law,* I added in my head—but eventually I caved. Not for me, but for him. So I agreed to a shopping outing. Especially after the tension Harper and I had been wading through the past two days. Shopping was easier than forcing stilted conversation over a meal at a restaurant, and I could easily wander off and browse by myself without injuring her dainty ego.

The best part was when Lane handed me his credit card and told me to treat myself to whatever I wanted. "With a growing belly, you'll probably need a whole pregnancy wardrobe," he suggested. *Don't mind if I do!*

I had never had someone who wanted to spoil me. I didn't dress in name-brand clothes or walk in expensive shoes, but Lane made me feel like a designer woman. *You deserve nice things,* he'd insist when I turned down his gifts, his face droopy and sad. *It makes me happy to treat you well.*

And so I let him. Soon I realized just how happy it made me too. I was his queen, he was my king, and I felt every bit the part.

"Don't you have your own credit card?" Harper asked.

"Nah, she can use mine," Lane said.

"But she can't forge your signature. That's illegal."

Oh Harper, ever the rule follower.

"You'd be impressed with how scary good her forgery skills are!" Lane laughed.

Harper frowned.

"When you don't have parents, you're forced to learn such skills to get by in life. Permission slips don't sign themselves," I joked, hoping Harper wouldn't read into it. "So, we all set?"

I plastered on a smile and off Harper and I went. As I stepped into the car, the movement of curtains above the front porch drew my gaze upward. A shadow passed across my bedroom window, and a chill prickled my skin. Lately I couldn't shake the feeling of being watched.

By the time we reached the mall, I'd pushed the stalker sensation out of mind and prepped myself for a shop-fest. The Streets at Southpoint in Durham, North Carolina, had a bit of everything for everyone. Urban Outfitters for me. Lands' End for Harper. Victoria's Secret for me. Maidenform for Harper. So when Harper parked the car and proceeded to hang at my hip from one store to the next like a parole officer, I couldn't help but feel claustrophobic. And when I felt smothered, I rebelled.

We wandered side by side through the mall, the cutesy storefronts made to imitate the street shops one might find in a quaint but lively 1950s town that no longer existed. Harper's watchful gaze followed me around every clothing rack, through every aisle, never giving me a moment's peace. You'd think the *sisterly* companionship would feel comforting, but instead it was unsettling and downright obsessive. Maybe it was because of the earrings I had pinched and hidden in my coat pocket. Or the stolen ring I brazenly wore, as if claiming ownership so publicly entitled me to that ring. I couldn't help my thieving impulse.

It wasn't about the items, because Lane's checking account

would easily cover the cost. It was about Harper—and her judgment as she looked down on me as *less than*. The moment Lane handed me his credit card I felt it. Harper thought I was a gold digger, but I didn't need or want Lane's gold. I could take what I wanted, when I wanted it, and so I shoved my sin in Harper's principled, entitled face. With pregnancy hormones raging through my body, I needed to feel normal again—myself. And *myself* was a rebel. A heart thief. And today, apparently, a jewelry thief.

Three hours and six shopping bags later, I could tell Harper was growing weary. Her gait had slowed, her eyes had lost interest in me, and her chitchat had gone stale. My advantage was being ten years her junior, which equipped me with the stamina to shop for hours on end without exhaustion. If shopping were an Olympic sport, I'd be wearing a gold medal.

"You ready to head home?" Harper asked me for the umpteenth time.

I felt sufficiently stocked up on all things maternal, so I agreed to cut the poor woman a break. She had given it a good run.

"Yes, I'm ready. And famished. I'm sure the baby is exhausted too. Let's go." I glanced at her empty hands. "You didn't find anything you wanted to buy?"

"No, nothing I needed." She eyed my full hands. "You didn't find anything you *didn't* want to buy?"

I couldn't tell if the lilt of her voice was attempting humor, accusatory, or simply annoying.

"All of it's for the baby," I answered.

"Well, not *all* of it." Her lips straightened in a line with the touch of a frown.

If she knew about my sticky fingers, at least she didn't push it. I imagined her whispering to Lane in secret tonight about my extracurricular thieving. I felt another she-said/she-said argument brewing.

Harper led the way outside through the automatic doors, to a large outdoor shopping and dining patio that stretched a good two blocks ahead. Between the rows of stores were street performers singing, fountains spraying water, and even a climbing wall where kids were clamoring to the cheers of their parents. One day I'd watch my own child's unsteady legs and chubby arms heft her way up the climbing wall. I couldn't wait for that day to finally arrive.

Harper halted in front of an Italian restaurant with a sandwich board announcing its specials for the evening. "Did you want to stop now for a bite to eat, or just make something when we get home?"

I couldn't stomach a long meal of awkward silence or awkward conversation with her.

"Let's just head home. My dogs are barking." I chuckled, and Harper looked confused.

"Your dogs are what?"

"My dogs are barking. You know, John Candy and Steve Martin in *Planes, Trains, and Automobiles*." Nothing seemed to register. "Wow, you've never seen that movie?"

"Can't say I have."

"Harper, it's from your generation, not mine. And it's a cult classic."

She shrugged indifferently.

"How about we have a John Candy marathon? We'll start with *Uncle Buck* and work our way down to *The Great Out-*

doors." My spirits lifted. Maybe we could actually bond over the big-hearted buffoon. "Oh, and we can't forget *Spaceballs.*"

Her grimace deflated all my hope. "Anything starring John Candy I wouldn't enjoy. I prefer documentaries, nature shows—more educated entertainment, not slapstick comedy. I'm guessing you found *Ace Ventura* simply riveting."

What kind of person didn't love John Candy? I almost felt bad for her, going through life with such solemnity, no humor to lighten her existence. It explained a lot about her, though. Her personality was as stale as her film choices.

We wove our way through the crowd, past a man strumming John Mayer's "Your Body Is a Wonderland" on a guitar, toward a fountain with bronze statues of children splashing one another. I touched my stomach where my baby swam inside me and thought about how she would one day run through a sprinkler, giggling as it sprayed her with water. In my heart, I just knew she was a she. Mother's intuition, perhaps.

"One second," I told Harper as I fished a penny from my purse. Lifting it to my lips, I whispered my wish, kissed the coin, then tossed it into the fountain. It made a *plop* before it sunk to the concrete floor where hundreds of other wishes glistened in the watery sun.

"What did you wish for?" Harper asked, sidling up to me.

"If I tell you I'd have to kill you." I smirked, but Harper frowned. "I'm kidding. Geez, relax. You're not supposed to tell your wish or it won't come true."

"I thought only children believed that."

I ignored her remark because the day had turned out better than expected and I wasn't going to let her sour it. Lifting her chin high, she took off, her back stiff and straight. I followed a beat behind her, the pregnancy drain hitting me suddenly. As I paused and leaned down to adjust the American Eagle shopping bag that had slipped from my fingers, a man wearing aviator sunglasses bumped into me, nearly knocking me over.

"Excuse you!" I yelled. "Watch where you're going!"

The man stopped and pivoted to face me, his body shadowed and just a silhouette with the sun sinking behind him.

"Maybe you're the one who needs to watch out." His voice was a low growl as he rushed off.

What did he mean by that? My stomach dropped inside me. My breath snagged in my throat. I shaded my eyes with my hand. It couldn't be *him* . . . my past coming to revisit me.

Before I could know for certain it was him—because maybe I imagined his voice, maybe I was wrong—please, God, let me be wrong—the man disappeared into the crowd. The panic followed me all the way to Harper's car, then all the way home as the gray ribbon of highway unrolled ahead of us, my thoughts drifting back in time . . .

* * *

Sweat and mothballs—that was the scent of the woman sitting next to me. Except not the sweet workout kind of sweat. It was the dank kind that soaked her armpits and collected under the folds of her neck when crammed into a Greyhound bus for six hours, wearing a hot-box knitted sweater that's a size too small.

The scenery outside my window whizzed by in a blur of crooked trees, open fields, and an endless highway. After riding through the night, I opened my eyes to a streak of cardinal red that melted into burning-ember orange. Kissing the sky was a dusty rose that receded into a swelling regal blue. It was the perfect sunrise for a perfect fresh start.

If only I was inhaling the hay-scented country air outside my window instead of the reek of offensive body odor. I would have switched seats if there were any other window views available. Instead, I curled up as best as I could into the cold vinyl seat and leaned against the glass, watching town after town drift into the background of my life. As I pulled my sleeve over my hand and covered my nose, I vowed never to return to my condemned love in my condemned city.

Every love had a story. Mine and Noah's started in death and ended in death. We were darkly poetic that way. He was the only one there for me when my parents died, picked up my broken pieces, helped me put them back together. But they never quite fit, no matter how hard we forced them. And those jutting edges that were left? Well, they cut me so deep I bled out.

I breathed a patch of warm dew on the window, then traced a heart in it. I didn't know if I would ever love another again—because no matter how dysfunctional Noah and I were, I still loved him deeply—but now I would begin to love myself. The sunrise pouring through the heart promised light. Light cast out darkness. No more feeling sorry for myself. No more swimming in the ache. I didn't quite know where I was going, but I would know when I arrived. Freedom was a lofty goal for a broken spirit, but I was a fighter backed into a corner.

Armed with nothing more than a single duffel bag, a pocketful of stolen cash, and a lie, I would leave my identity along with the pain behind. But instead of being another victim, this time I vowed to be the victor.

Chapter 12

Harper

It took one moment to break trust and a lifetime of work to rebuild it. I really thought Candace and I had shared a connection at the mall today. United over fashion, related over decor. Retail therapy! She even let me snap a selfie of us raising our banana-mango-kale smoothies, as if toasting the camera. I think she even smiled! We had started over, lemony fresh.

My gait was perky when I entered my bedroom with its stiff avocado-green wallpaper, the kind your grandmother would have picked out when she bought her first house in the 1940s. Trails of mustard-yellow flowers climbed in distressed rows where the sun chewed away at the paper. The scent of hardcover books and dust lingered in the fabric of the walls, telling stories that only ghosts remembered.

After our rejuvenating outing, I yearned for companionship. Friendship. I even felt more like myself, my face made up and hair curled. It felt good to feel pretty again, existent, alive. Picking up my phone, I stared at the black screen. It was time, time to free-fall back into society. Modern society, that is, where face-to-face human interaction was as rare as a monkey sighting in the city. Now, we all lived inside our phones, where our deepest human connections were tethered to our internet connections.

First things first, I wanted to look up that name Detective Meltzer had mentioned, the one Ben had opened up a bank account for. I found the envelope in my purse where I had scribbled it in the corner: *Medea Kent*. A quick Google search gave me nothing. Not a single result. Strange. The name sounded exotic on my lips. An international client, perhaps? Clearly I wouldn't find my answers today.

My Facebook hiatus had raised a lot of concern among my so-called friends. I hadn't posted on social media since Ben's death, only browsed my newsfeed a time or two and searched for Candace. After all the messages offering condolences and prayers, I figured I owed my friends a status update. It was the least I could do to show I still existed in the land of the living. Ben had believed that social media was the downfall of society. According to him, it turned everyone into agoraphobic preachers with their own personal pulpits to spout whatever nonsense bubbled inside them that day. Everyone now had a cause, but only behind the safety and anonymity of a screen where there was no accountability. But even I couldn't resist its draw. You could impulse buy, get your fake news, and make new best friends all in a matter of minutes, with just the swipe of a finger!

Initially, I joined the bandwagon to keep track of long-distance high school friends. Though maybe *friends* was a stretch when you hadn't seen or spoken to someone in person in nearly two decades. But it sated that gnawing curiosity—was the head cheerleader still prettier than you (there went her tight body after three kids!), does the captain of the football team still have that charm (look at that receding hairline!)? It turned out that even the most popular, good-looking kids in high school eventually did plateau out into normalcy, with flabby arms and beer bellies and wrinkles and bad haircuts just like the rest of us. Social media was a socially acceptable form of stalking and self-validation.

Today I had decided to end my Facebook lull and publicly grieve—and publicly heal, I suppose. It was expected when everyone knew your husband had passed . . . and those who didn't know deserved fair warning before they tagged me in marriage memes. I admit, I clicked on my Facebook app icon with trepidation. When Ben's murder hit the news, a lot of speculation had pointed to me, the black widow. It was inevitable, since even the police had their eyes on me. The questions. The accusations. The suspicions. When a spouse ended up dead, with no enemies to speak of, people tended to point fingers at the only obvious suspect: the one with the most to gain. A multimillion-dollar insurance policy was exactly that.

Considering all this, one couldn't blame me for hiding from public view. Wasn't that what guilty people did—hide? But I wasn't guilty. I just wasn't ready to face all the backlash or sympathy. Until today, when Candace had validated me as a human, spent time and shared laughs and smoothies with me . . . and it felt so good. I needed more of that, and I knew the first step was back into the virtual world if my healing was to start gaining traction in the real world. I wasn't the talk of the town anymore. People had moved on for lack of caring. After all, it was a well-off, middle-aged man who was murdered, not a woman or child. I'd bet most people assumed he had it coming.

As Facebook sprang to life, the first thing I noticed when I opened my account was the countless notifications, all comments about a post I apparently had made. But I hadn't posted anything. I clicked on my profile as thousands of pixels drifted into place, forming words that made me swell with horror. Shock soaked into every part of me.

"What the hell?"

Time-stamped this afternoon, an appalling post from Harper Paris, from my very own account:

Living my best life husband free!
#deadandgone #blackwidow

The backlash went on for more than two hundred comments and a thousand angry-faced emojis, the post shared dozens of times. Complete strangers from all over the globe told me what a murdering waste of space I was, questioned the state of my soul, insisted that I should rot in jail—wait, no, apparently I deserved the electric chair for what I'd done. And eternal hellfire. Some commenters with extra time on their hands to look me up even mentioned the baby:

First she killed her child, now her husband. Child services needs to get her other kids safely away before they're next.

I heard her two-year-old died last year. Think she killed that child too?

This woman needs to be behind bars before someone else turns up dead.

Get this #babykiller and #husbandmurderer off the streets!

The child died under suspicious circumstances. Then her husband turns up murdered. How have the police not arrested her already?

There's nothing more dangerous than a black widow who has everyone fooled.

Comment after comment attacking my character, charging me with murder, bringing up the baby. Maybe they weren't wrong. The two events were connected, after all. I was a killer in denial. Were my own children no longer safe with me as their mother?

The phone slipped from my fingers, landing soundlessly on the mattress. I stifled a sob, but I couldn't hold it back. The whole world hated me, despised me, called me a murderer. I could only imagine what the cops would think when they saw this. Because most certainly they would. And it would raise a whole slew of questions I couldn't answer. About Ben. About the baby's death—and the details of what had actually happened. I could never let that get out.

I inhaled a steadying breath. *Smell a flower, blow out a candle.*

Calm yourself. Don't panic. Just think.

Maybe I could fix this. They were just strangers, after all. Who cared what they thought of me? And yet I suddenly understood why teens were attempting suicide over social media bullying.

Smell a flower, blow out a candle.

I grabbed the phone and reopened the app, finding the post at the top of my feed. I clicked the corner icon to delete it, expecting the action to erase the hurt as well. A refresh later and it was gone—*whoosh*—into cyberspace. But the hurt was still there. No, it wasn't hurt. It was anger that burned into my skin. Hatred for the person who did this. I'd already lost so much. Where my heart once lived was now an empty cavity, as if you could reach inside me and feel nothing but cool, damp air. Who would want to break what was already broken?

No one came to mind, no one who hated me this much to pose as me and write something so evil. Had some anonymous scammer hacked into my account for fun, or was it personal, done by someone with access to my phone? I knew one thing—yes, this was personal. And that left only one person who could have done it. Who *would* have done it.

Candace. She had motive and means.

The motive: She hated me, for one. I was the thorn in her side, and the feeling was mutual.

The means: I never kept track of my phone. I always left it sitting around, or sometimes even let Elise play *Angry Birds* or *Escape Room* on it. Candace could have easily grabbed it and posted to my account since I didn't password protect my phone. Ben had often warned me about that. *What if your phone gets stolen?* he'd said a dozen times. I hadn't listened to Ben back then, and now I regretted shrugging him off. Never again would he warn me about the dangers of not password protecting my phone. Never again would I get the chance to tell him he worried too much, or anticipated the worst in people.

When would every thought stop leading back to Ben?

Focus.

The post was made sometime around my shopping trip with Candace. I couldn't be sure about the exact time we left, but it was close enough. My phone had definitely been with me in the car and at the mall, in my purse the whole time. And Candace had a secret ability, a superhuman power to commit wrongs without guilt. I first noticed it when I caught her wearing a ring she had stolen. She didn't think I had seen, or maybe deniability was a game for her. Whatever the case, she proudly wore that ring with a bold lack of remorse. If she could effortlessly pilfer jewelry, how much easier was it to borrow my phone and post something terrible? And just when we were starting to get along . . .

I couldn't imagine why Candace would want to hurt me to this extent. Sure, she came across a bit cold and aloof. But this was sociopathic. I needed to confront her about it, but I didn't know how to outsmart her and catch her in a lie. Without proof, I had nothing but my word against hers.

Sneaking down the hall toward Candace's bedroom, I stood by the door, which was cracked open, and listened. It was quiet inside, nothing but the occasional ruffle of pages. As I knocked, the door swung in, giving me full view of Candace eating chips in bed, a copy of *Us Weekly* magazine in hand. I cringed at the thought of all those greasy crumbs making their way into her wrinkled sheets.

She barely offered me a glance, her eyes remaining fixed on a page littered with pictures and celebrity gossip.

"Can I speak with you a moment?" I asked.

She groaned and glanced up, only her blue eyes visible above the magazine's horizon. "What's up?"

I hadn't considered how to word this without blowing things up. I figured the simpler, the better. "Did you post something from my Facebook account?"

She wiped her mouth with the back of her hand. "Why would I do that? I don't even have a Facebook account." There was no surprise in her eyes. No reaction at all.

"I didn't ask if you posted from *your* account. I asked if you posted from *my* account." The narrow glare she gave showed her clear dislike for my interrogation methods.

Closing the magazine and tossing it down, she cocked her head and smirked. "No, I did not post from your account. I'm not some vengeful teenager who uses social media to passive-aggressively launch an attack on a girl who stole my boyfriend, or whatever. I'm not into drama, Harper."

She picked up her magazine and buried her face back in it. Conversation over, apparently.

"I never said it was drama. I just asked if you posted something."

"I can only assume it's drama, or else you wouldn't be accusing me of doing it."

My face warmed with embarrassment. "It wasn't an accusation. It was just a question. Someone posted something from my account, and the only person who could have accessed my phone lives in this house."

"Maybe one of the kids did it. I always see Elise on your phone."

I shook my head. "This isn't something they would post. Plus it was posted when we were at the mall today. My phone was with me the whole time . . . and you were with me the whole time."

"So you think *I* would be that crazy to steal your phone while I'm with you? I have a life, Harper, and petty Facebook crises aren't part of it. Are you sure you didn't post whatever it is so that you could make me look bad to Lane?" She lowered the magazine and raised her eyebrows at me.

"What? That's ridiculous!"

"Is it really? Because ever since you met me you've been trying to break me and Lane up. Clearly you're out to get me, and I wouldn't put it past you to frame me so you can cry to Lane about what a mean girl I am." She rolled her hands into tiny fists, twisting them under her eyes, the universal sign for crying like a baby. Then she stopped and observed me, hard and cold, and I observed the floor, hard and cold. "But I'm not that easy to scare, Harper. I've dealt with way worse than you before."

This was it, the beginning of the end. No more playing house, no rewind, no more shopping trips and selfie pics. We were now sworn enemies. I was speechless. And afraid. Something about the way she had said it shook me. This was not a woman I wanted to mess with . . . but she was also not a woman I wanted my brother chained to.

"Are we done here?" Candace's gaze roved over me, unraveling me with her eyes. She sensed I was weak, and she preyed on that.

"Yeah, we're done." I nodded and left, but I had dealt with way worse too. As I shut the door behind me, I could have sworn I heard her mutter, "*Black widow.*"

Like I said, it was only just beginning.

Chapter 13

Harper

I loved laundry day. The solitude, the mindlessly busy hands. There was something relaxing and numbing about it. The idyllic repetition of folding and stacking, the soft strands of fabric running through my fingers. Sometimes I would put on my favorite show, hide in the bedroom, and fold the minutes— and the anxiety—away. My brain would shut down while I created tall, neat piles all over the bed. For me, laundry was a cheap, productive form of therapy. Certainly cheaper than the therapist I had stopped seeing months ago, despite what the judge ordered.

The wicker laundry basket that matched the wicker bins I had gotten on sale at Pottery Barn last year—back when I enjoyed shopping, or enjoyed anything, for that matter—sat on one side of me, the other side of me filled with short stacks of clothes. Elise's bottoms, Elise's tops. Jackson's bottoms, Jackson's tops. Lane's Windex-blue scrubs in matching sets. As I pulled out a button-down shirt from the bottom of the basket, I gasped.

Ben's Brooks Brothers oxford work shirt, one of his favorites. Despite its $150 price tag, he said it was worth every penny. So I'd bought him ten. I laughed back then at the frivolity. Now it made me nearly cry because I was homeless, broke, and desperate.

I set the shirt aside. I thought I had donated all of Ben's clothes to Goodwill, where some lucky bastard would be dressed to the nines in designer wear for the price of a cup of Starbucks coffee. I must have missed this one at the bottom of the dirty clothes heap. Pressing the collar against my face, I inhaled the scent of clean linen fabric softener. Ben's smell had been stripped by detergent, and maybe that was for the best. He didn't have a particular scent, other than the pungent sweat he soaked the sheets with each night, which I teased him about almost daily. I'd tell him he stunk up the bedding. He'd blame the dog. I'd laugh and remind him we didn't have a dog. It was our thing. Our banter. Ben was a hot, sweaty sleeper. What I would give for my sheets to be dank with his sweat again.

I wondered if his pillowcase held traces of him. I wondered if I'd find more of him scattered throughout the laundry bins. I wondered when the wondering would end. I hated this part of death, when the ghost lived in your head.

Reaching for another item, my fingers tangled in a pile of lacy underwear. A thong. Who in their right mind enjoyed the sensation of floss riding up their butt crack? Somehow

Candace's dirty clothes always ended up in my wash, which irritated me to no end. Didn't she realize laundry required organization? Like colors with like colors. Whites with whites. Delicates handled, well, delicately! When she threw a red wool sweater in with the whites, it turned everything pink and shrunk the sweater. It had served her right, but of course I'd been blamed for the sweater that now fit a newborn.

I laid the underwear on her stack of clean clothes, which was taller than the rest.

"Candace!" I yelled to a silent house.

When I got no reply, I glanced out the window and saw her swimming laps. Back and forth, back and forth, in a fluid rhythm of splashing arms and legs. With it only being late May, it was still early in the season for swimming, but *that's what a pool heater is for!* she had explained. Never mind that installing the heater had cost more than a car. Although summer was still a month away, it had arrived early this year with temperatures already in the 80s, but when the pool temperature hadn't yet risen to a balmy warm owing to the chilly nights, Candace had insisted on a heater. And a new pool patio. And a custom pergola. Like every other whim of hers, Lane had obliged and paid extra to have it installed that week.

I want to give her everything life has withheld from her. She's never had anything of value. Let me spoil her if I want to spoil her, Lane tried to explain when I brought up her extravagant spending. Nothing I said would open his eyes to the truth. I smelled a gold digger, but Lane only smelled her pheromones. At least it kept her out of my hair, her daily routine of sunbathe, swim. Sunbathe, swim. God forbid she spend the time washing her own laundry.

Picking up her teetering pile of clean clothes, I carried it into her bedroom where the bed was a mess and the floor barely visible under all the junk. Clothes, shoes, towels, shopping bags . . . she was a shameless slob. I couldn't stand my brother being forced to live like this, so I began tidying up her dresser so I could place the clothes on top. Opening her top drawer, I found it was crammed full of assorted clothing with no theme whatsoever. Socks, T-shirts, and shorts all mixed together. My God, the girl had no sense of organization.

As I moved things around, folding and coordinating as I went, a piece of paper crinkled along the bottom of the drawer. Pushing the clothing aside, I pulled it out through the folds of fabric. An ultrasound image. Why would she put a priceless photo like this—the first glimpse of her baby's face—in the bottom of her drawer? It deserved to be framed. Despite the war between us, our children would be cousins. Even if I couldn't be a happy sister-in-law, I could be a doting auntie. It wasn't the baby's fault her mother was a devious leech.

Maybe as a gesture of goodwill I would frame it for her. I already had an adorable ultrasound frame that would be perfect, a monkey swinging from a tree with the caption *It's a jungle in here!* My mother had gotten similar frames for each of my kids—an elephant and a giraffe—but the monkey frame remained empty in a box in my closet.

I examined the picture, remembering back when I had my first ultrasound with Elise. What an exciting day, seeing that blob floating around, a tiny head and arms and legs. And that heartbeat! Who would have known you could see it beating a mile a minute? It made everything inside me feel so . . . real.

At that moment I had planned my home, my life, and my future around that tiny person growing inside me.

Well, at least Candace wasn't lying about the pregnancy. Initially I had my doubts, but this was a good thing. Finally, a truth amid the lies! I traced the speckled white image of the baby against the black background. My brother's baby. I really was an aunt! If I was going to have a little niece or nephew, I didn't want a schism. I needed to smooth things over. We *did* have fun shopping together, didn't we? Anything was possible.

Taking the ultrasound with me, I headed to my closet and rummaged through several boxes until I found the picture frame at the top, dusty with time. I slipped the thin paper inside, adjusting it just right. As I checked to see how it looked, I noticed the date: the ultrasound was taken the day they got married. I counted the weeks in my head. The math didn't seem right. In fact, if the date was correct, it put her at almost three months pregnant. This meant she got pregnant a month before she even met Lane.

This meant she lied about everything.

This meant the baby wasn't Lane's.

This meant I wasn't an aunt.

This meant war.

I needed to tell Lane, but he was already overworked and stretched thin. I didn't know how he was surviving on the four to five hours of sleep he barely got, but at the rate he was going, he was doomed to crash. And crash hard.

I didn't want to add more to his already full plate of night shifts and home project to-do lists. He'd been picking up double shifts at the hospital to pay for all the extra baby "needs," as Candace called them. The weekly pregnancy massages, baby yoga classes, and $1,200 baby stroller were hardly necessities, though. If it wasn't a pair of Jimmy Choos that would last a lifetime, or diamonds that you could pass on to your kids, it wasn't worth the money. If the baby would spit up on it, poop in it, or spill food on it, you didn't pay $1,200 for it.

All of these demands for a baby that wasn't even his.

Before burdening Lane with this new information, I decided I'd do my own digging. I would winnow the wheat from the chaff, the truth from the lies. There were so many puzzle pieces that didn't fit together when it came to Candace, but what was her ultimate angle? I knew my brother was an easy target for any single woman looking to start a family. He made good money as a nurse, he was handsome and loyal, and he owned his own home, had saved a nice little nest egg, drove a reasonable car. Who wouldn't want a guy like him? And his best trait also made him the best target: he was trusting to a fault. Even I had taken advantage of that a time or two. But I couldn't let someone else, someone who wasn't family, do that to him.

I had two questions for Candace, and I suspected if I unraveled the answers to them, I'd unravel a lot more of her secrets. If the baby wasn't Lane's, whose was it? And why was Candace pretending it was Lane's?

Chapter 14

Candace

I could swim in your depths forever.
If only I could promise you forever.

In my previous life I didn't have a pool, so as a child, during the most brutal beatings of summer heat, I often had to go in search of one. Back then I found a lot of things, and I lost a lot of things too. When food was scarce, I hit up local soup kitchens. When my parents had an overdue bill, I stole money from my friends' parents to keep our electricity on. When I was lonely, I found love. But more often than not, I lost love. It was hard to love a rebellious, thieving orphan like me. Maybe that's why I settled for the wrong man. Or maybe that's why, when I found the right one, I wouldn't let him go.

With arms outstretched, I glided across the pool water,

faceup, squinting at the sun. Already my skin was tanning into a freckled bronze. With my ears beneath the surface, all I heard was the low hum of the pool filter. My belly hovered just above the water line, a small bump showing at last! I had eagerly waited to see the firm contours of my abs smothered in baby weight. I wondered if I'd need a pregnancy swimsuit, or if my bikinis would suffice for the rest of the summer.

Where I grew up in the sticks, people didn't have in-ground pools. We had cheap plastic baby pools that you could find at the Family Dollar store, just deep enough to soak in. If you had extra money at the end of the month—which my family never did—you could maybe afford the smallest aboveground pool, which you then paid for in installments. Luckily, the elderly lady two streets down from my house had that extra money to buy one. And, luckily, she always went to bed around eight o'clock, which gave me just enough time to night swim before my legal guardian noticed me missing from my bedroom.

After my parents died when I was ten, my grandmother took me in when she felt like it, and my legal guardian took me in when she didn't. My secretive nightly swims were the only structure in my life, the only time I could breathe, feel free. I was constantly being tossed back and forth between houses, which made me easy to lose track of. Maybe this lack of structure was the reason for my urge to swim. There was something therapeutic about water, floating as if outside of my body, defying gravity, unbound by physical restraints. On the ground I felt heavy with sadness. In the water I was uninhibited. In the water I was at peace.

In my northern hometown, only the privileged had pools,

and you were lucky to get a solid two months' worth of swimming in. But here in North Carolina, where you're battling 80-degree heat in May, every other house had one, and the swimming season was twice as long. I had escaped to the right place.

I paddled myself to the pool steps, ready for a snack. With the nausea popping in every couple of hours, I found myself snacking throughout the day, whenever I felt up to it. Whoever named it *morning sickness* had not given credit to the all-day plague that it really was.

I had barely toweled off when Harper came storming out onto the patio, her face splotched with anger, her hair wild with red fury, her lips an angry pink slit through her face. Her thin lips reminded me of a sideways parenthesis, always downturned. Her heart was a waste of space because it didn't feel, and Harper lived up to her name, because the woman harped on everything. Dishes in the sink. Dust on the furniture. Unmade beds. Her obsession with cleanliness was boundless. I wondered what expectation I had failed to meet this time.

"What now?" I grumbled.

And then I saw it.

A thin wisp of paper in her hand. A black-and-white blur. She waved it at me. The ultrasound photo. How had that snoop found it? I was sure I had put it back in my drawer after looking at it this morning, a routine I did daily in private. Starting the day with a shared moment together, face-to-face, mother to child.

Harper swung the pool gate open with force, and it nearly smacked her as it bounced back.

"Care to explain this?" She flapped the photo at me, her voice lifting in an accusing pitch.

"It's an ultrasound photo. I would have thought you'd be familiar with them after having kids."

The smart-ass in me was coming out, and I wasn't stuffing her back in. Besides, I didn't know exactly what Harper had noticed or not noticed, and I couldn't crack open her skull to find out, no matter how much I wanted to. So I continued drying off, scrunching my hair into wet curls.

Stomping toward me, she shoved the picture under my nose.

"You know what I'm getting at. The date on this image."

Okay, so she knew. I could tell her the truth . . . or I could lie. Either way, Lane was going to find out and I didn't know what would happen then. Or maybe I did know, and that's what scared me.

"Do you enjoy going through other people's personal things?" I dropped the towel, then reached for the paper. With a backward step, she hid it behind her back.

"Cut the crap, Candace. I'm done playing nice with you. And you're done playing house with my brother. Explain the date on this ultrasound, or I'm taking this to Lane. He should know the truth about your baby."

The truth? The truth was so complicated. I could hardly understand it myself, let alone explain it to someone else. That was the nature of feelings, wasn't it? A complicated series of moments, each one thrusting your heart in a different direction. It was a wonder we didn't all have vertigo.

"Sit." I pointed to a lounger next to me, shaded beneath the pergola.

137

"I'd rather stand," she insisted.

"It's a long story. Will you please just sit down so we can talk? I don't feel like being blinded by the sun behind you."

Without another word, Harper sat, arms folded neatly, the ultrasound tucked between her hand and body. Facing her from the opposite lounger, it felt like we were in a showdown. A twenty-first-century duel with words. I didn't know where to begin, where to end. I had my own version of my past, of what happened, much like we all do. We all created our own injustices and accomplishments, and we all ended up lying to ourselves and everyone else. *I was the perfect child.* No child was. *I was the star of the high school football team.* For one play, once. *My parents never hugged me.* They hugged you every night before bed. *We were never in love.* You just don't remember what love feels like anymore.

There were too many holes in the story I wanted to tell her, so many starting points to pick from.

"I'm guessing you noticed the date, which, based on how far along in the pregnancy I am, means the conception predates Lane."

Harper crossed her legs. She meant business. "Exactly. So I already know that Lane's not the father. What I don't know is why you entrapped my brother."

"First of all, I didn't entrap him. And second of all, no, I'm afraid he's not the biological father."

"So who is?"

I shrugged. "I had a one-night stand and got pregnant. I don't even know the guy's name. I was drunk and stupid. But then I met Lane shortly after, and we fell in love deep and fast. It wasn't just me, Harper. You have to understand this.

When he told me he wanted to have a family with me, it seemed like the perfect solution. This baby could be his."

She humphed. "It doesn't work that way, Candace. You can't just *make* a baby belong to someone else. There's a word for that—*adoption*. And there's a lot more you have to consider. Like the genetics, and the biological father's rights, and—"

"Just stop!" I couldn't stand her voice for another moment. As if she even cared about any of that. "A baby could give a crap about genetics. A loving home is all that matters. As a mother, you know this. You also know that Lane would make an amazing father, and together we could give the baby what every child deserves. Family. Love."

This baby was everything that mattered in life. A new beginning. Hope for a better future. Unconditional love. This child had connected two hearts, locked two people together.

"Lane deserves to know the truth."

And yet some people cared more about law than love. People like Harper. I needed to convince her in terms she would understand. "Do you love your brother?"

"You know I do," she answered.

"Then you know that telling him the truth will destroy him. Have you ever seen him happier than he is now? Why do you want to take that away from him?"

She shook her head, the gesture saying more than words. "Don't put this on me."

"You have the power to let him be happy or to break his heart. So it *is* on you."

"But it's all based on a lie!" she yelled, startling me. "Is anything you say the truth?"

"My love for Lane is true." I stopped, not knowing how to

cross the divide. "I know you hate me, but there is no room for hate in love. If you love Lane, you need to stop hating me."

Harper's skepticism rose with her eyebrow.

"Look," I continued, "I'm not proud of the things I've done. But I'm proud of what I have with your brother. I'm proud of the kind of man that he is and the kind of woman he inspires me to be, and I'll remind him of how I feel every day for the rest of my life. Where the sperm came from doesn't matter—what matters is that Lane's dream is coming true, and he's going to have the perfect family. With a woman who loves him more than anything else on this earth."

"Do you really? Or do you just love the idea of having your happily ever after at any cost?"

"Of course I love him. He's the best person I know. I would do anything for him—anything to keep him, Harper. Even if it meant hurting someone who tried to destroy what we have." I wove a threat through my words that I wanted her to hear.

Harper leaned forward, her gaze analyzing and critical. "I do believe that—that you'd do anything to get what you want."

Dropping the towel behind me, I stood, because I knew my height commanded respect. I looked down on her, letting her know I was—and always would be—above her. In life, in love, and with Lane.

"If you tell him, you'll hurt him more than I ever could. Could you live with yourself if you did that to the one person who has always tried to fill your void? Could you strip away his only chance at happiness? And if he did end up forgiving me, which I'm sure he would in time, do you really think I'd let you stay a part of our lives? Because I can be pretty convincing, and I can also be a mean bitch. Take the path of least resistance, Harper."

Harper was a woman who pulled. I was a woman who pushed. In the end, pushing got the job done and was a hell of a lot easier.

"So what are you going to do, Harper? Keep fighting against the riptide and die trying, or go with the flow for Lane's sake?"

It was the right question to ask, because Harper had no real choice. If she told Lane the truth, there was a good chance he'd forgive me anyway and we'd still end up together—without her. My tears could be pretty persuasive when I tried. Especially as my belly grew, an irresistible lure to a man with family fever. We both knew she would end up losing no matter what she did. Even though Lane could forgive much, I wasn't built that way. In fact, the last person who crossed me would never cross me—or anyone else—ever again. And I wouldn't stop when it came to Harper. I was ready to take her down.

"So what's it going to be, Harper?"

Chapter 15

Harper

I wasn't afraid of dying, but I was afraid of being alone when I did. It seemed both were inevitable.

When I was pregnant with Elise, I spoke a vow so solemn that it was unbreakable. I had been sitting in bed, awake with acid reflux and Braxton-Hicks contractions, unable to sleep. Holding my fat belly in my arms, I promised my unborn baby that I would be there for every important moment. The first word. The first step. The first boyfriend. Graduation. Wedding. Grandchildren. I would somehow conquer death, as if I had that power, to be there whenever my child needed me.

Oh, how naive I was back then. Back in a time of ignorant bliss, when the world was pure and simple and filled with hope. I never expected the crushing blow as life's hammer swung down and smashed my perfect little dreams into perfect little pieces. I had never anticipated crouching in those shards, waiting for another blow. That's all I seemed to do these days—wait for it.

Back then, every image I envisioned included me, Ben, and our children. I never fathomed life without him. Why would I? In my mind, I could singlehandedly defy death and divorce, with Ben by my side. It turns out I couldn't. And it turns out he wouldn't. Some days, single motherhood felt damn near close to death.

Single mothers are plainclothes heroes. Anyone who, after an exhausting day of work, can multitask helping the kids with their homework while figuring out what to cook for dinner that the kids won't grouch about, followed by kitchen cleanup, then an hour-long bedtime routine—all of this on her own—deserves a friggin' medal. Or at least a spa day. If you thought being a police officer or a firefighter or a doctor was hard, think about the single mothers out there. They are the toughest of them all. And I was now cursed to be one of them.

I tried my best, I always did, but there's a tipping point where no amount of effort seemed enough. I'd spent the past hour coercing Jackson to do his spelling homework, while Elise grumbled through her math problems. There were only a few more days left in the school year, but the kids were already mentally on vacation. It was an uphill battle to get them to do anything.

"Ew, what smells?" Elise whined from the kitchen island where she doodled in the margins of her homework. "Tell me that's not dinner."

"It smells like rotten eggs," Jackson chimed in with an opinion I hadn't asked for.

"Guys, knock it off. I haven't even started cooking yet. That's Candace's lunch you smell."

The fresh salmon I had purchased for tonight's meal had mysteriously gone missing, though the empty packaging sat on the counter next to Candace's empty lunch plate. Another dish to pick up, not in the sink where it belonged. As I rummaged in the freezer for something else to cook, rage hit me with the force of a Black Friday shopping mob. I envisioned slapping that sneer right off her face, marking her perfect skin with my perfect handprint.

The chicken and rice casserole I threw together for dinner ended up a disaster. With Lane working late and Candace tucked away in her bedroom bingeing on Cheetos and Netflix—and probably her salmon lunch leftovers—no one was there to help ease the mood that hung over the dining room.

Elise grimaced as I spooned the casserole onto her plate. "It looks like puke."

Jackson gagged as he pushed his food around with his fork. "It tastes like puke."

"You haven't even tried it yet," I said. I pleaded. I begged. I gave up.

For the second night in a row, Jackson had refused to eat a single bite of anything. The boy was already a child-sized Gumby, all knobby knees and elbows, but lately he looked even skinnier, like he'd been stretched into nonexistence. As if that wasn't enough to heap on my already huge pile of worry, Elise fought with me through the entire meal over not having any personal space, begging to move back home.

Home. What was *home* these days? Because nothing felt like home without Ben.

Jackson sits up and watches me all night, Elise complained. *He makes weird scratching sounds while I sleep,* she whined. No matter how much I tried to understand Jackson, what he was going through, he simply wouldn't tell me what thoughts rattled around in his head. I was almost afraid to find out.

I wanted to believe these were typical kid problems, but the truth was that all sense of normal had died along with their father. I had no clue how to help them or return to the place we couldn't return to—our old life. Our happy life. A life that only existed in my mind.

Because what husband killed himself unless things weren't what they seemed?

I sent the kids to the living room to watch television while I finished cleaning up. Just one more hour to go before I fell into my bed and into a book that would hopefully seduce me into its pages and release my chains to this world. If only I could stay within the chapters, in a story I loved instead of the reality that I hated. These days, I counted down the minutes to my nightly solitude. All day I pushed the feelings down, just below the surface, but at night, alone in my bedroom, I could let them rise and feel them all. The sadness, the loneliness, the heartbreak, the anger, the questions I wanted answers to: Why? Why? Why?

All the stages of grief were coming back in a single hit: isolation, anger, asking every what-if, giving up. Everything but acceptance. I wasn't there yet; how could I accept that he took his own life? Especially when he knew how hard I worked to break through the grief before. *Damn you, Ben!* As my hands slid up and down the casserole dish—sudsing, sudsing, sudsing—my mind wandered and slipped into a dark place. I needed a cigarette.

I didn't smoke. I never had, not other than the occasional cigarette over drinks with friends, and definitely not since I fell for Ben and he told me he'd never date a girl who smoked. But Ben wasn't here, and I needed a hit of something, anything, to numb me. I didn't know where Lane kept the hard liquor, so the pack of cigarettes I had bought the day after Ben died would have to do.

I slipped outside into the cool night air, the cigarette smoke contaminating the fragrance of roses that hung by the back porch. Every puff coursed through my lungs and into my bloodstream, my own little act of rebellion against the traumas of death and single motherhood. How did women do it? A woman was like calm water on the surface, but underneath the water's edge she was a gliding, hunting shark. I wanted to be a shark, but I was a jellyfish that lazily floated along, ready to be someone's dinner.

An eddy of smoke, with an undertone of burning leaves, clung to the fibers of my shirt. I'd need to remember to change clothes when I got inside.

The swimming pool glistened under a full moon. I looked up and met its hollow gaze, remembering how fascinated four-year-old Jackson had been with the man who lived in one of its many craters. I never had the heart to tell him the truth, that the stories were lies we told our children as we patted ourselves on the back for parenting well done. Yet those lies cultivated their imagination. If only all my lies had such a silver lining.

I traced Ursa Major with my eyes; my need for dark solitude was as insistent as the stars.

In the alcoves of my thoughts I heard the back door slide open, then closed. I didn't turn to look; I could sense my brother when he was near because he possessed a kind of calm that was almost tangible. I imagined it was like being in the presence of one of the Twelve Apostles. You just *knew* he was goodness. Lane must have sensed my dark mood and come to find me.

"Hey, Harp. You okay?" Lane sat beside me, blood speckling his scrubs, and held his hand out for a drag.

I passed the cigarette over to him, nodding at the bloodstains dotting his clothes. "Tough day at work?"

Lane took a drag and coughed. "Mm, smooth."

I chuckled. "Shut up. I should have warned you that they're an old pack."

"No, Betty White is old. This is archaic." He handed the cig back to me.

I gestured to his clothes. "You kill someone?"

He glanced down at his shirt, as if only just now noticing it. "I didn't have a change of clothes in my work locker. I need to catch up on laundry."

"Isn't that Candace's job? You know, since she's home all day doing nothing."

"It's not a big deal for me to do it."

"You know how I feel about that. Anyway, I washed your clothes so you don't need to. What happened at work?"

"Eh, same old, same old. One of my patients fell and cracked her skull on the floor. Lost a lot of blood, but she's okay. I'm more concerned about you, though. You don't smoke."

"I do today. I don't know what to do with myself anymore, Lane. I feel so alone."

Wrapping an arm around me, he hugged me into his side. "You're not alone. I'm always here for you."

I straightened and pulled away from him. "Not anymore, Lane. We both know it. You've got your wife who needs you. There's not enough of you for the both of us."

He nudged me with his shoulder. "That's ridiculous. You and I are a package deal. Our lives will always twist around each other; we're twins separated by a year. Besides, I can be a husband and a brother at the same time. Millions of people do it every day."

"Not really, Lane. Not the kind of brother who shows up to help his sister frame her husband's suicide as a murder." I sucked in a long draw and exhaled a puff of smoke. "But I'm done asking for favors. I'm going to find my own apartment, something small and affordable, get a job, and get out of your hair."

"No, you're not. You've only been here for a little over a week. You're going to stay as long as you need to, Harp. Give yourself time to heal. The baby isn't due for months. There's no rush for you to leave."

We both knew it was time, though Lane would never admit it.

"I do have one last favor to ask, though."

"Anything," he said.

"I just need a hug from my brother."

Lane took the cigarette from my fingers and put it out on the patio floor. Lifting me up with him, he hugged me, a hug so enveloping and warm that it wrapped me in love. It was the hug of two little children who couldn't bear to be separated by even a sliver of space. It felt safe to be a child for once and not always the adult. I closed my eyes to relish it to the fullest. When I opened them, there stood Candace, jaw clenched and eyes narrowly watching us from the kitchen window.

I jolted and stepped back. Candace slowly drifted out of sight.

"I've been meaning to ask you. Have you been taking your meds?" Lane asked.

Not this again. "I don't need them anymore."

"You know that's not how it works. You have to keep taking them consistently."

"I don't like how they make me feel. Like the walking dead."

"Then the dosage needs to be adjusted. But don't just stop taking them. I'll go with you, if you want. We can talk to the doctor together. I'm very familiar with this stuff, you know. It's what I do for a living."

I nodded, wordlessly following him into the house where, like a good girl, I would take my medicine to silence the wailing inside my head. I checked the time. Bedtime at last! I found Jackson coloring at the coffee table while Elise watched reruns of *Scooby-Doo*. I remembered fondly watching the show as a kid myself on Saturday mornings. How times had changed. Kids these days had instant access to everything they wanted, while us old folks had to wait until the weekend for our favorite shows. And God forbid a child sit through a commercial!

Glancing over Jackson's shoulder, I expected to find an explosion of creativity the way Before Jackson used to be. Before Jackson would create a flurry of scribbles and scissor cuts as he turned an elephant into an elf. Instead, I found the entire page colored black with red squiggles. I thought of death and blood. What else would have crossed a mother's mind at such an image?

"Hey, buddy, whatcha drawing?" I asked warily.

"It's dirt."

Oh, that wasn't so bad.

"What are these?" I pointed to a red squiggle.

"The worms."

"Worms?"

"Yeah, like the ones eating Daddy in the ground."

My chest tightened and I moved to hug Jackson from behind. But my arms wouldn't obey. I couldn't touch my own son. What child considered the worms ravaging his father's corpse? He scared me; the child I had borne—part me, part Ben—was untouchable. Every maternal bone in my body yearned to wrap myself around my tiny boy, but my muscles tensed and grew defiant and rigid. Instead, I placed my hand on his shoulder. Yes, I could handle that.

"Jackson, why would you want to draw that?"

"I dunno." He shrugged, as if I had asked what he wanted for a snack.

"Do you think about this kind of stuff a lot?"

He nodded, shifting away from me. He always shuffled out of reach. Away from physical contact. It was becoming as worrisome as my inability to touch him. The mother in me yearned to close the gap between me and my son; but the mother in me also couldn't because of what he had done. The one thing I couldn't forgive him for.

"Sweetie, why won't you let me touch you?"

"I dunno."

The same two words he used to answer every question. I knelt down, meeting him eye-to-eye. "Please talk to me. I don't know how to fix it if I don't know what you're thinking. Are you upset with me?"

He peered at me with eyes that had seen too much, robbed of all innocence. "I guess."

"Why, bud? I'm trying my best."

"Because you're the reason Daddy's dead." His voice was thin, like a strand of silk choking me.

"Why do you say that? I loved your father."

And I did. More than anything.

"No, you didn't. Or else Daddy would still be alive."

I felt the pierce of grief all over again.

"You think I killed Daddy?"

"Yeah. It's why the policeman keeps coming to talk to you, isn't it?"

I hadn't realized Jackson had been paying such close attention. How could I explain a murder investigation in a way a six-year-old child would understand?

"No, bud, the policeman is just trying to figure out who did it."

"Will the person who killed Daddy come after me next? Is that why we have to live here, to hide?"

Oh no. The conversation was unraveling faster than I knew how to handle. I couldn't tell Jackson that his father had committed suicide. But thinking his father was murdered wasn't any better. How long had my son been fearing for his life?

"No, sweetie, it wasn't like that. No one is after us."

"Then why did you force us to live here? I hate it here. I miss Daddy. I wanna go home!" Throwing down the black crayon that had been clutched between his stubby little fingers, Jackson jumped up and ran upstairs, leaving me alone with my heartbreak.

I wanted to chase after him, squeeze him until he giggled like we used to. *I love you the size of a peanut,* I used to say, and he'd laugh. *I love you the size of the ocean,* I'd amend, but he'd shake his head and say, *Bigger!* Tickling him, I'd compare my love to the moon, the earth, the sun . . . and at last to the ever-expanding universe, because that was our love. Ever expanding. Endless. Our whispers would float through the night-lighted bedroom while his spider legs wrapped around my waist.

I missed my boy who wore superhero underwear, who chewed his bottom lip in concentration, who moved in a whirlwind of motion, who laughed endlessly at his own fart jokes. Where did my son go, and what sad creature had taken over his body? His flame had been extinguished too soon, his passion and zest for adventure and color gone before it had fully arrived.

After several breaths, I headed upstairs, readying myself for a conversation with the son who blamed me for his father's death, who thought a killer was after us. I needed to set things right with him before he recklessly pieced more faulty bits together. His bedroom door was shut when I got there, and when I jiggled the handle it was locked.

"Jackson," I spoke against the wood, where curls of white paint flaked off. "Can we please talk?"

The doorknobs in the house were outdated glass, lacking modern safety features. Kids back in the day could lock themselves in and you'd have to bust the whole door down to get through.

I knocked lightly. "Please unlock the door, or I'm going to have to take it down."

A moment later I heard the approach of footsteps, then the click of the lock. When he opened the door, I smelled the faint scent of smoke.

"What's going on in here? Why do I smell smoke?"

I dashed past him into the room, as Jackson wrapped his short arms halfway around my waist, begging me to stop. I charged through his tiny bodily blockage.

"Please don't be mad, Mommy!"

Behind his bed, in a cheap plastic—and meltable!—garbage can, I found the remnants of a photograph burning to ash.

"What is this?" I screeched, blowing it out. "You could have burned the whole house down! Was that you who set off the fire alarm last week?"

Jackson broke into tears, muttering something about ghosts visiting him in his dreams. I picked up what was left of the photograph; only half of our smiling faces were intact, but I recognized the image immediately. The day was still fresh in my mind. Taken a year and a half ago, it was one of the last pictures of our family whole and happy. In this perfect moment on a nature hike at the Cape Fear River Trail, we had no idea what horror was to come.

"Calm down, honey." In a pile at the bottom of the garbage

can were other pictures, some depicting people I didn't recognize. "Why are you burning these?"

He caught his breath before speaking, his words quivering with his body. "The ghost told me to."

"What ghost? The old lady who died here?"

He nodded. "She told me if I burned the pictures I wouldn't have to remember Daddy anymore."

"Why would you want to forget Daddy?"

"Because it makes me sad."

"Oh, honey." I pivoted him toward me, his body stiff and unwieldy, and held his hands. They were the only part of him I could hold. "It's okay to be sad. You'll always remember him, and you should. It's good to remember the people we love. Daddy is just waiting on the other side for us, so you don't need to be sad. We'll see him again in heaven someday."

We stood together in angsty solitude, his fingers locked in the grooves of my knuckles. Eventually he wilted onto the floor, and I lifted him into bed, pushing aside Elise's notebook and Nancy Drew mystery she was in the middle of reading. My mother had lent Elise a copy she had grown up on, the cover cartoony and faded. After settling Jackson in, I kissed his forehead, my lips warm against his cool skin.

"It's going to be okay, bud." I clung to the promise that it would, fighting against the probability that it wouldn't.

I grabbed Elise's notebook and saw that the lined page that it was open to had two words on it. A username and password. More specifically, my Facebook username and password. How had she even found that? And more important, why?

"Do you know why Elise has my Facebook login information, Jackson?"

"She got it off your phone to talk to a boy she likes."

"What boy?" My little girl was into boys already? When had I missed this? I was a worse mother than I thought, oblivious that my daughter was growing up and I couldn't see it beyond my own self-importance.

"I dunno."

Any boy on Facebook would be too old for her. We hadn't even had the birds and the bees conversation yet. Was she even ready for that? Or was *I*?

I set the notebook down, tucking the bedspread around Jackson's tiny frame. "Do you know if Elise ever posted anything?"

He chewed his bottom lip in thought. Ben used to do the same thing. "I know she let Miss Aubrey post something that day she was babysitting, 'cause they wouldn't let me see."

"Was that the day I went out shopping with Aunt Candace?"

He nodded. "Before you left. I remember 'cause it made Elise cry real bad but Miss Aubrey couldn't delete it before you left."

Shoot. I had been wrong. I had been so certain it was Candace, so quick to blame. I felt horrible about my accusation. Even worse that Elise knew and was afraid to tell me—about the post, about the boy crush, about everything going on in her life, apparently.

Once Jackson had drifted off, I remembered that Elise was still watching television, so I headed down the hallway toward the stairs, passing the bathroom. Behind the door I heard sobs—but not a child's sobs. A grown woman's.

"Candace?" I whispered to the closed door. "Are you okay?"

I knocked softly, unsure if I should intrude. It went quiet

within, except for a gasp and the shuffle of feet. A moment later, the shower turned on and drowned out her weeping. A hard pass to my question.

"Mommy?"

I whipped around at the sound of a faint voice and found Jackson standing in his doorway. Hadn't he just fallen asleep?

"Yes, sweetie?"

His gaze burned with intensity. "We're not going to see Daddy in heaven. I don't think God'll let us in."

"Why would you think that?"

"Because I know you killed Daddy, just like I killed my sister."

I couldn't deny it, because I knew he was right. Some sins are unforgivable.

Chapter 16

Candace

When you need to laugh, let me be your joker.
When you need to cry, let me be your shoulder.
When you need to yell, let me be your endless sky.
When you need to fall, let me be the arms to catch you.

"Candace? Are you okay?"

I ignored the muffled question and subsequent rap of Harper's knuckles on the bathroom door. She didn't deserve to know why I cried. She would have judged me for it anyway. A grown woman crying from a bad dream. Only for me it wasn't just a dream; I had relived one of the worst parts of my life. Harper wouldn't understand; hell, even I didn't understand it sometimes, how I let myself steep in the abuse, then again subconsciously chose to relive it.

In this moment I was glad for the inches of wood that separated us. I turned on the shower to make her go away. Staring my reflection down, I watched streaks of tears cut a snail's trail through my makeup. I rested my hand on the mirror and leaned against it, the steam from the running water slowly spreading across the glass. Soon I began disappearing, the mist taking my shoulders, then neck, then finally my face. Then I was gone in the haze, merely a faceless shape.

Ever since I discovered I was pregnant, I couldn't stop crying. Over every sappy commercial. Over the growing pile of laundry. Over a text message from Lane saying he was held up at the hospital. Over an argument with my sister-in-law who hated me. The saddest part was that I *wanted* her to like me, and I *wanted* to like her back. It was an unexpected want because, up until now, I had hated her from afar, eager to wedge distance between us. She was the competition, after all. But I empathized with her struggle against grief. We shared those same tears, that same loss, the same heartbreak. Kindred, anguished souls. Initially, I thought we could heal each other. They say to keep your friends close but your enemies closer. What happens when you want your enemy to become your friend?

After all the other pregnancies, and all the subsequent miscarriages, I had never experienced *this* part of pregnancy. It was like my sensations were heightened to superhuman capacity—my feelings, my sense of smell, my voracious hunger. Everything except for my physical strength, which felt sapped, like my body had been drained of all its lifeblood, leaving me limp and helpless and hungry and nauseated. How could I be both sick to my stomach and yet starving? Pregnancy hormones made no sense whatsoever.

Along with the unexplained weeping came anger. My rage became flesh. Sometimes I could visualize wrapping my fingers around a neck and squeezing the life out of the person. Harper had been my target for that whimsy. Countless nights I had crushed her throat to shut up the nagging and the criticism, imagining watching her eyes bulge until I choked out her words. The images slipped into my dreams. Then I'd awaken loathing myself for the hatred I couldn't contain.

The dreams were another thing altogether. Some nights they featured strange sexual fantasies with my best friend from high school, a short, pimply, plump girl who looked just like you'd expect a girl named Enid to look. Other nights were plagued with nightmares about losing the baby, me reaching down between my legs, my groin soaked in blood. All of it was so horrifyingly graphic. The wild cards were the flashbacks in time. I never knew what I was going to get, whether nostalgic or traumatic. The recurring theme of my pregnancy dreams tended toward reliving my worst experiences, scratchy sandpaper memories. Like the one I couldn't shake out of my head.

After undressing, I felt the shower water running hot and stepped inside. The water sluiced down my back, and I sobbed until I didn't know what was water and what was tears. Little streams of sorrow circled the drain, then were gone.

I closed my eyes as the water ran over my face and let the memory wash over me . . . praying it would circle the drain and disappear with my tears.

* * *

I flinched as the front door slammed shut behind my love, now my hate, while my tears dripped on the yellowed linoleum floor. Noah had left, and knowing him, he wouldn't be back for hours. Grime had collected in the crease near my bare toes where the wall met the baseboard. This was my corner, where the dust and hair and grease settled into the edges of the kitchen. And me— the dirtiest of them all. This corner was my hiding place when Noah's fists got riled up. Not that I could hide from him, but at least it protected me from the fullness of his wrath. Noah usually gave up when I cowered in the corner with a kitchen chair blocking me in and him out.

Noah Gosling believed in what he called the "Rule of Thumb." This was the width of a stick with which husbands were allowed to beat their wives. He'd read it on Wikipedia and felt the ancient practice was worth adopting as his own. If you thought the eighteenth century was long gone, you'd be wrong. Noah thought he was burying my will. He didn't know I was a seed growing roots.

With Noah gone, I breathed. My hand rested on the barely noticeable bulge of my stomach, as if clinging to the life inside. But the blood seeping into the crease of my jeans told a different story. A story where the man I loved, the man whom I created a child with, hated me more than I hated myself.

He hated me so much that when I told him about the baby he called it entrapment. *As if our nuptials years ago weren't already a contractual bond, dumbass. He slapped me for that comment. Maybe I did want to trap him into a future with me because I loved him to a fault. Maybe I wanted to trap the best pieces of him with the best pieces of me in a tiny, beautiful, pink-skinned, better whole.*

Despite the fists and the cursing, I loved the son of a bitch. Because with the darkest lows came the brightest highs. Euphoria when he held me, cradled me like a sad child, then kissed me with all the passion of a thousand lovers. I was never an open book, but with Noah I let him consume my every page. When it was good, it was mind-blowing good. But when it was bad, I bled, I died inside. And now my baby was dying with me.

No one understood my addiction to Noah. Not even me. If you asked me to explain it, I couldn't. It was as if he had entranced me. He had charm, and a lot could be forgiven of a charming man. I was cursed to be in love with a monster. But that monster knew how to bring me to orgasm, he knew how to play with words that lured me in, he knew all of my secrets and I knew his. We were secret-keepers, dark soul mates, a tornado meets a hurricane, wrapped in a typhoon. I loved being devastated by his love.

But now I had another life to think about. The baby's. I would give up orgasms and wordplay for the tiny human growing inside me. I had to this time. There was no other choice. If there was any chance this baby would make it, I needed to get out. Now or never. Over the years I could never do it for myself, but for my baby, I would.

I had contemplated killing Noah. Many times, in fact. It would be easy to claim self-defense, with my bruises as my witness. But every time I felt the urge, made a plan . . . I simply couldn't. I loved him too damn much. He had saved me when I lost my parents. I owed him enough to let him live.

I stripped off the bloody jeans and panties, leaving them in the corner behind me. I found a pair of stretchy yoga pants in the laundry room, ones that comfortably fit my rounding belly.

I grabbed a handful more, along with underwear and several oversized T-shirts, then grabbed the biggest duffel bag I could find in the bedroom closet. Noah's old, faded green military duffel, one not earned but purchased at a thrift store—he'd never served a day in his life. "Independent thinkers like me don't make it in the military. We're leaders, not followers." Except that Noah was neither of those things. Noah just *was*.

I shoved the clothes I could grow into, along with the barest of necessities, into the bag with the hopes that I would indeed keep growing. If I lost the baby, there was no point in me leaving, was there? Because I had nowhere to go and nothing to go to. I was never strong enough, or brave enough, to forge my own path, but for my child I would be strong and brave. As I buckled up the only possessions I could heft over my shoulder, I vowed never to let Noah find me. Or to let him lay hands on me, or my baby, again.

Next, I needed cash. The little that we had saved up could get me an Uber and a bus ticket out of town. It could get me a few nights in a seedy motel until I found something more permanent. To my benefit, Noah didn't believe in banks. "That's how the government keeps track of you," he warned ominously. "Money is how they control you." Noah was passionate that way. When he believed in something, or was against something, he followed through. So, instead of depositing his paychecks into the safekeeping of a federally insured bank, he cashed his checks and hid the money in a red Folgers Coffee can on his dresser, the first place a thief in the night would look. Popping the lid off, I grabbed the entire wad of cash.

A dollar for my tears? How about interest?

Almost $500, I counted. Enough to catch a bus to the coast.

Find a small town where I could start over. Raise my baby somewhere safe, and beachy, and sun-kissed. Somewhere far away from Noah.

I pocketed the bills, pausing to look at a picture sitting on my memory box, as I called it. The image contained me, Noah, and his parents back when we first started dating as teenagers. He'd been my friend through childhood, helped me survive losing my parents. Somewhere along the way the friendship turned to young, dumb love. I couldn't leave behind my small wooden memory box, the only nice thing my father ever made me, full of both happy and crappy memories, so I placed the picture inside it and slid it into my duffel. Tossing the bag over my shoulder, I walked out the door, following the cracked concrete sidewalk toward an unknown future. I didn't know where exactly I was going, but I knew where I was coming from. And I would never go back. My old story had been told, a tale about a victim. As my stride grew more confident, and the sidewalk more level, I wrote a new story. A story for my baby and for myself about a woman who became the victor. No matter what—or who—it cost.

Chapter 17

Harper

Because I know you killed Daddy, just like I killed my sister.

Jackson's accusation clung to me like tar, binding and sticky. My son's blame hurt more than Ben's death. It hurt more than Ben's suicide letter. Nothing compared to the lash of my child's words against my skin. All of the pain, all of the guilt, all of it Jackson heaped onto my shoulders for me to carry the rest of my days. But that's what mothers did, didn't they? They carried the burdens of their children.

"I already told you, I didn't kill Daddy," I whispered, the statement lodged in my throat. "That's why the police are helping to find out who did."

He shook his head, but it was more of a tremble. "I don't understand. You said someone else killed Daddy, but I know you made Daddy so sad he killed himself."

Jackson knew? He knew about the suicide. But how?

"Where did you hear that?"

I had done everything in my power to ensure the kids never found out. It was far easier to explain a home robbery gone wrong than to tell them their father simply gave up on them, that they weren't enough of a reason to stay alive. Who the hell would have told them otherwise? Certainly not Lane. And no one else knew the truth. Unless he told Candace, and Candace told the kids . . .

"I dunno."

"Jackson, honey, whatever you've heard, it's not true. And I always tried my best to make your daddy happy."

"Then why were you always sad? And why was Daddy always sad?"

Deep insight from such a young boy. When did Jackson grow up and how had I overlooked it? He had always been mature for his age, highly intelligent and well-spoken. By age four, he was reading proficiently. At age five, his kindergarten teacher bumped him up into first grade. I remember the sense of pride I felt watching him surpass his peers. But now, now I missed my baby. I missed the days when his curiosities lingered on making slime, or a worm's anatomy. My mother had warned me about this. When life gets too perfect, God kicks dust in your eyes, blinding you with misery while He steps back and watches you fumble ahead blindly. I thought that was her resentment talking, the unquenchable bitterness over my dad's disappearing acts. But maybe she was right all along. Iron was forged with fire, after all. And I had long ago lost my faith in God.

Struggle makes you stronger, Mom had told me, *and it gives you character.* But I had enough character to last two lifetimes.

I wanted to trust God, that all the death held some higher meaning, some bigger purpose. I wanted to be grateful, like the mothers I saw on Facebook who stared Death in the face and, proud of their war wounds, claimed, "Where, O Death, is your victory? Where, O Death, is your sting?" I yearned to show my children the light, but I couldn't find the light for myself. I was merely a child playing with matches.

"I'm sorry, Jackson. You're right. It's my fault. After what happened with your sister, I was never the same. I couldn't find a way to get better or a way to be happy. Then Daddy got sad too. Being sad is contagious. Do you know what *contagious* means?"

"It means it spreads."

"Exactly. The sadness spread. That's why we're here with Uncle Lane now, to try to stop the sadness from spreading anymore."

Jackson considered this for a moment, then looked at the floorboards. His expression was hard to read in the dim hallway.

"How did he do it?"

"Do what?" I wondered aloud.

"Kill himself. How did Daddy kill himself? With a gun? Or a rope? Or did he cut himself with a knife?"

Oh, God, had Jackson actually been imagining all the various ways his father offed himself? And where did a six-year-old get such ideas? Certainly not from the limited age-appropriate internet access he had on his tablet. Jackson continued naming his list of possibilities, but I didn't hear the words above the wails inside my head. I covered my face with my hand, as if I could hide from this conversation. I wasn't an angry person, but there it lived, right beneath my grief.

"Or did he drink poison? Or—"

"That's enough!" I yelled, cutting him off. "I don't want to talk about this anymore." I couldn't listen to another word. I had spent the past year burying bad memories along with the pain. How dare Jackson unearth it with his cruelty?

Jackson stood there, unmoving, his chalky eyes growing damp.

Oh no, what did I just do?

"I'm so sorry, sweetie."

My icy anger thawed into remorse, and I rushed to Jackson, aware of how I was treating my son. My young boy was so traumatized that he conjured a list of causes of death. He was still a child, and I expected too much from him. Some days I forgot that Jackson and Elise were kids, their emotions just beginning to evolve, their minds still blossoming and innocent. Why did I force them to carry the weight of little adults? I wasn't being fair to either of them.

I knelt at Jackson's bare toes. "Please forgive me." I held his cheeks, the bones jutting into my palms, and begged him with my eyes. My arms twitched to pull him against me, but instead I remained stoic.

"Okay. But, Mommy, when can you forgive *me*?" His voice was tiny in the long hallway.

I've never blamed you for what happened, I wanted to say. And yet I couldn't utter the words. It wasn't true. And until I forgave him, I couldn't cross the chasm between us.

"Forgive him for what?" Candace's voice broke into the somber moment.

I released Jackson's face and popped up on my feet. "It's nothing," I said, ushering Jackson back into his bedroom. When I had finished tucking him in and calling for Elise to come upstairs and brush her teeth, I stepped into my bedroom and found Candace sitting on the bed, hands folded on her lap, waiting for me. Beside her sat the monkey-themed ultrasound frame I had planned to give her, the ultrasound placed neatly inside.

"Was this for me?" She picked up the frame and pressed it to her chest.

"Yes, as a peace offering."

"I love it. Thank you." She stood. "I know you heard me crying."

"Yeah, I wasn't trying to intrude. I just . . ." I just what? Cared about her?

"I know." She smiled, and for the first time I thought she was pretty when she smiled.

"Was that about our argument earlier? Because I'm sorry, but I also felt the need to protect my brother. I wish you'd understand that."

Candace stood and walked into the hallway, then waved me to follow. "I need to show you something."

Once in her bedroom, she led me around piles of laundry, crumpled fast-food bags, and stacks of junk mail. Every surface was covered with garbage or mess. I hoped my inward cringe didn't reach my face. Shoving her rumpled blankets and last night's pajamas aside, she sat on the bed and patted a clear space beside her. I sat.

She opened the bedside dresser drawer and pulled out a wooden box. It was rough, the lid slightly crooked and clearly handmade, and stained a deep cherry. Carefully opening it, she moved a stack of letters aside, then flipped through a pile of photos and pulled one out.

"Are those love letters from Lane?" I asked, glancing at the top letter.

She pushed them under the photos and shrugged. "You'd be surprised how poetic a guy can be when he's in love. But as beautiful as words can be, Lane doesn't need words to profess his love. He does it daily in the way he takes care of me."

Shutting the box, she handed a photo to me.

The paper was torn on one edge and creased down the middle. Based on the Backstreet Boys *Millennium* poster that hung on a wall in the background, and the girl's zebra hair highlights, I guessed the photo to be taken in the early 2000s. I recognized a teenage Candace in fishnet stockings and camo dress with Doc Martens, sandwiched between a woman who looked to be in her forties and a sullen teenage boy, who stood almost a foot taller than her, wearing flannel over a Kurt Cobain T-shirt with grunge Johnny Depp hair and a ring piercing his lip. An older man stood behind the boy, his hand on the boy's bony shoulder.

"Is this your family?" I asked.

"No. These are my ex's parents. And that's my ex, Noah." She pointed to the boy. "After my parents died, I was shuffled around a lot. When I turned fourteen, Noah's family took me in. He was a childhood friend, then my boyfriend since ninth grade, and his parents were so good to me. They basically raised me, and Noah and I became inseparable. I loved him more than anything."

She took the picture back from me and spoke as if to the people in the picture.

"I thought we were end game."

End game. The popular teenage term reminded me just how worlds apart Candace and I were.

"But he turned out to be an abusive, controlling asshole."

I was coming to realize that men could be a lot of things. Abusers. Cheaters. Liars.

"I understand . . . on some level. Ben hurt me pretty badly too, when he cheated on me." Candace didn't say anything, so I continued to fill in the empty air. "It makes me wonder what else he was hiding that may have resulted in his death."

"What do you mean?"

"Well, everything around his death is suspicious. God only knows what the police will uncover."

I realized this conversation was becoming all about me. We were sharing a moment, and here I was stealing it from Candace. "So what happened with Noah?"

"After I couldn't take it anymore, I left Pennsylvania and came here."

"Pennsylvania? I thought you said you were from Ohio."

"I moved around a lot. But Pennsylvania was where I ended up with Noah."

Her life was a Monet painting. From a distance I only saw the big picture of a woman manipulating my brother with sex and lies. A closer look at her life was a lot messier. A tinge of guilt hit me for judging her so harshly. I hardly knew anything about the woman my brother had married, and I wondered how much he even knew.

"Did Noah . . . physically hurt you?"

She held out her forearm and traced a jagged scar that ran up the skin.

"He did this during one particularly emotional fight. It wasn't usually this bad, but still . . ."

It was clear we were exchanging secrets as she opened a door so private that there wasn't a key for its lock.

"That was brave of you to leave him."

Candace shrugged and rested the picture on the nightstand. "Maybe. Or maybe it was cowardly. But in the end it worked out. I met Lane, and he rescued me. He made me believe in love again. I know you question my motives with Lane, but after the life I've had, all I want is to have love and happiness and a family—things I never got growing up. I have it all now, and I'm not going to let anything take it away from me. Do you understand what I'm saying?"

I nodded. I did understand. It was all any of us wanted. But not as easy to hold on to.

"I don't want to fight with you." I touched her forearm, a gesture of sincerity. "You're my sister-in-law, and I hope we can start over. Be actual sisters, friends. Would you be open to that?"

She sat in dense contemplation. What was she thinking? Then she reached across the gap between us and hugged me. It was the answer I needed. When she pulled away, a new connection strung us together.

"All I ever wanted was to be enough. Smart enough. Pretty enough. Good enough."

This, coming from a woman who demanded attention by merely existing. "But you're gorgeous. How could you ever think you're not pretty enough?"

"I'm talking about true beauty, the kind that doesn't wash off. The beauty that gives power to move mountains and the stamina to create a diamond from coal. I have nothing to offer the world. I want purpose. I want the furor, everything I've been through, to mean something."

Weren't we all searching for meaning?

"Then you've got to endure and find those lessons in life that will lead you toward your destiny. I believe that if you hold on tight enough to this life, it will guide you to where you're supposed to go." I was preaching to myself.

"Is that what motherhood is? The purpose we're looking for?"

"I don't think it's enough. While it's everything, it's also nothing. One day the kids are gone, and then where does that leave you? Empty. Motherhood takes every bit of you, and some days it's hard to smile when you've given your all and have nothing left for yourself."

"You make it sound complicated."

"Sometimes it is."

As Candace propped her new ultrasound frame up beside her bedside lamp, my eyes were drawn to Noah's picture. It could have been his popular nineties heartthrob looks—a throwback to *My So-Called Life*-era Jared Leto, yum—but a familiarity seeped into me. How did I know this man? *Why* would I know this man?

"Does Noah know where you and the baby are?"

"I don't know, but if I ran into him, he'd never get the chance to hurt me ever again." Her hand curled into a fist. Candace was capable of more than she gave herself credit for. It was frightening what a cornered woman was capable of.

Chapter 18

Lane

The *click . . . click . . . click . . .* of a man in a walker shuffling past the open door of Ms. Eidenschink's hospital room blended with the *beep . . . beep . . . beep* of her heart monitor. The man's open-backed hospital gown gave ample view of his wrinkled ass connected to bony, ashen legs. His body was mere parts, unusable and ready for donation. In this job, I was reminded daily of the fragility of life.

The patients I tended to were like ghosts, just waiting to fade away. Only a year ago Ms. Eidenschink had been living on her own, tending to her cat, Lucy, in a cluttered house fit for *Hoarders*. One bad fall and a broken hip cursed her to a bedridden life in a hospital room with little more than a television and the occasional visitor. Every once in a while a woman named Ari Wilburn would stop by and dye

173

Ms. Eidenschink's snow-white hair the inky black that she preferred. It was the little things that meant a big deal to people bound to their hospital beds.

"How are we doing today, Ms. Eidenschink?" I greeted her at the foot of her bed.

She smiled up at me, her full lips painted red, along with one of her teeth. "Doing well, Lane. Doing well. Where have you been? I missed seeing you."

What she meant was she missed flirting with me. Any *cute young stud*—their words, not mine—was a welcome treat on this floor. Everyone needed a hot-blooded interest in their life, even if it was the interest of a thirty-something married male nurse.

"I've missed you too. You're looking good today."

She waved me off. "Nonsense. I look like Frankenstein's bride."

With the black hair and red lips, it wasn't much of a stretch.

"How is the new bride? Marriage is good, yes?" Her accent—possibly Polish, though I wasn't a language expert—covered her words so thickly I felt sorry for her mouth.

She extended her arm for me to take her blood pressure. Where needles probed her veins, her skin had turned into a stormy black and blue. When I finished taking her vitals, she stood, the chair squealing across the tile. Despite every effort, the inch of makeup couldn't hide the sallow hue of her face.

"Yes, everything's good," I replied after a beat. "Although I'm still having a little trouble with my wife and sister getting along. I'm not sure why they're at each other's throats."

She nodded, as if that was to be expected. "Jealousy does that. I can help. I know much about female relationships."

"Oh, that's okay. I'm sure it will work itself out." The poor woman didn't need to be burdened by my family drama.

She clicked her tongue at me. "You young people assume we know nothing about life. But you wrong. I know heartbreak, jealousy, *revenge*. My past not filled with wispy sepia emotions that have been long forgotten. No, quite the opposite. At my age, the past is all I have. I feed off memories. Pass me your troubles. I help."

"Revenge, you say? What do you know of it?" I asked. She didn't strike me as the vengeful type.

Beneath penciled-in eyebrows her pupils slipped back and forth, watchful of eavesdropping ears. "Oh, that is story for another time. But I will tell you this: revenge is natural form of survival. Your sister and wife both protective of you. They fight to the death for you. Your job is to figure out way to keep them both thinking they are number one."

We were interrupted by the squeal of the lunch cart being wheeled in by a food service worker. From the looks of him, he spent most of his time around food. Angling sideways through the door, he wiped the perspiration of a workout from his brow.

"Lunchtime!" he announced in a thunderous baritone.

While he doled out the food tray, the television hanging in the corner of the room flashed the local news. A ribbon of words scrolled across the bottom. Something about Benjamin Paris. Finding the remote on the bed, I turned up the volume.

"Durham police have caught a break in a local murder investigation that had been cold for almost two months," the news anchor began. "In April, investigators received a call to the home of Benjamin and Harper Paris on Hendricks Way.

When emergency workers arrived on the scene, Mr. Paris was pronounced dead from a knife wound to the chest. A murder investigation was then launched but quickly stalled, owing to lack of evidence and suspects."

"We had a body and the weapon, but no leads." Detective Levi Meltzer's mustache wiggled as he spoke to the camera. "Sometimes a witness doesn't step forward—out of fear, usually—but we're fortunate when they do."

The screen flashed back to the news anchor. "Neighbor Michelle Hudson heard the crash of glass the night of the murder."

The wrinkled face of an old lady filled the television, and in the background I saw Harper's house, slightly blurred. "I am considered the neighborhood watch because I don't sleep much. I always keep an eye out on things. That night, when I heard glass breaking across the street, I naturally looked to see what it was. To be honest, it didn't make sense what I saw, so I never said anything. At my age your brain can play tricks on you, you know? But eventually I figured I'd tell the police what I saw and see if they could make sense of it."

"The Durham Police Department hasn't disclosed further details at this time, but they are confident it will help identify the killer and close the case."

The ongoing repartee between Ms. Eidenschink and the food service worker slid into an absolute, cold silence. My thoughts turned like the gears of a clock, *tick tick tick*ing down to some inevitable tragic conclusion. Outside the window, the clouds joined into an army of raindrops, like a billowing iron curtain. Lightning streaked across the gray.

The neighbor had seen us. *Boom.*

Another flash.

We'd be charged with insurance fraud. *Boom.*

And I was pretty sure that tampering with evidence was a jailable offense. I would miss my child's birth, first breath, first wail. I'd never have the joy of waking to his screams just as I'm falling asleep. Or watching her chest rise and fall while she sleeps, ever nervous that her frail life hung in the balance of each breath. My sister had damned my life along with hers.

I had everything. And soon I'd have nothing.

I pulled my cell phone from my scrubs pocket and slipped into the hallway while dialing. Harper picked up midway through the first ring.

"Did you see the news?" I whispered before she got a full *hello* out.

"No, why?"

"They interviewed a witness—Michelle Hudson—who saw us that night. What if she identifies us to the police?"

"Michelle?" Harper scoffed. I could almost hear her eyeroll. "I can't imagine that she would have seen anything but shadowy figures, if that. She's as blind as a bat and a gossip fiend. I'm sure that's all this is—a lonely old lady's way of getting involved and feeling important."

"How can you be *sure* she didn't see us?" I needed more than Harper's assumption. I needed certainty.

There was always the chance that Ben was in fact murdered, and Michelle Hudson saw the real killer. But I couldn't hang my life on a *chance.*

"Do you want me to go ask her?" Harper offered. "I can talk to her, find out what she told the police."

I considered it for a moment. "Do you think she would actually come out and tell you to your face that she saw you?"

"Like I said, the woman is starved for attention. She would probably serve tea and scones while telling me she thinks I'm a killer. But really, Lane, she may have seen *something*, but there's no way she saw *us*. I'll talk to her if it will make you feel better."

Who knew what would happen if Harper confronted Michelle. If the police were watching, it could put Harper back under suspicion. I couldn't risk it. "No, don't do anything yet. I'll take care of it."

If only I knew *how* to take care of it.

Chapter 19

Harper

Lane told me to sit tight and he'd take care of the Michelle Hudson situation, but I'd never been good at sitting tight. I probably should have listened to Lane, but I knew Michelle. We had been neighbors for years. What harm could possibly come from a quick chat?

When I arrived at Hendricks Way, my first stop was to pick up my mail. It was odd that the mailbox was empty, because even after forwarding it to my new address, I still got advertisements and coupons almost daily. I didn't think much of it before heading down the sidewalk to Michelle's, waving at Mr. Radcliffe, a friendly enough guy who lived across from me. He was the kind of neighbor who barely spoke two words in passing, but would mow your lawn out of the kindness of his big, quiet heart.

When Michelle answered the door, her hair neatly coifed and linen outfit pressed, it almost looked like she was expecting someone.

"I suppose you're here to find out what I saw that night." She stepped aside, inviting me in.

"You always were to the point, Michelle." I stepped inside, prepping myself for the worst. If only I had known the worst was yet to come.

* * *

By the time I was done at Michelle's I needed to pick up the kids from school. A year ago, I would have welcomed the kids home with freshly baked cookies and questions about what they had learned. With crumbs scattered across the counter, they would chatter about the friend whom they played with or the answer they got right. But ever since "the accident," they came home to an empty kitchen and silence. It wasn't fair to them, I knew this. But sometimes I simply didn't have the energy to do better. Today, however, I did. I could climb mountains today.

Once upon a time my love for my children was endless. Until one day my son did something so unspeakably horrible that it tore right down the middle of that love. Now, my love had edges. To make up for that, I rarely said no to them. Especially when all they wanted was some dollar store candy.

One tended to spoil children after losing a loved one, especially when that loved one was their father. Maybe it was out of guilt, or maybe it was out of empathy, or maybe it was just to stop the whining. Regardless, candy seemed to make things better, if only for a moment. But that single moment was priceless.

The line at the dollar store reached halfway down the hair accessory aisle. This gave Elise ample time to ponder the merits of headbands over hair bows while the cashier checked out customers with the speed of a corpse. My hair dripped on my shoulders, still wet from our mad dash across the parking lot in an impromptu downpour. I couldn't wait to get out of my damp white oxford shirt, which I was certain now showcased my bra.

The cramped store—where everything was $1 or under!—was the only place I could afford to shop for unnecessary extras, like candy or toys. Without a job, or Ben's income, or my savings account, or the life insurance payout, money was tight. No, not tight—invisible. Suffering didn't get you much more than sympathy and a prayer these days, neither of which paid the bills. I was still paying a huge mortgage on the house, and I wouldn't see my first rental check for another month. And I couldn't—wouldn't—accept Lane's numerous offers of financial support. He was already giving me room and board for free; I couldn't take his money on top of that. I had stretched the cash I had on hand for the past seven weeks since Ben died, but I needed money. Fast.

It was the last place I wanted to work—I preferred the company of plants over most people—but when I saw the *Now Hiring* sign posted in the dollar store window, I had decided to stop in. With half a dozen résumés sent out for more fitting jobs—secretary work, greenhouse manager, craft department supervisor—but no hire yet, I couldn't afford to be picky. After handing the store manager my application for a job as a cashier—though, based on the current staff, possessing all of my teeth probably made me overqualified—I let the kids wander. Two minutes in, they were both whining for candy. My "no" lasted another minute. By minute five they had each picked their favorites and were bumping into the legs of a cardigan-wearing man in front of us. When he scolded the children with a soft-spoken "how would you like it if I took your candy, little girl?" then peered at Elise with buggy eyes made buggier by inch-thick wire-rimmed glasses, I was convinced he was a child abductor whose fashion sense was inspired by *Mister Rogers' Neighborhood*.

The grandmother behind us wrestled with her grandson's cowlick, slicking the tussock of hair down with a wad of spit. Her impatience at his endless babble was stamped on her face, a face wrinkled by exhaustion from raising her negligent daughter's kid. At least that was the story I had made up for her.

Jackson counted the caramels in his bag while Elise fumbled with the packaging on her Sour Patch Kids gummies.

"I thought you didn't like the sour ones," I commented.

"I didn't used to, until Miss Eileen got them for me. I liked the ones she gave me."

The name didn't ring a bell. "Who is Miss Eileen?"

"Grandma's neighbor, duh," Elise said, as if I should have known whom my mother hung out with.

"When did you meet Grandma's neighbor?"

Elise thought for a moment. "The night Daddy died. Grandma dropped us off at Miss Eileen's house after you left. And she gave me Sour Patch Kids."

"Oh."

It was more of a concerned "oh" than a satisfied "oh" because I couldn't imagine why on earth my mother would have dropped my children off at a stranger's house when she was supposed to be watching them. What could she have possibly been doing that was more important than ensuring her grandchildren's safety? And more pressing, why didn't she tell me?

"Can I have one?" Elise asked, pointing to the bag of lollipops I held in my hand. A peace offering for Candace. I remembered during each of my first trimesters being constantly queasy, but lollipops seemed to offer a short-lived cure during the worst of it. I figured maybe it could help Candace too.

"You'll have to ask Aunt Candace. These are for her."

It was the first time I had referred to her as *Aunt* Candace to the kids, and it felt comfortable, like a fuzzy sweater. My sister-in-law—there, I said it!—was still a mystery, but after she had opened up about her past to me, we connected. We had both been broken by someone we loved. Maybe we could heal together.

A feisty woman with a small frame but a big voice, standing in front of the child abductor, began arguing with the cashier over the price of an item, insisting it was two for a dollar. I was cursed to always pick the wrong checkout line. It happened at every store I shopped; I could switch to a faster-moving line, but whichever I chose, the curse would follow. The cash register would malfunction, or the cashier would go on break, or a customer would pay with a *check*. Who used checks in this day and age? The curse had given me every possible line-stalling scenario. This was new, however, finding the one person in the universe who would argue over a price at a store where *everything was a dollar*!

Shaking my head, I pulled out my phone. After my chat with Candace, we had left things between us in an awkward space.

We hovered in the void between acquaintances and friends. She had been through some real tough experiences, and I wanted to trust her, to like her. But this nagging feeling . . . it tugged at my shirt like an insistent child. Something was off. The little details, like where she was from. Every new answer poked another hole in her time line. Before, she had told me the baby was from a one-night stand. Her revision implied Noah was the baby's father. Which was the truth? Which was the lie? How did one even sift through them to find out? Plus she hadn't yet been honest with Lane about the baby not being his. If I could just find something to prove she was who she said she was, I would feel so much better.

By now, the manager and two cashiers were huddled around the feisty shopper, trying to get to the bottom of the pricing fiasco. I still had to wait through the child abductor's cartful before it was my turn. The kids were occupied with hair scrunchies and a rainbow paper windmill. Opening Google on my phone, I searched for *Candace Moriarty, Pennsylvania*. Or was it Ohio? I had lost track of facts, if there were any. I expected an old address listing to pop up, or a White Pages listing. But there was absolutely nothing except a record for a woman who had passed away years ago. If there was no history of Candace Moriarty, did she even exist? Or did she go by another last name? Maybe Noah's.

My online search came to a stop when the phone beeped with an incoming text from Lane: *Is Candace with you?*

I texted back: *Who dis? New phone.*

Apparently Lane didn't find my joke funny: *I'm serious. Have you seen her?*

A moment later Lane's name, along with his profile picture—

a shot of us taken on a beach trip four years ago—flashed on the screen. My pregnant belly was cut off from the bottom of the image, but I remembered the trip like it was last week. The five of us filling the three-bedroom beachfront condo, sand toys scattered across the deck while our towels, hanging from the railing, whipped back and forth in the salty ocean breeze. Lane carrying Jackson on his shoulders, Ben carrying Elise and the beach chairs. I had been forbidden from carrying anything but the baby inside me. With our backs to the ocean and our faces to the sun, Lane held out my camera and captured a selfie of the two of us in a perfect day.

I picked up on the first ring, the urge to tell him everything bursting out of my seams. Had I promised not to say anything to Lane? Or was I bound to secrecy by an unspoken sisterly pact?

When I answered, Lane sounded out of breath. "Hey, Harper. Do you know where Candace is?" The tip of his question rose with hope that my answer would be yes.

"What do you mean? Isn't she home?"

"No, and I haven't seen her at all today. I was hoping she was with you."

"Sorry, she's not with me. Why are you so concerned? And why are you out of breath?"

"I, uh, just got back from a jog. But she was gone when I woke up, and I haven't heard from her all day. That's not like her."

And jogging was not like Lane. Certainly not in a downpour. And it didn't sound like Candace to just disappear all day without a word.

"I don't know what to tell you. Maybe she's just been out shopping all day. Or she's out with friends?"

"She doesn't have any friends . . . that I know of."

There's a lot you don't know about your wife, I wanted to say. "Look, it's still early in the day. She'll probably turn up this evening. I'm sure she's fine. She's a grown woman, and grown women go out sometimes. It's nothing to worry about."

"You're probably right. I wouldn't have given it a second thought if she'd just answer my calls or texts. She never takes off without touching base. And she left her purse with her wallet inside. How could she go shopping without it?"

That information would have been helpful earlier in the conversation.

"Are you sure she took her phone with her?"

"One sec." The line rustled with the sound of Lane rummaging through her purse. "I don't see her phone, and when I called it I didn't hear it ring. I can only assume she has it on her. So she left with the car and presumably her phone, but no purse. Is that normal for women to do?"

It was not something that *I* would ever do, but who was to say Candace wouldn't? I gasped, hand to mouth, at the worry that crashed into my head. My dread hopscotched from Candace to Noah. A humiliated man was the most dangerous man. She had left him, crushed his ego, stolen his unborn baby. If he had found out he was the father, it wouldn't surprise me if he came after her. With Candace, nothing would surprise me.

"Lane? I might know who Candace is with."

"Who?" He sounded relieved, but he shouldn't have been.

"I'll be home shortly. We need to talk. There's something about Candace you need to know."

Chapter 20

Lane

It was almost eleven o'clock at night before headlights streaked across the steel-gray wall as Candace pulled up the driveway. Up until this moment I had been worried about my missing wife. Now I was pissed beyond words.

"It looks like she finally decided to come home." Keeping me company with distressing conversation, Harper watched me while I watched the front door. "You ready for this?" Harper asked.

"As ready as I'll ever be."

Harper knew better than to press. She pulled out a *Better Homes & Gardens* magazine from beneath a stack of mail, examining it. "They still haven't updated my address." She glanced over at me. "Why did you pick up my mail from the Hendricks Way house? I stopped by today and the mailbox was empty."

Damn. I hadn't thought she'd notice. "Oh, um, I was in the area."

"Doing what? That's totally out of the way."

"Does it matter? I was trying to be nice."

She tossed the magazine down and glared at me. "Calm down, Lane. Why are you acting so defensive?"

"You're attacking me for getting your mail for you. I'm sorry for thinking of you."

"No, I'm sorry." She paused, as if she was caught in a mental fog. "I'm just on edge since Michelle Hudson made her statement. I thought maybe you had been over there to see her and I panicked. I just want that whole thing to go away."

Harper's instinct was sharper than I expected. I *had* been over to see Michelle. But I couldn't tell Harper—or anyone—about it.

I sat forward at the sound of a car door slamming shut outside. I glanced at Harper and nodded in the direction of the stairs. Knowing what was coming, Harper excused herself from the sofa, her hand pausing on my shoulder as she passed.

"Accept no more lies, Lane," Harper warned. "And remember, this is about her, not you. And do *not* tell her about what we've done, or she will bury you with it."

"I know, I know. We've gone over this a million times."

She leaned toward me, our faces this close. "You can love her more than you love yourself, but it's going to cost you everything. I would know."

Then she left.

I found it ironic that I was supposed to squeeze the truth out of Candace, yet I hid way worse secrets from her. Like tampering with evidence. Staging a murder. Or what I had been doing all afternoon. I hadn't even told her about the black sedan I noticed sitting two doors down from our house with a man clearly watching us. Earlier today I had pretended to take a jog past his car, but he knew what I was up to and took off before I could get a look at his face.

All evening I had expected the police to show up with two sets of handcuffs, one for me and one for Harper. Maybe it would be a relief. I was physically and emotionally exhausted from the perpetual state of panic I lived in. All the plotting, the preparing for worst-case scenarios . . . no matter how many times I talked myself in circles, I came back to the same conclusion: there was simply nothing we could do but wait.

And not tell a soul.

That was the deal I made with Harper.

I had thought Michelle Hudson's witness testimony about the night of Ben's death was the worst of my problems, until Harper hit me with news of her own after she put the kids to bed. Apparently my wife was a liar. The worst kind too. Candace had reeled me in with hopes and dreams, but they belonged to another man. A dangerous man. She had run from him into my arms. Was I merely an escape hatch? Or did she genuinely love me? I could never tell the truth from the lies with her.

Did I really have room to judge her, though? I was a criminal in the making, after all. In the end, I was left with an unsettling feeling that I had betrayed Candace, not the other way around. As Harper's feet padded across the upstairs landing, the front door creaked open.

I was so relieved that my wife was alive that I could have killed her. The house was dark, except for a single lamp on the coffee table beside me. After quietly shutting the front door, Candace tiptoed toward the stairs, then paused when she saw me. My heart raced, as if something frightening or surprising was about to happen. It reminded me of the day I asked her to marry me. I had no idea if I was going to get a yes or a no, and it terrified me. Much like how I felt now, wondering what terrifying truth she'd reveal tonight.

She marched into the living room, a shopping bag swinging from her arm. I barely recognized her, wrapped in pale, washed-out skin. The bronze glow had been replaced with dark scoops beneath her eyes.

"Hey, babe." Her voice was tinged with an unspoken apology. "You're still awake."

"I've been waiting for you. I called you a dozen times today. Where were you?" No *hey, babe* this time. I was angry, and I wanted her to know it.

"Out." She lifted her Nordstrom shopping bag up as proof. "Shopping."

I had caught her in lie number one. "Until almost midnight? And without your wallet?"

"What? Are you stalking me?"

"Answer the questions, Candace. No lies this time."

She huffed, and I knew stalling when I saw it. "First of all, I'm not lying. And second of all, I used Apple Pay on my phone, you asshole, to buy your sister a thank-you gift, then I got a pregnancy massage, and after that I was craving Korean so I grabbed dinner out. Would you like to see all my receipts? You can check my mileage, if you'd like." She thrust her hand onto her hip and cocked her head, and I recognized the sarcasm too late.

Maybe I had overreacted. "I'm not trying to start a fight. I just didn't know where you were all day and you wouldn't take my calls. I was worried."

"I'm a big girl, Lane. I don't need a babysitter."

"I know, but it was so out of character for you to just . . . disappear, without a note or text or anything." *Especially when your deranged ex, whose baby you're carrying, might be looking for you.*

She exhaled an exasperated sigh. "Sometimes I need a little space. The pregnancy hormones make me sick all the time, and angry when I'm not sick, and sad when I'm not angry. And with all the people in the house, it can feel overwhelming."

"I get it. But I did have something I wanted to talk to you about. Can you sit down for a minute?"

She glanced away, then looked past me. "Um, do you mind if I grab something to eat first? I'm starving."

"I thought you already ate dinner."

"I did, but I felt too sick to finish. Now I'm hungry again."

Was it the pregnancy, or another lie because she hadn't actually gone out to eat? I would never know. Everything that came out of her mouth was lies. I couldn't trust the woman I married. I didn't even *know* the woman I married.

"Food can wait. This is important. We need to talk. Now. I'm not asking anymore, Candace. You owe me a conversation."

Her silence was so loud.

"Excuse me?" Her jaw clenched, and her words came out taut and angry.

"I know you lied. You lied to me about everything—about the baby being mine, about where you're from, even about your name, Candace *Moriarty*! How about you tell me your real identity, for starters."

"Lane," she said, owning my name. "Who told you all this stuff?"

"Does it matter? Who are you really?" The hope-filled boy in me wanted to cry, but the wiser man in me held it back.

Candace dropped her bag on a chair and sat beside me, her knees angled toward mine. She scooted closer, generating heat between our legs, our arms. I was still in love with her, and I didn't even know her. I choked on her silence. Finally, she had the courage to look me in the eyes.

"I guess Harper told you everything?"

"She's my sister, and clearly the only one who cares about me. I want the truth, Candace. From your lips, not Harper's."

"I had hoped to leave all the pain in my past. I just wanted to move forward with you into the future. Why is the past so important?" She was pleading with me, her voice intense and wobbly.

"You can't just walk away from it, Candace. That's not how it works; because it's not the past if it's still the present."

"What's that supposed to mean?"

"I know about Noah. About the baby not being mine. So it's not the past, is it? He's still looking for you, isn't he?"

She sighed, her gaze dropping. "I'm sorry for not being honest. I'll tell you everything. But I need one thing from you first."

I wouldn't give her a damn thing, but if it got the truth out of her, I could lie. "What's that?"

"I just need you to listen and not react until I'm done."

I could give her that. I nodded.

"First, I want you to know I love you. More than anything. That's why I lied, because I was afraid the truth would make you leave me. And I hope you'll still want to be my husband after you hear it all."

I raised my hand to stop her. I was too angry to suffer through her emotional preamble. "Enough precursor. Get on with it."

"Sorry. Okay. Well, my name isn't Candace Moriarty. It's Candace Wilkes. Well, sort of." She lifted a finger to stop me from asking what *that* meant. "That's my birth name. Born in Cleveland, Ohio. Eventually we fled Ohio after my dad's arrest warrants piled up, and we ended up in Pennsylvania where my grandma lived. After my parents died when I was ten, I moved around a lot. That's when I got close to a guy named Noah Gosling. His family took me in when I was living on the streets, and eventually we became high school sweethearts. We got married very young and I became Candace Gosling. Young and dumb, I thought we'd live happily ever after. Well, he ended up becoming an abusive jerk, but I stuck by him because I was afraid to leave . . . until one day I decided I couldn't risk losing another baby. That's when I left. Then I met you. I wanted to tell you, but I didn't know how. Or if you'd be willing to accept another man's baby."

Realization boiled slowly, but when it came, my anger was hot and spitting.

"So he really is the father of your baby?"

She didn't answer at first. The stretchy minute gave enough time for the humiliation to claw into my flesh. I had been a fool for love.

"Yes, unfortunately it's his. But I had gotten pregnant several times with him and none of my other babies survived the stress or the abuse . . . until this one. I took the beatings for years, until I just couldn't anymore. I had been so stupid and weak and foolish and hopeful that he would change. I preferred the devil I knew to the devil I didn't know—homelessness and being alone, living on the streets and potentially ending up dead. All I wanted was a family, a man who would take care of me, not hurt me. Noah clearly wasn't the answer. But you were."

I wanted to buy what she was selling: Hope. A future together. But I couldn't, because it was all fake goods.

"So you got pregnant with his baby and then ran off. Does he know?"

"I don't know. Does it matter? He never wanted to be a father. You did. That's when I realized everything could work out okay."

"Only because it's all based on lies." When she frowned, I instantly regretted the dig. "So who is Candace Moriarty?"

Tears wet her eyes, and I almost felt sorry for her. I couldn't imagine what she had gone through, but right now I was too fuming to care.

"I created a new identity after I left. I knew a guy who could make me a fake ID. I was afraid Noah would find me, so I picked a name from the obituaries. At that point I never thought about the lie catching up to me. After I met you, it was too late to come clean. I didn't want to lose you. Would you have stayed if you had known the truth?"

I couldn't answer that because she had never given me the chance to find out. I sat in stunned silence. I didn't know what to say or what to feel. All I felt was betrayal and heartache.

"We'll never know, will we? You knew how much I loved you, and yet you kept this huge secret part of yourself from me. You just assumed I wouldn't accept your past. Instead, you deceived me, lied to my face, told me I was a father . . . you never thought about anything other than yourself. How could you spin lie after lie about your whole life, *our* life? Is there anything that's true?"

Her gaze hung on her hands, stiffly clenched.

"The way I feel about you, that's true, Lane. I love you more than anything. I want a future with you—you, me, and our baby. That's all true. Please forgive me. Please, I'm begging you. I can't lose you. It'll kill me." She dropped to her knees, kneeling before me, gripping my hands like her life depended on it. In a way, it did. "I knew if I told you the truth you'd never think I was good enough. All I want is to be good enough for you. Surviving without a mother broke me, but you helped build me back up more resilient than before. I want to be strong enough to forge a better future for us. For *our* children."

"You mean *your* children. Not mine."

"Please, Lane. I thought you, of all people, would be understanding."

"Oh, I understand plenty. I understand that you lie easier than you tell the truth. I understand that you're selfish and will do anything to get what you want."

"Wow. So that's what you think of me." She rose to her feet, glaring down at me. The passion sharpened her tongue into a knife. "Apparently you're no different from any other man. I should have figured as much."

"Don't blame me for what you've done to us!" Slamming my fist on the coffee table, I stood to meet her, eye-to-eye. "You thought I was the kind of man who judges someone based on their past. Well, I have a past too, Candace, and I would have never held your mistakes against you. So, then, I guess neither of us knows each other. We're two strangers, not two united souls. You've pushed me away with your secrets and broken me with your lies. There is no *us*. It's just you. And me."

"No! You don't get to split us with a word. It doesn't work that way. You promised your future to me. You can't just take it back!" The air vibrated with her rage.

"I married Candace *Moriarty,* not you."

"You can't leave, Lane."

"Watch me!"

I stormed across the room, unable to cork the tears that I didn't want her to see. She didn't deserve my anguish over her. Candace ran after me, reaching for me, but I shoved her back. Too hard. She fell to the floor, crying out as her rear slammed against the wood. I stopped, wanting to scoop her up and offer a million apologies, but I couldn't. My rage held me hostage.

I regretted every moment as I watched my wife splayed out on the floor, holding her belly, sobbing my name. I hated myself as I grabbed my car keys and headed for the front door. Everything in me screamed, but the voices were too loud. I needed to leave. As I reached for the doorknob, a movement drew my gaze upward, where I found Harper standing at the top of the stairwell, staring at me with eyes full of pity.

You can love her more than you love yourself, Harper had said, *but it's going to cost everything.*

She was right. I could forgive a lot. My sister knew just how much. But the lies and deceit and entrapment . . . It was too much to be able to forgive. As I slammed the door shut behind me, it was the beginning of the end, when the girl breaks the boy and the boy seeks revenge.

Chapter 21

Candace

Love is brutal. Love is bliss. Love is hard. Love is
forgiveness.
I hope you can forgive me for loving you so hard.

Seek and destroy. That seemed to be my mantra these days. Everything I sought—love, family, hope—ended up in ashes. I hadn't seen Lane since he left yesterday. I hated myself for scaring away the only man who ever truly loved me.

As I sat on the front porch in the dark, the chirp of crickets reminded me how alone I was. I glanced down at the black screen of my phone. Every hour of silence as Lane ignored my calls and texts terrified me—I felt him slipping from my grasp. Harper and his mother hadn't heard from him either. Unless they were lying to me, which was more likely. I wondered where he would have gone, and if he was ever coming back.

It was hard work learning to love someone the way he needed to be loved. Lane needed honesty. I needed forgiveness. Separately, they were two simple things. Together, they were impossible. We had too much clutter between us, a skyscraper of barriers. His undying servitude to his sister, the demons chasing me from my past, the secrets we both tucked in our back pockets. I knew Lane had secrets, just like I did. I read it in the earnest way he touched me and his quick, nervous glances. Lane was a dog-eared book; I had read and scribbled notes on every page of him. I knew him better than he thought. Maybe even better than Harper did. I also knew Harper was the reason everything was falling apart in my life.

I understood why she clung to Lane. She needed him, just like I did. No one loved selflessly. We all had expectations and demands from a relationship, whether it be from a lover, friends, or family. None of us were so pure-hearted that we gave of ourselves endlessly. The heart could only beat so much for someone else before it wanted something in return. Harper needed affirmation; I needed adoration. Lane only had so much to give.

A car passed by, its headlights skipping over me. I sat up, hoping and praying Lane had returned home. As the vehicle continued on down the road, I exhaled, unaware I had been holding my breath. Damn, I missed him, and it had only been a day. When had I fallen so far for him? I thought back to the day we met, a day that wouldn't stand out to me until much later. He had left only a small imprint on my life back then, but now he was the mold I wanted to fit my life into.

When I decided he was The One, I had already given my heart away, so I lent him mine to borrow; I didn't expect him to keep it. It had been too easy to fall for each other. We both had empty gaps that needed to be filled, so he picked a needy, jaded woman and I picked an easy target. But it became real somewhere along the way, despite the secrets.

The mug of tea on the bistro table in front of me had turned cold and bitter. Like my heart had become, thanks to Noah. Then I found a second chance. But now I'd lost it. Now everything felt wrong and nothing felt right, and all my anger and pain and regret and loss swirled inside my skull like a tornado. The iron frame of the bistro chair dug into my lower back. I needed sleep. I cupped my tummy and felt a swish inside me. Was that the baby kicking back at me? A fighter— she got that from me. The baby needed sleep. But I needed Lane more.

I counted my mistakes along with the stars and held my breath while waiting for a sign that everything would be okay. I was a rear-window hostage, crying in the back seat while watching home dwindle into the background. Lane was home. It was my fault that I lost in love, wasn't it? Every mistake was a noose that I wrapped around my own neck. I held the end of the rope. I kicked the chair out from under me. I squeezed until I died, then squeezed until I brought myself back to life, only to repeat the process.

My grandmother once told me that heartbreak makes the heart stronger, if you play your cards right. But I had never been good at poker, at pretending I was strong. I gave too much and loved too deeply. I got overinvolved. It was a bad habit of mine, letting love control me.

Closing my eyes, I remembered my second-grade crush, Damian. It was the first day of school, and he smiled at me and said he liked my dress. The dress came from a secondhand store, but in that moment, I felt like a princess. I told my mom about my feelings for Damian as she tucked me into bed that night.

Mommy, I'm in love!

She had laughed it off, like she did every time I had fallen for a new boy since kindergarten. *Your heart is like a bottle floating in the sea, letting the tide of emotions take it where it wishes,* she told me. We were sitting in my bedroom on my rainbow, tiger-print bedspread. I was always crushing on someone new, but Damian felt special. By the fourth day of school I'd discover he wasn't. *You fall too easily,* she added. *You can't give boys control over your heart. That's yours to keep, darling.*

Words of wisdom, Mom. Sitting up, I decided I wouldn't let Lane do this to me, make me wait for him, pine for him. I didn't need him. I might not have ever really wanted him. He was a convenience, that's all.

The penny in my hip pocket dug into my thigh. I was outgrowing all my clothes lately and loving it. I pulled it out and stared at its brassy polish. There was a wishing well in the town I grew up in, a forlorn wooden well that needed a paint job and some TLC. When things were hard—harder than usual—Mom would take me to the well, hand me a penny, and tell me to make a wish. I wished for all sorts of things: a pony, Mom and Dad to stop fighting, my current crush to like me back. I now realized true love was like throwing a penny in a wishing well and believing it would make a difference: a fantasy.

I had been blinded by the beauty of make-believe, but I

wouldn't toss my penny in again. It was mine now, and it would stay in my pocket. I was finished with fairy tales. I had thought our love stood a chance when Lane reached out to me, a needy woman who wounded with words and ceramic plates. I was heavy in his arms, and he had held me anyways. But the reality was there was no "till death do us part." I would always be one mistake away from losing him, and I had only myself to blame.

It was the fastest slow-fall from grace.

Another flutter of movement inside my tummy startled me. My eyes opened as I pressed my fingers against the quickening. The baby was moving, swimming inside me. Shifting uncomfortably on the tiny cushion, I propped my feet up on the bistro chair catty-corner to me and relished the tremble of tiny arms and legs stirring within. Then the utter stillness of the street, the call of crickets, and the Sherpa blanket draped over me lulled me into sleep . . .

* * *

With $500 and a mishmash of clothing stuffed in the duffel bag at my feet, I watched my derelict small town in rural Pennsylvania blur into wheat fields and rugged hills outside the Greyhound bus window. My breath left a moist patch on the glass, and in it I drew a heart. Love—that was my goal. All I needed was already buried within me, inside my womb.

This time I wouldn't fall in love. I would choose carefully, a man I could control. I didn't want another Noah, who mirrored my darkest fears, then reflected an illusion of love back at me. That's how he got me in the first place—all tricks and smoke and mirrors.

As the window heart evaporated, my cell phone buzzed from

deep in the bag. After wrestling with some garments to free the phone, I pulled it out and swiped to read the text:

Where are you? And where's my fucking money, bitch?

If only Noah knew I wasn't coming back. I'd need to get a new phone and new number along with my new life if there was any chance of escaping my past. Everything I had was tied to Noah. My phone, my life, my baby. The only way to cut the chains was to get as far away as possible, become someone new, someone better.

I opened my web browser and searched Best places to raise a family and clicked on the first article that popped up. I scrolled through the list, weeding out anything west of the Mississippi. I only had $500 to get me to where I was going, so it had to be affordable to get there and live there and survive there. Then I saw it:

Durham, North Carolina: Affordable living, growing community, job opportunities, decent schools. The perfect destination for young families and settling retirees. Idyllic. It sounded perfect. I now had a destination. All I needed was a plan.

* * *

It was the time of night when the moon sleepwalked across the sky, slowly intensifying, creeping up on the sun. I woke to a stiff neck and moonbeams crisscrossing through the tree branches, landing on my face. Lane still hadn't come home, and I had an unsettling feeling that when he did, it would be the end of us.

I headed upstairs to bed, careful to avoid the creaky steps. I reached the top of the landing and turned the corner toward my room. The hallway was windowless and dark, lined with closed doors. I paused at the sound of scraping floorboards and found a moving shadow at the end of the hall. A tiny silhouette stood by my doorway.

I jumped back. "What the heck?" I yelped.

I flicked on the hall light switch, pouring white light on Jackson's ghostly form. No squinting. No blinking. Just a bored, disconnected gaze.

"Jackson?" I was afraid to say his name, and I didn't know why. I was certain I was stuck in a horror film.

He didn't answer, didn't flinch.

I reached for the doorknob to Harper's room, cracked the door open, and peered inside. "Harper," I whispered harshly. She didn't move. I took a step past the threshold. "Harper!" I called louder. Still nothing. A deep sleeper like Lane, apparently.

I glanced over my shoulder to look for Jackson, but he was gone. Disappeared. I imagined him slinking back into his hollow. Way too creepy. I shut Harper's door, turned off the hall light, and ran into my bedroom, my back pressed against the closed door while my nerves settled.

I was disappointed to find the bed still empty, in the same rumpled mess I had left it in from the night before. This was bad, maybe even unreconcilable. Lane was angry. Angrier than I had ever seen him. It was in that solitary moment when I realized what I stood to lose. My home. My medical benefits. My future I had so carefully planned out. Damn Harper and her big mouth! Everything was unraveling, and the thought of birthing the baby on my own, becoming a single mom, finding a place to live, securing a job . . . it was all just too much. Worst of all, I didn't know how to win Lane back, if it was even possible.

I stood in front of my dresser mirror, hands propped on the edge, staring at a sad reflection. Who was I? What purpose did I have? Empty blue eyes looked back at me, examining me and finding nothing but a picture of disheveled hair and deepening frown lines. I didn't deserve Lane, and I didn't deserve a happily ever after. Love, family, hope—they were flimsy dreams that scattered on the wind like scraps of paper.

My scars told my past and my future. A jagged line ran up my forearm where Noah had cut me during a fight. The first fight. I hadn't learned how to fight back until after I left. Although the score in my flesh had faded into a pale slash, it served as a permanent reminder of where I had been and where I would never go again. The blemish was my journey from death to life, from pain to promise. But then I went and screwed up my second chance, my third chance . . . When would I learn? Maybe my father was right all along. I didn't deserve happiness, or love, or anything good. I was born of misery and would die in misery. Suffering was my birthright.

A pair of scissors rested on the corner of the dresser, and I picked them up. Held the cold metal in my palms. Slipping my fingers through the handle holes, I opened and closed the blades, the slice of the edges cutting through the air in a soft *whoosh*. Grabbing a handful of hair, I held the blade up to it and cut through, watching the black tendrils fall to the floor. Another handful, another slice, and again, a blue-black puddle of hair and tears collecting at my feet.

With each *whoosh* I self-destructed, cutting my hair with Noah's words: *Bitch. Whore. Useless. Worthless.* I would wallow in my sadness, sink in nice and deep until it swallowed me whole. Glancing at the tragedy I had made of my hair, I saw my running mascara as my war paint, as a figure approached behind me in the mirror.

"What are you doing?" I jumped at the sound of Lane's voice as he rushed toward me, hugging me while pulling the scissors from my grip. "Don't do this to yourself."

There was nothing I could say. No future to hope for. No past to redeem. Any courage I had left was somewhere back in Pennsylvania.

"Why not? I don't deserve you," I answered, the sobs coming suddenly. "I don't deserve anyone." My proclamation hung in the air. I was afraid to look at him; I couldn't seem to find a place to rest my eyes.

He lifted my chin with the crook of his finger, then handed me a humble bouquet of flowers. Fragrant daylilies, one of my favorites.

"I'm sorry it's not nicer, but finding a quality flower arrangement at this hour is harder than you might expect. It was either these or gas station carnations."

I wiped my nose with the back of my hand and sniffled, choking on flowers and self-loathing. I set the flowers beside the scissors on my dresser.

"You chose well." I felt my dry lips peel apart in a smile. "Can I ask where you've been?"

"No, you don't get to ask me questions."

"Then why did you come back? Other than because it's your house and all."

His pause seemed to guard thoughts he didn't want to utter.

"Because after a day of missing you, I realized I love you more than I hate what you've done."

"You . . . you forgive me for lying to you about the baby?"

He glanced behind me before answering. "I'm not quite there yet. But I understand why you did it. I'll need time—"

"I'll give you all the time in the world if it means there's a chance we'll stay together."

"I admit, Candace, I'm not sure how to feel. Everyone thinks I should leave you, that you're bad for me. But I've never felt so good as when I'm with you. I don't know what to do with that."

It was everything I wanted to hear, except not. His family hated me—hell, *I* hated me—and yet he still chose me. There was something he wasn't telling me.

"Why do you still want me? I'm nothing special. You could have anyone you wanted, but you pick me, a messed-up woman who's pregnant with her ex's baby. Why?"

He shrugged. "It's hard to explain. But when I'm with you, you're beauty and perfection and belly laughs, and shattered plates and insanity and passion. And I love it all. I guess I feel alive with you."

I scoffed. "You're so full of it, Lane. You can smell the trailer park on me a mile away. I'm no good for you, no good for my baby, no good for myself."

"Hey," he soothed, placing his hand on my shoulder. "That's not true. Clearly you'll do anything for your baby . . ." His palm slid up my neck and his fingers intertwined with my hair. "And by the way, hacking away your hair won't fix things. What were you thinking?"

My reflection showed the horror I had made of it. Half flowed down one shoulder, the other half hung in uneven chunks. "If I can't look beautiful for you, I don't want to be beautiful for anyone else." I didn't know how to explain it, my self-destructive tendencies. It was as though I wanted to punish myself for failing.

"Well, you're out of luck, because I still find you breathtaking. And I think we should try again."

"Try what again?"

"Try finding out who we are together with all of the secrets out of the way."

His words dripped into my ear. Slowly, they started to fill up my brain . . . then my heart. More than anything, I wanted to find us again, rebrand our love, our own version of it. Fights were a marital rite of passage. So we cry and throw plates and cut our hair, vowing never to make the same mistakes again. Then we make up, and it brings us back to life. In the end, the misery of the low was worth the high.

The thing was I had never intended to love him, only to use him to fill me back up. Then I found myself liking him, adoring the way he pulled out his sparse gray strands of hair in order to cling to his youth. And the way he screamed music lyrics while mowing the lawn. I knew it was love when I watched him clean up the piles of toenail clippings I left on the coffee table. No nagging. Just consistent kindness. I looked forward to the moments he snuck into my shower for a quickie. I hated him with all my soul because I loved him with all my soul.

"Yes." With that one word I became honest and vulnerable and terrified. "I want to try again too."

Trailing his fingers down my arm, his touch sparked goose bumps in its wake. With the other hand, he fiddled with his phone, then set it down on the dresser while the Gin Blossoms' "Til I Hear It from You" began to play. Old school and before my time. And perfect.

He kissed my forehead, holding me against him while we moved in unison to the music.

"I've had a chance to think, and I know you've been through a lot. It wasn't right for you to lie to me, but I understand why you did." I felt his words sink into me, then grow inside me.

"You do?" I looked up at him with an unspoken plea that this was real.

"Maybe you were scared I wouldn't accept you or the baby. Maybe you found out you were pregnant after we were already together. I don't know the details of what exactly happened, and I'm not sure I want to. All I know is that I love you, Candace, and I want a family with you. On one condition."

"Of course. Anything."

We continued drifting back and forth, feet touching, arms enfolding each other.

"You never lie to me again. About anything. I want the truth going forward. If you lie to me again, it's over. Can you promise me total honesty going forward?"

I wanted so desperately to say yes, to make that promise. But it would be yet another lie. Telling the truth, though? No, I couldn't do that because it was unforgivable. The "yes" tasted sour, but I swallowed it anyway. Then with every ounce of conviction I could muster, I lied.

"I promise. No more secrets." The song ended but our dancing resumed. "Can I ask something of you?"

Lane kissed me, and as his lips drifted away, his eyes hooked on mine. "Of course. Anything." He winked, and I realized what he was doing. Imitating me. I owned him again. I bet I could ask for the moon and he'd give it to me.

"I want to start putting the nursery together. For *our* baby."

He didn't reply at first, then he chewed his lower lip. "Okay. Let's do it. I will ask Harper to leave. I think you're right, that we need time together, alone. It's been one problem after another since she arrived; I think we've earned a break. I'll talk to her about it in the morning."

"Thank you, Lane." I nearly jumped into his arms, I was so happy.

I grabbed his cheeks and pulled his lips to mine, ripping his shirt off as I scraped my fingers down his chest. Little blossoms of pink budded everywhere my kisses touched. I licked down his naval—his body was my canvas and I wanted to paint it with my tongue. He was the purpose for my hungry lips, my grazing fingers, my bated breath. The sex was intense, passionate, full of apologies and forgiveness. As we sat up, heaving and sated, he looked at me and laughed.

"What's so funny?" I asked, laughing but not knowing why.

"You look like a zombie."

I sat up, checking my reflection in the mirror. Mascara trailed down both cheeks, along with smears of eyeshadow across my temples.

"I'm thinking of trying out goth. You like it?"

Cupping my hand, Lane led me to the bathroom, then held a washcloth under the faucet until the water ran hot. After soaking the washcloth, he pressed it against my face, wiping away the salty residue of tears and makeup. Lane polished me clean, inside and out.

When we returned to the bedroom hand in hand, I scooped up the pile of hair from the floor and the dresser. Only then did I notice that the scissors were gone.

Chapter 22

Harper

There was no light where we were going. Only darkness ahead. At 6:42 I bolted awake with the residue of a nightmare clinging to me. In my dream, the police had arrested me, charged me with murder, and my children had to watch me get hauled off in handcuffs. At 8:26 I finally put my phone down after exhausting every possible internet search for news updates on Ben's investigation, Michelle Hudson's testimony, and affordable criminal defense attorneys. At 9:03 I was officially asked to move out, with nowhere to go.

Nothing I said could convince Lane to leave Candace, my sister-in-law from hell. She was bitter, scheming, and selfish. He saw broken, passionate, and unloved. She was completely untrustworthy, and yet when I came downstairs to find them flirtatiously making pancakes together—a dollop of batter on the tip of her nose, a smear across his cheek, then licking it off each other—my stomach dropped.

I'd overheard enough last night to know that Candace had mastered the art of manipulation. I couldn't weed the truth from the lies, the woman was *that* skilled. A true politician, she'd earned the sympathy vote. Knowing how my brother could overlook an abundance of sins—I knew from personal experience testing this—I decided I'd do my own digging. See for myself what the truth was if Lane wasn't going to bother.

First thing first was this Noah Gosling character. Who was he *really*? Candace had painted him as an abusive ex-lover, the father of her baby. But I knew there were always two sides to every story. I wanted to hear his side, and I would.

"Want some breakfast?" Candace asked between giggles as I made my way to the cupboard behind them to grab a coffee mug. I'd need it extra strong today.

I rolled my eyes. "No thanks. I see you both dipping your spit-soaked fingers in the batter."

"Oh, c'mon. We're family. It's not like we have cooties," Lane teased.

"God only knows what you both have," I muttered.

Carrying my java in a laughably large soup-bowl-like mug, I headed outside to the back porch and sat on the swing I had bought Lane as a housewarming gift. It was Amish made, from the foothills of Pennsylvania Dutch Country. I wondered if that was anywhere near where Candace grew up . . . allegedly. Mockingbirds chattered as they scattered across the sky. A pair of cardinals hid in a Japanese maple tree, their red bodies blending with the leaves.

Three gulps later, I was ready to do some research. I opened my Facebook app and did a cursory search for Noah Gosling. Several accounts popped up, so I narrowed it to Pennsylvania. Two accounts, but one looked like an aged version of the boy from Candace's picture. Cute guy. Tattooed. Lip piercing. *Bingo*. Bare-chested in his profile picture, and I wasn't looking away. He lived up to the Gosling name.

I clicked to message him, not sure what to say. So I began typing without thinking:

> *Hi, Noah. You don't know me, but I think I know your ex-wife, Candace Moriarty. I was wondering if we could talk sometime? I have a couple questions I'd like to ask you. Thanks, and I hope to hear from you.*

As May was nearly over, we were leaving spring and heading into summer, and already the air was ripe with thick heat. Southern heat was moist and suffocating, with a persistence that stalked you in the shade. Through the open windows upstairs I could hear Elise yelling at Jackson about something or other. While her grievances always changed, the volume of her yelling stayed the same.

Except this time, it was different. Two unified shrieks cut through the air. I jumped up and ran inside, taking the stairs two steps at a time and throwing open their bedroom door.

"Mommy, Mommy, Frankie winked!" Elise screamed and ran behind my legs while Jackson idled at my side.

"What happened? Frankie . . . what?"

"The doll, Mommy." Jackson's fingers trembled as he pointed to an old doll.

"Where'd you find that?" I asked.

"In the attic above Uncle Lane's bedroom. There's a secret entryway in their closet," Elise confessed.

"You're not allowed in their bedroom, let alone their closet. If Candace had caught you, it'd be off with your heads!"

At least with the mess Candace made of her closet there was little chance she'd notice that two kids had rummaged through it. The doll appeared old and could be valuable, so I didn't want to toss it out, no matter how creepy it was.

"You named him Frankie after Pappy?"

"Yeah, before we knew he's possessed," Elise muttered into my side.

The kids had named it Frankie, my grandfather's name. They'd never met him, but I'd spoken about him and they had seen pictures of him throughout our house.

"The doll is not possessed."

"It *winked* at us! Jackson saw it!"

Okay, this was getting ridiculous. First, ghosts in the house, now, possessed Chucky dolls.

"Calm down, guys. I assure you that Frankie did not wink at you on his own. You probably moved him. Look." I walked over to the doll, its eyes half open. I lifted the doll and tilted him backward and forward, showing them how his eyes blinked as I moved him. "See?"

"But we were both on the other side of the room when his eyes moved, Mommy. I think the old lady lives in him now."

Jackson's lower lip twitched, as if undecided whether to curve up or down.

"Mom, that doll is scary!" Elise insisted.

"How about I take the doll and put it in my closet. Problem solved, okay?"

"What if he comes out at night and tries to kill us?" Jackson asked.

"That only happens in scary movies, not real life. I promise he won't come alive. I'll put him in a place he can't get out of."

The kids seemed satisfied enough with my solution as I took the doll and headed into my bedroom. As I pushed it up on the top shelf, I could see how it creeped the kids out. One glassy blue eye remained half closed and sleepy, the other wide with half the lashes missing. The plastic lips, a pink worn by time, pouted for a bottle or Binky or thumb. It wasn't a thin plastic doll either, like the cheap ones you might find at the store. This doll had substance, weight. Almost like it was full of something. The old lady, perhaps?

I shook the notion away. The therapist had explained some of the symptoms of traumatic grief; we had been down this road before, but it seemed to be getting worse. Post-bereavement hallucinations. Night terrors. Paranoia. And now I was catching it too.

My Facebook Messenger app beeped. I sat on my bed and opened the app. A reply from Noah:

Candace Moriarty? Do you mean my ex-wife Candace Wilkes? And you've been misinformed. We're legally still married.

And the plot thickened. Candace was apparently still married. Which meant she wasn't married to Lane. Which meant he had no obligation to her! I couldn't wait to tell him he was free, free at last! There was no mention of Noah's unborn baby. Perhaps Candace never told him.

Well, she supposedly married my brother. Any idea why she would lie about who she is?

I waited while three dots ran across the message bar as he typed:

No idea, but tell that bitch to return what she stole from me.

Was the baby what she had "stolen" from him? I typed a hasty reply:

She stole from you?

Three dots blinked across the screen as he continued. Then his reply came through:

What she took doesn't matter anymore. I would have reported her to the police, but I figured I was better off without her. Where is she now?

Damn, the man was bold. If I told him, it'd lead him straight to Lane, and God only knew what kind of person Noah was. I didn't want to answer in case he really was as dangerous as Candace made him out to be, so I lied:

I don't know.

He didn't buy it:

Yes you do. You said she married your brother.

Crap. What had I gotten myself into? I was about to close the app when another series of dots ran across the screen:

I already know everything I need to know about you, Harper Paris from Durham, North Carolina. It won't be that hard to find you and get her myself.

He was becoming more aggressive by the reply. I was only trying to protect my brother from his psycho wife, not get everyone killed in the process. I may have hated her, but I didn't want her dead. Unless she had made it all up and Noah was the victim, not her. Who was lying and who was telling the truth?

Tell her I'm coming for her.

In a panic I closed the app and set the phone down. What had I done? Now Noah only had to look up my address—he had my first and last name, my city and state, probably even Lane's name via Facebook now—to find out where I lived and come after me to get to Candace. What had she stolen? And how was I going to tell Lane what I had done? If Noah didn't kill me, Lane certainly would. He had already given me a warning shot about causing any more *girl drama*. As if we were two teenage girls fighting over who got to use the bathroom first. This was serious. I had set off a shitstorm, and there was no way we weren't all going to get dirty.

I needed my mom.

Chapter 23

Harper

"You look terrible, Harp." My mother had never been one to bite her tongue and I rarely appreciated her brutal honesty.

My body was exhausted from trying to claw myself out of the grave I had buried myself in. It was only a matter of time before the police came knocking on my door. I had researched every possible outcome for myself, and it all ended the same: jail, and a fine that would throw me into bankruptcy. The judicial system didn't take kindly to tampering with evidence and insurance fraud. Of course I'd refute Lane's involvement and spare his future, since he'd be the one taking custody of the kids. God forbid I let my mother spoil them worse than I already had.

"I'm sure I look as terrible as I feel, Mom." You know you're in it deep when your mother is the only person left whom you can trust.

Elmo's Diner was packed as usual, but it was always worth the wait. It had a menu that catered to Mom's particularities for meals that she couldn't make at home, coupled with my preference for tried-and-true dishes; it was the happy medium one rarely found in life. Across the austere table, Mom looked overdressed in a silk blouse with a cream blazer. Her blond hair was styled up in full waves, her go-to style when her gray roots were growing out, and it framed a face perfectly made up. The woman literally put her face on when she applied her makeup.

"Would you like a refill on your tea, ma'am?" the waitress asked me, carrying a sloshing pitcher full of southern sweet tea.

I definitely shouldn't. I didn't need the extra calories.

"I'd love a refill, thanks."

Outside of our booth's window the sky brooded, like acid-washed jeans. I pushed my home fries around my plate, my stomach already full after eating the quiche and drinking two—now three—glasses of sweet tea, which Mom had clucked at. *Sweet tea this early in the morning?* she had scoffed when I placed my order. But it could be the last time I enjoyed sweet tea, because who knew if they offered it in jail? So I drank my fill, with Mom tsk-tsking in the background.

While I overindulged on tea, Mom picked at her salmon cake and eggs, a slow-eating trait she must have passed down the line. I'd lost count of how many times Jackson came home with notes from his teacher saying he needed to start eating lunch faster at school. Eventually the teacher sat him at a table by himself so he'd stay focused on his food, but he still took his sweet time eating, like a grazing cow with nothing else to do. When I found out my little boy sat all alone in a buzzing cafeteria packed with energized kids, my heart broke a little, and that's when I had started popping by the school for lunch to join Jackson.

"Thanks for meeting me today. How's your meal?" I asked Mom.

She held up a finger, a gnarled twig tipped with cherry blossom–pink nail polish, while she finished swallowing her bite. "Delicious, thank you. How's yours?"

"Good." But there was no good transition into what I wanted to tell her.

"Have you given any thought to what you're going to do with your house?" Mom could always fill the dead air between us.

"What do you mean?"

"Certainly you don't want to keep it . . . after what happened there."

I swallowed a bite. "I'm renting it out. I have a family getting ready to move in."

"Rent it? Why not sell it?"

"I'm not ready to part with it. All our family memories are there. I still feel Ben there, in the cushions of the sofa and the reflections of the mirrors."

"But it's been almost two months since he died, honey. It's time to start healing and moving forward with your life."

"I know, but he hasn't disappeared yet, no matter how many times I clean the rooms. I'm not sure I *want* to move on yet."

"Harp, you can't do this to yourself again. Hasn't enough bad happened there? It's time to let go."

"How can I? I'm not sure I want to say goodbye forever. Besides, I'll be getting monthly rent checks to help pay the mortgage, so that gives me time to see how I feel about it a year from now."

Mom slapped the table and my half-empty glass of tea trembled. "You want the burden of that house for a whole year? Renting is a pain, let me tell you. And it rarely turns a profit. Why weigh yourself down with the bills and maintenance of a large house like that when I could sell it quickly for you? It's a seller's market right now. I could get you top dollar for it."

She grew more heated with each word, as if my holding on to my house was a personal affront to her.

"To be honest, Harp, I don't think you should ever return to that murder house. It's not safe. What if the killer comes back? And besides, why would you want to be surrounded by the ghosts of the past? That sounds terribly painful."

"Just stop, okay? I don't know why you're so quick to forget Ben and—" I stopped, unable to say her name, or else I knew I'd break down into tears that wouldn't stop. "I know you never really liked Ben, but he was a good husband and a good father. We might have had our rough patches, but what couple hasn't?"

"What you two went through wasn't a *rough patch*. It was a devastating loss, and he never truly supported you through it. I never even saw the man cry after she died. What kind of man doesn't cry at his own child's funeral? Especially when he's to blame!"

"Enough! I'm done talking about this. You blame him for what happened, but it was just as much my fault as his."

"Nonsense. The blame lies solely on him for her death. You know that, I know that. And at least you didn't go cheating on him afterward. The man deserved to die, if you ask me. Clearly whoever killed him felt the same way."

A diner was no place for this conversation. And I was in no emotional state to keep it civil.

"What about me? Did I deserve to lose my husband? Did the kids deserve to lose their father? No, because even if he made mistakes at the end, it doesn't erase all his goodness before that. I don't know how you can be okay with the fact that he's dead. Because I'm not."

She shook her head and fingered the collar of her blouse. She looked just as uncomfortable with this argument as I felt. "Maybe you should be okay with his death. It'd help you move on with your life. Find someone better, who doesn't destroy everything he touches. I just want to see you happy, that's all. And getting rid of that house of haunts could be part of that process."

And we were back to the house again. "I'm not saying I won't eventually sell. But unloading that house is the least of my worries. Right now, my focus is to find a job, find a place to live, and get my family back on its feet."

She huffed. The same huff she always did when the topic transitioned to me working. "What kind of job does a girl with no degree or career path find? Maybe working at a garden center or plant nursery again? I just don't want you ending up like me."

"What's wrong with how you ended up? You're a successful real estate agent, Mom. That's something to be proud of."

The corner of her lip curled up in a doubtful look. "But it wasn't my dream. I want better for you. You know, it's never too late to go to college and pursue your passion, which you could have done if that husband of yours hadn't pressured you to start having kids instead."

It was I who wanted kids right away; it was my choice, not Ben's. But Mom never missed a chance to guilt me about it, as if college were going out of business.

"Can we not speak ill of the dead, please? He was my husband, Mom, the father of my kids and your *son-in-law*."

"Well, he was no son to me, leaving you and the kids with no security. At least you should be getting your insurance payout soon, I hope. Have they found any leads yet on who killed him? It worries me that his killer is still out there, running free."

"No, they haven't given me any names yet." And I knew there would never be any. I wanted to tell her everything. She was my mother; it wasn't like she'd ever turn me in. I felt it in my bones. It was time to come clean. "I need to be honest with you. I've done something bad."

She dabbed her napkin to the corners of her mouth, tinting it with pink lipstick. My mother, so prim and proper, even amid a scandal.

"We've all done bad things, dear."

"No, this is *really* bad. I might end up arrested over it."

She dropped the napkin and aimed a sharp gaze at me. "What are you talking about? What could you have possibly done?"

I leaned across the table and whispered, "Ben wasn't murdered. He killed himself."

223

Mom gasped and her eyes lit like the neon lights stretching across the ceiling.

She shook her head. "No, not possible. What makes you think that?"

"A suicide note he wrote. It mentioned something only Ben knew about, and it was definitely his handwriting."

"Why didn't you tell the police that?"

"Because I would have lost the insurance money, so I staged it to look like a murder. It's only a matter of time before they figure that out and arrest me." I couldn't tell her about Lane's involvement. As far as she knew, it was only me . . . and it would stay that way, just in case the police questioned her. No way was I going to risk Lane's freedom.

"If the police haven't turned up yet, there's a chance they never will. It's been almost two months. And besides, knowing what kind of man Ben was, murder isn't out of the question."

Her conspiratorial tone made me question everything I thought I knew. What kind of man did she think Ben was? I wanted to ask her the question that had been bugging me more and more as the police investigation unraveled. It was ludicrous to even consider, but my mother had a way of getting what she wanted. She had always wanted Ben out of my life, then one day, *poof,* he was.

"Do you know something I don't?" I wondered aloud.

Glancing away, she avoided my eyes, her fingers frantically fidgeting now. Avoidance—wasn't that a sign of guilt? Then she sighed wearily. A weary, weighty sigh. What secret was she carrying?

"Mom, did you have anything to do with Ben's death?"

"Are you asking if I murdered your husband?" With a glare she dared me to answer. "Geez, Harper, what kind of person do you think I am?"

"No, I'm not saying you killed him. But did you say something to him that might have shaken him up? Something that might have made him want to *disappear*?"

Raising her palms in surrender, she pursed her lips. "Fine, I might have threatened him a bit when I suspected him of cheating, but that's all, dear. The man needed to know he wouldn't get away with hurting my baby girl. I would make sure of that."

Her explanation wasn't good enough. There was more. I could feel it tearing its way out into the open.

"Where were you that night, the night I found Ben? Because I know you weren't home with your grandkids the whole time. They told me you left them with the neighbor, Miss Eileen. Which I'm pissed about, by the way. Don't ever leave my kids with a stranger again."

"Eileen isn't a stranger. She's a dear friend. And I simply needed to run to the store for something. Don't make such a fuss about it. Eileen loved the company and the kids loved the candy. No harm, no foul."

Except I sensed a foulness that filled me with fear.

She waved the topic away, then waved the waitress over. The woman was Princess Di, ever decorous. "Let's not talk about such dark things. How about dessert?"

"I thought it was inappropriate to have dessert for breakfast."

She chuckled. "Well, you're already drinking sweet tea, so why not?"

"Mom." My urgency held a force that crushed her smile. "If

I end up in jail, promise me you'll help Lane take care of the kids. I'm terrified about what's going to happen."

"Honey." She grabbed my hands in a surprisingly fierce, wrinkled grip, as if her words weren't enough to hold me. "You've always been the strong one. Even more so than your brother. You will get through this, your kids will be fine, and no matter what happens"—she squeezed my hands for emphasis—"I will take care of my family. You have my word."

"Thank you, Mom." Despite all our differences, Mom knew how to fight, knew how to get back up, and she had taught me that same resilience. "Speaking of Lane, I wanted to talk to you about him."

"What's going on with your brother? Is everything okay?"

"Not really, no. You know how I suspected something wasn't right with Candace?"

Of course she did. We were of like mind when it came to *Candy*.

"Well, it turns out I was right. She's on the run from an ex-husband named Noah, and the baby she's carrying is his, not Lane's."

"No!" Mom puffed, covering her gaping mouth with her hand. Blue veins coursed between the jutting knuckles. "Are we living in some kind of soap opera? Where did you hear all this?"

"She told me."

"Does Lane know?"

"Yes, she told him and they had a big fight about it and he left. But this morning they were all lovey-dovey, so I guess he forgave her."

"But . . . why? Why would he want to yoke himself to a liar? Or to a child that isn't his?"

"I don't know, but there's more. She lied about her name too. She's using some alias that she found in an obituary. Honestly, Mom, I don't know what's true anymore. And I don't trust her not to hurt Lane. He's in love, and we all know how irrational love can be."

Love had caused me to stay with a husband who was cheating on me. It had caused my mother to suffer the continuous neglect of my father. Mom and I both knew just how treacherous love was. We sat across from each other, her brown eyes burrowing into me, flickering with a dark mischief that sparked the hairs on the back of my neck.

"I'll tell you what I know about love. Love is a dangerous weapon, and it robs us blind. It makes us weak, because when we're in love, we live in glass houses where everything feels open and shiny and clean. But all it takes is a tiny crack and the whole house shatters."

"So how do we crack Candace's glass house?" I asked.

"All you have to do is find the right stone and throw it."

Chapter 24

Candace

Life with you is a risky, exciting game where we're both winning.

I don't particularly like kids. As a child I never cradled baby dolls while pretending to be a mother. As a teenager I never took babysitting jobs. In fact, children downright annoyed me. My own, however—the arms and legs poking around inside of me like a tiny alien—I already adored. It's an unexplainable connection when you have something so precious growing inside you, a love so deep and pure it's beyond words. Harper's children, on the other hand, I found not just unlikable, but downright evil.

Thirty minutes into it I regretted my offer to watch Elise and Jackson while Harper joined Monica for brunch. I didn't let it show that the lack of an invitation hurt. I was Monica's daughter-in-law, after all. And let's not forget that my darling sister-in-law stabbed me in the back with her betrayal, so an apology meal would have been appreciated. The sharp prick of my humiliation was that I had actually thought Harper and I had made the shift into friendship. Sisterhood. Instead, I swallowed my embarrassment, smiled, and nodded as Harper left me instructions for handling lunch for her kids, reminding me three times before walking out the door that they weren't to vegetate in front of the television all afternoon.

Of course, these rules didn't apply to Harper, as I caught her children spending many an afternoon comatose in front of their various screens. Yet I was required to entertain the brats, unpaid, mind you, which had turned into the fiasco I was dealing with now.

I had suggested playing the game of *Life* to kill some time. I didn't expect it to turn into *Risk* or *Battleship*. The kids couldn't go a minute without fighting. A half-empty bowl of popcorn sat on the corner of the coffee table, with red Solo cups of Dr Pepper—which the kids also weren't allowed, but I had sworn them to secrecy—in front of each of us. Jackson and I sat on the sofa, and Elise knelt on the floor. The game board was open in the middle of the table. We had spent a solid forty-five minutes playing, and we hadn't even completed the career-choosing opening of the game! Every occupation card one of them complained about; every salary card the other contested. If ever anyone needed a hefty dose of birth control, these two kids incentivized it in the flesh.

"It's not fair that Jackson gets the higher salary when he's got a crappier job," Elise whined, tossing her salary card on the floor where she had dropped a mound of popcorn kernels.

"I hate this game," Jackson grumbled, throwing himself back against the sofa. "It's not like life is really like this."

I had a foreboding feeling we weren't playing a game anymore.

Shifting closer to him, I rested my hand on his bony shoulder in a wooden effort to comfort him. "True, life isn't as easy as spinning a wheel and finding bliss. But, much like this game, life can throw you some pretty fun curveballs."

"What do you mean?" Jackson asked.

"Well, like how I met your uncle Lane when I least expected it. And we fell in love so quickly and now I have a baby in my belly. Life is unpredictable."

"What about when life is always horrible? And scary?" Jackson met my eyes, something he never did. In them I watched a memory flicker to life, sparking, stiff gears turning. This was where Jackson and I understood each other. Death haunted us both. "Are you talking about losing your dad?"

"Yeah, and about when I killed my sister."

"Jackson!" Elise yelled, thrusting her fist into his rib cage. "You're not allowed to talk about that! That's a secret. We don't tell secrets, remember?"

Jackson shot Elise a glare, rubbing the spot where she had hit him. "But Aunt Candace is family. I thought family was safe."

"Not *her*," Elise whispered just loud enough.

"What's he talking about?" I wanted to know, and yet I didn't. Since the moment I met him, Jackson had struck me as an odd kid, a little too quiet, and mostly creepy. Lately, the weird factor had gotten worse, his black eyes rimmed in sleepless circles, his unwashed hair hanging over his ears. His pale skin gave him a ghostly appearance that reminded me of *Children of the Corn*.

"Nothing." Elise stood, hauling Jackson up off the couch with her. "Let's go outside. I need to talk to you"—she shot me a look—"in private."

Excluded from the family yet again. It was probably something I should get used to. My phone dinged with a text while I scooped up the popcorn bowl:

I'm coming for a visit. I think it's time we had a chat.

The text came from a blocked number. So I replied:

Who is this? How did you get this number?

No reply. I debated texting again, then thought better of it. Don't engage.

I cleaned up the board game and drained evidence of the soda while the kids shuffled outside. While they conspired—or whatever it was they were doing—I decided I'd get some swimming in. Heading upstairs to change into my swimsuit, I passed Harper's open bedroom door, stopped midstride, took a step back. A peek wouldn't hurt.

Everything was in obsessively neat order, not a single item of clothing out, as if the room were only intended to be photographed, never lived in. Bed wrinkle-free, pillows perfectly fluffed, floor swept clean, even her nightstand dusted and sparse, with only a lamp, a hardcover copy of *All You Ever Needed to Know About Plants*, and a small, leather-bound book centered on the table. A journal, perhaps? A glance inside could give me insight into what crazy rattled around in her brain.

I picked it up. Checked behind me. Clear. I heard the kids chatting outside below the open window. Just a quick look.

The scribble wasn't that of an adult but of a child. So it was Elise's journal. I wondered why Harper had it. I flipped through pages of idle musings from a little girl's perspective. The boys she liked. The bully she hated. The friend who betrayed her. Common themes that draped over all our lives from childhood into adulthood. I paused to read an entry about her brother, chuckling as she recounted how he'd farted in her face. Where was this version of playful Jackson? When had he turned so withdrawn and bleak? I continued leafing through the pages, pausing at a drawing of a black broken heart. Beneath it were the stains of teardrops, tiny circles of discolored paper dotting the page:

> I feel so empty inside. I hate my brother. He took my sister away, and Mom said she's in heaven, but I don't want her in heaven. I want her here, beside me, so I can give her belly kisses and braids and paint her nails. Then she can paint my nails, even though she never did it right. She always ended up painting my entire finger. I'd let her paint my whole hand if she would just come back. It's Jackson's fault. I saw him, but Mom says I don't know what I saw. I know what I saw. I saw him kill her, and I can never forgive him.

Jackson killed his sister? I dropped the journal on the bed, my stomach churning. Harper had secrets darker than mine, and that was quite an achievement. Either Lane was protecting them for her, or he didn't know. But this . . . this was a big one. Harper was raising a budding murderer.

I had to keep her and her deranged kids away. I had my own child to think of. What if Jackson hurt my baby? If there was one thing I carried with me from my childhood, it was a tactical method of survival. Kill or be killed. Everyone had a weakness, and now I knew Harper's and exactly how to destroy her.

Chapter 25

Candace

I could swim in your depths forever.
But forever isn't long enough.

Some days it felt like I watched my life happen around me. I paddled and paddled, but I couldn't break through. Monica loathed me; it was evident in the way she greeted me with a harsh, insincere *Candy.* Harper was jealous of me, as evidenced in her aloof demeanor toward me. Lane was her possession, and God forbid anyone threaten that. I saw the hate in the way she examined me, as if she were inspecting a bug squished between her fingers, but hate suited me. It inspired me to win. As for Lane, well, he was the only good thing going in my life, but he was hiding something big. A secret for his sister. For himself, maybe. Whatever had happened, whatever mysteries he harbored, he'd locked them up tight.

When I mentioned offhandedly in bed the night before about my conversation with the kids, he was quick to slam the door on it.

Why would Jackson say that he killed his sister? What was he talking about? I had asked.

The worried look he gave me, guilt mingled with alarm, got filed in a place I couldn't access.

Jackson's been . . . obsessed with death since his father passed, he had tried to explain. *He makes things up. It's become a problem. He hasn't been dealing well.* But I noted the lies between the truths.

Why isn't he in therapy? He should be seeing a doctor if it's that bad. You should have heard what he said . . . and how he said it.

It's not our place to judge. The kid has been through a lot. Just cut them some slack, okay? And don't read into it.

How could I not? The kid practically admitted to murder.

He's not acting normal, Lane. He needs help.

Can you please let it go?

Slam! The door had become my enemy, locked and unbreakable. I had dropped the conversation then, not for me but for Lane. I didn't want to burn our love into ashes by lighting a fire I couldn't put out. But I worried it was too late. We had sex that night, but it was dispassionate and friendly, like fuck buddies, not lovers. He couldn't cross the chasm that had come between us. So I decided, after flopping onto my side of the bed, Lane curled up with his back to me, that to fix our relationship I would need to start by fixing myself.

Me time self-care was the perfect place to begin.

A nine o'clock prenatal massage followed by a hair appointment was just what I needed. Jet-lagged from drama, a makeover could cure just about any ailment. Harper would scoff at the $150 price tag of my Swedish massage and the $120 haircut on Lane's dime, but fixing the damage I had done to it was worth every penny. I admit, chopping it off in a panicked act of self-loathing wasn't the best decision. But the new short, layered style was pretty cute, if I did say so myself. I had never had it chin-length before, but I could get used to it. If I could get used to the sister-in-law from hell, I could get used to anything.

Bella Trio Salon was a riot of color and chitchat. A splash of burgundy on one wall. A Tuscan yellow on another. A cucumber water station in one corner, and beyond the entrance a marbled staircase leading to a second story where the masseuses made their magic. With hair dryers blowing, brushes beautifying, and dye setting, you could walk in as one person and walk out as another.

Standing behind me, dusting the clippings from my shoulder, was Gisele, her arms rattling with jewelry and her lips puckered in entitlement. From her designer boots to her flawless makeup, I would have admired her if I didn't hate her. Even her name was designer—Gisele. She looked like the type of woman who stole husbands. A football helmet of platinum hair and clothes tight like a second skin, she was about six inches short of the stereotypical home-wrecker. But men didn't care how tall she was. They only cared where she came up to on her knees.

Gisele handed me a mirror, along with some advice. Her southern accent was as potent as her Versace perfume. "Hon, women like us have to be careful these days. Look at the madness in the news! You just don't know what kind of crazy people are out there."

I didn't know what *women like us* entailed, or what it had to do with the news she was referring to, but the advice was sound. We *did* need to be careful. And there was a whole lotta crazy out there.

Hanging on the wall in the corner was a huge television, the sound muted, but closed captioning ran across the bottom of the screen. A Deaf hairdresser two chairs down signed to Gisele:

Isn't that the same woman who was interviewed by the police a couple days ago?

I still remembered the sign language my mother had taught me after she lost hearing in one ear during a battle with meningitis. My insecure father had forbidden us from signing in front of him, but my mother and I took advantage of any chance we got to use it when he wasn't around. It was our secret language.

Gisele signed back, her wrists jangling and my surprise piqued. She didn't look like the . . . bilingual type. Especially not one well versed in American Sign Language.

I think you're right. That's her.

The Deaf woman continued, her hands animated:

They think she was murdered in her home.

Murdered? I recognized that sign right away and looked up to catch the tail end of the news brief:

"Police are investigating after Michelle Hudson, neighbor

of victim Benjamin Paris, whose murder case is still ongoing, was found dead in her home late last night," the closed caption read. "When a local resident of the quiet neighborhood came to check in on Hudson, she found the front door unlocked and called 911. Responding emergency workers pronounced Hudson dead at the scene. Investigators have classified the death as suspicious, given Ms. Hudson was a witness in the Paris murder. Police ask that if anyone has any information that might help in the investigation to please come forward."

Scary! So much evil people are capable of, the Deaf stylist signed. *I hope they catch whoever did it soon.*

Gisele replied, *I know. I hope they catch him soon too.*

I wondered if Harper had seen the news. Or if the investigating detective on Ben's case would notify her. It was a strange turn of events. And a little too coincidental that the only witness in her husband's murder was now dead.

After generously tipping Gisele for proving my stereotype about her wrong, I waved goodbye and headed outside, running my fingers through new, short black layers tipped in pink. The bob was sassy, like me. The sun dappled my face, and my flip-flops smacked the concrete sidewalk. At the end of the plaza was a gluten-free, soy-free, taste-free bakery, so I figured I'd pick up a muffin for Harper and then hit the doughnut shop to grab a cronut for myself. I wasn't done trying to make amends with Harper, no matter how much I wanted to give up. And the baby insisted on sugar and starch, so sugar and starch I would give her.

As my sandals *smack-smack*ed along the sidewalk, a movement in my peripheral stopped me midstride. I glanced behind me, sensing eyes watching. Observing. Idling in the parking lot was a black car, sitting in the middle of the road like it was waiting for someone. I couldn't tell the make or model; I was no automotive aficionado. My knowledge of cars was as basic as my knowledge of tools: black car, white truck, hammer, unbolt-thingy. The only screwdriver I was familiar with was one I could drink.

By the time I reached the no-taste bakery, the car had drifted forward along with me, but the reflection of sunlight on the window cast a glare I couldn't see through. I thought I caught a glimpse of aviator sunglasses through the glass, but I couldn't be sure. First, the sighting at the mall. Now, a vehicle tailing me. All signs pointed to a Harrison Ford action movie.

It wasn't until after I slipped into the bakery, bells on the door jingling as it slammed shut, that the car slowly rolled past. The driver turned his head toward me, I could see that much, but his face was hidden beneath the sunglasses. I was slammed with a sudden sense of familiarity as the incident at the mall revisited me.

Noah. He must have found me.

I didn't want a cronut anymore. I wanted to survive. Survival was a battle, one I knew how to fight, because I had been training since the day I left home. I wasn't afraid of Noah anymore; I was afraid of what he brought out of me.

Chapter 26

Harper

"What do you mean there's another name on my husband's life insurance policy?"

My hand was giving my phone a death grip. Nothing the insurance agent said made sense. I had called to get an update on the status of the funds, just in case they were able to start processing the check. It was wishful thinking, I know, but worth a call. I didn't expect to find out that I was the recipient of only half of Ben's policy.

"There are two benefactors listed for the policy, ma'am." I could tell that the girl on the other end of the line was losing her patience with me, but I was losing my patience with her as well. None of this made sense.

"Who is the other benefactor? One of my children?"

"I'm sorry, but I'm not at liberty to say."

I didn't know why this hadn't come up before. It was infuriating! Not only did the life insurance company make me chase it down for my entitled payout, but then it wouldn't release the information on who was on the policy.

"Please, I've just lost my husband a year after we lost a child and I'm only trying to get our finances in order. Can you just bend the rules this one time and tell me which of my children is on the policy so that I can start trying to get my family taken care of?"

The lady inhaled in my ear, and her voice grew soft with sympathy. "I'm so sorry for your losses. But my hands are tied."

There had to be a way to get this woman talking. All I wanted to know was whom my husband was giving half *my* money to—our kids' money, their future.

Could it be the same person Ben had created a bank account for? I couldn't pull the name from my memory; it was a strange name. Not one I'd ever heard before. I had written it down somewhere. In my purse, maybe?

"One second," I told the agent, stalling while I rummaged through my purse contents. The crinkle of an envelope told me I'd found what I was looking for. I reread the name I had scribbled on my to-do list during my chat with Detective Meltzer: *Medea Kent*.

"Is the other beneficiary Medea Kent?"

"That's correct, ma'am."

Medea Kent. Medea Kent. Her name kept popping up everywhere like a bad case of whack-a-mole. Who the hell was Medea Kent? And why was she listed on Ben's policy? God help me, was this his mistress? Did he have the balls to leave his lover half the life insurance policy that belonged to me and his kids? We were his *family,* for crying out loud! Unable to wrap my brain around what all of this meant, I tried to slow my thoughts.

Smell a flower, blow out a candle. But it didn't work. I was flooded with a mix of confusion and anger and sadness. How could Ben have done this to me, betraying me all over again from beyond the grave? I couldn't handle another secret; I was sure this one would break my back.

"Are you still there, ma'am?" the lady asked hesitantly, pulling me out of my hysteria.

I wrote *Who is Medea Kent?* on the paper where I had been jotting down notes from my call with the insurance agent.

"Oh, um, yeah. Can I also verify that the address you have on file is correct? We just recently moved so I wanted to check on that."

I heard her fingers tapping a keyboard, then a minute later she spoke. "Yes, ma'am. I have Summer Lane listed as your primary mailing address."

Summer Lane? Why did that sound familiar? Opening the envelope, inside was the scrap of paper with the address *3 Summer Ln* written in Ben's print.

"Yep, that's the right address."

Beneath Medea's name I wrote *3 Summer Lane?* Closing my eyes, I found my breath again. My thoughts stopped whirring just long enough to catch a thought. I needed to know who this Medea was, why my husband had decided to leave her a million and a half dollars. Certainly the sex couldn't have been worth that much.

After a weak thank-you for all her help, I hung up and cried.

"Damn it!" I slammed my cell phone down on the kitchen

counter, realizing I'd cracked my screen after the fact. I couldn't take another lie, and now my cell phone had a splinter running up the corner.

"How could you?" I screamed, waiting for an answer from Ben's ghost that would never come. With fists clenched, my wail grew into a solid wall of sound. I yelled until I ran out of voice.

While I threw my grown-up-sized fit, Lane snuck up behind me and pulled me into a bear hug. Part of me wanted to shrug him off, punch him in the gut because I just wanted to hit something, but I knew I needed a hug more than a fistfight.

"Hey, you okay?" he asked.

"Eff my life!"

"*Eff my life*, huh? You must be pretty pissed to start talking teenager."

I laughed as I cried, because Lane had a way of doing that to me. He could turn sobs into snorts. It was his gift.

"What's going on, Harp? If you're about to have a mental breakdown, no one would blame you. You've been through a lot." He pulled out a barstool and sat beside me.

"It's everything, Lane. I just found out Ben's mistress is listed on his life insurance policy for half of it. A million and a half dollars, Lane! I mean, why? What did she ever do for him other than a few months of screwing? I gave him my heart, my entire life, his children, his home . . . and that's what he leaves me with? A final act of betrayal—seeing her name listed next to mine as if we're equals! I don't understand, Lane."

I wept in Lane's arms as he held me, my sobs soaking into his shirt. "It's okay."

It didn't feel okay. Not even on the same continent as okay.

When I found my voice again, I looked up at him through the tears. "Everything is falling apart. And I got a call from Detective Meltzer, who wants me to come down to the station to discuss some 'recent developments,' which I'm sure is code for an arrest warrant."

"Pornstache called you? What exactly did he say?"

"He told me that Michelle Hudson was found dead in her home. Murdered."

Lane's eyes widened with shock. "Murdered? How?"

"I don't know. He won't tell me, but I'm starting to wonder if Ben didn't kill himself after all. Do you think someone killed him and staged it as a suicide—y'know, before we restaged it as a murder?"

"You want me to be honest, Harp?"

I sensed our conversation was taking a deeply personal turn. "Always."

He dropped his gaze to the marbled countertop, then sighed. "Ben wasn't the man you thought he was. I know you know this, but it was worse than you can imagine. He hurt people, people who trusted him. Was it bad enough to get him killed? It's possible. I've been wondering that since the night you called to tell me he had died."

I had no idea what Lane was talking about, and that scared me terribly. "What kinds of things did he do? Am I in danger? And the kids?"

"No, nothing like that, Harp. I just think the best thing for you, for the kids, would be to get as far away from all of this crap as you can. Forget the life insurance money, sell the house, and start over somewhere new."

"You're starting to sound like Mom."

Lane glanced up at me with an urgency. "Maybe Mom could go with you. She's always wanted to retire in the Midwest with all that open space. It'd be a perfect place to raise kids."

I shook my head. "Why the sudden push to run away? You're talking nonsense." Unless it wasn't nonsense. Unless Lane knew something I didn't. Was Mom connected to Ben's death?

He didn't answer at first. Then the words came softly. "Because I'm afraid if you don't leave, something bad is going to happen. I just want you safe."

What if *safe* wasn't possible? That thought plagued me daily. "It's not like I can leave until the investigation is over. I'm scared, Lane. First Ben's dead. Now Michelle. And after the baby's death last year . . . what if the cops start thinking I'm some serial killer or something?"

"Hey, take a breath. It's okay. You're innocent, which means they can't prove you've done anything. And Kira's death was already ruled an accident; there's nothing they can pin on you. The only thing you could possibly get in trouble for is tampering with evidence, which would probably be a slap on the wrist. You're not a killer. You're a scared widow who lost her child last year, then did something stupid in a moment of panic when you found your husband dead. Who would ever want to convict you after all you've suffered?"

I may have appeared blameless on paper, but I didn't feel innocent. "The only good thing about Michelle's death is that she won't be talking anymore."

A curl of horror lifted Lane's lip. "Did you really just say that? Who *are* you? I thought you liked that lady. You sound like you're glad she's dead."

"I'm not trying to be callous, Lane, but she could have put me in jail. I'm not happy she's dead . . . but it does kind of relieve the burden a little."

"So you'd rather she die than you go to jail?" His face was disappointment marred with judgment.

Two months ago, Lane was my salvation. Now he was my damnation.

"Please don't put words in my mouth. I'm not saying that. I'm already dealing with enough. I don't need you adding more guilt to the circus of emotions I'm already feeling."

The problem with evil was that it was sticky. It left a residue that you spent every waking moment trying to wipe off. But you couldn't. It stained your soul. And over time it spread, making you ugly to the point where you didn't recognize where you ended and the evil began.

Lane shifted away, creating a distance I felt growing.

"I'm sorry," I apologized. "I don't know what's going on inside me anymore . . . if it's grief, or fear of getting caught, or what. I just know I feel utterly helpless and hopeless."

"I understand"—I must have pulled him back in, because he squeezed my shoulder affectionately—"but you have to trust that everything will work out. Just try not to react. That's when people make mistakes."

"Yeah, I've already filled my quota of them."

Lane picked up the paper I had written notes on from my call with the insurance agent, along with Medea's address. "What's this?"

I tapped my pen against the granite. "Basically, the reasons why they're not paying me yet. And Ben's mistress's name and address."

"Yikes."

He slid the piece of paper back toward me:

Autopsy still in progress; needs to be completed
Need death certificate to get payout
No suicide death benefit; murder still has to be determined
Who is Medea Kent?
3 Summer Lane?

Until the autopsy was completed and cleared as a murder, I couldn't get a death certificate. Without a death certificate, I couldn't begin the claims process. Detective Meltzer told me it could take up to twelve weeks just to get started on the autopsy, then it would be another sixty days after I had the death certificate before the payment processed. In total, at least five months would pass before I'd see a payment. Five months of struggling to pay my mortgage, the astronomical attorney fees, plus rent and groceries and gasoline and utilities and my cell phone plan. Five months of hell, and that was the best-case scenario.

"What does all this mean?" Lane prodded for an explanation.

"It means the murder investigation is still under way, so I have no idea when—or if—I'm going to see a dime. And I can't afford to ask my attorney to intercede, since I'm broke. I can't believe they're doing this! I'm a grieving widow unable to pay my bills until they pay me what I'm entitled to. Ben has been paying into it for years, and they're going to dare dispute my payout until a killer is found? Because we both know, Lane, that no killer will ever be found. And if they can't find a killer, they might not rule it as a homicide. If suicide is determined, that means no money—not now, not ever."

"Don't worry about the money. I'll cover you until you're on your feet. I won't leave you hanging."

Lane never left me hanging, that was the problem. He had helped me commit a crime. There was no coming back from that. So many memories together, but the night of Ben's death alone defined us. That one decision followed us. And it would track us through the remainder of our years, scuffling behind us day by day as we tried to pretend it away with birthday parties, and holidays, and family dinners. But it would always be watching us, always haunting us, always binding us.

"I'll go down to the police station with you and we can talk to Pornstache together. If Michelle had identified you, don't you think they would have hauled you in already? It's an elderly woman with failing vision peering into pitch-black. How accurate could she have been?"

"Accurate enough that someone killed her. I spoke to her."

"You *what*? I told you not to get involved!"

"Well, I had to know what she saw. And she saw me, Lane. Though she hadn't mentioned me by name specifically to the cops yet. She merely told them she'd seen two people breaking into the house. She told me she suspected it was me after she read about the life insurance policy online. All this time she was convinced I had killed my husband."

Lane didn't reply at first, and I wondered momentarily if he thought *I* had killed Michelle to shut her up.

"I didn't kill her, if that's what you're thinking." I couldn't believe we were having this conversation.

"I know you didn't, Harp. Regardless, you can't act guilty.

Go to the station like an innocent person would do. And it wouldn't hurt to pressure the police to finish the autopsy since you'd like Ben's body released so you can have a proper burial."

I shrugged in agreement. He was right. Lane always was. I exhaled the tension gnawing into my shoulders and lower back. It sounded like the only logical thing a blameless person would do. I began to write *Request Ben's bod—* when the pen ran out of ink. After a futile scribble in the corner of the paper, Lane rooted around the junk drawer, then handed me another pen.

"Here, try this one."

Accepting the pen, I noticed the writing on it: *The Durham Hotel. A chic boutique hotel with a midcentury modern vibe.*

"Where'd you get this?" I asked coolly.

"No idea. It was in the drawer."

"Have you been here"—I held up the pen—"to this hotel?"

He read the name, then shook his head. "No. I probably just picked it up somewhere."

It couldn't be a coincidence that Lane had a pen from the very same place Ben spent the last night of his life before coming home and killing himself. The only other person who knew where I was going that night was my mother. Had she told Lane? Had she followed me there after dropping the children off with Eileen?

I couldn't think about this now. I had a home-wrecking whore to track down and a detective to deceive.

"So what's the plan for how to deal with Detective Meltzer?" I asked. I imagined the two of us storming into the Durham Police Station, where Detective Meltzer undoubtedly ate lox and bagels, crumbs clinging to his mustache, while watching Adam Sandler movies on his iPhone.

"I'll make him an offer he can't refuse," Lane said huskily, then narrowed his eyes and flicked his hand under his chin with Marlon Brando flair. I laughed, because after all these years he still didn't know it was Al Pacino who said the line in *The Godfather,* and there was no chin-flicking flair when he said it.

"You are going to misquote that line until you die, aren't you?"

"Yep," he said with a wink.

As I headed out the door, my phone rang with my mom's Glamour Shots–esque image flashing across my cracked screen.

"Hey, Mom."

"Hi, Harper." A din of background voices nearly drowned her out. "I'm down at the police station again."

"I thought they already talked to you about Ben?"

A short pause filled with noise. "It's not about Ben. I'm being questioned about the murder of Michelle Hudson, and I need your help."

Chapter 27

Harper

Some days I went hours before I remembered that I was a widow. Then it would come in a flash, *Ben is dead,* but there was his nose on Elise, there were his lips on Jackson. Other days, like today, it was the first thought that awakened me and the last thought that followed me into my dreams.

The moon smiled down on me, its crescent wide like the Cheshire cat's. I wasn't smiling back tonight. I had just spent the last three hours at the police station while Detective Meltzer pelted my mother with questions about her whereabouts the night of Ben's death, the day of Michelle's murder, what her relationship with Ben was like. I watched her fumble over her lies, saying that she had been watching her grandkids all evening. The kids had been given a tour of the police station and a cruiser by a friendly officer who felt bad for them when he saw them slumped in the corner of the waiting room amid two prostitutes arguing over which street corner belonged to whom. For the first hour, Elise and Jackson whined about going home. For the next two hours, they followed the young officer, oohing and ahhing, asking a bajillion questions until Elise decidedly told me she wanted to be a cop someday. A touch of irony, since her mother was a criminal.

I had graciously thanked that officer for entertaining my kids as I herded them out the door. At least they hadn't been in the interrogation room to deny my mother's statement.

That's when the big news came out—during the interrogation—and that's when I saw just how corrupt my husband had been. Losing his mother-in-law's life savings in a bad investment. Then taking a large chunk of Lane's savings too. Ruining his own *family*! No wonder my mother had hated him. It was a wonder Lane didn't. Now my conversation with Lane made sense; I didn't know Ben at all, a man capable of stealing from the people who loved him, from the people he was supposed to love back.

As the details were explained to me, Ben sold it as a promissory note investment, where Mom and Lane—and a handful of others whose names weren't disclosed to me—could buy back some of the debt to save Ben's investment company. Except it wasn't Ben's company per se; sure, he had helped start it with the CEO, Randolph Whitman, but he had no control over it or ownership. He simply didn't want to have to start over, so he figured saving a sinking ship might work. It didn't. Especially not when Randy ran off with all the money. Ben died the same night that Randy fled, gone in the wind. And now I was more confused than ever.

After taking the kids home and putting them to bed, I needed to clear my head. So many worries rattled around up there in my skull. Only one place really gave me clarity—beneath the weeping willow tree in my former backyard.

In one hand I held the keys to my Hendricks Way house. In the other hand I held the leather diary containing my daughter's darkness. What I had read disturbed me greatly. What eleven-year-old wrote such graphic depictions of blood and death? Enfolded between pages of friend drama and school pressures I discovered a horrifying account of a little boy named Frankie—I assumed he was named after the doll that they had made such a fuss about—murdered by his reflection. The reflection kept luring the little boy with gifts, but with every gift the boy accepted, he lost a bit of himself. First it was not eating, then it was seeing things. It sounded awfully reminiscent of Jackson. Finally, at the end of the story, the little boy disappeared into the mirror and became the reflection, stuck behind glass with no escape.

Elise had titled it "The Boy in the Mirror," as if it were just a story, an Aesop's fable, except evil and unhinged, like R. L. Stine on steroids. I had read the story again and again, hoping to uncover some deeper meaning within the images of darkness folding over each other. All I found was a child in great need of hugs and therapy. Just like Jackson.

I stood in the backyard of the house I had called home for years, now a vault holding memories and secrets. The air was unseasonably crisp for a late May evening, which felt good after the day's pitiless heat. My skin yearned for the cold to clear my head, to sharpen my focus. I needed single-mindedness now more than ever as the police were beginning to ask questions I couldn't answer. Well, perhaps *couldn't* wasn't the right word. *Shouldn't.*

Michelle Hudson, the only witness in my husband's murder case, was dead. Did I know anything about that?

Of course not, I'd insisted. *How tragic! She was such a nice old lady.*

Unfortunately—yet fortunately for me—she hadn't gotten a good look at the two—yes, two!—intruders who had broken into my house the night of Ben's death. But the police now had a lead—and it most certainly was connected with Michelle Hudson's death—and they were looking for two suspects.

I hope this can get us answers finally, I exclaimed.

The evidence they had found at Michelle Hudson's house would tell everything soon.

Oh good!

Oh crap.

Evidence? What evidence? It was only a matter of time before the lies came undone. The truth had a way of doing that. If you just kept pulling on the end of the string, eventually the whole knotted ball unraveled. I could sense the time for goodbyes approaching, which brought me here. Home.

Sliding the key into the keyhole, I unlocked the back door and headed inside, inhaling the musty scent of unlived-in space. I paused at the antique nineteenth-century Victorian mirror, a gorgeous piece in an elegant oak frame with applique carved vines and flowers, which I had left hanging in the hallway as it was too heavy to move. The renters arriving next week needed mirrors too, didn't they?

In the gray I looked younger than my thirty-eight years. I didn't mind the threads of white hair beginning to pop up amid the red. Or even my thin dash of chaste lips. I'd never considered myself a great beauty, but I had always been happy with who I was. You can forgive a homely face when you have a good heart. But I had lost that, the thing that truly mattered. I could no longer look into my own eyes, they were two black holes that sucked in all light, all hope.

It was strange how death took only a moment, but it changed everything forever.

I crept into the living room, careful not to disturb the dust. I didn't want to wake the ghosts that lived here. I was surprised to see the sofa Ben had died on still here. I had insisted that the cleaning company dispose of it; who would want to keep such a deathbed? But for whatever reason, they had cleaned it and left it, along with the harsh recall of seeing Ben's dead body sprawled out across it. I sat in the place Ben had taken his last breath, tracing the bronze nailhead accents, my vision drifting back in time. A pool of blood flowered at my feet, rolling across the wood, seeping into the cracks between the boards. A swell of nausea churned in my stomach, and I jumped up and ran to the powder room.

Splashing water on my face helped abate the stomach sickness, but not the heart sickness. I stepped into the hallway, remembering all the details Ben and I had put into our Hendricks Way home. I lived through art, decorating each room with passion and pain. The burgundy living room painted after I lost my baby so that my house bled along with my heart. Bone-white furniture I'd bought when I vowed to start fresh and move forward, pure like snow. The memories were doomed to tarnish, but I would hold on to them as long as I could.

I headed upstairs for one last look. The bedroom was as I'd left it, our California king four-poster bedframe against the far wall. Curling up on the naked mattress, I inhaled the lingering scent of Ben's cells. It wasn't the cool patch of Egyptian cotton we had slept on, but he was still here. I could feel him.

Pulling my purse closer, I rummaged inside for the note Ben had left me, his last words. I hadn't told Lane that I'd kept it. I was supposed to have destroyed it, the only tangible evidence of his suicide that existed. But I couldn't part with it. It was all that was left of my husband, his last message to me. For some reason probably rooted in self-loathing, I wanted the reminder of what I had caused him to do. The guilt felt deserved, and it was mine to keep.

I skimmed the letter, then closed my eyes, allowing the exhaustion to suck me in. And as the edges dulled to black, I thought of that terrible night, the night Ben died and I was forced to live. The details of what I had seen, the truth I had discovered, clawed their way out . . . loosening the memory free, then rising . . .

* * *

The retirement neighborhood that Mom lived in was the quintessential place to grow old. Modest one-story brick homes, yard maintenance provided. With a community pool—No Kids Allowed!—a fitness center, and even a cute general store, it was more a village than a neighborhood.

Although Grandma loved visits with the kids, her neighbors, not so much. Any disruption to the quiet unsettled their fragile nerves. I glared at Elise and Jackson, both wandering off the front stoop of my mother's house, and shot a warning.

"*No fighting, you two. Grandma is looking forward to your sleepover, so you best behave. Do you promise you'll be respectful and listen to her?*" *Threats didn't mean much when they came from Grandma, but they knew I always meant business.*

"*We promise,*" *Elise moaned.* "*You've said this, like, a hundred times already.*"

I shifted my eyes to Jackson. "*And you?*"

"*Fine,*" *he said, drawing the i out with annoyance.*

Mom's footsteps shuffled toward the door after the first knock, her cheery voice calling, "*Coming!*"

When she answered wearing a sweatshirt and jeans, I nearly choked on my shock. Mom never wore casual comfort; Mom was glitz and glamour. As a real estate agent she was driven by appearances—look like success and you'll attract success, she had always told me.

"*Get in here and give your grandma a hug!*" *she exclaimed, dragging the kids in and engulfing them in her arms.*

"*I appreciate this, Mom. I'll be back in the morning after breakfast to pick them up.*" *I planted a quick kiss on Elise's and Jackson's heads, then turned to the door.*

"*You won't stay for a bit? I just put the kettle on for tea.*"

"*I'm sorry, but I've gotta run. I'll check in later, though.*"

She grabbed my arm with a shaky but firm grip. "*Is tonight date night? What's on the agenda?*" *she asked with a raised eyebrow, then sent the kids off to the kitchen for homemade chocolate chip cookies.* "*Go help yourselves to cookies while your mommy and I chat!*"

She always spoke with such enthusiasm to the kids, even over the simplest things.

A moment later the din of Elise and Jackson fighting over the remote, followed by the headache-inducing sound effects of cartoons, filled the small house.

"So?" Mom probed in the sweet-and-sour way she always used to bait me for information. "Do you have a special night planned for Ben?"

"You could say that." Or I could say the truth, which was that Ben had a special night planned, but not with me. But I had a surprise of my own for him.

"No need to lie to your mother." She possessed the unique ability to see through me. I spent my adolescence trying to mask my tells, but she had maternal X-ray vision. "You can be honest with me. I know you're"—she cupped her mouth and lowered her voice to a whisper—"having marriage troubles."

"Mom, we're fine. We just need to figure some things out."

"Like how to keep his dick faithful?"

"Mom! The kids!"

She waved off my protest. "Oh, they can't hear anything over the racket of that television. I just wish you'd leave that man once and for all. I know what he's doing behind your back. Lord knows after being married to your father I can sense such things, and you deserve better."

"I don't want better. I want Ben. And we're going to work things out. You'll see."

Mom's lip curled down in a scowl. "Whatever you say, dear. Tell Ben I said hi. Or go to hell. Whichever suits you."

"Mom—"

"Don't defend him. I know what you're doing, and you better not cut him any slack, Harper. That cheating bastard doesn't deserve it. Neither does the home-wrecker he's sleeping with."

I heaved a sigh. "What makes you so sure he's cheating?"

Glancing at the beige carpet, she fluffed her hair, fiddled with her necklace, anything to avoid looking at me. "I wanted to tell you, honey, but I didn't want to break your heart. A couple weeks ago I saw him . . . with a blond tramp. I spotted them out at lunch when I was with a client."

"What? How could you not tell me?"

Mom rolled her eyes. "I didn't want to say anything until I knew for certain. It was lunch and it could have been his secretary, for all I knew. Why cause drama if there wasn't any? But I think all of these late nights 'working'"—she air-quoted the word—"is proof enough of what he's doing. I would know. Your father did it to me too."

I sniffled back the pain threatening to leak from my eyes.

"And what if it's true, Mom? I don't want to lose him. I've already lost so much. I don't know what to do."

Mom frowned at me, anger in the stern clench of her jaw. "I'll tell you what you should do. You show that man no mercy."

Chapter 28

Candace

Does it scare you that I watch you when you sleep?
Does it frighten you that I inhale you when you're close?
Sometimes it terrifies me how intensely I feel about you.

There are three rules to successful stalking. One: Stay out of sight. Two: Be discreet. Three: Don't drive a car that your stalkee would recognize. Apparently Noah hadn't read the handbook, because he was breaking all three rules. But I would not be shaken by a man who didn't even know how to properly stalk me.

I had just finished my afternoon laps in the pool, minus a few due to pregnancy fatigue, and had thrown on my cover-up and sandals. The mailman had just made his rounds, and I couldn't wait to open the package of custom baby onesies I had ordered online. Harper called them extravagant, I called them adorable.

The path along the side of the house led to the driveway, where the mailman had left the package. I picked it up and headed toward the mailbox to grab the rest of the mail. Across the street an old man sat on his John Deere riding mower, zipping up and down his lawn wearing nothing but jeans, a cowboy hat, and his wrinkled skin for a shirt. Two doors down a Chihuahua yipped frantically at a car parked in front of the house. Something felt familiar about the car. A black sedan, strikingly similar to the one from the hair salon. Although it faced away from me, I could make out a silhouette in the front seat.

How blatantly suspicious.

I had just about enough of this crap, and I was fuming for a confrontation. Noah's passive-aggressive threats were no match for the new me. The stalking, the text, now showing up at my house! Hell no. I had endured his fists, his anger, his fake apologies for years. No more! Since leaving him, I had found the fight within me, and I was finally ready to use it.

Tugging my cover-up down to hide my bikinied rear end, I marched across the street toward the car, my sandals angrily flapping against the concrete. The suburban cowboy watched me storm past his freshly mown lawn and lustily leered— *yuck*—and the dog ran to the corner of its yard nearest to me, still yipping, but stopped at the edge of the grass, as if held back by an invisible fence.

The sideview mirror was angled away from the driver's face, and the sunlight streaking across his window sliced him into fragmented shadows. By the time I reached the bumper I was jogging, my sandals nearly sliding off my feet with each step as I clung to the mail with both hands. When I closed in on the back door of the car, he took off, his tires squealing, leaving a black patch of tread in their wake. The mail dropped to the sidewalk as I flipped him off with both hands.

"Coward!" I yelled at his blinking taillights as he took the turn off my street, blowing through the stop sign with barely a pause.

I stomped all the way back to the house, ready to call Noah to give him a piece of my mind. I wondered if he had changed his phone number, considering the text I received came from a blocked number. It wouldn't matter; I still had his parents' digits memorized. When I blew into the living room, slamming the front door behind me, a faint whimper echoed from the dining room. I peeked in and found Harper crying at the dining room table, a piece of paper soaked in tears beneath her elbows and a bottle of wine with only a mouthful left swirling around the bottom. No wineglass? This was *bad*. It was hard to stay angry at a sobbing woman.

"Hey, you okay?" I asked, grabbing a box of tissues from the pantry and pulling out a chair beside her.

She shook her head. I passed her the tissues. She pulled out two.

"What's going on? You're not pregnant too, are you? Because I've never cried more in my life." I grinned weakly and she chuckled drunkenly. We were quite a pair of emotional messes.

"Yeah, pregnancy hormones are a bitch." She blew her nose and glanced over at me, her eyes rimmed in drippy mascara. "But no, I'm not pregnant. I'm just having a hard day. Nix that—a hard week."

"Is this about your mom's visit with the cops last night?" I knew the feeling well, wondering if my mom was okay. My entire childhood was spent worrying about my mother.

"Yes, partly that, and this." She turned her gaze to something in her hand. A pen. She examined it, then set it down. "The stupid pen."

"Please tell me you're not crying because you ran out of ink."

"It's not that. I'm just . . . dealing with a lot of memories lately. And this pen brought them all up . . . again."

I picked up the pen, flipping it over so I could read the print.

"The Durham Hotel. Was that a special place for you and Ben?"

She sniggered, a harsh, bitter sound. "No, it wasn't a special place for me, but it was for Ben."

"What do you mean?"

She didn't speak, not at first. Then the sounds formed words and the words formed sentences as the story poured from her lips. "It was at this hotel where I . . . I found . . . him . . . Where I found out for sure that Ben was cheating on me. I saw him there with another woman. It shook my world."

"Oh no." I rested my hand on her shoulder, almost afraid to touch her through her grief.

We sat in silence for a long time, so long I shifted to get up, figuring the conversation was over. She needed time alone. Then she spoke, her story forcing me back into my seat.

"It started with a strange credit card charge from this hotel. I didn't even usually check the credit card statements, but that particular day I did. So I called, thinking it was a mistake. We hadn't been to a hotel in ages, and never that one. When they told me that it was accurate—they even line listed the extra room charges for me—I thought maybe the credit card had been stolen. Never in a million years did I think my husband would cheat on me. Not after everything I'd been through, all we'd been through together. So I activated alerts on my credit card in case it was used again. Then one day I got a notification text that the card had been charged. Same hotel."

Harper raised the pen to eye level, fixated on it.

"I needed to know for sure, so I went there. I had to see for myself. There I was, standing at the front desk asking the check-in lady what the person who used the card looked like, when she pointed him out. Across the room in the lounge stood my husband, arm in arm with another woman. A young blond home-wrecker with a tight body. How cliché is *that*? Well, I couldn't face him, not like that, so I ran outside and down the sidewalk. I ran and ran and ran until I couldn't breathe. I thought I was going to die that day. Part of me wishes I would have. That was the last time I saw my husband alive."

"Oh my goodness, Harper. I'm so sorry. I can't even imagine . . ." And yet I could.

"It's unimaginable." She lifted the wine bottle to her mouth and emptied the remnants in one long gulp. "To discover the man you love with all your heart has betrayed you in the worst possible way. It's . . . worse than death. I thought I'd been through the worst after losing a child. Well, I was mistaken. That day I met parts of myself I never knew existed, and I could only feel darkness inside of me. Now I have no idea who I am anymore. I lost the best parts of me because he took them from me. I'll never be able to trust someone ever again." She paused. "Other than Lane, that is."

"I understand." And I truly did. "Betrayal changes you." It

was like falling into a pool. The initial shock is cold and un-familiar, but as you get used to it, it starts to become part of you, soaking into you. "I feel terrible that you had to go through that."

"If it would have ended with Ben's death I might have been able to move on. But it didn't. I ended up doing something terrible that I can't fix, and now I don't know what's going to happen. The irony is that Ben's cheating was nothing compared to what I've done."

"What do you mean?"

She stopped. Realization sparked in her eyes. She hadn't meant to share that, had she?

"Sorry, I don't know what I'm saying. I really should have kept that to myself," she hastily muttered.

What sin could a throw-pillow-loving, gluten-free home-maker possibly have committed that she couldn't come back from? I wanted to Heimlich the details out of her, but her mouth was clamped shut. Conversation closed.

"Did you ever confront the woman he was cheating with?"

"No, I was too shaken up at the time, and honestly, if I ever did meet her again I'd probably kill her. So it's for the best I never got the chance." She pushed her chair out and stood, balling up the used tissues and grabbing the neck of the now empty wine bottle.

"I had no idea you had been through so much. And then, after all that, losing your husband . . ."

"I lost him a year ago, Candace. I had been trying to save a marriage that was already dead. When I found out he was at that hotel with another woman—when I really *knew* it—I couldn't bear to see Ben or my kids or my mother or Lane. I was humiliated and broken. I spent the rest of that night crying in my car wondering why I had lost him. Wondering what I could have done to prevent him from cheating. You know what conclusion I came to? Nothing. I couldn't have done a damn thing differently."

"And that's on him, not on you. You didn't force him to cheat."

"No, but I pushed him away. I didn't realize it at the time, but I made his life a living hell, just as he did to me." She shrugged, walking toward the kitchen. "In that way I suppose we were perfect for each other."

I didn't know what to say, how to console her.

She paused, her back toward me. "I'm sorry I'm so protective of Lane." When she turned to face me, her cheeks were wet with tears.

"I understand that."

"And I know it's not right of me. I judged you wrongly from the moment I met you, and I'm sorry. I can't seem to let my brother go, and I don't know why." The tears came fluidly now, and I rushed to her side.

"Hey, I get it, okay? You don't need to apologize anymore. And you don't need to cry over it." Emotions made me uncomfortable. Maybe it was because my father never allowed me to have them.

"It's just . . . I love him more than I love myself," she sniffled, "and I'll do whatever it takes to make him happy. But I'm sad over what that has turned me into."

As Harper tossed the bottle in the recycling bin, I returned to the dining room to pick up the paper she had left on the table, not meaning to read it as I carried it to the kitchen. I paused in the doorway, my eyes glued to the letters and words in front of me. A last message from Ben to Harper:

My darling Harper,

You saw this coming, didn't you? You knew one day you'd walk into our home and find me like this, taken by my own hand. You had to, after all the suffering. All the secrets. All the pain . . .

And I wondered why the police hadn't seen this yet.

Chapter 29

Harper

Now that I was starting to sober up, I could feel the regret. Why on earth did I open up to Candace? God only knew what she thought of me after discovering that my husband had cheated on me, so I had stalked him, and now he was conveniently dead. I might as well have confessed to murder.

It was too late to take it all back or plead drunken rambling. Note to self: Never drink a whole bottle of wine alone. In my defense, the alcohol had done most of the talking, and some of the conversational details were a little vague. I wasn't one hundred percent sure about what I had said or left unsaid, but as snippets of the conversation pieced together in my head, the big picture was concerning. I had said too much.

I checked the time. Candace was down for her afternoon nap, and Lane was working at the hospital until dinnertime.

I still had a couple hours before the kids were due home from school, so I grabbed my keys and headed to the car. I couldn't stand another minute in this house. I stood beside the car, aiming my key fob at the moving target as the world tilted back and forth. Damn, maybe I wasn't as sober as I thought. My first attempt at unlocking the car failed as I hit the lock button on my fob, then the alarm.

"Come. On!"

As the alarm blasted throughout the neighborhood, I punched every button on the fob until it shut off. In the haze of slippery thoughts I knew this was a bad decision. A terrible decision to drive. *Don't drink and drive.* I'd heard the slogan repeatedly since I was a teenager. But right now, in this moment, I didn't care about anything, because chances were high I was going to be arrested soon anyway. Might as well go out with a bang.

It took four tries for me to properly insert the key into the ignition. Then two tries to successfully back out of the driveway. It took so much focus I strained my eyes, igniting a headache. The stretch of street before me was wobbly and blurred, so I leaned forward in my seat, nearly pressing my face to the windshield. As I turned onto the main street, a police cruiser pulled up behind me at the stoplight.

"Crap!" I shouted to the dead air. How long had he been following me?

Concentrate, I reminded myself. *Just drive normally.* Except that the street was swimming and swaying and making it hard to drive normally. Turn right. Blinker on. Green light. Slowly hit the gas. It was like being sixteen, learning how to drive for the first time, with my mother screaming directions at me from the passenger seat: *Put your blinker on! Accelerate slowly! Red light half a mile ahead! Slow down before you kill us!* Every instruction an exclamation point.

I prayed over the next mile as the cop car followed me, mumbling, *"Pleasedon'tswerve pleasedon'tswerve pleasedon'tswerve."* Several glances in the rearview mirror later and he was *still* there, *still* following me. Two turns, always behind me. Was he tailing me on purpose? Had Detective Meltzer told him to keep tabs on me?

A burst of blue and red lights sent my heart into overdrive. The siren cut through my concentration. He was pulling me over. My first DUI. I slowed to a crawl, aiming the car toward the berm, and prayed he wouldn't give me a Breathalyzer test. If I could talk my way out of it, I still had a slim shot of not getting caught. I hadn't broken any driving laws . . . that I knew of, at least. As I mentally prepared my defense—*I thought I was going the speed limit, Officer. I used my signal for every turn, sir*—the cruiser shot out from behind me, flying into the open lane beside me, careening ahead with siren blaring and lights flashing.

It hadn't been for me after all. Thank God for bigger criminals than me. Heart attack averted!

At last I reached the turn-in to my mother's subdivision. Exhaling a breath of relief—had I held my breath the entire drive here?—I passed my mom's house twice before crookedly pulling into the driveway.

I stumbled my way out of the car, up the walkway, and onto the porch stoop and dizzily knocked. Mom answered in a huff.

"Harper." Ouch. Her shrill voice hurt my ears. "What are you doing here?"

"I . . . I need you, Mommy. I need your help."

"Oh my God. Are you drunk?"

So I wasn't hiding it as well as I thought.

"Nooo," I blurted out, then tripped over my own foot while just standing there. "Okay, maybe a little tipsy."

She exhaled an annoyed sigh and dragged me inside by my arm. "Get in here. I'll make you a coffee. You can't possibly drive home like this. You're lucky you made it here alive."

The fragrance of lilac assaulted my migraine-sensitive nose.

"Sit," she ordered.

Wobbling my way into the living room, I fell into the first armchair I came to. From the kitchen I heard her tinkering with coffee mugs and the coffeemaker.

"You hungry?" she asked. "You should probably eat something to help soak up the alcohol."

Silly Mom. I was already two sheets to the wind. No amount of food was going to soak up the wine flowing through my veins. But I was craving something salty, so I shouted, "Got any chips?"

"Lord help me," she mumbled. "What is *wrong* with you?"

"I heard that!" I yelled. "Are you mad at me?"

A clatter of ceramic later, Mom entered carrying two mugs of coffee and took a seat on the sofa across from me. While I sobered up on black coffee, Mom topped hers off with cream and sugar.

"No, I'm not mad at you. Disappointed, though, yes."

"Don't pull that motherly disappointment on me. I wrote the book on it." I often used that same line on Elise when she disobeyed. I wonder where I learned it from.

"So what's going on that has you drunk as a skunk in the

middle of the afternoon?" she asked, resting her hand on her bare collarbone.

"Where's your necklace?" I asked.

"Oh, I must have forgotten to put it on today. I still need to fix that clasp before I lose it. So . . . ? Don't deflect, Harper. Spill it. What's going on?"

"Everything's gone to shit, Mom."

She narrowed her eyes at me. "Language, Harper. You know better than to talk like that."

"Apparently I don't know better. I told Candace about Ben."

"What about Ben?"

"That he had been cheating on me. That I saw him at the hotel with the other woman. I don't think—now I could be wrong, because the details are fuzzy—but I don't think I told her that Lane and I tampered with the scene that night. But God knows what all I said. The whole conversation is a blur."

"Oh, Harper." She plunged back in her seat, shaking her head. Coffee sloshed onto her pants. "That is bad. Please tell me you're kidding."

"I wish I was."

"Certainly you didn't tell her *everything*?"

"No, I don't think so." I wasn't sure at all, to be honest. "But more than I should have. I can't imagine what's going through her head right now." I groaned. As Julia Roberts so aptly said in *Pretty Woman*, "Big mistake. Big. Huge."

Sipping the black coffee, I winced at its bitterness. "At least I didn't tell her about Medea Kent."

"Medea Kent? Who's that?"

That's right, I hadn't told Mom about that fun little discovery. "Oh, the other beneficiary on Ben's life insurance policy. The name of his mistress."

"He named his *mistress* on his life insurance policy? You can't be serious."

"Yup, I have officially hit an all-time low."

I set my coffee on the white-painted table between us. A lilac-scented candle flickered like a jagged talon, its spear point hot and alluring. I stared at the flame, my vision glazing over as a disk of wax pooled at the base of the wick. While my mother's voice *wah wah wah*'d in the background, my thoughts drifted back to Jackson in his bedroom, setting the pictures aflame. I wondered what it felt like to be engulfed by fire, to watch everything burn, and for the first time I understood my little pyromaniac.

"Harper!" Mom's stridence shook the daydream loose. "Where'd you go off to inside your head?"

"Sorry, my brain keeps wandering."

"As I was saying, there's nothing you can do except to regain the upper hand. And you can only do that by gaining Candace's trust, restoring family order."

I grinned. *Candace.* So Mom *did* know her preferred name.

"Ha! Family order? What order do we even have? I'm probably a suspect in my cheating husband's murder, Lane married a pathological liar, my son is now an arsonist, my daughter has become a horror enthusiast, you're being questioned about Michelle's murder, and Ben's mistress is taking half my money. If you have any idea how to restore *family order,* I'm all ears, Mom. Because I'm feeling clueless right now."

"Stop your wallowing and do something about it!" Mom was missing the part of the heart that doled out empathy. "First things first, we need to get Candace out of the way. She's no good for your brother. Then we need to sell your house and take care of your family. Use that money to start over. Help each other heal. Then, when you're emotionally ready, you can move forward again. But like I said, Candace has *got* to go. By any means necessary. Do whatever it takes."

"Mom, you're sounding an awful lot like you did when you talked about wanting Ben gone. And now he's dead."

I eyed her warily, the dark overture sobering me more than the coffee ever could. She stared into her cup. Avoidance. What wasn't she telling me?

"I just want you to get back to normal, and you can't do that with a manipulative liar in your midst."

I shook my head. "I can't afford to piss her off. Lane blindly loves her, for better or for worse, and if I get on her bad side I'm afraid I'll lose him. Plus, Candace knows too much. And I already told you I'm not selling my house. Not yet. Maybe not ever. What is your obsession with me selling it?"

"I haven't been totally honest with you." Mom raised her hands, as if surrendering the truth. "I've found myself in some-what of a . . . financial predicament. I was hoping you would be willing to sell the house so that you could loan me a little money to pay off some bills."

"I would if I could, Mom, you know that. But it's too risky for me to try to sell the house anyway. What if they seize my assets on top of everything else? Then I would be left with nothing. Literally. They haven't unfrozen my bank accounts yet. And it might be months before I get my insurance payout. Have you asked Lane?"

"He's already given me so much. I hate to even admit this, but things with my real estate work have been slow. And as you found out during my interrogation, Ben scammed me out of every dime of my retirement money."

"I still can't believe Ben would take his own family's money." Incoherent words tore through my throat. "Detective Meltzer told me he had a secret bank account set up in another name. I'm assuming it was for Medea. How did I not see this side of Ben?"

"As sure as he's dead, the man was pure evil. The lies he spilled came so naturally too. He offered me this great *business opportunity* to double my investment return. Why wouldn't I trust my own son-in-law? So, of course, I invested. I lost everything, Harp. Every. Last. Penny. For the past six months I've been working two jobs, fourteen-hour days, and I still can't make ends meet. No one wants to hire an elderly real estate agent when all these fresh faces around here offer the moon and the stars."

She took a shaky breath, wiping the wet corners of her eyes.

"This is embarrassing for me, but I'm burned out, honey. I need a break. I really thought your insurance money would come through, or at least that you'd have access to your bank accounts by now."

"I'm so sorry, Mom. I had no idea you were struggling for that long. Why didn't you say something sooner?"

"Oh, honey, I didn't want to start trouble with you and Ben after he screwed me over. The lies . . . That man ruined me. And to be honest, I wanted him dead. But I couldn't go saying that to you, now, could I? And since then it's all been pretense, my dear. I didn't want to worry you and Lane, but I can't hide it anymore. I'm looking at foreclosure if I don't catch up on my payments."

"I know Lane's got extra money. And I'll be employed soon and can help out. We'll be happy to help get your bills caught

275

up." I couldn't speak for Candace on the matter . . . well, I actually could. I knew she'd put her foot down, but I hoped Lane still had enough of his balls intact to stand up to her for the sake of our mother, who had sacrificed so much for us when we were growing up. "And as soon as I have access to my bank account again, I'll pay him back and get you on your feet."

"No, I can't ask your brother again. I already mentioned it to him, and Candace shut it down. She said they need the money for the doctor bills and baby stuff. I'm not going to push it. I'll figure something out."

"I'll take care of it. Don't you worry."

And I would. Even if I had to drag Candace down kicking and screaming, I was not going to let my mother suffer any longer. Hadn't she suffered enough? I just hoped she hadn't done something to deserve it. Our sins did have a way of coming back to bite us.

"Mom, I have to ask you something. And I need you to be honest with me."

Her brown eyes flicked upward, earnest but guilty. The look lasted so long it rattled me, forcing me to glance away.

"Did you kill Ben because you found out he lost all of your money?" I searched her face for any sign of truth.

Her gaze hardened. "Did you kill Ben because you found out he was cheating on you?"

Though we both swore our innocence, every cell in my body lit on fire with a knowing that my mother was capable of a lot more than she would ever admit to. Like mother, like daughter, after all.

Chapter 30

Harper

My newborn baby was warm and light in my arms, her chubby flesh so real. Resting in the crook of my elbow was her head, so perfect and kissable and pink. Frantic arms pumped the air, and squishy legs wriggled like she would take off running if I let go. I stood with her in her nursery; I recognized the scene. It was the day I had given birth. The ghost pains between my legs lingered from pushing her out, delivering her at home in the shower while Ben held me upright and the midwife caught the baby as she fell.

Double-checking the nursery, everything was as it should be. Crisp white crib in the corner. Clean linen scent in the air from the freshly washed bedding. Bold, uppercase letters with pastel polka dots painted across the wall: KIRA.

The down of her red hair—just like mine—tickled my forearm in wispy strands, like a ghost's fingers playing with it. She was here, so very tangible . . . and yet not. My arms felt light. No, something was wrong.

I blinked, and I couldn't feel the weight of her anymore, only the mirage. I pawed at the fading image, wondering, How did I conjure my baby here? How do I get her back? *But my questions disappeared along with her form into empty space.*

"No!" I cried, my arms cradling nothingness.

"Kira!" I screamed, but my voice only echoed back at me.

Another blink. The nursery was gone. Instead I stood in my backyard, the place I had called home. The pool was calm like ice, unmoved by the breeze. Carefully I stepped toward it, watching my reflection in the water follow me. A splash across the pool broke my image. I ran to the other edge, searching the water for the source. My reflection swirled beneath the water's chaos.

My face in the water morphed into something else. Someone else.

"Kira?" I called out.

But it wasn't her creating the churning. It was Jackson, with two-year-old Kira lying limply in his arms. He handed me her still body, then looked up at me, blood seeping from black eyes tainted with darkness.

"What did you do, Jackson?" I screamed and begged for an answer, but he replied with silence. Then he walked away, his body dripping wet, leaving tiny footprints across the patio, as I held my dead child in my arms and wept.

* * *

Morning was the exhale after a night-long held breath. As the streetlamps died and the horizon came to life, another nightmare ended as dawn chased it away. Covered in sweat and tears, I bolted upright from under the bedding, overwhelmed with relief and fear. I didn't know where one emotion began and the other ended. It wasn't real . . . and yet it was. I had held her—Kira, the child I had lost. The toddler I still mourned a year after her death. She was a part of me that I would forever mourn, a broken part that could never be fixed.

The damp covers twisted around my legs and I kicked myself free. My pillow smelled rancid with perspiration. I sniffed my armpits, grimacing at the oniony odor. Another night terror, another load of sweaty sheets. I wondered if the dreams would ever stop, or at least fade. But if they did, would Kira's face fade with them?

The worst part about losing Kira wasn't the gaping void in my life since her drowning. It wasn't the haunting memories following me like specters. It wasn't even the endless daily grief I felt waking each morning missing her, or the dread of another exhausting night dreaming of her. Such things were the nature of death. They were to be expected, balanced by the hope of seeing her in heaven. I believed in our future reunion, I truly did, with every part of my devastated soul, and that faith was my saving grace. Without that promise of eternity together, I had nothing. Her death cut me deep, but that wasn't the worst of it.

No, the worst part wasn't being left behind. The worst part was that losing Kira cost me my love for my son. Missing her, crying for her, hating the void of her, turned my love for Jackson sour. My love for my daughter caused my hate for my son. What mother says or feels such a thing? A monster! It was unnatural and grotesque. But it was true, no matter how horrific the reality was. I could never forgive my son for what had happened that day. For what he had done, even in his innocence.

I had never told Jackson he couldn't take his baby sister swimming. I never imagined he would pick up his two-year-old sister in his tiny arms, carry her into the pool, then drop her. He didn't know better; he was so young. In my head I blamed myself for not anticipating it, for not watching them that day, for not putting up a fence before it was too late, for not protecting my children. But my heart, well, it resented Jackson deeply.

That inability to forgive—*that* cost me everything. My marriage. My relationship with my kids. My ability to feel or heal. The only thing it hadn't cost me was my capacity to function. That knack to compartmentalize I got from my mother.

Forcing myself out of bed, I grabbed the bedding and balled it up, then tossed it in the laundry basket. I opened the window blinds and was greeted with happy sunshine flowing into the room. *Bake me with your happiness, oh sun!* I wanted it, but I couldn't have it.

With robotic routine, I peeked in Elise and Jackson's room to find them still asleep, then collected their dirty clothes, adding them to the pile. It was amazing how much we could accomplish with the weight of the world on our shoulders. Heck, three days after Kira's death I was already grocery shopping, as if a trip to the store could reset my life. I hadn't thought to avoid the diaper aisle, and it took two employees to lift me up off the floor when I broke down crying, clutching a package of wipes, unable to see through my tears to find my cart. After that episode, I isolated myself at home for a couple more weeks, until the isolation drove me mad. That was when all the pent-up feelings poured out into my everyday interactions. It leaked out in my reactions . . . or overreactions, as the case may be.

One month after Kira's death it started to become noticeable. And very public. I had been living in a trance, but when the trance wore off, fury took over. Everything was a great personal offense. Especially the woman at the supermarket yelling at her two-year-old daughter to calm down and behave. Two, the same age Kira was when she drowned. Two, too little to know how to behave in a supermarket. Two, an age far too young to be yelled at like the mother was doing. Something buried inside me—grief, anger, injustice, pain—snapped, and I unleashed it on that mother that afternoon.

Remembering it now, it happened in fast-forward. But that day, those minutes felt like slow-motion. It was the cereal aisle, as I vividly recalled. I was in the middle of a discussion with Elise on the health merits of Cheerios over Cap'n Crunch. Down near the Cocoa Puffs a mother had been screaming, red-faced, gripping her child's cheeks between her talons: *You behave right now or you'll be getting a spanking you won't forget!* Strung within this was a handful of curse words.

I didn't think twice—heck, I didn't even think once—before I walked straight up to her, removed her hand from the girl's face, and shoved my finger an inch from her eyeball.

Don't you dare treat that child like that. You're going to hurt her!

The woman knocked my finger away, then leaned forward. *Excuse me? Don't you tell me how to parent my child.*

Except in my mind that wasn't her child. In my grief-stricken delusion, it was Kira who needed protection. So I raised my hand and slapped that woman so hard it left a red handprint on her face. Elise's mouth dropped open at the scene, while Jackson hid his eyes beneath his hands. The woman cowered, then called, *Help me! This woman is attacking me!*

Attacking implied repeated hitting. I only slapped her once.

Two weeks later, a judge slapped me with a sentence for grief counseling. I was lucky it wasn't worse, but when the judge found out I had just lost my daughter, he figured I needed therapy more than a night in the slammer.

If you've never lost a part of yourself, you wouldn't understand this. But there is no cure for it. No amount of antidepressants or antianxiety drugs can make you antihuman. When a piece of you breaks off, it can't be glued back on. No matter how many drugs a therapist thinks will help. All the medicine did was inflame stomach issues and blunt my personality as it coated my mind in gluey syrup. It didn't remove the vision of finding my dead daughter in my son's arms, and that visual controlled the whole vicious cycle.

I knew I shouldn't blame Jackson. I told myself this every day. He was a five-year-old boy when he led Kira outside the back door. He only wanted to play with her when he held her hand, their two tiny palms cupped together, and guided her toward the pool. He didn't realize that his two-year-old baby sister couldn't swim when he lifted her up, cheeks puffed out as he strained to carry her, and stepped into the water. He didn't understand the gurgling was a cry for help as she sunk under the surface.

I shouldn't blame him, a child, for killing his sister. And yet I did. Every day I blamed him, because I didn't want to blame myself. I should have been watching. I should have insisted Ben put up the pool fence, no matter how many times he told me he'd "get to it." By the time he "got to it," my baby girl was already gone and buried. I should have known something was wrong when the house went too quiet. When the chatter between Jackson and Kira paused. I should have, I should have, I should have.

And yet I didn't. Until it was too late.

From Elise and Jackson's bedroom doorway I watched them slumber, appreciating the preciousness of it. Elise stirred at the creak of the door; Jackson curled up into a tiny lap-sized ball. I wanted to forgive my son for leading Kira to her death. I wanted to forgive the ghost of my husband for not putting up the fence sooner. I wanted to forgive myself for not being omniscient.

But the truth of the matter is this: a heart that is broken doesn't work anymore, and so it can't forgive. All it can do is ache.

Chapter 31

Lane

"Not a soul on earth will convict me when I murder your sister, Lane!" After a long day taking blood pressure, administering medicine, and monitoring patients, I had barely made it through the front door before Candace's verbal assault began. "Because the jury will feel so bad for me—a pregnant, newlywed wife who simply wants a little space—that they'll applaud me for doing right by my husband."

Not this again. It was the sixth time—yes, I'd counted—in two days that Candace had asked me when Harper and the kids were moving out. I didn't have an answer because my sister didn't have answers. We were in the middle of a double-murder investigation and Candace was more concerned about painting the nursery than catching a killer.

I couldn't blame my wife for feeling this way. Every day her patience was tried in new and creative ways. Yesterday, she found the pool skimmer clogged with Barbie doll heads, which led to a $500 filter repair. The day before that, Jackson had dropped a gallon of milk on the floor and left it for Candace to clean up. And don't even ask me how or why Jackson's underwear ended up clogged in the toilet.

All the spills, the toys everywhere, the noise . . . it was a normal life with kids, but not a life we were ready for. And the moment Candace reprimanded them, Harper got defensive. The last straw happened this morning on Candace's way down the stairs when she stepped on a toy that sent her tumbling onto her stomach. She had finally calmed after an emergency visit to urgent care to ensure the baby was okay. It was a lot for her to deal with, and I knew I was asking too much of a new marriage, letting my sister and her kids live with us for this long.

"I know I promised you they'd be gone by now, and I'm working on it," I said as I set my keys on the entryway table and headed upstairs to change clothes.

Candace followed me up the stairs to our bedroom, where I changed out of my scrubs into joggers and a tank top that Harper would make fun of. My whole *hipster* wardrobe had been customized to Candace's taste, and my sister had something to say about all of it. Between the two of them, I couldn't win. Where one was approving, the other was critical.

"You keep saying that, but they're still here. It's a simple conversation. Why are you making this so difficult? All you have to say is, *Harper, it's time for you to get your own place.* See? Easy," Candace ranted on.

"Honey, this is my sister. I can't just kick her out like that.

It takes a little . . . finesse." It was the same answer I had given to her yesterday, and the day before, and the day before that. "Besides, I don't want her alone right now. She's still mourning her husband, and no one has hired her yet, so she has no money to pay for a place to live."

"Yeah, about that job search, what the hell is taking her so long? And why hasn't she already found something? Her kids are both in school—she should have already been working during the day."

"She's only been here two weeks, babe. Besides, you don't understand all the stress she's under." She didn't. She couldn't. She wasn't in Harper's shoes.

Candace would never understand just how much Harper had suffered after Kira died. How she had gotten a job to distract herself, but the medicine she'd been prescribed numbed her to the point where she couldn't focus, which led to her getting fired from the plant nursery. The monthly anniversary of Kira's death had led to breakdowns in front of clients, which led to her being fired from her secretarial job. Firings number three and four were inevitable because some mornings she couldn't get out of bed. She wasn't ready for the workforce, and I wasn't going to push her.

"So help me understand, Lane." Candace sounded sincere.

"Harper has had . . . a rough year, to say the least. Last year she lost a child, her two-year-old daughter. She drowned. And it wasn't Harper's fault, if that's what you're thinking. Her husband blamed her, and she took it upon herself, but the reality was that it just happened."

Candace's face softened. "Oh, I didn't know all the details about what happened with Kira. I'm so sorry."

"And even if she did make a deadly mistake, does she deserve to suffer for the rest of her life over that? You can't judge it unless you've been through it. Anyway, after that happened, Harper changed. She was never quite the same. I don't know if she can even hold a job with how messed up she is right now. Grief does that to you. It changes everything, and until she's had time to heal, I don't think shoving her into a hostile, lonely work world will help."

Candace touched my arm, sorrow in her gentleness. Sympathy.

"Add in losing her husband and, well, would you be able to function after all that?"

She shook her head sadly, then wrapped her arms around my waist. "I feel terrible that she's gone through so much. I'll stop bugging you about it. I know it's hard for everyone."

With her head tilted up to me, I kissed her forehead, her nose, her lips. Then trailed down her neck as she pulled me against her.

"I'll show you hard," I murmured into her collarbone.

Sliding her fingers through my hair, she pulled my face to hers, her kisses eager and bossy. I picked her up, she straddled me, and I carried her to the bed. Dropping her on her back, I stood above her, ripping off her clothes, pulling her panties down to her knees, then paused to admire her perfect body. The swell of her belly, teeming with life. Love welled up inside me, in the eagerness of my hands as I unclasped her bra, and the force of her legs around my waist pulled me closer. I climbed on top of her, gazing down at the woman I adored, and pressed my fingertip to her lips when she tried to speak. I didn't want words to intrude on this moment.

"The door," she said as my finger muffled her speech.

"What?" I asked.

"Someone's knocking on the front door."

And now I understood how passion deflated when kids entered the picture. Kids—or strangers knocking on your door—were the needle to the balloon. *Pop!*

"You have *got* to be kidding me." I climbed off Candace, slid off the bed, and pulled my pants back up, wondering how I was going to hide my bulge.

Candace patted my groin and chuckled. "Better luck next time, babe." Then she threw on her clothes and trotted to the stairwell. She paused at the top of the stairs, then backtracked to the bathroom. "Actually, I'm going to grab a quick shower. I'll be down when I'm done."

I kissed her on the cheek in passing, and she squeezed my ass. By the time I headed downstairs, still pulling my hipster tank top on, I found Detective Meltzer in my entryway, Harper welcoming him inside.

"What's going on?" I asked.

"I'm here to speak with both of you," the detective answered. "Mind if we sit down?"

"Not at all." Harper led the way to the living room, then, compelled by etiquette, offered, "Would you like some coffee or tea?"

"No, thanks. I hope we can make this quick."

Detective Meltzer sat and unzipped a black duffel that he had set at his feet. Pulling out a clear plastic bag, he handed it to Harper. It looked like a piece of jewelry inside.

"Do you recognize this necklace?"

Harper examined the necklace through the plastic, then

huffed as she passed it back to him. "Where did you get this? It's my mother's necklace, an heirloom."

"We found it at the crime scene of Michelle Hudson's murder. We pulled prints off it, and we lucked out and found a match. Your mother's prints were in the system from when we took them after we questioned her about Ben's murder. She's currently down at the station, but I wanted to have a chat with both of you as well."

"Are you saying my mother had something to do with Michelle's murder? I thought she was already cleared when you brought her in before," I interjected. My face heated with an urge to protect. "Because I know my mother. She could never kill anyone."

"That was before we found this." He lifted the bag with her necklace. "Money is a pretty big motivator for murder. Especially the person who stole her entire retirement fund and left her penniless, and the one witness who could identify her," the detective added.

Harper shook her head, waved her hands, her entire body a denial. "There is no possible way my mother could have overpowered Michelle Hudson, let alone Ben. My mother is frail. As for the necklace, I don't know how it got in Michelle's house."

"Let's say your mother didn't do it." The detective folded his hands, cocking his head. "Follow some logic with me. Michelle said she saw two people at your house the night of Ben's murder. You claimed you were with your mother and kids at her house, and Lane was at work until around midnight, which, based on the time of death, was after Ben died. We confirmed Lane's alibi, but your alibi, Harper, is awfully convenient now that we found your mother's necklace at a murder scene. You do realize how that looks?"

He was right. Even I was beginning to question things.

"What about Medea Kent? Have you looked into her as a suspect?" Harper blurted out.

"Yes, and she checks out. But you and your mother . . . I still have a lot of questions."

"Detective, please understand I would never kill Ben. Never. Think about it—he was far more valuable to me alive. He had a great-paying job. Why would I want to ruin that?"

"You tell me. Did you know his business was failing?"

"No, I had no idea until you told me. I'm telling you, Detective, as far as I knew, everything was fine with his job, and with us."

"So you're saying your daughter's drowning didn't cause any problems at home? Because usually something so traumatic can break a family up. And I know you had some . . . anger issues that you were taken to court over."

"I was grieving. I was angry about losing a child, not angry with Ben. We still had two kids to stay together for. In fact, we were finally starting to heal as a family when . . . it happened."

Detective Meltzer watched my sister crumble, his posture stiff and eyes calculating. Harper looked at me, her eyes wide and pleading. I could almost read her mind: *Do we confess what we did? What do we do now?* I subtly shook my head. Not yet. We needed to talk this through first.

"Harper"—Detective Meltzer shifted his body—"can you tell me what you were doing the afternoon of Ms. Hudson's death? Because Mr. Radcliffe, your neighbor, claims he saw you in the neighborhood that day."

Oh crap. I didn't like where this was heading; it was somewhere I couldn't navigate, because I didn't have a clue what my sister had been doing there beside "talking." I heard the fear in her answers. Could the detective tell that he'd rattled her nerves by the way her leg twitched?

"Detective, I have been nothing but cooperative with you," Harper bristled, "but I did not kill anyone. I stopped by to grab my mail, that's it. Then I picked up the kids from school and took them to the dollar store. Then, that night, Lane and I watched a movie with the kids. Feel free to ask them. We had stayed in because of the storm that came through."

It was a relief that Harper remembered the details of the day, almost too many details, because I sure didn't. But from the sound of it, we were safe. We weren't murderers after all.

"What about your mother? Do you know where she was that day?" he pressed.

"Working two jobs, I assume," Harper answered. "I'm sure her bosses could vouch for her—"

"Mom's working two jobs?" I interrupted. "Since when?"

Harper shook her head to shush me. It clearly wasn't the time, but we had some catching up to do.

"Look, as you know, we've been working Ben's case for two months now without a solid lead." The detective dropped the necklace in the black bag at his feet. "This is the first link we've gotten that connects both murders—and they lead back to you and your mother. I'd be remiss if I didn't look into it. Benjamin Paris was responsible for losing a lot of people's money, but the only ones without a solid alibi are your mother, who was taken for her life savings, and you. And now we find her necklace at the scene where the only witness we had was killed.

I know it's hard to imagine an elderly lady killer, but you'd be surprised what people can do when they're put in a corner." Hefting the bag strap over his shoulder, Detective Meltzer rose from the sofa and moved toward the door. "I'm sorry to tell you this, but the evidence is enough to make an arrest."

This was getting out of hand. My mother couldn't go to jail for something she hadn't done. I wanted to tell the detective everything, that Ben hadn't been murdered, that he had committed suicide. My mother didn't know that Harper and I were there that night, so she had nothing to gain in killing Michelle Hudson. But then why was her necklace at Michelle's house?

No, it was better not to say anything until I talked to Harper in private.

"I'll be in touch," the detective said as Harper led him out the door.

"Should I call Mom to warn her?" Harper asked me.

"No, we can't do anything that will piss off the cops. We need to cooperate for now."

I considered all the knowns and unknowns. Ben had screwed over a lot more people than I had realized, including my mother, who vocally hated him. Could she have hated him enough to kill him? Then Michelle Hudson turns up dead, the only person who had seen anything, with my mother's necklace at the scene. Add Ben's mistress beneficiary to the mix, and it led me in circles. Medea Kent could have been connected, but apparently she *checked out*, whatever that meant.

The steps creaked as Candace came downstairs. "Everything okay?"

"No, not really. That was Detective Meltzer. My mom's been arrested for Michelle Hudson's murder. I'm going to have to hire an attorney and figure out how to get my mom out of this mess."

"Oh my God, Lane. I'm so sorry. Anything I can do to help?"

"Do you know how to get out of murder charges?"

"No, but I know how to give a good hug." Candace pulled me into her arms, tucking her head under my chin. I kissed the top of her head, noticing that her hair was dry.

"What happened to your shower?" I asked.

"I got sidetracked with checking my email." Leaning back, Candace gazed up at me. "Hey, everything will be fine. Okay?"

I nodded, while all kinds of thoughts swirled together as I mentally grabbed at scenarios and facts and conversations, until one thought in particular struck me from behind. I had never told Candace Kira's name, and Harper was tight-lipped about it with anyone she didn't trust. I couldn't imagine Harper sharing something so painful and personal with a woman she loathed. If neither of us had told her Kira's name, who did?

Chapter 32

Harper

After Detective Meltzer left, Lane headed to the police station to deal with my mother's arrest while I waited at home until it was time to pick up the kids from school. As much as I wanted to support Mom, I couldn't go down to the station again. It was the last place I wanted to be, facing my likely fate behind bars. I had dealt with enough police and attorneys in the past year; it was time for Lane to take the reins.

Instead, I hid in my bedroom to shove my face in my pillow and ugly cry. The stress was getting to me, and I was one bad moment away from a nervous breakdown. It was only a matter of time before they hauled me in, but for murder, not tampering with evidence. I had no way to prove my innocence, because my "alibi" mother was now being arrested for murder also. I knew I hadn't murdered Ben. And I knew my mother had no reason to kill Michelle Hudson. So who did?

With the tears exhausted—for the time being—I got up and straightened the bed. Cleaning helped clear out my thoughts. The detective didn't seem to know much about Medea Kent, other than coming across her name when looking into Ben's financials, but it was odd that he didn't mention anything more about her. Like how she was a skank home-wrecking whore. During the investigation he had pulled our cell phone records, credit card statements, everything. How could he *not* know about the affair? Unless he knew but wasn't telling me. After all, as Lane put it, he had no desire to *give* information to me, only to *pull* information *from* me.

Hoisting a box from my closet, I rummaged through it until I found what I was looking for. Ben's work cell phone. The police hadn't taken it for some reason.

It made sense that he used it to hide his calls from me. I pressed the power button, but the battery had long ago died. My cell phone charger wouldn't fit, and I didn't remember finding a charger with it. It was probably at the office, which had shut down two months ago. There was nothing more I could do, so I returned the phone to the box and shoved it inside the closet. I didn't know what I had hoped to find amid Ben's old texts to Medea. Anything that would free me from suspicion, I guess.

I stood in my sparse bedroom, worried and confused and terrified. The scrap of paper Medea's address was on teetered on the edge of my dresser. I'd spent the past two months running, which was getting me nowhere. It was time for a new approach. There was only one way to face a problem, and that was head-on.

* * *

3 Summer Lane led me to a run-down house in an even more run-down neighborhood. The two-story brick home could have been semidecent, if not for the mountainous pile of trash next to it, or the tires with dog fennel weeds growing up through them scattered throughout the yard. A row of rusted propane canisters sat at the foot of their personal landfill mountain, where everything from clothes, to shoes, to car parts, to household garbage climbed a story high.

I knocked, wondering how anyone lived like this. As I raised my fist to knock again, the rusty squeal of the doorknob turning stopped me. When a brown-haired woman with a plain face, about my age, answered the door, I didn't know who I was looking at. She didn't look anything like the blond bombshell I had seen with Ben at the hotel.

"Medea Kent?" I asked, expecting a yes.

Instead I got "What do you want with my daughter?"

Medea was this woman's *daughter*? How perverted was Ben? If she was my age, her daughter couldn't have been much older than eighteen or nineteen. A child!

"I'm sorry, I don't even know where to start." My brain was idling. I couldn't bring myself to tell this woman her daughter had been sleeping with my husband. "Do you have a minute?"

"What's this about? Did Medea get into some kind of trouble?"

"No, well, I don't know. Can we talk?"

"I suppose." She eyed me warily. "My husband is inside

sleeping—he works nights," she added, as if I required an explanation, "so we should probably speak out here."

She gestured to two green-painted metal rocking chairs at the end of the porch, the kind my grandmother had spent many years sitting on watching the street like it was her post. These would have been considered vintage if they weren't rusting through. Plastic pots lined the railing, full of dry, cracked dirt and crunchy brown leaves. A black cat hopped down from the chair as I approached. I sat, and—I realized I hadn't gotten her name yet—the woman sat catty-corner to me.

"I'm sorry to show up like this, but my name is Harper Paris, and I believe my husband, Benjamin Paris, knew your daughter."

I didn't know why I was here anymore. I didn't know what I was here to find out.

"Benjamin Paris? I never thought I'd hear that name again."

"You know Ben? Well, *knew* him. He passed away two months ago."

Her hand flew to her heart as she gasped. "No! Benny died? He was so young—not even forty yet, right?"

Benny? I'd never known anyone to call him Benny. It sounded foreign to me. "How did you know Ben?"

"Oh, gosh, that was a lifetime ago. Benny and I dated in college, right before you came along, actually. He broke up with me for you, you know. You were something special to him."

"Really?" I realized then that I had no idea who this woman was. Certainly not the villain I came for. "I'm sorry, but I didn't catch your name."

"Natalie. Natalie Simmons, but Benny knew me as Natalie Kent."

The black cat jumped up on my lap, purring as it settled into a fat, fluffy ball. I ran my hands down its silky back.

"Styx likes you." Natalie grinned. She was pretty in a classic way. "So apparently you found out about Medea. I'm her mother. I guess Benny told you everything?"

I had no idea what Ben should have told me. "No, actually, Medea is listed as a beneficiary in Ben's life insurance policy. I have no idea who she is, or why her name is on there."

"Oh." Natalie shifted stiffly, and she glanced away. Her fingers tapped a metallic beat on the arm of the chair. "Well, I suppose you should know the whole truth. Medea is Benny's daughter. He got me pregnant right before he met you, and when he wanted to break up, I told him about the baby. But I didn't feel it was fair to either of us to yoke him to me and a child that he didn't want. So I gave him an out and he took it."

Ben had another child? My heart felt like it was ripping apart. Not only did he have an affair, but he had managed to hide a whole other family. He made a bastard out of an innocent child. This didn't align with the man I knew, a father who so tenderly hugged his kids every night before bed, who propped them on his shoulders for chicken fights in the pool, who kissed their boo-boos.

My breath shook as I tried to speak. "I'm sorry he did that to you and Medea. I didn't know—"

"Don't apologize. He's financially supported Medea for the past seventeen years, sending her money every month without fail. When the last two payments didn't arrive, I admit I was a little confused, but I never contacted him about it. I figured he had given enough. He always made sure Medea was provided for. It was his way of accepting responsibility, I guess."

"Does Medea know he was her father?"

"Yeah, she's aware. In fact, Benny was the one who named her when I found out it was a girl."

How could he have not mentioned this to me when we were dating? The deceit had started from the very beginning. It was heartbreaking to discover my whole relationship was built on lies.

"I wasn't fond of the name *Medea* at first, until he told me the significance of it," Natalie continued.

"Oh really? What was the meaning behind her name?"

Natalie smiled, taking years off her face. "Medea was a figure in Greek mythology. She was married to Jason, they even had kids together, until one day Jason renounced her. He said she was no longer his wife and instead he wanted to marry the king's daughter."

The similarities were eerie. It sounded a lot like mine and Ben and Natalie's triangle.

"I know what you're thinking, and yes, that probably reflected Benny's own choices, which was why he suggested the name. Anyway, in an act of vengeance, Medea killed all of their children and flew away. Luckily, none of our children were killed as they were in the myth"—she chuckled at that— "but there are definitely some interesting connections there."

But one of our children *had* been killed, and now I couldn't help but wonder if Ben's betrayal had played a part in Kira's tragedy. Was it Fate's punishment for what Ben did to Natalie? Did this story intersect more with our life than I knew?

"Well." Natalie slapped her knee as she rose to her feet. "Medea had hoped to reach out to Benny when she turned eighteen, but I guess that won't happen now. I'm sorry for your loss, by the way. Benny was a great guy, and crazy about you."

Tears tickled the corners of my eyes. Yes, yes, he was—during the highs of our marriage, at least. And while he hadn't been truthful with me about a lot of things, at least he cared enough about his daughter to ensure she was taken care of. I had always seen the goodness in his heart; I hated that a few bad choices had soured a lifetime of love. Maybe focusing on the fact that Ben cared so deeply about his children could help me reconcile the liar and the lover.

"Yes, he was one of the good ones."

I rose to my feet, thanking her for her time. I felt bad for what Ben had done to me, but worse for what he had done to Natalie and Medea. He had betrayed me after years of loyal love, but he had completely neglected her from the beginning, leaving his pregnant girlfriend, then never even setting eyes on his own child. There was no way to make up for it now.

"Before you go"—Natalie's voice halted with hesitation—"you mentioned something about a life insurance policy?"

Or maybe there was a way to make up for it, to the tune of $1.5 million.

Chapter 33

Candace

When you want to hide from the world, hide in me.

There was something about an unexpected knock at the door that sent a jolt of panic through me. Like Pavlov's dog, but in reverse. Instead of hearing a bell and drooling, I heard a doorbell and hid. It could have been PTSD from all the childhood evictions I experienced when we were forced out of home after home. Landlords are rarely kind when they're hauling you out on the street. Or it could have derived from the vivid recall of cops showing up at these various temporary homes to drag my dad off to a night in the slammer for yet another domestic assault. It tended to leave an imprint on a child's memory. It even crossed my mind that it could be just because I didn't want to be caught in my pajamas on a Wednesday afternoon, but that sounded way too normal and conventional an excuse for me. Whatever it was that had turned me knock-phobic, it meant I never liked surprises. I always wanted to know what to expect.

Deep down, I knew the real reason. It was because I was always running, always hiding. Always waiting to be found. It's like swimming in the ocean at night, when you suddenly start to wonder what's underneath the surface of the water. Because you're always certain there's a shark circling your legs.

I was in the kitchen making a snack when the first knock came.

I was in the living room peering through the curtains when the second knock followed.

By the time the doorbell rang, I was running to the entryway.

My lungs snatched for air. I threw open the door and saw Noah standing on the porch, resolute in the way he cocked his hips, his gaze roving my body. Not in a seductive way—the scrutiny was pure, naked hatred. He wasn't going to leave until he'd had words. I knew this from sharing years of life with him. Was he here to drag me back into the nightmare of my past? Because driving eight hours from Pennsylvania to North Carolina seemed a bit extreme just to collect on a $500 debt.

Noah didn't scare me anymore. In fact, *he* should have been scared of *me*. I was tougher now, a seasoned fighter, thanks to him. There's a point in life when you simply won't let yourself get knocked down anymore. I had finally passed that point.

"Is someone at the door?" Harper called from somewhere inside the house.

I didn't want Harper finding Noah here, tattletaling to Lane about it. "I got it. It was just a delivery!"

I sucked in a steadying breath and stepped out onto the porch, pulling the door shut behind me. Seeing Noah was like traveling through time. I had been preparing for this moment since the long Greyhound bus ride away from him. And finally, here I was, ready to take him on. I'd wasted my youth idolizing him, but now, he was just a tarnished piece of junk that left gilt on my fingers.

"Noah Gosling. I never expected to see you again."

"You don't look happy to see me."

"Did you expect otherwise?"

My ex, in the flesh, wearing ripped jeans that hung loosely from bony hips and a frayed Def Leppard T-shirt worn so thin that it looked like had gotten it at an actual Def Leppard concert in the 1980s. He still had the lip piercing, but I no longer found the poor-boy grunge look sexy. I had matured. Now I found money, success, and true love sexy.

"After all our years together I hoped for a little nostalgia. Anyway, Candace *Moriarty* . . . or whatever last name you're going by now. I found that pretty clever, by the way, you being a Sherlock Holmes fan and all."

"Uh-huh. How did you find me?"

"Don't you know you can find just about anything about everyone online these days? All I needed was your new alias, which your sister-in-law so kindly gave me."

Harper, of course. I would have to remember to thank her with a slap to the face.

"The rest was simply filling in the blanks on where you lived and a search on a public records database. Did you know you can even find cell phone numbers online . . . for free? That was an unexpected surprise."

"So that was *you* who texted me that lovely little threat. What was it you said again? *It's time we had a chat.*"

"I thought you'd appreciate the heads-up." He sneered. "Now here I am, an eight-hour drive later, face-to-face with the woman who stole my money and publicly humiliated me."

"Is that why you're here? Over a measly five hundred bucks and some embarrassment?"

"Hell no. You're not worth the energy." He exchanged his grin for a crooked frown, the lip ring weighing down half his mouth.

"Then why are you here? And why have you been stalking me?"

He laughed, but I didn't find this conversation funny in the least.

"Stalking you? You need to get over yourself. No one's stalking you but the demons you're running from. You should trust the hairs on the back of your neck. There's a reason you have them. I'm not here for you; I'm here for me."

No surprise there. Everything was always about him. "I'm listening. What do you want?" I was ready to be done with this conversation, done with Noah. For good.

He pushed against the door behind me, and I stepped forward to block him.

"You've got some balls, standing up to me."

"I learned to fight back after I left your sorry ass."

"Oh, come on. Where's your hospitality? Let's go inside and have a nice little chat." He wasn't asking, though, as he shoved his weight forward.

I rammed him back a pace. "Screw you. I don't owe you a chat. And I'm certainly not letting you inside my home."

"Why? Are you ashamed of me? Or is it that you don't want your new little family to find out about me? I'm your dirty little secret, aren't I?"

Not so much a secret anymore as a shame I didn't want to introduce them to. I hoped Harper wouldn't come looking for me. I just needed to find out what he wanted so I could get rid of him.

"I saw your new man. He doesn't look very good in bed." I heard the insecurity between the folds of his words. He was picking a fight because he was jealous.

"I thought you weren't stalking me. That sure sounds like stalking."

"I bet having sex with him is like doing community service, isn't it?"

Noah wasn't exactly wrong. The first time with Lane was polite rom-com sex. I almost had my doubts about being with him after that, a man who always read the fine print and respected speed limits. But then things changed, like he had something to prove. It had intensified from PG family-friendly sex to passionate put-a-baby-in-me sex. I brought the animal out in him, and he brought the love out in me.

"That's none of your business. Just get to the point, Noah. Why are you here?"

Clawing at his wrist, I dragged him to the corner of the front porch where we'd draw the least amount of attention. He coiled his tattooed arm around my neck like we were buddies. I hated him for coming here. I hated his ugly thoughts that turned into ugly words that spewed from his ugly mouth. I shoved his arm off me.

"I know you have to go back to playing house and all, but I have a gift for you." He handed me a large manila envelope that I hadn't even noticed him holding this whole time.

"What is this?"

"Open it and find out."

I unclasped the seal and looked inside. Sliding a thin stack of papers out, I read the top line aloud: "'Divorce Agreement.'" It tasted so sweet to say it. "You're giving me a divorce?"

"Yup."

"What's the catch?" Noah always had a catch.

"While you were off stealing my money and playing hide-and-seek, I met a girl. I want to marry her. Legit, unlike your fake little family. But to do that, I need a divorce."

There had to be more than this. Noah didn't care about convention or propriety. Certainly no girl was worth all the hassle of finding me, coming all the way down here, and arranging for this divorce agreement just so that he could make an honest woman of her.

"What's so special about this girl?"

"What's so special about your guy? When it's love, it's love."

"That poor girl has no idea what hell she's in for with you."

"No, Candace, I'm a changed man. True love brought out the good in me. You and I, we were toxic. But this girl pulls me apart like taffy. That darkness that used to own me, she's the light that makes it scatter."

Who was this person speaking? The pretty prose didn't match the skull tattoo on his arm.

"Waxing poetic over her, huh? You really *have* changed."

No, Noah loved no one but himself. There was something else. "It can't be that she's *that* good in bed. She has something to offer you. Something no one else can give you."

Noah's jaw dropped in mock offense. "You think so little of me."

"That's because I know you."

And that was when the puzzle pieces clicked into place. "You finally found yourself a trust fund girl, didn't you? You always told me you would."

He laughed. "You *do* know me."

Of course. There was the catch. A rich girl, someone who could give him a fresh start. I wondered if perhaps she could give Lane and me a fresh start too. We could run away to some exotic beach together, or maybe a cute little farm in the rural foothills where we'd raise our child on fields of flowers. For once, Noah could be my ticket to something better.

"Fine, I'll sign this. But only on one condition. I want paid. I want recompense for all the pain you caused me, all the babies you took from me, all the scars you left me with."

I watched to see if he understood me. He did.

"How much is all that worth?"

"How rich is your new girlfriend?"

He scoffed. "Wow, and here I thought you had changed into a nice girl. How about ten grand?"

"Ha! I don't think so. My autograph is worth way more than that. I'm thinking closer to ten . . . times ten."

"One hundred grand? Are you kidding me with that? Hell no. I'll just tell your new cuddle buddy that his wife isn't legally his because you're still married . . . to me. See if he still wants you then. You'll be out on the street with nothing."

"Oh, I don't have anything left to lose. But it sounds like you do. A rich fiancée is your path to a perfect life. What's a perfect life worth to you? Because I'll need at least one hundred thousand dollars to get myself settled."

He considered. He pouted. He shook his head. Finally he caved.

"Fine, a hundred grand."

"When you have the money, I'll have the signed divorce papers." I lifted the envelope, flapped it in his face, and headed toward the front door.

"I got your money." He pulled out a checkbook with a pen tucked in the fold. Sure enough, his name, along with his fiancée's, was printed across the top, and below it a new address in a town I didn't recognize. He scribbled hastily in the blanks, then handed me the pen. "Now give me my divorce."

It seemed awfully convenient that he had that much money accessible from his pocket. "How do I know this is a real check for real money?"

"Cash it and find out. When have you ever known me to own a checkbook? Like I said, life is good. And I can make yours good too if you trust me."

I had no other choice but to trust him. He turned around and leaned over, and I placed the papers on his back, signing where each sticky note told me to.

"Looks like we'll both have it all—the perfect house in suburbia, a nice car, and a fat bank account. Oh—" He glanced down at my belly. "And a kid on the way. Congratulations on the rug rat."

He had to go there, didn't he? After all the miscarriages that he had caused, the rage wrapped itself around my body, curling my fingers into fists. The violence of my thoughts shook me, and it took every ounce of self-control not to slap him right then and there. To hurt him like he hurt all my babies before this one. But instead, I stood stoically, burying the anger inside, because I knew if it came out, it would never stop.

"Oh, and by the way, now that we're square, stop following me. You think you're so clandestine in your black car and aviators. You're such a cliché, Noah."

He squinted in confusion. "What are you talking about? I don't have a black car." He pointed to the monstrous gas-guzzling blue truck parked on the street with wheels so big it could have crushed my tiny four-door. The truck looked to be more expensive than the single-wide trailer we had lived in for most of our marriage. "And I certainly don't wear aviator sunglasses."

If Noah hadn't been following me, who had? And why?

Folding and pocketing the check, I wondered if my bruises and scars were worth a hundred thousand dollars. No, there was no price high enough, but at least this afforded Lane and me a new beginning. As I headed to the door and Noah headed down the walkway, we both turned back one more time. The last time we'd share a glance. A final goodbye, forever.

"Hey—" Noah said, the word catching me at the stoop. "Nice hair. I like you better with it dark."

Dark, just like my soul.

Chapter 34

Harper

"Nice hair. I like you better with it dark."

I lingered by the open bathroom window a little longer than I should have. I wasn't eavesdropping, because eavesdropping was intentional. I just happened to be at the right place at the right time to have it confirmed: Candace was still married to someone other than my brother. My eyes followed the man she called Noah back to his tacky blue monster truck. I recognized him as the same guy from the Facebook profile, with a little more wear and tear.

It wasn't a surprise that he had tracked Candace down, just like I tracked Medea Kent down. That's what desperate people who want answers do. Except Noah apparently got what he came for, while I still had no idea who the blond skank home-wrecking whore was. One of Ben's clients? Or his secretary—Jenny, Jan, something with a *J*—who flirted with him in front of my friggin' face at last year's Christmas party? She was about the right age, with the same taste in whore clothes, and blond. Maybe I needed to let it go; Ben was dead, after all. What did I have to gain from torturing myself over this? I had to accept that I would probably never find out. It wasn't like I could ask the police to investigate for me, since adding infidelity to my list of motives to kill my husband wasn't exactly my goal.

After washing my hands, I checked the clock. Almost time to start dinner. Lane would be home soon, hopefully with good news about my mother, and we'd need to have a sit-down with Candace. It was exhausting keeping up with all the lies.

I wondered how much more Candace had neglected to tell Lane about. Lies on top of lies. So Candace was in fact still married, like Noah had told me; this was a good thing. It would be a lot easier to get rid of her with no legal contract binding them for better or for worse. But it begged the question: Why hadn't she mentioned the baby was Noah's? If anything, it was a free pass to a lifetime of child support, especially now that he was some rich girl's boy toy. I would have thought she'd jump at the chance.

A compulsion to protect my brother kicked in as I realized Candace would likely go after Lane's assets once he kicked her to the curb. I imagined her fumbling for an excuse for what she had done. What was the tally of lies up to now? A fake name. A baby that wasn't Lane's. They weren't even married. There was no way I was going to let her manipulate her way back into his arms or his bank account.

I heard the glass door that led to the back patio slide shut, and I rushed into the kids' bedroom where I could view the backyard. Elise and Jackson sat in one corner, Elise building a fort out of patio chair cushions while Jackson watched. Near the pool, Candace tossed her clothes into a pile on the lounger, about to begin her afternoon swim. She dipped a toe in, then slipped into the water. This would give me about thirty minutes to do a little digging.

Slipping past the kids' bed, my stride was stopped by what I saw in the middle of the bedspread. Scattered photographs, each of them cut apart into scraps of faces and backgrounds. Picking up the metal scissors, I wondered where they'd found them. I had never allowed the kids to use grown-up scissors after I caught Jackson running in the house with a pair, point facing out.

I picked up a photo, its edge burned and curled, holes roughly punched out where the eyes should have been. I realized it was Candace, with Noah's arm around her. It looked familiar, but why?

The memory congealed. The day I found Jackson burning up our family picture, I had seen this in the wastebasket, amid the pile of photos that Jackson was about to set on fire. That's where I recognized Noah from; that's why he looked so familiar to me when Candace showed me her old pictures. I had thought that Jackson aimed all his pent-up anger against me, but this pile of chopped-up pictures were mostly of Candace. The eyes were poked out in every single one. He *hated* her, probably more than I did.

But why?

It didn't make any sense.

Maybe Jackson knew something I didn't. Maybe I'd find an answer in her bedroom.

Taking the scissors with me, I headed down the hallway. I didn't know what I was looking for exactly, but whatever it was, I'd know it when I found it. Something in my gut led me, directed me, urged me on. Her dresser was cluttered with magazines, makeup, and food remnants. I set the scissors beside an empty chips bag surrounded by a few tufts of hair clippings from when she had mutilated herself. I had a shot in hell of finding anything amid the junk.

Her dresser mirror was scribbled with lipstick messages. *I only have eyes for you*, with a heart beside it. *You're mine forever*, with a lip print. So that bathroom message that had shaken Jackson so bad was a message from Candace to Lane. It would have been sweet if it wasn't so psycho.

I opened drawers, flipped through papers, dug in her closet while minute after minute ticked by. On her bed lay a self-help book, which was odd, considering I never saw Candace read anything but the tabloids or something to do with Meghan Markle. I flipped through the pages, stopping to read an underlined passage she had made a note about:

The blood of the covenant is thicker than the water of the womb.

Beside this in the margin Candace had scribbled:

Meaning: The blood shed in battle bonds soldiers deeper than family. Our marital vows are our covenant. If Lane's family is against us, I must fight to push them out.

So she *had* been plotting against me. I wasn't overreacting after all. Glancing out the window, I saw Candace had stepped out of the pool. I had a couple minutes of her drying off, maybe a few to spare if she laid out for a bit before she headed upstairs to change. As I turned from the window, I noticed her jewelry box, a gorgeous, antique white piece with five drawers in the front, a mirrored top that opened up to a velvet-lined compartment, and two sides that swung open to hang necklaces. Not sure what I hoped to find, I lifted the lid, the mirror catching the light, and picked up a handful of bangled bracelets. So here's where she kept all her noisy boho jewelry.

Drawer by drawer, I opened one after the other, looking at rings and necklaces and bracelets. So much jewelry for one set of wrists. At the last drawer I almost didn't bother, but my fingertip hooked on the curve in the tray and slid it open.

That's when I saw it. A charm bracelet. At first it seemed so ordinary, until the shine of gold caught the sun, and I read the words crossing the metal band:

True love waits

The letters crashed against my trembling fingers as I dropped it back onto the velvet pad.

Why did that phrase sound so familiar? There was some sort of malfunction going on with how fast the earth was spinning. Minutes went by as quick as seconds once did. And then I remembered—

"What are you doing going through my stuff?" If my skin wasn't attached, I would have jumped out of it as I caught

Candace's dripping reflection in the jewelry box mirror, standing right behind me. I turned to find her half naked and burning with anger—or too much sun exposure—with her hands on her bony, bikini-clad hips.

The floor creaked as she stepped toward me, almost into me. She was too close. I was scared. My skin told on me, erupting in embarrassed red splotches.

"Why. Are. You. In. My. Room?" She punctuated each word, growing more severe with each syllable.

All I needed to think about was the bracelet to fuel my fire. "Where did you get this?" I picked the bracelet back up and dangled it in front of her.

"I found it."

No explanation. No excuse. No getting caught. She was a gifted liar.

"Don't lie to me, Candace, not after all we've been through. I know where this came from. I just want to hear it from you."

"Hear what? That I found it at a pawn shop? You have no idea what you're talking about."

Candace tossed her towel on the floor and reached for a rumpled T-shirt on the bed.

"You got this from Ben, didn't you? You were the woman sleeping with him, the woman from the hotel. Except you were blond then. That's what Noah meant when he said he liked your hair dark."

She cackled, and it was almost painful to watch her crumble. "So you're snooping *and* spying on me. Wait until Lane hears all about your delusions."

"Don't worry, I plan on telling him everything. About how you're still married to Noah. And how you were Ben's mistress.

I can't believe I've been sharing a home with the woman who tried to steal my husband! Did you kill him too?"

She didn't speak, and I couldn't read if it was denial or blame on her face.

"But why Lane? First you stole my husband, then you stole my brother. Was it a personal attack against me? What did I ever do to you?"

Her eyes widened, her bottom lip trembled, and I knew I'd caught her. But she wasn't giving up. She was a fighter, like me. "First of all, don't flatter yourself. You are nothing to me, so all of this"—she waved her hand in a circle—"is not about you. And secondly, I didn't steal your husband. He came to me first. I didn't even know he was married in the beginning. And by the time I found out, things were already pretty . . . serious between us."

Serious? No, it couldn't have been more than a fling for Ben. Someone temporary to fill the emptiness. Unless . . .

"Is Ben the father?" I pointed to her stomach.

I didn't think she was going to answer me, until she did.

"Yes, he's the father."

"Oh my God. Is that . . . is that why you killed him—because he didn't want the baby?" Before everything I now knew about my husband, I would have never thought he'd abandon a child. But now I knew better. He had done it before with Natalie. And he had done it again with Candace.

"Why would you assume I killed him? We both know it was a suicide . . . which you covered up. I saw the note."

"No, that suicide note—that wasn't Ben. It couldn't be."

Ben's last words were engraved in my head. I had read the

letter dozens of times, slept with it under my pillow even after Lane told me to burn it, because it was everything I thought Ben wanted me to know. I punished myself with his lyrics. And somewhere inside I knew it wasn't his voice from beyond the grave, but I had doubted myself. One should never doubt instinct.

"You want to know how I knew it wasn't him?" I continued in the fury of the moment. "Because I knew Ben, and you clearly didn't. Ben didn't say things like *vanquish the cruelty of life.* I always thought that was the weirdest thing for him to write, and now it makes sense. You killed him, then staged it as a suicide. How ironic, right? That you would stage it and I would unwittingly undo your handiwork."

I snickered, not at the humor of it, but at the paradox of life. Candace stood there, buttoning her shorts as if we were discussing the weather, waiting for more. So I gave her more.

"And Michelle Hudson? It was a pointless murder because the poor woman hadn't seen you after all. But framing my mother for it? That's an all-time low."

"Oh, that was just too easy. It literally fell into my hands. You can thank the broken clasp on her necklace for that. I found it in the living room the night of our dinner. It was fate opening a door for me, I guess."

"Why my mother—your own mother-in-law?"

"Why'd she keep calling me Candy? Why did she hate me? Why did she try to push my buttons and tell Lane to leave me? There are always reasons for everything we do, some understandable, others not so much." Candace didn't flinch, didn't move, didn't show an ounce of remorse.

"I understand all of that, I do. But Lane—why him?" It was the only unanswered question I had. "I just want to know why you picked my brother. You owe me that much."

She waited a long minute, the gears shifting in her head, then she spoke, each word slow, sure, mindful.

"I'll tell you why I picked Lane. I think you both have earned the right to know. You see, Lane and I have history. But before I get to that, I want to set the record straight about Ben, because you've misinterpreted most of what happened. You want to blame me, but you really should be blaming yourself."

"Oh really? How so?"

"When I met Ben, he was in a really dark place. After we spent some time together he finally told me why. He had lost Kira and his wife in one fell swoop. While you wallowed in depression, he was expected to carry all of you on his own. But you never considered his loss. I did, though."

"You know nothing about our marriage!" I screamed, spittle spraying.

"I know I didn't go to him looking for love; he came to me looking for healing. He never mentioned being married until later, so it wasn't like we plotted the affair together. He got drunk at a bar; I made sure he got home in an Uber. When he came back to that bar looking for me to return the favor, I agreed to a dinner. Dinner turned into dessert. And well, after that . . . it's hard to turn a rich, handsome, attention-starved man down. At that point I still thought he was single."

"So you're saying you had no idea he was married? I highly doubt that."

"Believe what you want, but it wasn't until after we started seeing each other that he told me about you and your daughter. He never gave me much detail—it was clearly too hard on him to utter it out loud—only saying that he blamed you. And that after it happened you changed. You wouldn't touch him or let him touch you. You were constantly angry, picking fights with strangers even. You destroyed that man. I loved Ben because you wouldn't. You were too wrapped up in your grief to notice him and his grief, so I did. I met the needs you weren't willing to meet."

The sound of skin on skin stopped her accusations. I watched it happen, unable to stop it, as my hand connected with her face. Her head whipped back in a seamless response as her palm covered the mark on her cheek.

"You know nothing about grief," I said, emotions flooding me. "You couldn't possibly understand loss, because you love nothing but yourself." The tears were coming, and I wouldn't hold them back. She needed to see my sorrow in the flesh. "When I held my lifeless child in my arms, all of my heart and all of my joy bled out of me. My hands will forever be painted red with her death, because I can't forgive myself. I don't want to forgive myself. Because love requires everything. Why do you think I took the blame instead of letting it fall on Jackson? I lied to everyone—the police, Ben, even Lane—about what happened, out of love for my son. I told everyone it was on my watch that she wandered to the pool, fell in, and drowned. I wanted to protect everyone else more than I wanted to heal myself. Love is sacrifice, Candace. What have you ever sacrificed for another person? Nothing!"

"You don't know me." Her arm—the one scarred by Noah—dropped to her side, and her eyes burned like hot coals. "Oh,

I've had loss. More loss than you could imagine. So don't claim the victim card all for yourself. Ben was grieving too, and you pushed him away because you didn't want to share your misery. Well, congratulations, Harper, now you own it all. You lost your child and your husband . . . and this clingy thing you have going on with Lane? Well, that will be gone next."

"No"—I shook my head—"Lane would never abandon me. Family sticks together."

"You have no idea what that man is willing to do for me. Or what I'm willing to do for him."

"You're fighting for people who don't want you, Candace."

As soon as the words left my mouth I saw the rage bubble up inside her. I had gone too far. Her gaze darted from the floor to the door to the wall, while I tried to keep up with it. She lunged toward her dresser, the motion so swift that my brain hung back. A heartbeat later she held the pair of scissors in her fist, aiming the point at me as she leaped forward. Covering my head with my arms, I ducked and shuffled back, but she bulldozed forward, her body slamming into mine. I screamed as the tip of the scissors bit into my stomach. I cradled the gushing open wound, trying to cup the blood back inside. When I looked up at her, she held the scissors above her head, aiming them at my face.

"Mommy!" The voice barely cut through the white noise buzzing in my ears. But it was loud enough to hold Candace back for the second I needed to scramble toward the bed. Behind Candace, Jackson pummeled her with his fists, but it was like a fly buzzing around her face. A mere annoyance, not a threat.

Jackson rammed through her legs toward me and protectively hugged me. His short arms cradled halfway around my body, as he screamed, "Mommy! Don't hurt my mommy!" My baby boy risked his life for mine. Everything I thought I'd lost—my heart, my soul—inflated fully, the love bigger than ever before. Pulling him under me, I kissed him and held him and wept into his hair as I shielded him from Candace and all the evils in the world. I would never let go again.

I crouched over Jackson in the corner as Candace threw down another blow that grazed my back. I cried out at the surge of pain coursing through my body, begging her to stop. Her arm swung down again, the point hitting my forearm as I blocked her. Then, again, her arms rose, both hands clutching the hilt, this time aiming for my shoulder where I hunched over Jackson possessively. I couldn't watch her stab me to death, so I tucked into a ball with my son in the center, waiting and bawling and calling for help.

Waiting for the next strike . . . but it didn't come. I dared a glance at her. With the scissors still in midair, a memory seemed to flash across her face. Tears filled her eyes, the blue irises becoming unnaturally bluer, then dribbled down her cheeks as some distant pain stayed her hand. But only for a moment. She blinked back to now, her arms trembled, and I saw the hatred return.

When I should have felt the slice of metal into my flesh, I instead was hit with her full weight as she dropped onto me. I yelped and shoved her aside, crawling across the floor with Jackson scuttling ahead of me, only to bump into a pair of legs. My view traveled upward to find Lane standing above me holding the now bloody turquoise-and-gold urn containing Kira's ashes.

Chapter 35

Candace

There is nothing I wouldn't do for you.

"You have no idea what that man is willing to do for me. Or what I'm willing to do for him." I meant every word of it.

The incredulity on Harper's face made me want to smack it right off. She had watched my life go up in flames while she held the matches. Not anymore. It was my turn to win. I had proven that I could take whatever I wanted of hers and make it into something better, more beautiful. Ben had been depressed with her, sullen, dull. I turned his misery into a work of art, passionate, colorful, and exciting.

And wretched, doomed Lane, chained to obligation to his sister and mother. He lacked luster, and independence, and a zeal for life, and I hand delivered all of that to him. I reached into his lonely heart and pumped it back to life with my own hands. How dare Harper belittle all that I did for them, or question the love I was entitled to.

Unlike Harper, I never had loving parents dote on me. I never had a man who adored me above everything else, tending to me like a beautiful flower. I never had children to look up to me like I was their sun and moon. Harper was so fortunate and she didn't even see it. I did, and that's why I deserved it, because I appreciated it.

"You're fighting for people who don't want you, Candace."

The bite of her words went deep. I didn't know why I lunged at her. Anger at her truth. A fight for self-preservation. It was a familiar fury I couldn't control—pure vengeance swirled into a tornado I couldn't stop. I first felt it at the hands of Noah, but back then I was too scared to stand up for myself. Then when Ben rejected me and his unborn baby, the one still growing within me, that righteous anger resurged. I wanted him dead, because he had made me as good as dead to him. I felt it again when Michelle Hudson threatened my last chance at happiness when she'd gone to the police. And now I felt it with Harper. All I knew was that once that wildfire was lit, it burned out of control.

I leaped forward, sinking the scissors into her body, slicing through muscle and sinew. The quick little coward scooted away, so I tried again.

"Mommy!" Jackson's distraction took just long enough to pause the Red that blinded me as he thrust his tiny fists into my legs. I imagined those same little hands drowning his sister and my compassion for him was gone. He ran toward his mother, just as I dropped another swing that pushed her back. Another one hit her forearm. No more missing the mark. *End it now,* the Red commanded.

A tinge of brief regret hit me as Harper wrapped Jackson up beneath her, cowering and begging for mercy. The image pulled me back into my memories of my father beating my mother while she covered me, protecting me from his fists. For an awful moment I had become my father, and my core trauma came to life. Only this time, I was the villain.

All I had ever wanted was to love and be loved. All I got was rejection and pain. I thought of how my father chose death over me. And how Ben chose Harper, then Lane chose Harper. Why wouldn't anyone choose me? The Red returned, then just as swiftly it was snuffed out as something hit me against the back of my skull. Deafening silence, like high-altitude pressure, pressed against my eardrums at the same time darkness pressed against my eyes.

I felt myself falling more than I saw it, then everything went away, the anger and the regret, swirling into the black hole that the rest of me was floating toward. Somewhere in the bits and pieces of my thoughts, I drifted into my past, into my mistakes, into my fate.

* * *

I opened my eyes after several blinks, unsure of what I was seeing. Could it be true? Had I finally found my happily ever after?

I was more familiar with this plastic white stick than I cared to admit. So many pregnancies. So many positives. All ending in negative. Loss. Miscarriage. Pain. Anger. But this time . . . I knew this time would be different because it wasn't with Noah. It was with someone who wanted a baby, wanted me, wanted us.

It was with Ben, my future.

I pulled up the delicate white panties I had bought for his eyes only. Black lace was for sluts and red lace for lust. White was for the woman you wanted to marry. Pure. That's who I was. I adjusted the matching bra and slipped on the floral silk kimono that he liked on me. He mostly liked slipping it off my shoulders, watching it drop to the floor in a pool at our naked feet.

I flushed the toilet and washed my hands with the tangerine-scented soap the Durham Hotel provided. Where did they get this? I was in love with the fragrance. Checking my hair and makeup in the mirror, I fluffed up the waist-length blond tendrils just right and dabbed a shimmer of gloss across my lips. Ben loved my hair, often telling me he wished his wife didn't insist on cutting hers short. He especially loved to pull it during sex when the animal in him came out.

I rubbed the free, trial-sized lotion on my hands and bare legs, picked up the pregnancy test, and opened the bathroom door. When I slipped into the hotel room that had become "our spot," Ben was lying across the modern platform bed holding a bottle of postcoital wine. We always drank and cuddled and talked after sex, and sometimes I liked it even more than the orgasms he gave me. He wagged the bottle at me—oh, not wine but champagne! That was new—and smiled.

On the contrasting red bedside table were two fluted glasses, each one half full and fizzling with bubbles.

"What are we celebrating today?" I asked, climbing across the navy comforter toward him. I wondered if he knew. Was I already glowing? I'd have to remind him that I couldn't drink alcohol.

"Us." He said it so matter-of-factly that it gave me all the assurance I needed to share my own celebratory news.

"I have something else to celebrate."

"Oh yeah? What's that?"

I took the champagne bottle from his hands and set it on the table beside the glasses. Sidling up to him, I wove my fingers between his. I needed to be close to him as I told him. This moment would last forever, we'd recount it to our son or daughter someday—I was pretty certain it was a girl—and I wanted it to be perfect.

"Us."

I held out the pregnancy test for him to take. But he didn't. Instead he just went still, gawking at it, looking anything but happy.

"What is that?"

"It's a pregnancy test, Ben. I'm pregnant. We're pregnant."

Only now did he look at me, and it was with clenched-jaw anger. Only now did he take the plastic stick, and throw it against the crisp white wall.

"How is this possible? You told me you were on the Pill."

I had told him that, hadn't I?

"It's not always one hundred percent effective. I guess this baby was really meant to be. Our little miracle."

"No." As if that word simply erased the baby's existence.

He pushed me away from him. Not our little miracle, apparently.

"You're not happy." I stated the obvious.

He slammed his fist into the mattress, then rose from the bed, running his hand through his hair like he was trying to rip it out.

"Of course I'm not happy. I'm married, Candace. How the hell am I supposed to tell my wife I'm expecting a baby with another woman? She'll never forgive me."

"I thought you and I would get married and—"

"You and I are nothing!" he yelled over my voice, over my dreams, over our future together.

I felt the embarrassment of tears. How could I have made the same mistake twice, loving the wrong man, a man who didn't love me back? How could I fall for a man who used me, tinkered with me until he broke me?

Ben stomped across the blue carpet, blue like the water I wanted to drown myself in. I slid off the bed and threw on my clothes while Ben fumed back and forth. When he paced himself out, he spoke, as if he had come up with a logical solution.

"You have to get rid of it. There's no other choice. I'm not raising a baby with you, and I'm not leaving Harper. I don't know how you could be so irresponsible."

As if I impregnated myself. As if he had no part in it. He turned to me, glaring with such hatred that I felt it seep into my pores.

"I'm not getting rid of my child, Ben. You'll just have to come clean to Harper and tell her what happened." I grabbed my purse from the red nightstand, knocking over the champagne flutes, and headed toward the door. "Or I will."

His hand reached out, jarring me backward. Flinging me around to face him, he leaned toward me, his face inches from mine. "This is your one warning, Candace. Fix this problem, or I will."

The fingers pinching my muscles tightened until I yelped. "You're hurting me!" I whipped my arm away, finding five oval bruises where his fingers had been. Ben wasn't the knight I had thought he was. He was another Noah.

Chapter 36

Candace

The words exchanged in the hotel room cut me badly. But the letter Ben tucked under my windshield wiper later that night ripped my heart out.

I had given him time to reconsider as I drove home from the hotel and spent the next hour weeping in solitude. Flipping through the countless letters Ben had written me over the months, I reread his poetic professions of love, hating how he had entrapped me with his words:

There is nothing I wouldn't do for you.

When you want to hide from the world,
  hide in me.

To my beautiful Candace, whose name means "clarity."
You've given my life clarity and purpose: to bring you joy.

I wake up to exist for you. I open my eyes to see you.
I breathe to inhale you. You are my reason for each
moment.

You once told me that you felt broken beyond repair.
Let me mend you. Let me make you whole again.

And so many more, all garbage. All lies. All ammunition for the hatred burning inside me, begging me to end the pain, end the rejection. Except I was tired of being the victim and just taking it. Driven by a fury and desperation I had never felt so strong before now, every cell of my body demanded justice.

Resting my hand on my stomach, I refused to lose a baby again. I had fought far too long for a child, and no fickle, selfish prick was going to take it away from me. I had brooded enough over Ben's dismissal of me. I wasn't some rag he could toss in the garbage, and his unborn baby wasn't some mere inconvenience he could ignore. Maybe if I said the right thing I could win him back. So I texted him, but his curt replies only scratched at the wound.

We need to talk, I texted. I couldn't let Ben end things. I needed to fight for him.

There's nothing left to say, he replied.

You can't walk away. We're having a baby together,
whether you like it or not.

You can't prove that. And if you try to tell Harper about it, I'll take the baby and you'll be left with nothing. No court would give a child to a single, broke psycho, but an upstanding family man with the means to give the child everything . . . I always win, Candace.

And then poof! That was it. He ghosted me. For the next couple hours he ignored my texts and calls, and with the lengthening silence my anger swallowed me deeper inside of it. He was under the false assumption I would tuck my tail between my legs, admit defeat, and walk away. Boy, did he have a thing or two to learn about me. I'd been a doormat before, a punching bag, but at least that man had had the balls to marry me. Noah might have beat the hell out of me physically, but emotionally I was still intact because I knew I could leave him if I wanted to. It had just taken me time to build the willpower.

But Ben . . . oh, Ben killed my soul. He gave me hope, then ripped my emotions right out of me and charred them into black ash. And now he had the gall to pretend like I didn't exist? To go on his happy way with his miserable wife, stuck in a life of affectionless grief? I had lost babies. My grief was as wide as the ocean and as deep as the canyons. I knew what it felt like. And here I was offering him a new life, a better one with me, a woman who adored him and would do anything for him. How quickly he turned it down when I offered him my heart. No, he didn't just turn it down. He squeezed it until it popped.

Big mistake, Ben.

He could hide behind the safety of his phone, but he couldn't hide from me standing in front of him, face-to-face. Somehow through the exhaustion I made my way to my car. Somehow *through the tears I saw the letter he left, tucked under my wind-shield wiper. I pulled it out. It was written on the Durham Hotel stationery. He must have written it after I left, not even giving it a full night to reconsider destroying our future! His handwritten goodbye was a loosely veiled threat. As I read the words over and over, the devastation to my soul felt more complete. It was the finality of our relationship, the death of our love.*

He carpet-bombed all my hopes and dreams. I had trusted him with my life. I had given him my future. Ben was Noah all over again, a lying, manipulative, egotistical monster who didn't care how much damage he caused as long as he won.

I tucked his letter in my back pocket. It was torture to keep it close, but it was also fuel for what I needed to do. I was terrified as I got into my car. Panicking as I drove the short distance to his house. Then, somewhere between parking down the street and the walk to his backyard, I felt resolve mixed with indignation. It was the right thing to do. The only thing to do.

Fate was guiding me. I knew it the instant I found his wife's car missing from the driveway. I would listen to that little voice this time. I knew where his wife parked, what she drove, where they kept the spare key, and my way around the house from the times Ben had snuck me in for a quickie when his wife had her weekly therapy appointments. When she stopped going, we were forced to get creative. Thank God for hotels.

No more second chances for Ben. No more fake apologies or excuses. He had used up his last. From the back porch I could hear the television blaring. He would never hear my entry above the sound, hopefully neither would the kids. I looked around, wondering how I could sneak in and sneak out undetected. I lifted the planter that he usually hid the key under, finding an empty space with a dirty outline of where the key had been.

The jerk! He was already wiping his slate clean of me. We'd see about that.

A narrow, rectangular window with an old-fashioned floral pattern etched into the glass was close enough to the back door that I could reach the lock to the doorknob. A soundless entry was out of the question. I pulled off my shirt, wrapped my hand in it, and punched through the glass, holding my breath for a full minute before daring to breathe again. No movement inside, no other sounds beside the television. I hadn't alerted anyone.

With the shirt still attached to my wrist, I fiddled with the lock until I heard it click open. After shaking any glass shards from my shirt, I slipped it back on and entered the house. I followed the sound of Ben's obnoxious snores, mixed with the voice of the host from Mad Money, coming from the living room, something I would have adored, once upon a time. I had never had the bliss of sleeping next to him until morning, feeling the rumble of his snores against my back, and I never would.

I tiptoed up to Ben's sleeping form on the wheat-brown leather sofa that should have been ours, watching him so peacefully ignorant in his narcissism. How could he sleep so soundly after destroying the woman he proclaimed to love? How could he slumber so deeply after betraying the wife he vowed to love faithfully? Maybe I was doing his wife a favor too. Though the woman deserved nothing from me. She was the reason he came to me, yes, but she was also the reason he refused me.

I padded into the kitchen, careful not to touch anything. A hand towel hung from a bronze rod, so I grabbed it and selected a knife from the cutting block. The thickest handle would be the biggest blade. *Easy peasy. I'd never stabbed someone, but how hard could it be? Especially when they weren't fighting back.*

Returning to my lover's side, I blew him a kiss and made a wish. I wished that he'd find happiness in the afterlife. As much as I hated him, I had loved him twice as much. But I also couldn't let him destroy lives without consequence. This was the price one paid. I positioned myself above his rising and falling chest, then raised the knife over my head. I'd need enough force to kill him on the first try. I aimed at his heart, then stopped.

I couldn't do this. I couldn't kill a man.

A light blinked on the phone on the coffee table, then a second later, it buzzed with a text message. I picked up the phone and read it:

You can call me the Problem Solver, buddy. About your little problem, I know someone who can make it go away. I'll be in the wind tomorrow, but you can reach me on this burner phone if you need me. —Randy

Had Ben asked this Randy *person to make me go away? What the hell did that mean?*

I searched for his text history, but it had been erased. Just like he'd erased me from his life. I deleted the text and set the phone down.

Show no mercy. *My father's words echoed inside my head. Ben didn't deserve mercy, and he didn't deserve to live. His heart became a pin at the end of a bowling lane, and with every angry cell I aimed the knife, then plunged the blade down into his chest cavity. I immediately let go and stepped back, waiting for something to happen.*

With a gasp, he jerked up in response to the impact, mouth open in a macabre circle, then he reached his arms out toward me as blood seeped into his shirt. His fingers were close enough to move the air above my skin, and the fine hairs on my arm prickled at the near touch.

Our eyes locked for the last moment as I watched the man I loved die. It was awful and liberating and soul-ripping and powerful being there for his last flittering moments on earth. His arms dropped to his sides, his eyes closed, and gravity lulled his head sideways. Goodbye, my dark prince.

A commercial for Mr. Clean Magic Eraser—replace your grime with shine!—blared on the television behind me. An omen? Somehow all the mess I'd made of my life would be made clean? I found the remote tucked in the wrinkles of a blanket imprinted with Ben's children's smiling faces, and I imagined Ben and I wrapped in the smile of our own child's face. It was a fantasy that would always remain just that—a fantasy.

Turning off the television, I dropped the room into stark silence. Much better. I needed quiet to focus on how to replace my grime with shine.

I found a bottle of bleach under the kitchen sink and got to work cleaning off all traces of me, going strictly based on what I had learned about forensics from watching thriller movies and police procedurals. God willing, most were accurate enough that I didn't leave any evidence that would lead back to me. After wiping down the knife with a paper towel soaked in bleach, I placed his hands on the handle. Finally, I wrote a goodbye—a goodbye that would prevent any suspicion of murder.

I knew Ben's handwriting intimately from the many notes and love letters he had written me over the months. Forgery was a gift I had practiced a lot as a teenager when I wanted to excuse myself from school. I had never imagined putting that talent to use by framing a murder as a suicide. I considered what Ben would have wanted to say, then I remembered he had already said it. To me.

From my back pocket I pulled out the letter he had written to break me. I examined the straight, capital letters, rigid and formal, that he had penned:

Candace,

You saw this coming, didn't you? You knew one day it would have to end between us. You can't blame me for this. You put us here, after all, with your choices and entrapment. It was only a matter of time before we closed this chapter, because it was all that was left to do. You're not my true love; you never were, you never will be. I tried. I really did. But in the end, trying isn't enough. I'm not able to manufacture love. We lived on lust, and that's about it.

You'll spend the next year hating me, but then you'll have your baby and move on and be better off without me. You're tough. But raising a baby together isn't an option. If you choose to come after me for support, I'll take the baby and raise it with Harper. You know I have the means to take everything from you, and you can say goodbye to any happily ever after. So take this chance to have your family and move forward. I don't say that as a threat, but a warning and a promise. I won't hurt you if you don't hurt me.

I love Harper, and that love is enough for me.

Ben

Then I began rewriting it, tracing his penmanship as best as I could, specially adjusted for his beloved Harper, so that she felt the same sharp pain that I did. How darkly poetic that his cruel goodbye to me would be passed on to his wife:

My darling Harper,

You saw this coming, didn't you? You knew one day you'd walk into our home and find me like this, taken by my own hand. You had to, after all the suffering. All the secrets. All the pain.

You can't blame me for this. You put me here, after all. It was only a matter of time before I escaped the pain of this world, because it was all that was left to do. I couldn't carry on anymore . . . not after what happened. What you did. What I could never forgive. I tried. I really did. But in the end, trying isn't enough. It's not enough to erase the past. It's not enough to blur the memories.

You've spent the last year hating me, and I've spent the last year missing you. We're not who we used to be, and I realize now we'll never find ourselves again. When you lose too much of yourself, there's no way to rebuild. Moving on without you wasn't an option, but this was.

I loved you, Harper, but love isn't enough to vanquish the cruelty of life. Death is, though.

Your ghost for eternity,

Ben

It was believable because it was true. The investigation would end quickly. Recently lost a child to a horrible accident. Mentally *ill wife. Suicide from depression was written all over this. With everything cleaned up and staged as best as I knew how, I headed toward the back door where I would disappear forever. Start over, me and my unborn baby.*

Glass crunched beneath my feet. Shoot. The hole in the window—a dead giveaway of a break-in. Where would they have kept the broom? I opened a closet door in the hallway as a car headlight passed over me. Was the car turning up the driveway? I couldn't tell, but it didn't matter. I had already spent too much time here; I needed to leave before his wife returned. I couldn't worry about the broken window. I'd let someone else deal with the aftermath.

A wicker box of toys sat against one wall, so, careful to keep my hand covered, I lifted the lid and grabbed the first hard toy I found. A metal truck. Perfect. Closing the lid, I set it beneath the broken window. Kids threw toys through windows all the time, didn't they? It sounded believable enough to me.

On my way out, I bumped a small table next to the back door with a framed picture on it. The picture tipped over, and covering my hand with my shirt, I picked it up. Two adults surrounded by palm trees and white sand, arms around each other, huge hopeful smiles often found on the faces of the rich and entitled.

I recognized Harper with her red hair, standing next to a good-looking shirtless man in swimming trunks. I clucked at his muscled stomach—nice—then felt a familiarity about him. No, it couldn't be. I held the picture closer to my eyes, examining the man's facial features. Yes, it was him! It was my savior the day I arrived in Durham, North Carolina. How did Ben's wife know this man? Was this fate acting on my behalf yet again? The man's name slipped around in my skull until I caught it.

Lane Flynn. His genuine kindness to me back then gave me hope for a better future. He had been sweet, gentle, and seemed interested in me. Lane Flynn. The one that got away.

I'm coming for you.

Chapter 37

Candace

The morning after Ben's death, I had expected to find Benjamin Paris's name in the obituaries, but not in the news. And not like this. After all, suicides didn't usually make the front page. But murder did.

> *Durham police are looking for multiple suspects in an armed robbery and murder investigation, the police department announced earlier today. Benjamin Paris, 39, was fatally stabbed following a home invasion on Hendricks Way late last night. Paramedics arrived on the scene to find Paris already dead, the perpetrators having stolen thousands of dollars in valuables and artwork. The police believe two suspects*

*are involved in the murder and ask that anyone with
any information please come forward.*

How the heck had the cops figured it out so quickly that it
wasn't a suicide? What had happened to the note? To the staging? And what's this about multiple suspects stealing stuff? What
was going on?

As the significance of the article sunk in, I knew I was in it
deep. A murder meant a lengthy investigation. It meant forensics
and DNA and looking into Ben's extracurriculars and phone call
logs and credit card charges. The risk was high that I would end
up dragged into this. Someone would recognize me. Or had seen
my car parked down the street. Or caught a glimpse of me
wandering through their backyard. A new hairstyle and dye job
could take care of some of that, but I needed more. With a baby
growing inside me, I couldn't risk going on the run. I needed
health care and security. I needed to stay just inside the outskirts
of the investigation so that I knew how to protect myself and
the baby.

It was possible Harper had restaged all my efforts. After all,
she had the most to gain from a murder. A suicide meant no
insurance payout, and men like Ben—no matter how much of
a cheating jerk he was—always provided for their family. Men
like Ben were prepared. Men who lived in mini-mansions with
six-figure incomes bought the best death benefits. That, at least,
could be to my advantage. Harper would be suspect number
one. It was only fair that if I didn't get a dime for my child's
future that Harper didn't get one either. I refused to be left with
nothing while Harper buried her husband and got rich doing it.

My brain rumbled through every step, every touch, every

action at the crime scene. What had I missed? I had been so careful, thoughtful. I didn't know what the investigators had found that would suggest anything but suicide—the window I had broken, most likely—but I would find out. Lane Flynn was my inside source.

I could never forget the day I met Lane, the first day I arrived in Durham, North Carolina, after a grueling bus ride. After leaving Pennsylvania, I had bled the entire trip, until finally arriving in the town described as having the best medical facilities in the South, and being "culturally dynamic while holding on to its historical significance." The town had good medical care and was small and clean and modern and cute. It was the perfect mix of youthful innovation and mature taste. Welcome home!

My first night at the cheapest motel I could find ended with a night in the hospital when the spotting gushed into bleeding. That day I lost Noah's baby but gained a friend. The miscarriage made me a wreck, but my attending nurse, Lane Flynn, was kind, compassionate, and sincere. He helped me through the loss.

We exchanged small talk and deep talk. He liked to unwind with karaoke, and I liked to unwind with swimming. He shared his desire for a family, and I confessed my knack for screwing such things up. He told me I was perfect, and I told him he would make someone a lucky wife one day. He stood by my side as I prayed for the life of my baby, then wept as I lost her. He hugged me when the loneliness crushed me, and brought me flowers before I was discharged with empty arms that should have held my child.

I hadn't thought much about Lane in the following months, only that he was the perfect example of what a man should be, but I was stupid back then. I hadn't yet figured out that there were only two types of men—the Noahs who crushed you, and the Lanes who built you up. I was still stuck on adventure and bad boys. I hadn't yet been awakened to security and love. My stupidity had instead led me to Ben. But now that Ben was dead and I was pregnant with Ben's baby, I needed someone with no baggage. Someone ripe for love and a family.

The answer to all my problems had been right in front of me on the day I arrived in this town, and he lived inside the four walls of the quaint, suburban three-bedroom house with its promise of better things. Lane Flynn wasn't bad-looking either. And he made decent money as a nurse. And he wanted a family as desperately as I wanted to give my unborn child a father. He was perfect.

Months had passed since we had met, and I doubted he would remember me with my new hairstyle. If anything, it was better that way, starting fresh. All it took was a "chance" meeting at the karaoke bar that he often frequented, a lot of flirting, two chocolate martinis, and a little destiny to bring two lost souls together . . .

Chapter 38

Lane

The crack of the front door being thrust open, and the subsequent swarm of emergency workers storming a house, was something you'd expect to see in a movie. You'd never expect it to happen in your own home.

It didn't happen exactly like that, but it felt pretty damn close in the moment, minus the guns blazing and the SWAT team breaking down my door.

After Candace went down, I ran for my cell phone to call 911. I didn't know how long she'd stay unconscious, but hopefully long enough until the cops arrived. Most of what I relayed to the emergency operator was lost in the recesses of my brain. I was in work mode, delivering facts: *Sister stabbed multiple times, at least one abdominal laceration. Wife attacked her. Wife unconscious. Possible skull fracture. Please send EMTs soon.*

Pressing a balled-up shirt against Harper's stomach, I carried her to the bathroom, where I stockpiled gauze and bandaging. While tending to the gaping hole in her abdomen—the most pressing of her injuries—the tread of boots rumbled into the entryway.

"Paramedics!" a voice called out.

"We're upstairs!" I yelled. "Hurry!"

Harper faded in and out, then winced awake as I pressed a bandage to her wound. The footsteps trudged up the stairwell, two paramedics appearing at the bathroom door, ready to attend to her. I handed her off to them, assured Jackson and Elise that their mom would be fine as I led them out of the way into their bedroom, then went to search for the cops. Just as I descended the stairs, Detective Meltzer walked through the front door, wearing jeans and aviator sunglasses, his badge clipped to his belt. His bulk filled the entryway, at odds with the warmth of the sunlight that spilled in around him. I waved him over to follow me upstairs. He flipped his sunglasses on top of his head, and I talked while we walked.

"I . . . I don't even know where to begin. I just found out that my wife killed my sister's husband." The shock hadn't yet settled.

"I can't say I'm surprised," Detective Meltzer replied. "I've been looking into Candace Wilkes for a while now."

I stopped and turned around. "Was that *you* who was watching my house?"

"Yep, and you almost caught me that day in the rain—the day of Michelle Hudson's murder when you approached my car." Detective Meltzer aimed his finger at me like he was pointing a gun. "It's a damn shame too. If I had followed

Candace instead of watching your house, Michelle Hudson would still be alive."

"You think Candace killed Michelle?"

"I bet I'll find evidence in her belongings that proves she did."

"How did you figure out she was involved?" I asked as the detective trailed behind me up the stairwell.

"Of course I started looking into you and Harper when Ben was first killed. It was only recently that I came across your marriage certificate to Candace Moriarty, though, and when I looked into it I found a dead woman's records. That was enough to start watching her."

"And you never said a damn word to us about it?"

"I never said a lot of things to you. It was an ongoing investigation, Lane. You know the rules. So where's our suspect?" We arrived in the upstairs hallway, and he glanced around, looking for her.

"In my bedroom."

"And what exactly happened?"

"She attacked my sister with a pair of scissors. I knocked her out with an urn."

He humphed. "An urn, huh? That's a new one," he said as we reached the doorway.

We both stopped short when we entered the empty room. No Candace. Just a smear of blood on the floor.

"What the—?" I rushed to the other side of the bed. Where could she have gone? I checked the window, but the screen was intact, and there was no way she could have slipped past me in the hallway without anyone noticing. At least I didn't think so.

"Check the bedrooms!" the detective yelled to another uniformed officer who joined us in the hallway.

While the detective pulled out his radio, using code words I didn't understand, I pondered how she could have escaped and where she would have gone.

A couple minutes later the officer called back, "All clear!"

No, no, no!

The detective left me with my confusion while he consulted with another officer who had arrived. With his gun steadily aimed, he stooped to look under the bed, then muttered something as he stood up. From his pocket he slipped a latex glove on his hand, then reached under the bed. What on earth had he found? When he pulled out a Nordstrom bag, I recognized it from the night Candace went "shopping" for a gift for Harper. The same night Michelle Hudson was killed. Detective Meltzer lifted a bloodstained shirt from within.

"Get forensics up here!" he yelled.

How had I been duped so badly? Nothing that I thought I knew was real. Not Candace, not our feelings, not our future. It had all been lies from the start. How could I have fallen so easily for her? I had forgiven the lies she fed me, but this was beyond anything I could have anticipated. My thoughts whirred at a wild pace, and I felt sick, like a hand had reached inside my stomach and was rummaging around in it.

I had married a killer. How strange it felt to become one flesh with a person I've never met.

Except I did know Candace. I had spent two months with her, learning her ways and diving into her mind. I recalled the first day I'd brought her into my home. She had been fascinated with it, its history, the hidey-holes and nooks. She explored it like it was a lost treasure. And her favorite feature—the attic.

Of course.

I opened the closet door and shoved the hanging clothes aside. The waist-high door was cracked open just a sliver, enough to allow a thin stream of imprisoned hot air to escape. I crouched down and pushed against the wood, and it swung open. Crawling through cobwebs and a cloud of dust, I entered the cavity. Dusty boxes climbed one wall, and scattered across the wide-planked floor were generations of previous owners' forlorn possessions. Piles of hardcover books created a make-shift fort in one corner around a collection of toys and doll clothes, presumably belonging to the Frankie doll the kids had found up here. It was apparent that Jackson and Elise had spent some time secretly exploring and playing.

Although it was dank and dark, I could see Candace pressed against the far wall where a tiny circular window, covered in an inch of grime, allowed in hazy light.

"I knew you'd find me." She was so casual as she wiped her hands on her legs, then walked toward me, the soft pad of her bare footsteps barely audible. Then she stopped and stood in front of me. My body stiffened as she grasped my hand. I let go. I didn't want her touch. She had killed Ben and an innocent old lady, and nearly killed my sister.

"I'm sorry for everything I've done, Lane. I know I'm messed up in my head. I don't know what snapped inside me . . ."

"Ben, I sorta get, because he hurt you. But Michelle Hudson? What kind of monster are you?"

She wiped a tear that rolled down her cheek. "One that doesn't deserve your forgiveness. One that's really damaged,

Lane. I wanted so badly for us to be together, and when I thought Michelle was going to get in the way of that, I went too far. I can't explain what I was thinking, because I wasn't thinking. I was only feeling panic."

"You know I have to turn you in, right? And you're going to rot in jail for what you've done."

"Yeah, I know. I'm at peace with that. It's what I deserve. Honestly, I'm tired of running anyway." She stood on her tip-toes and kissed me on the cheek, and part of me wanted to hold her, but the bigger part of me needed to let go.

When she stepped away, she held me captive with her blue eyes.

"My biggest regret was hurting you," she whispered. "I really did end up falling for you. You're the first person who made me the victor, not the victim. I'll always love you for that."

Her voice was rich with conviction, the rhythm of our breath quiet and insistent as a pulse. I had only one last question for her: "Why?"

Why me? Why frame my mother? Why attack Harper? So many whys.

"I just wanted love, Lane. That's all. Why is it so hard to find?"

If only I knew the answer to that.

"It's time to go," she said. "I'm ready to face the consequences. Just promise me one thing."

"Okay," I whispered.

She placed my hand on her belly. "Take care of the baby for me. Raise her to have a pure heart like yours. Show her what family should look like—what you and Harper have."

That was the Candace I longed for, the one who loved deeply. Too deeply in the end, though.

I let her hand graze mine, then led her down the attic stairs and out the door into the bedroom. Our parting was as quiet as a falling snowflake. Then the flurry began. Detective Meltzer stormed in, another officer following him, while reading Candace her rights:

"Candace Wilkes, you are under arrest for the murder of Benjamin Paris and Michelle Hudson. You have the right to remain silent . . ."

The rest of the words were a blur as they grabbed my wife by the shoulders, turned her around, and handcuffed her. She didn't say a word, didn't fight back, simply let them. I had fallen in love with not just a liar, but a murderer too. Even in knowing this horrific, gruesome truth, I still loved her. I hurt for all the pain she had suffered in life. As Harper had explained it to me, Noah had taken the biggest part of her, then Ben took what remained. It left the spot empty where her heart should have been. She had only wanted the same happily ever after that everyone else wanted, I guess even more so. She was willing to kill for it.

As I watched them haul her down the stairs, out the door, and down the walkway to Detective Meltzer's waiting black sedan, I realized that she wore her darkness so well that all I saw was light.

Epilogue

Harper

Today was a hopeful day, stuck in the middle of two less important days. It wasn't the beginning or the end, but a happy middle. It was the day Lane got custody of Mercy Kira Flynn.

The newborn baby was swaddled in a pink hospital blanket, resting in the crook of my arm while I sat by the fire in my new house. When Candace announced her name—Mercy Kira—I wept. A tribute to the daughter I lost, a remembrance that she was alive within us. I liked to think that Kira was smiling down from heaven, approving of the name. I would live in a way that would make my daughter happy as she watched on from her heavenly perch and help raise Mercy to live up to Kira's name. Holding her against my chest, I gave the baby the sum of all my parts—my life, my soul, my word to always protect her as best as I could.

Maybe Candace wasn't so evil after all. Candace had vowed to give Lane the family he deserved. And for once she hadn't been lying.

"How do you like the new place?" Lane asked me between sips of hot cocoa.

I glanced around the living room, where the Christmas tree lit up one corner in silver and blue sparkle. Garland wrapped around the banister leading upstairs to the kids' rooms. Three bedrooms, one for me, one for Elise and Jackson to share—which they insisted on, to my surprise—and a nursery for Mercy when she was here. I figured that while Lane worked I could take care of her. My niece-stepdaughter. Well, I'd need to work on what to call her. For now, I just called her Mercy.

"It's starting to feel like home. Especially now that the kids have scattered their toys all over the place. And it's affordable." My mother had found me the perfect deal.

Jackson ran—not shuffled, not skulked, but ran!—into the room squealing. My son was loud again! Laughing again! The noise was a song. His rambunctious destruction was a melody. Therapy helped taper his irrational fears of possessed dolls and haunted homes, grounding him in a sense of reality and hope. And I learned what patience and understanding should look like. He abruptly stopped at my knees, kissed the baby on her forehead, hugged me, then took off for the kitchen. We were hugging now, daily, sometimes hourly. A little love went a long way.

"Did you close on the sale of your other house yet?"

"Yep, Mom finally sold the *Murder House*." I raised my glass of white zinfandel—the only wine I could afford on my salary working at the botanical gardens while I was taking horticulture classes at the ommunity college—and I clicked it against Lane's, saluting good riddance to the house and its awful nickname. "Not exactly Mom's dream house sale, but it's done and she got a nice fat commission out of it. And I ended up turning a small profit, so I can't complain. At least Mom's happy."

In the modest kitchen, which was about two people wide, Elise baked cookies. Though judging by the smell, she was more likely burning them.

"Check the oven!" I called to Elise. "And don't set the house on fire."

We could chuckle now over the fire alarm scare way back when. Jackson swore never to play with matches again, and I swore never to stop loving him even if he did.

Mercy cooed, her blue-black eyes wide and expectant. She looked so much like Ben, with the same little dimple, like God had pressed His thumbprint in her chin. Her *chimple,* I called it. And the same thick dark hair. Every minute I loved her a little more. With a mother in jail, a dead father, and no other family to speak of, Lane was the best—and only—option as a parent. I would help him, because if Lane could somehow look past the betrayal and damage Candace caused him and still love Mercy with every fiber of his being, then I could support him in raising this little girl. When Mercy smiled, well, it was an easy yes.

Mercy, the perfect name for a child who was born out of suffering but destined for something better. Life had a way of doing that, stripping you naked and vulnerable, then leaving it up to time to heal you.

On the table beside me was the letter Candace had mailed me from jail. I had been nervous when I pulled it out of the mailbox, wondering what she could possibly want to say that hadn't been addressed in court already. I read it, breath held and hands trembling:

Dear Harper:

Do you remember that time we were at the mall and I threw the penny in the fountain and made a wish? Well, my wish was that somehow you and I would be able to forgive each other, to become sisters for real, not only for me, but for my baby's sake.

I know the damage I caused devastated you. But let's be honest and admit that you were devastated long before I came into your life. My point is this: Don't let life devastate you. You are the strongest woman I know, and you've lost more than any person should suffer. But you have a bigger faith than anything life throws at you. You know there's hope ahead. Live in that hope. Don't fear death, face it. Remind it that it holds no grip on you, because one day we'll all be on the other side of death wondering what all the fuss was about. I hope one day I'm in heaven with you, even after all that I've done. Maybe put in a good word with God for me, will ya?

When you and Lane took Mercy in and made her your own, you did that for me. Thank you for making my wish come true. I love you like a sister. And I'll cherish your obsessive neatness, your annoying criticisms, and your helicopter parenting from afar. I won't even mind your love of throw

pillows. Because that's what sisters do. We love each other despite our crazy differences.
    Much love,
    Candy

I smiled at the signature: *Candy.* She had finally embraced it. As I had reflected on the past year, I had come to realize that we all wanted to be unwrapped and seen and loved. When Candace and I had peeled back each other's layers, we both found heartache and distrust and anger. But the point was that we cared enough to keep peeling. That was the nature of living.

Acknowledgments

Sometimes writing the acknowledgments is harder than writing the story. There are so many people I'm grateful for who have supported me, lifted me up, made my words clearer, bought my books, shared with their friends, and encouraged me to keep going. I thank God for planting the seed inside me, and my husband for helping me water it. No, Craig, this doesn't put you on the same level as God, but I'm thankful He gave me you. No one else could put up with my midnight tapping on the keyboard and writing getaways like you do, especially with four kids always needing something or other. Thank you for being a single dad when I need to meet a word count.

Katie Loughnane will always be one of my absolute favorite people on earth, not just because of her editing brilliance, but because of the way she roots for me and strokes my tender author ego. Thank you for believing in me since book one and forever after. I still owe you my firstborn child for all you've done for me. Beth Wickington, I cringe to think what errors would slip through without your incredible eagle eye along with Elle Keck's. Avon Books and I both are so lucky to have you both on our side. To my William Morrow counterpart Tessa Woodward, thank you for seeing my vision with each book and bringing it to life.

Behind every great publisher is a great marketing team. You know who you are, Sabah Khan, Ellie Pilcher, Kaitie Leary, and Brittani Hilles. All the articles and interviews and publicity and reader reviews you secured for me impressed me every time. All those five stars out there are because of you. You're what gives a book wings to fly, and I'm grateful for all of your hard work and creative efforts.

My editors at Proofed to Perfection Editing Services always deserves a clap of praise, because they always get first look at my completed manuscript for a reason. Thank you for being the best editors in the biz!

A writer is like a tree, the fruit being the books, but the roots being family and friends who nourish us. Emily Sutton and Jessica Young, I don't even need to put last names in there because you both know just how much you mean to me. I wouldn't know how to write about the depths of friendship without Em showing me what it is for the past twenty-four years (how can it be that long—we're still in our twenties, aren't we?). You're my favorite cheerleader, and you make that cheer outfit look good! Jess is a constant inspiration for how to grab a dream and hold on, especially when I see her passion for my dream as she's demanding a bookstore manager to put my books out front and center. Thank you for being passionate for me when I'm too shy. I only hope every reader can find friends like mine.

To Mom who passed down her writer gene, Tim who inspired me at age ten to start writing, Dad who gave me his smarts, and Tracy who taught me how to find myself, thank you. To Diane who gave me her son, thank you for being the mother-in-law who loves me even when I drive your son crazy. To Michael and Lauren and Paul, I'm honored to share genes with you. To Angie, Missy, and Jamie—my sisters-in-law—I love you for not being Candace to my Harper. I'm blessed to have nice ones!

My children, Talia, Kainen, Kiara, and Ariana, you guys keep Mommy on her toes. Thank you for the endless supply of kid anecdotes to include in my books. Every child character has a little bit of you guys in them, and one day when you're old enough to read my books I'll tell you which events are actual excerpts from our real lives!

I could go on and on, but your eyes will tucker out. Thank you to everyone who buys my books, demands them from their libraries, asks bookstores to put them front and center, shares posts on social media, and writes a book review. You are why I keep writing, and to you I owe my dream.

PAMELA CRANE is a *USA Today* bestselling author of almost a dozen novels. She loves writing about flawed and fascinating heroines. When she's not cleaning horse stalls or changing diapers, she's psychoanalyzing others.

You can find out more about her at pamelacrane.com.